BLUE & GRAY

CROSS

CURRENT

By
Dan & Suzanne Chilton

Best Wishes,

Dan & Suzanne Chilton

Dedicated to the descendants of:

Thomas Boggs Chilton
Thomas Coot Chilton
Charles Truman Chilton

TABLE OF CONTENTS

PROLOGUE

A RELIC strange, from my bachelor hoards,
You show me with crimsoning face;
A little thimble of silver fine—
Art thou not wondering, bride of mine,
Whose finger it used to grace? [2.31]

John J. Chilton pulled a chair close to his desk and gazed at his wife with a look that clearly meant sit. The spry codger with battle-worn knees and an impeccable white moustache was a leftover from an era when chivalry did not need a name because it was synonymous with manners. A man of words, he liked nothing better than an audience.

"When the Civil War began, I was four years of age and she past twenty," he chuckled. "Infatuation for Lizzie seared her unusually attractive image into my heart."

He opened the desk drawer overflowing with papers tied with twine. "My memoirs of the war include hushed events of her life and that of my childhood hero, Alexander." He paused, lifted the top packet from the stack, placed it on Christine's lap, and then simply said, "Read."

With the tarnished silver thimble on the third finger of her right hand, she untied the string and began.

True Tales of Bygone Days by John J. Chilton.

CHAPTER 1

ADJOINING FARMS—1850

Hath it a history? Yes, ah! yes,
For she who that relic wore
Every pulse of my soul could stir
With a look or a touch, while I, to her
Was a cousin—a boy—no more. [2.31]

E lizabeth Clementine Davis laid her banjo aside when she first
saw Alexander as he topped the riverbank, rode slowly through
the pasture, and slid off the big red roan, a strong hold on the lead rope
of the trailing calf.

Her father, Samuel, met the lad with a handshake and words she
could not quite make out from the steps of the cabin porch.

"Yes, sir, Mr. Davis." Alexander took another quick glance at the
girl on the porch.

Samuel turned toward the cabin. "Lizzie, come meet your cousin
Alexander."

Lizzie skipped down the gravel path and leaned on the hitching rail.
"Hello, Alexander. I am thirteen years old today, and we have cake. Do
you want some?"

He paused, looked at her straight on, and nodded. "First, I must
take the calf to the barnyard." He led the calf to the gate and into the

barnyard where he removed the lead rope and set the calf free. He closed and latched the gate.

"Race you to the porch," Lizzie challenged.

Alexander gave fair warning. "I'm fast."

"One, two, three, go!" Lizzie knew she met her first friend in Shannon County because he refrained from declaration of his footrace win. From which family of her many Chilton cousins he came, she did not know.

Her mother stepped to the porch, dried her hands on her apron, and attended to the matter right away. "Hello, Alexander. I am your Aunt Betsy's sister Issabella. These two youngsters are your cousins Thomas and Caroline.

"Pleased to meet you, I'm sure, ma'am. Aunt Betsy said you arrived last week from Tennessee. Our farm adjoins Uncle Joshua and Aunt Betsy. We live some ten miles up Jacks Fork."

"You are very brave indeed to bring us the calf from so far off. Your folks must have great confidence in you. You cannot be more than ten or so," Issabella said.

Lizzie noticed Alexander look at his boots with a sideways grin. She was glad her mother seemed so proud of Alexander. Why, he might be the most courageous boy she ever knew. Probably the strongest, too, figuring the way he could run.

"Truth be known, my older brother and a cousin traveled with me. We also brought a calf to Grandpa Coot. Safety on the river in twos and threes, never swim alone, and stay out of the angry crosscurrent." Alexander stated river rules with confidence.

Lizzie added her wisdom. "Yes, the crosscurrents pull you under and drag you on the river bottom until you drown."

Not to be outdone, her brother scrunched his face and hands. "Then you float up after three days, all bloated and wrinkled."

Little Caroline covered her ears and screamed, "Stop! Make him stop, Mama!"

"Mr. Davis, please draw up the water, and let us commence with this party." Issabella chuckled and set the sweet apple cake on the table. "Then, we can sing awhile on the porch."

"I play banjo," said Lizzie. "Grandpa Davis gave me his banjo when we left Tennessee. Do you play an instrument? All the Chiltons are musical, Mama says. You can sit by me."

Her brother pointed to the space next to him on the bench. "I want to sit by Alexander. Boys sit here, and girls sit over there."

Alexander took a place on the bench next to Thomas. "Yes. I play guitar and my sister and brothers play fiddle. Some people call it a violin, but with Mama being Irish, we fiddle at our house."

"You came the perfect day. You are a special cousin now. Our very first friend."

Her mother reached into her pocket. "Hold out your hand." She placed something round and cold into the palm of Lizzie's hand. "This is a special birthday. My mother's thimble belongs to you, now, my grown-up girl."

She placed the silver thimble on the third finger of her right hand. "I loved to borrow it on days when we quilted with Granny Davis, even though she later removed my big stitches. Thank you, Mama, but Caroline must receive a special present."

"Do not worry. Caroline will receive a special gift on her thirteenth birthday, same as you."

Young Thomas asked, "What about me? What about my thirteenth birthday?"

"Your father will tend to that matter when the time comes."

Lizzie noticed her father's impatient scowl. "Time for the blessings," she quickly added. She folded her hands and bowed her head, but she could not resist a peek at Alexander.

Their eyes met, but she dared not giggle during the blessing.

Then Alexander blurted out. "I'm going to marry you someday. I never saw anyone as pretty as you."

Lizzie pulled the last of the bed sheets from the kettle of boiling water set over the outdoor fire pit. "Steamy day, steamy laundry. I am so thankful you and Uncle Joshua took us in when Papa and Mama died.

My thirteenth birthday lies vivid in my mind because of it. I turn eighteen today, you remember."

Aunt Betsy replied, "I remember and well recall those troubled days. Sinking sickness spread across the county like wildfire. You stood your ground when the aunts thought it best to split the three of you between us. Now, here you are, a proper lady."

"Sometimes I am that woefully scared child, what with Caroline gone first to Grandmother Chilton, then to Granny Davis in Tennessee; and Thomas at F. M.'s farm. In the end, we went separate ways. I could never leave them, and deep down, I wonder how they could leave me. Oh, my! I must see to something special for Caroline's thirteenth birthday!"

"What if we send her Grandmother Chilton's brooch? Caroline lost father, mother, and grandmother at such a young age. I believe she needed more mothering than I had time to give. She was one among many in our large family. A sister, a child herself, can't provide such, my dear."

"I know you are right. Moreover, Thomas did stay until he could earn his own way as a very young man. Uncle Francis Marion sees to Thomas like a father. Training me as midwife and nurse serves me well to earn my way, come what may. I am forever grateful. Sometimes I just get silly lonesome in our host of loved ones. How can that be?"

As if summoned, Alexander rounded the corner of the house. He rode bareback and led a saddlebred bay. "I wrote a new song. Best one yet," he teased. "Get your banjo, Lizzie; we're headed to the river."

Without a blink, Lizzie tossed the corner of the half-hung wet bed sheet toward the fence, caught-up her banjo from the porch, and leaped on bareback. "One, two, three, go!" She caught him by surprise, but the race was on.

"I swan to my time," Aunt Betsy called as she walked to the fence to finish her niece's task. "Alexander can charm you into anything. Always could, always will."

Barefoot and wearing an old muslin day dress, Lizzie held her banjo high overhead, galloped her horse into the swift clear river at the shallow ford, and crossed to the shady tree-lined bank. A deep blue swimming hole beckoned where the river slowed. "I win!"

"Cheater!" Alexander responded. He stopped at the ford, slid off his horse, sloughed off boots, shirts, and pants; he kept on just enough to remain decent and waded in waist-high water with guitar held high. "Rocks get sharper every year. Miss 'wild-hair' chose the best plan after all." He placed his guitar by her banjo, and then he swam to where she and a host of cousins treaded water in wait.

She turned to escape downriver. To no avail because she felt his hands press her back, dunk her proper, and follow her underwater to watch her surprised face.

Not to be outdone, Lizzie grabbed him by the shoulders and planted a big kiss on his mouth. Then she pushed him even farther under and swam to the surface for air.

So surprised by the kiss, he gulped water and came to the surface choking and coughing. "Dang, girl, what did you do that for?"

"I felt like kissing, and it felt good!" She looked toward Nelson in definite challenge.

He swam upriver as fast as he could. "We're first cousins and kissing will not do, no, ma'am."

When she saw Nelson wade out of the water, sit on her dress, and dry his hands and arms with the skirt-tail, she shouted, "Put down my dress, you skunk!"

"Nice towel. A bit dirty though." He tossed her somewhat-splashed dress into the river.

She screamed and swam toward her floating dress before it sank in deep water. She swam upstream on her back to shallower water, pulled the dress over her head, and latched the hooks and eyes; and then, without mercy, splashed Nelson.

Nelson pleaded, "Peace? Peace! Let's sing."

She sat on the bank and watched Alexander swim to and fro. He joined the line of cousins for a turn on the grapevine, swung out over the water, scrunched into a ball, and dropped into the water with the biggest splash he could muster. He swam to a half-sunken log wedged between large boulders across the river from Lizzie, and he pulled himself up top. He seemed to savor the moment, from the looks of his sideways grin.

She decided there was nothing better for her than the river. Gray limestone bluffs rose more than fifty feet above the water and stretched downriver for a mile or more. Cedar trees, columbine, and ferns struggled between the high crevices. Blue ageratum, white and yellow daisies of several heights grew in the fertile folds in the bluffs where room-size chunks cracked away and lay in the deep water.

Stone ledges jutted out some ten to twenty feet under the water. The deep pool, glazed like blue glass, belied a rush of current below the surface.

A long wide bar of sand and gravel edged the other side of the river, and gave way to lavender horsemint under pink wild roses of five petals. River cane stood tall and swayed in the breeze. Grasses grew thick in the tree-lined pasture of rich and sandy loam deposited from ebb and flow of floods. Rises of twenty-five or thirty feet of violent and swift muddy water were common two or three times a year. The floodwaters returned to their banks and cleared after four or five days.

She absorbed every element of the scene. Sometimes she felt like the floods: violent, muddy, and over the banks. Music settled her, cleared her thoughts, and washed away her fears born of loss and isolation as an orphan.

Lizzie squeezed the water from her skirt and petticoat and strummed her banjo. Before very long, her fifteen cousins lined the river's edge. Youthful voices carried along the river, and the hollows rang with joy.

"I do so wish this moment could last forever. So many people to love." She turned onto her stomach and stretched, fully warmed by the sun on her back. She loved Alexander, his sisters, and his brothers and their wives. To her left sat his youngest sister, Elizabeth, John and Elizabeth, William and Mary, and lastly, his sister Mary Louisa and his cousin Nelson.

Except for Nelson, the cousins with whom she made her home sat to her right: Susannah and W.T. Orchard, Rebecca, Perry, Susan, Anne, James, and Francis.

She waved to Jesse Conway and Sam Nesbit, who stayed in the hired hands' cabin during planting and harvest seasons. "Come for a swim? Today the water flows as warm as above the Alley Spring."

"Sure it is." The two young men exchanged looks, removed their boots, hats, and belts, and walked toward Lizzie.

"Oh, no!" she said, and rolled to her back to sit up.

She tried to kick and flail, but one lad gripped her hands and the other, her feet. She felt the near-frigid water soak her backside, slowly rise to her shoulders and knees as her captors waded deeper and deeper into the river. She yelled, "Torture-ers!" Then she screamed as she felt herself launched into the air and splashing into water deep enough to cover her face.

Her feet found the gravel bottom, and by the time she stood shivering in the hot sun, she thrilled to see the banks clearing in a blur of cousins. A water fight of the finest kind commenced and drenched everyone.

"Yes, this moment could last," she sighed, just before two palmfuls of water splashed her face. "Forever!" she sputtered. She wondered if the war on the border with Kansas spread eastward, who gathered here today would return to swim their beloved river.

Lizzie brushed Aunt Betsy's hair and pinned it back for the workday. "I waited forever and ever for a dance at the cave! A brush arbor meeting at Blair Creek surely means a dance at Square Dance Cave up the valley from the cemetery."

She looked at the two women reflected in the mirror. She knew she favored the Chiltons more than she did her Welsh father: a straight nose, an abundance of black wavy hair, and large wide-set eyes as deep blue as Fancher's Blue Spring. Her face was square with wide cheekbones. She looked more like her uncle Joshua and his daughter Susan. Often mistaken as another of Joshua and Betsy's eight children, she never regretted the decision when orphaned to them—not one ounce.

Aunt Betsy clapped her hands and laughed for joy. "I know well the arbor and dance, with preaching in the valley and liquor on the ridge. The cave opens high up where springwater flows out of the mountain a ways below the mouth of the cave. Then it splashes over gray limestone rocks a mile or more along the steep hollow to the valley floor. Beautiful! From the ridge, you climb down the steep slope over large moss-covered rocks into the small mouth of the cave. About fifty feet along the sandy-floored corridor, a wide room opens up, large enough for four squares. Cool in the summer and warm in the winter, play parties occur for months on end."

"Now just how do you know so much about Square Dance Cave?"

"I lived on Current River long before your birth. We spent some days. My, but your mother loved to sing and dance. We spent some days. And I know to advise caution." Aunt Betsy sparkled with the memories of her youth.

"Tell me about the brush arbor meeting. Neither the circuit preacher nor Father Hogan builds an arbor?"

"A brush arbor meeting gathers when a preacher shows and fires up the congregation's joyous shouts, songs, prayers, and music. Leafy limbs and brush lie on the posts and crossbeams to form the roof. When the pine torches sputter out, the preacher's altar call ends the rail against sin."

Lizzie pulled her aunt from the chair by her hands, and they swung around in noisy jigs and boisterous shouts. "Living on the river savors your soul and washes away your sins. Let's cuss a bit so the Good Lord takes notice of our fall from grace and need for redemption!"

Aunt Betsy slowed the pace, "Don't be impertinent about grace and redemption, girl."

"I apologize. I just meant to be playful. I take salvation something serious as my daily source of joy." However, her joyful face saddened, and her eyes darkened with her mood. "Papa's motto lies firm in my soul: 'When you have nothing, God is enough.'"

Her faith spilled out of the hole in her heart.

The trip downriver to Blair Creek reminded Lizzie of a dance, but she failed to remember the words and steps. "Sing us 'The Brush Arbor Meeting', John. We need to practice."

Over the course of two days, Lizzie, her Chilton cousins, the Nesbit brothers, and other hired hands sang their way down Jacks Fork and Current River, and then up Blair Creek. Other joyful music drifted down the road from a mile off the destination. Lizzie knew the songs and wanted to stay at the arbor for a little while but remembered that the wagon driver, John, allowed as to how he held other plans than a revival meeting.

The wagon stopped at the Blair Creek Graveyard in the valley, the brush arbor meeting well under way. Lizzie helped John's wife lead her three little ones to their grandparents, who sat under the arbor on the wagon seat, removed for the occasion.

It took quite some time for John's wagon to pull up the hill to the ridge over the steep washed-out road. She noticed a large crowd, mostly men, gathered above the cave. Just as Aunt Betsy described, Lizzie gathered her skirts and began the climb over the boulders down into the cave opening, a drop of about ten feet. When she reached the sandy floor, Alexander handed her the banjo and turned to climb out of the cave. Lizzie felt abandoned and frightened at first. "I thought you brought your guitar."

"I brought it, but go on and play your music awhile."

"But I want to dance." She crossed her arms and assumed a petulant pout.

"I will come in later to dance and hear you sing."

Lizzie eased her way around the dancers. The squares swirled. She looked for her cousins, who visited along the way to the cave room. She leaned against the cool damp cave wall until the music stopped and the set ended. She edged her way next to a young woman who played a banjo. "Hello. I am Lizzie Davis, and I brought my banjo."

"Join us and get tuned. I am Mahala Jane Sutterfield and this here's my baby, Eliza Jane." Mahala scooted over to make room on the large flat boulder for Lizzie to sit. "We are distant cousins, you know. My father was a Davis and my mother was Cherokee.

"Cousins from Tennessee?" Scared as could be, Lizzie tuned her banjo to Mahala's, and a song took off. Lizzie failed to keep up at first, and then her fingers found the roll. She missed a few chords, but nobody seemed to notice. She beamed. Her daydreams awoke at last.

"Alexander, do I smell whiskey?" Lizzie turned away but gasped, even more shocked when he eased beside her on the large smooth rock and kissed the back of her neck.

"Let us take a dance. I waited years for this dance."

He led her to the Chilton's square. John, as the oldest cousin, always called the steps. Now, some families bounced around, or skipped, or marched stuffy-like, but the Chilton bunch really kicked it up.

At all the Chilton gatherings, Alexander and Lizzie set a fast pace with their guitar and banjo, and his brother and sister played fiddle. A child measured dance-worth by a jig on the right foot, graduated to jig on the left foot, then up in the air and alternated toes to the ground. The true rite of passage—jig backward!

When Lizzie danced the wrong direction, she felt Alexander grab her shoulders, turn her around, and swing her around the room, skirts flying.

The music ended with "bow to your partner." Out of breath, eyes shining, she placed her hand on her heaving chest and squealed with delight, "You're a dancing fool, Alexander."

The next dance tuned up. Other cousins rose to take their places, so Alexander took her hand and led her off the dance floor.

"Are you thirsty? I will go outside and bring you a cool drink," he said with a sly smile.

"I just bet you will." She collapsed on the rock, her hand to her throat; she felt her heart beat fast blood through every vein from her toes to her hot, flushed cheeks. "What a play party!"

Mahala chuckled and placed the baby in Lizzie's lap. "I will be right back."

She watched Mahala make her way among the crowd with a gentle, kind way, and she obviously enjoyed the friendly banter. She seemed to know everybody. Mahala wore a white and black polka dot blouse tucked into a black skirt. She drew her black hair back and a white feather emerged from the thick bun. Lizzie remembered her mama say the Davis cousins married with the Sutterfields. The thought made her feel she was among family. Her mama's grandmother was part Cherokee, named Sapphira, and her mama's sister, Sophia, was a namesake. Lizzie certainly saw her own heritage in her mirror.

Her attention shifted to Eliza Jane when the baby's dimpled hand grasped an escaped lock of her hair. As babies do, the little girl brought her tiny fist to her rosebud mouth. Lizzie released her hair from the baby's firm grasp and squeezed the baby close, cheek to cheek. She caught the sweet smells of soap and water, and of wild violet bergamot secured as a halo on the white homespun linsey-woolsey bonnet. *Perhaps a baby proves more joy than dread*, she thought.

She watched Mahala weave her way back to retrieve the baby and lay her on the colorful pieced quilt on the damp sand floor. "Lizzie, sing one of your tunes."

"Oh, no, I dare not sing a peep. Your banjo plays well."

"Yes, it is the family treasure. My mama gave her banjo to me, and someday it shall be Eliza Jane's banjo. It must not leave the family." Mahala swiped an escaped tear away with her sleeve. "Mary Louisa says you write your own songs and sing at home all the time. People need a rest, and most folks visit between sets. She says your Missouri song may be the prettiest she ever heard."

"I want to live on the Missouri River some day. Papa told all about it when he came as a boy with his father. The Delaware Indians led them. The Osage brought them to a stop before they pushed very far west. They returned to Tennessee." She paused. "I will sing, if you play along with me. In G."

Self-conscious and pleased when Mahala and the other musicians picked up the tune and harmonized on the chorus after one listen, she noticed several of the young men laugh and eye her intently. She flushed with embarrassment and missed a few words. She decided to end the song with the chorus, thankful another singer began the popular fiddle tune, "The Soldiers Joy." These chords and rhythms ran swiftly. Lizzie took her turn, timidity long gone, and sang a verse of the old Scottish song.

Alexander made his way down the ridge to the arbor and hitched his horse to a sturdy tree limb. He saw the girl who earlier gave him a "come hither" with her eyes and fan. This time, he followed her into the dark woods and down a path to the spring branch that trickled from the cave to the valley floor.

He ventured a kiss, returned in full. When she released the buttons of her bodice, his knees went weak. Aroused, but shy and unsure, after a few minutes he said, "Come with me to the square dance."

"Oh, my Papa frowns on dancing."

In seconds—what seemed like hours—he decided. "Well, then, we best get back to the preaching."

She chuckled, "Yes, let's." When she reached the arbor, she flashed him a knowing look in the light of the torches and joined her friends at the back.

He paused. A strange feeling of "got caught" swept over him. He backed into the shadows.

One of his cousins met him where he tied his horse. "I got all I wanted from that one. Best steer clear."

"Then she is just what I steer for, next arbor meeting." Halfway embarrassed and defensive, Alexander swung into the saddle and rode back to the ridge.

Lizzie heard a commotion at the cave entrance and saw Alexander push his way through the crowd.

"Come quick, Lizzie. Sam Nesbit."

"What happened? Is he hurt?"

19

"Get your banjo; we need to leave, now." He shifted his guitar to his back and adjusted the woven-string strap across his chest.

She passed her banjo to Alexander, who held her hand as she climbed up the rocks and out of the cave. He dragged her along so fast she stumbled on her skirt-tail, fell on the slope, and tore the flesh on her left hand. "Slow down or we fall to our death in the dark!"

He led her to the top of the slope near their horses where she saw Sam Nesbit. He lay on the ground, doubled up from pain with his arms across his stomach. "Sam, when people drink whiskey, they get sick to death."

"Not whiskey-sick, knifed." Alexander gently held Lizzie, maintained a tight hold on her hand, and the weight on his arm jerked as her knees gave way.

"Fine, fine, stand back. Give me whiskey to wash the wound, then bind him and get him home to Aunt Betsy. She can stitch him up, and he will heal. He will heal."

Sam reached for her hand. "He said dishonorable things about you. I straightened him out, and you can recognize him tomorrow by his bloody nose and black eye. Now, get me to aaghhhhhh."

Lizzie poured the whiskey on the wound and revealed the cut, deep and long. She ripped a long strip from her petticoat, tore the dirty bottom away, and began to wrap his shoulder and middle. A dark splotch spread ominously on the white cotton like a cloud across the silver moon above.

"Thank goodness for John's wagon." Lizzie climbed in the back of the wagon and folded quilts thickly to absorb the inevitable bumps on the rocky mountain road.

When Alexander and his cousins lifted Sam to the quilt bed, Sam passed out from the pain.

"Alexander, help Lizzie. William, go find the Nesbit brothers. John, bring the horses." Nelson stepped down on the wagon tongue and doubletree, jumped to the ground, and slapped one horse's rump to head out. "Nesbits are a hot-headed bunch when full of drink and bound for the Hulseys when news spreads. We best catch them up to their brother where they belong. I think Sam slashed himself during the struggles. Knives are for the hunt, not for the fight. Now, get along."

After Lizzie settled down, she realized the trip to Jacks Fork and Aunt Betsy took hours. They needed somewhere to stay the night. "Stop at the arbor. I can stitch him up if we find needle and thread. Many women bring their needlework to gatherings."

John said, "We're headed off the ridge now. Hold him steady."

Lizzie knew John drove the heavy wagon as carefully as he could, but it made for a rough go. Rain washed out deep ruts and exposed rocks as high as a foot or more.

The pitch-pine torches at the brush arbor gave a warm welcome, and prayers began over Sam's still body. Lizzie borrowed thimble, needle, and boiled horsehair threads. She ripped a thin piece of her ruined petticoat, wrapped it around and around until the thimble fit her tiny third finger. She stitched with precision from the inside out, just as Aunt Betsy taught her. The sharp earthy smell of blood made her gag, but she kept her self-control. *Let the blood flow a bit to wash out the fever*, she thought.

She saw the preacher leave the pulpit and come to lay on hands. "You should remain here until morning, when the young man can travel stronger. Many of us came prepared to stay the week."

Lizzie heard the two rowdy Nesbit brothers rush through the crowd. However, seriousness prevailed when Lizzie leaned aside for the newcomers to comfort their wounded brother in the firelight.

She lay by her patient and listened to the preacher lead prayers and sing well into the night.

The next morning, Lizzie offered water to Sam when he stirred. She helped him with the water and crumbs placed on his cracked lips.

Sam whispered, "We would make quite a pair."

"You rest now." Lizzie slowly sat back on the quilt, and silently wept on Alexander's shoulder. "Sam wants excitement and works to avoid trouble, but he's like a bucket, full to spilling over the brim. I could see the knife cut deep. I stitched several wounds, seen mamas and babies die. Nothing prepared me for this violence, nothing." Lizzie bent forward with her hands over her eyes as if to push away pain from memories of lives lost under her care; lives such as her mother and father when she was untrained, only thirteen, and miles from any neighbor. Loss engulfed her and she moaned. She felt Alexander's protective embrace and finally drifted into a fitful sleep.

A few hours into morning, Alexander shook Lizzie's shoulder. "Come with us to the campfire for something to eat. A nurse needs to keep up her strength." He helped her out of the wagon and led her to a wood stump, which served as a seat by the campfire.

Lizzie sat down, disoriented. "Thank you." She felt revived after her meal. She filled a tin pan for Sam, and walked to the wagon.

"If I make it through, I promise to stop fighting, even for fun." Sam winced as he raised himself higher on the blanket to accept Lizzie's embrace and assist to a drink of water.

"You rest and live. You live a long happy life and stay by your promise."

The business of the Senator Joshua Chilton farm kept everyone engaged and an abundant kitchen table filled three times a day for the large family and three hired hands. One, the injured Sam Nesbit, took up the habit to help Lizzie clear the dishes to the washtub on the bench by the back door.

"Thank you, Sam. An iron teakettle full of hot water can be dangerous going. Now, do not fill it too heavy. You are not fully healed."

"Glad to help out. I know a big family—three sisters and two brothers; well, three, if you count Thomas Allen. All orphaned, like you. When the Suggs wanted children, they took all seven of us in about 1840, and we're glad of it."

"How old are they now?"

"Willoughby and Sara? Oh, Willoughby passed, and Sarah, more than seventy. My sisters count near twenty, same as me. Matthew and

James, nineteen and seventeen, prove some help, if you keep them separated. They take to the turkey woods at every chance."

"And you would know about turkey woods." Lizzie laughed aloud, tossed the gray water and coffee grounds to the herb beds, and nodded to Sam to carry another kettle of hot water. "But I tell you true, Sam, you may be the kindest man on the face of the earth."

Lizzie tended to Sam's recovery in Aunt Betsy's kitchen, and he helped with more indoor chores as strength returned. She and the others loved Sam's gentle ways and his humor. However, she could see Sam looked at her in a lover's way.

It came as no surprise when, as he helped her lay laundry on the fence, he proposed marriage. "Marry me. When the Graduation Act lowered prices below two bits an acre, I bought a parcel of land in Newton Township, near Current River and the mouth of Sinking Creek. We can build a one-room cabin to start with, and add more rooms as needed."

"Oh, now, you need time. My patients always fall in love with me."

"I spent time with thoughts of you long before the dance."

"Elizabeth Clementine Davis Nesbit. I like the sound of the name. You may be the kindest man I know, and rightly handsome to boot."

"You must not joke about marriage with me." Sam seemed uncharacteristically serious or perhaps fearful of her true feelings for him.

"But, consider all the Republicans on upper Current River?" She teased and joyfully pushed Sam aside, ran through Uncle Joshua's pasture toward Jacks Fork, with just enough backward glances to invite him to give chase.

She stopped by the river's edge and turned to accept his embrace. The warmth of his arms around her spread a feeling of safety to her toes. When he kissed her, she heard a low moan. She liked his kisses. She liked it all.

Lizzie and Sam married in the fall of 1856. Chilton cousins, Nesbit brothers, and north-county neighbors, including the Deatherages, built the promised cabin before the snow rested peacefully on the pines and melted in the streams.

She wondered why Alexander was nowhere to be found the day she moved up Current River some twenty-five miles.

Lizzie gave birth to William Samuel Nesbit on a sunny brisk afternoon, October 13, 1857. "Oh, not so good. His head, so pointy, he looks like a possum. I counted his fingers and toes, and his ears lie flat to his head."

Aunt Betsy, the midwife, tidied the bedclothes, "Settle down and rest. You know pointy heads go with a hard labor."

"But you know I'm narrow at the hip. I fear a birthing will be the death of me. Until now, I was impatient when the mothers screamed. Nevermore shall you hear another scold from me. Did I rip much?"

"You both came along fine. Let me comb your hair and then call Sam."

Lizzie soothed when Aunt Betsy found the comb and lovingly smoothed the wet wisps with the dark strands gathered in a long black braid. "There. You look lovely. Issabella's Lizzie, a mother. She would be so proud of you." Wiping away tears, Aunt Betsy stepped to the door. "Sam! It's a boy!"

CHAPTER 2

A CALL TO ARMS—1861

She wedded. And I a frequent guest,—
Flung on a couch with my books,—
With jealous pangs I could scarcely hide,
Have watched his gestures of love and pride,
And the answering joy in her looks. [2.31]

L izzie pulled up the last of the fall vegetables and stowed them in
grapevine baskets, destined for the root cellar. She heard Sam's
whistle get closer and closer behind her and waited for his arms to circle
her waist. "I like strong arms around my middle."

"Looks like these strong arms need to carry grapevine baskets to the
cellar."

"Yes, but first you must plant three kisses on my lips." She turned
slowly within his arms and placed hers around his neck. "Hello, Sam."

"Well, hello, Lizzie." Kisses bestowed and more than three, Sam
picked up a basket, headed for the cellar and whistled a slightly different tune.

Baskets in the cellar held potatoes, sweet potatoes, various squash,
and turnips. She wove the large three-foot-round by three-foot-deep
baskets from wild grapevines gathered from their woods at last year's
wild-grape harvest. She asked Sam to cut handles from a main cordon

about two inches in diameter, and she bound it in the last six rows of the baskets. She collected ten baskets of wild grapes, plus the first crop of tamed Norton grapes she started three years before in her garden. Chilton men passed cuttings along since they left Virginia for Tennessee and then Missouri. After the grapes boiled up, with the crabapples for pectin, she sweetened the mix with maple sugar cakes for jam. The baskets would stay the winter with the vegetables. The fall of 1860 saw abundance in the woods and the fields.

She heard William wail from his tall, blanket-filled basket by the garden. "Out. Out!"

When Sam scooped William up and onto his shoulders, he picked up one side of the basket; Lizzie grasped the other cordon handle, and the trio made their way toward the one room cabin. She stepped around Sam's passel of hound dogs, up the split-log steps to the porch, and into the dark, cozy room. Herbs and vegetables bubbled in the cast-iron pot that swung over low flames in the rock fireplace. She breathed in fragrances sweet and earthy from bundles of herbs hung to dry from every rafter corner to corner. "Mmmm, I love my physic garden."

She settled in her mother's chair at the end of the "good table" from Tennessee. Sam's chair, William's tall stool, a cradle bed, and a corn-shuck mattress on a wooden rope bed completed the furnishings. Her sunbonnet and quilted linsey-woolsey medical bag hung on a peg by the door, ready for calls from her neighbors on the upper Current River, even the Republicans.

Lizzie's cousins in her Uncle Truman Chilton's family lived on a farm in nearby Spring Valley, and like her husband, howled "yellow-dog Democrat." He would rather vote for a yellow dog than a Republican.

She came to understand most of the other neighbors, a mix of Ohio, Indiana, and Illinois homesteaders, included neighbors David B. Smith, a civil engineer from Maine, and Amos and John Worthington, who came from Pennsylvania with mining interests and abolitionist views.

A few families on the west side of the county owned slaves, and nobody wanted the terror reported from the western border at Kansas for several years. However, she worried when Alexander and his brothers came upriver to visit cousins because David Smith always got wind of it and came spoiling for a fight. Alexander obliged and fought with a grin.

With the Chiltons, a gathering meant a dance and a crowd. Lizzie and Sam decided a new house called for a dance. When her cousins came early, she spent a joyous week getting ready. "Who came? The host does not see everyone. How does Aunt Betsy do it?" Lizzie was breathless with details, work, and excitement.

Alexander's sister, Mary Louisa, teased her. "Aunt Betsy birthed three daughters specifically to help with the dances."

"Since they are well practiced, get your fiddle, and get this dance underway. Sam knows my whereabouts if I am needed." Lizzie took off her apron, grabbed her banjo, and skipped down the path to the bottom of the slope. She greeted family, friends, and neighbors who sat on blankets and stools along the way. "Aunt Polly, you took charge of my William. Thank you."

When she arrived at the flat area, Alexander and others were tuned up and singing. He stopped at the end of a chorus. "Lizzie and Mary Louisa, get this party livened up!"

Alexander took note of the arrivals during the afternoon, a mix of all creeds and sympathies. He prepared for trouble and prayed for peace. "At the break, I am off to the table laden with the ladies' best and the hunters' bounty."

When he filled his plate, he walked to the edge of the gathering and leaned against a tree, with his left foot against the trunk to brace his balance. "What the...?" His plate swerved through the air and fell several feet away.

"Steal my horse, but do not think you get by without a fight for its return or the profit." David Smith shouted and looked as angry as a hog with one leg roped.

"Whoa, now, you make a serious charge. I stole no horse, not yours, not anybody's. Chilton men pay for their stock. Now, what horse disappeared? I personally will join you in its recovery; right after this party ends at dawn."

"You were seen leaving my property. Then my horse came up missing. Seem suspicious to you?"

"I did not venture north of Sam's place. But with my good looks and fine stature, one rarely misidentifies me." Alexander looked around and joined with the laughter of others. He knew they were waiting for a fight, and he took pride in landing the second shot, a decisive punch to the nose.

"You young smart-mouthed—" Smith stopped and ran toward Alexander, head down like a charging bull, caught him around the waist, and threw him off balance to the ground.

"Yahoo," Alexander yelled after he caught his breath, and then kicked and punched with all the strength he could muster. He felt Smith's heavier weight pin him to the ground, and knew his only hope was distraction. "You sure married a pretty woman!"

"Keep my wife out of it!" Smith shouted, pulled back his elbow to throw a punch and leaned to the downhill side of the squabble.

"Right pretty woman!" Alexander pushed his assailant away with a kick of his feet and raised knee. Then he felt his arm and fist free to punch. His fist crashed Smith's nose and blood squirted over his shirt. He pushed Smith to the side and back where three or four men helped him to his feet but held him from the fight.

"That's enough, now. Fun seems gone out of this wrestling match." Representative Alfred Deatherage, a nearby neighbor, stood between the two.

"Get back with the women," Smith shouted to someone behind Alexander.

Alexander knew he should not laugh, but it struck him that Smith was a jealous husband. Something certainly seemed different anytime Mrs. Smith stepped closer. He muffled a laugh, but when he met Smith's gaze, it was one of pure anger bordering on hate. Perhaps Smith did not understand that the sport of men of the Ozarks ran rugged, and a fight proved one's mettle. No good came from hate in the squabble. People die when passion prevails. He decided to give Smith a wide berth.

He returned to the stump where he left the guitar and joined the dance tune already in progress. Some people did not miss a beat during the fight, and he liked it just that way. He said, "Pearly Mae," and nodded to Mary Louisa whose bow carried the melody, and Lizzie's banjo strummed softly. "I caught this song from a good ol' boy up on Sinking Creek." [7.2]

After the last tune of the evening, Alexander listened to Jackson Herrin, one of several Herrin brothers in Moore Township on Big Creek, who recruited convincingly. "General McBride from Houston and Captain Freeman from Salem pack for the west a hundred miles, to a place called Wilson's Creek. They say there is room in the Third Infantry in Price's Missouri State Guard. Guard units protect our borders from invaders and stay within the state. Capt. Shadrach Chilton enrolls recruits at Alton in Oregon County, and we rendezvous to travel with the Reynolds County boys tomorrow."

Alexander noticed Lizzie move near Sam, who spoke quietly to avoid her hearing. "If we stay in the state, I stand strong for protection. Meet you in the morning at the rendezvous site."

Alexander breathed an honest sigh of relief when the neighbors and cousins bedded down or packed to leave. A gathering proved dangerous these days, when abolitionists or unionists mixed company with neutrals or secessionists.

Little William woke Lizzie at dawn, and upon their return to the house from the privy, she helped him climb into Sam's bed and snuggle under the covers. Then she closed the door. "And where might the rendezvous site be, my dear?" She whispered and her dark blue eyes snapped with fear, disguised as anger.

"Now, Lizzie, darling."

"Don't 'Lizzie darling' me. I want to know."

"The disagreements might only last a few weeks. I know you stand strong for the Union and abolition of slavery. However, I walk with pride to my duty to my state. I leave at dawn."

"Disagreements? War, Sam. War. You side with the rebels and leave us here alone with abolitionist neighbors? I am an abolitionist; however, people ascribe a woman's views with those of her husband. Our house will not last a week. I pack for Aunt Betsy's house. Leave, I will." She lifted William from the bed, whirled, and stomped to the river with little William in tow so fast he whimpered.

"Fall down. Fall down."

"Oh, my darling William, we walk too strong to fall down."

"We strong."

Lizzie, in tears, sat on the gravel riverbank and drew almost-three-year-old William into her embrace. "We strong."

She heard the crunch of gravel, recognized the boot, and felt Alexander sit beside her. "Do you rendezvous with Col. Lucian Farris tomorrow or with Farris' son, William, sometime hence?"

"Capt. William Farris," he whispered and took her hand into his.

Sunrise lifted the fog off the spring-fed river like a wispy shroud. She shivered.

At age eighteen, Alexander stood six feet tall and weighed 215 pounds. His reputation: win and win clean. His wicked good looks, mild manner, and sideways grin misled an outsider bent on trouble. Like other Chilton men, his straight aristocratic nose, high cheekbones, and wide, square face softened ladies' hearts. He took his fair skin, light blue eyes, and curly reddish-brown hair from the Harvisons, his mother's people from Ireland.

One late afternoon he sat on the front porch and played his guitar; an old camp song, but he could not quite remember the words. He looked up and saw a stranger, who reined his horse toward the house, and stopped at the hitching rail.

The man placed his hand near the rifle scabbard. "I hear the Chiltons are the best fighters in the county. I'm here to prove this right or wrong."

Alexander stepped off the porch and into the yard. "News of such traveled around lately. Now, we want no trouble. Go on down the road. Trouble enough comes uninvited."

"Oh, I mean a friendly fistfight. Prove your mettle." The young man dismounted but kept his hand on the rifle scabbard.

Alexander ambled to the hitching post. He ducked the first swing. One quick jab to the stranger's nose took the fire right out of the squabble. "Now, I may be known as a good fighter, but you ought to go up against my pa. He is strong as an ox and can whup a bear. Did so, I tell you. Saw it myself. *Deus spes mea*, I think I broke your nose." He kept his hands up to protect his own nose.

"Say what?"

"'God is my hope.' I heard the motto often enough, and with good reason, from my mama. Stay for supper and let her look at that nose. Did you say your name?"

The stranger wiped his bleeding nose with his kerchief. "Joe Butler, hired hand over at the Warrens. I'm from Tennessee."

"Most folks around here came from Tennessee or Virginia. Fighting your main business this fine evening?" Alexander lowered his fists and gave a sideways grin to the young stranger.

"No. Trouble's brewing at the subscription school, and the boys said you never missed a good brew." Joe picked up his hat from the ground and wiped his nose again. "I don't believe my nose is broken. Blood's staunched already."

"Schoolmaster James M. L. Jamieson resumed teaching the young ones to be northern sympathizers, did he?" Alexander stated the matter, more than a question.

"Reckon your pretty sisters ought to know. I watch the two pass the Warrens' farm every morning on their way to the school."

Alexander gave thought to the matter. "Mary Louisa knows better than tempt Papa's ire with the teachings. Papa says if Jamieson continues his Unionist ways, he invites escort out of the county."

"Then consider yourself invited." Joe swung into the saddle and raised his hand to tip his hat to the women at the door.

Alexander trotted to the porch and grabbed his hat and coat. "Going to the Warrens' with Joe Butler, here. Be back soon."

Alexander's mother called to her son." Be home before dawn, now, you hear?"

He was already in the barn. He threw on the blanket and saddle, tightened the girth, and with a deafening whistle, kicked his horse into a race with Joe Butler, three miles upriver to Mahan's Creek.

Night fell pitch black with the new moon, but they could make out fifty men or more gathered in the Warrens' yard. Alexander and his racing partner drew up their horses to a walk. "Bob-bob-white," Alexander whistled.

Someone ahead answered his call.

"It's safe to proceed. Same in Tennessee?"

"The very same." Joe Butler chuckled and followed Alexander to the edge of the gathering.

"Nelson." Alexander greeted his first cousin, dismounted, and dropped the reins.

"Alexander. No guns. Told us lads to stand clear and learn something."

By 1861, Alexander considered himself more than a lad. He followed close behind the center group of men, while the other two young men walked on either side and separated further as they made their way down the road to Jamieson's house and school.

Alexander watched the men surround the house, but he stayed back near the road.

Someone at the front of the mob shouted toward the door. "Jamieson! Gather your hat and coat. Step to the porch with your hands in the air!"

Silence prevailed. Then, Alexander saw the sliver of a light as the door open slightly.

"I am coming out. Hands up. My wife and young ones are inside. Do no harm, you hear?" Jamieson sounded firm but cautious.

"No harm intended for you or your family. A guard will follow you to Salem or Pilot Knob. Your family can stay. You will not see us, but rest assured we follow."

"What is the problem?" Jamieson inquired, and then turned toward the door. "Sarah, no. Get back into the house. Now!"

"You know the problem. We warned you to stop teaching the children controversial northern ways. Get smart with us, and the butt of a gun will smash your mouth. Now, move!"

Alexander whispered, "Never heard of a running-off before."

"You are a foolish man, James. Every man here owns his private sympathies, and only claims rights to protect his property from outside influences. Take your horse and walk him slowly ahead of us to the river ford."

A loud protest erupted from many men who surrounded the house and swept past Alexander, with talk of hanging and whipping.

"Enough!" The leader of the escort shouted more emphatically to the mob.

Alexander jumped at the shout and prayed all would heed the warning. "Here he comes. Give a wide berth."

Alexander flushed and his mind lost all reason when his eyes met those of his former teacher who gave a slight nod of recognition as he passed. He watched the vanquished proud man walk his horse down the road northward toward the river, as ten men on horseback followed a musket-shot distance behind.

"I learned my letters well from the schoolmaster. I know to listen when my uncles advise. Crying shame to lose a learned man. Trouble sure came uninvited this night." Alexander followed far behind the escort all the way down Mahan's Creek to the river, and then he and his two companions turned toward his home.

Taught to keep his own counsel, he wondered when his time came to protect his own kin, whether he would lose his temper, or find himself as brave and honorable a man as tonight's leader. He knew hill country ways. He would never learn the leader's name.

Alexander saw his father shudder when he heard the details of Jamieson's escort. Alexander asked, "Do you think Jamieson will hold hard feelings enough to exact revenge?"

His father answered with a question, "His escort came for him in the dark of night, did they not? However, time will tell. Joshua and I want you boys to start early for the Jamiesons in the morning. Miz Sarah needs help to load her belongings in her wagon—and both of our wagons, if necessary. Pack one with your mama's blankets for her six children. Then, you boys are to drive her and her family to Salem to join her husband."

"Escort the Missus? Surely, the insult must sting all the worse?" Alexander looked perplexed.

"Nay, you will find other Masonic sons there to help load. His wife and family are not to suffer for the beliefs he holds honorable, however misguided others judge him." Shadrach scooted his chair closer to the table. "Draw up everyone. Alexander, pray over this fine meal."

Alexander settled into his chair and took up the blessing. "God Almighty, we thank you for the good crops, but some rain to break the heat would be welcome. For our families and survival of the grippe, and for the bread and abundance on our table, we give thanks. Amen."

"You make a good prayer. A man takes pride in a prayerful son." Shadrach started the bowls around the long wooden table, made smooth and dark brown from years of soap, water, and beeswax.

After the much-delayed supper, Alexander, his two guests, and his family gathered on quilts spread over the grass. His brothers lit the pitch and pine torches.

His father took a place on the bench. "Trouble enough with the Jayhawker invaders on the western border, now we must refuse to get dragged into South Carolina's cotton gin. Made us take on the Reeds in fifty-eight and vote neutral with the rest of the legislature, excepting one. Accused me as a Know-Nothing and Mama, here, Irish."

He paused, patted the knee of his red-haired wife, Patsy, and addressed young Butler. "You know about the Know-Nothings?"

Joe shook his head, and looked down at his hands.

"The bunch of immigrant-haters gathered from the Democrats and Republicans. You can spot one when you seek an opinion, say, on secession or states' rights. 'I know nothing,' they respond. One cannot accuse me of faltering an opinion. However, another vote is coming, boys. Since the birth of the Republic, secession talk surfaced over some spat or another, generally in the Massachusetts Commonwealth or South Carolina. Some general or other will puff up, shoot into a crowd, and fire up 'Little Dixie.'" He sat taller against his pillows and took a sip from the jug.

"Little Dixie, Papa?" Mary Louisa, his fifteen-year-old daughter, knit her brow and adjusted his pillows, eyes all the while on the two visitors.

"Little Dixie, the land along the Missouri River from Saint Louis across the state to Westport, boasts fine farms so large they call them plantations. The wealthy planters own slaves and wield a powerful force in Missouri. Even so, many do not favor secession and sit in powerful political positions to keep Missouri in the Union."

"Slaves helped build the sluice for the mill. The boys sneaked up and watched." Mary Louisa gave a quick glance at her brothers and Nelson when she realized her breech of confidence. "Are we a wealthy powerful force?"

"By hill standards, yes, a powerful force in some quarters, however, we own no slaves, mind you. The laws find liberty, but in time for all of Missouri? That is the question. Joshua's vote counts as much as anybody's does. No need to worry, darling." Shadrach reached for Mary Louisa's pigtails and bestowed reassurance on his beloved daughter.

Alexander said, "Cousin Louisa may be more to handle than any bear when she hears about the schoolmaster. The Sinclairs and the Jamiesons are mighty good friends. I like a woman with some spit and fire."

"Louisa claims strong views, all right. The farther north you go in the county, the more people hold abolitionist views."

"Tell us the stories when Grandpa Boggs fought in the wars with General Jackson." Alexander, then one son or another, egged him on.

"And tell about Great Granddaddy Mark, and Stephen, Thomas, and James with their uncle John, who served with General Washington in the Continental Army."

Shadrach waved the boys off and respected his wife's fears when he heard her sigh. "Girls, take up your needlework and stitch of love and beauty."

"Good night, Mr. Butler. Good night, Nelson." Mary Louisa said.

Joe Butler quickly stood, hat in hand. "Night, Miss. Good night, Mrs. Chilton. Thank you for supper."

Alexander would long remember his father's smile of tenderness toward his mother, as she and his three sisters and two sisters-in-law disappeared up the steps into the house.

He whooped when he saw his father turn with fire in his eyes toward his three grown sons and nephew. "Boys, we weave battle stories, full of slashes, gore, flags, and medals—a glorified fistfight!"

"Col E B Alexander Provost Marshal General Dear sir I now sit down to address a pen to you concerning my friend James M L Jamieson...I have always known him to be an honorable high-minded gentleman & he was broke up in the beginning of this accursed rebellion & had to leave his family in the midst of their enimys & flee to Pilot Knob to keep a band of rebel ruffians & black gards from taking him out of his own house & hanging him just for being a true blue union man...."
—Louisa Chilton Sinclair [2.21]

Lizzie laid aside a copy of her Aunt Louisa's letter after reading the first few words. She refused to allow political sympathies to spoil the dance. She dressed most carefully in the upstairs room of the Senator Joshua Chilton house. "Mama always said she might as well stain the linsey-woolsey with berries and grapes at the start because other stains appeared at the end before the dress wore out." She layered three petticoats to try to give effect of the fashionable hoops of the east that cost cash money.

Susan said, "The silks of the east are of the finest expensive fibers in deep rich colors. Someday I shall wear silk." The women of her family spun their own cotton, flax, and wool; then dyed, wove, and fashioned lovely dresses of natural hues. The married women dressed in darker colors, the young women in lights and whites, and the children in serviceable walnut and butternut browns and berry-stain dyes.[1.90]

Lizzie pulled a dark yellow dress over her head and fastened the hooks and snaps. The dress had yards of pleated skirt to the floor; and long fitted lower sleeves which, when removed for summer, left short puffy sleeves much like a ball gown. She tucked the collar inside the neckline, placed a white, tatted collar around her neck, and then attached her mother's small oval brooch.

Her seventeen-year-old cousin, Rebecca, parted Lizzie's black hair down the center, and pinned the long unruly locks into a dark-yellow crocheted snood. "Lovely, lovely. Susan, you are next, then Anne."

Lizzie stood and motioned for Susan, age thirteen and dark haired like Lizzie.

Anne was eleven with light-brown wavy hair that streaked with white in summer sun and the largest brown eyes. She was destined to be a real beauty.

There were also four brothers. Nelson was nineteen, sturdy and dark like his father. Perry, more slender with brown wavy hair like his mother, was quite the charmer at sixteen. Young James was nine, Francis was seven, and Thomas was three. The three youngest engaged in a fair amount of mischief.

As Lizzie took note of her cousins' lovely summer dresses and preparations in the upstairs rooms, a sense of loneliness descended. Her sister, Caroline, was eighteen and gone to Tennessee to her Davis grandparents, after her Chilton grandmother died in 1859. Her brother, Thomas, was twenty and no doubt handsome as could be in his dark-blue Union Army uniform, somewhere near St. Louis. Both siblings looked like a Davis, with light sandy hair.

She looked at herself in the mirror and pinched her cheeks. With her petite stature and trim waist, she could pass for a woman of eighteen instead of twenty-two years. The sound of a melodious "Mama, Mama" broke her reverie. She gathered her young son into her arms and then set him on the floor. The two carefully descended the steep stairs to the dogtrot, a wide center hall between the large kitchen keeping room and the downstairs bedroom.

She smiled at Alexander, who stood at the foot of the stairs, hat in hand. She hummed a tune and stepped to the rhythms as if a princess descended the stairs toward her protector.

"You strike quite a pose, Cousin dear." Alexander offered her his arm and led Lizzie and little William to the porch and into the crowd gathered in the yard.

Lizzie stomped her foot in disappointment and anger at the back of the gathering, well out of hearing distance of strangers. "I make good on my promises. Sam will return from war only to find wife and son gone. He should be here on this important day."

Her cousin and best friend, Mary Louisa, said, "All the more reason he knows where to find you after his three-month enlistment. Maybe it won't turn to war here." Alexander's sister picked up her fiddle, retuned with a few strokes of the bow across the strings, and she and two brothers started another tune for the dancers gathered in the yard.

Lizzie felt her cheeks cool from red to pink as her mood lifted, and her fingers rolled and clawed her banjo strings with joy.

At the end of the song, Alexander handed his guitar to a cousin, walked toward Lizzie, and bowed. "May I have this dance, milady?" He took her hand and laid her banjo aside. "A waltz will do, sister, dear," he said over his shoulder, but his eyes stayed locked on the woman in his arms.

Lizzie tripped on her skirt tail, so she took up a hank of skirt and petticoat and stepped with Alexander into the crowd of dancers. "I love dancing with you. We just sail over the grass."

"We could sail to the end of the continent and be fine with me." He felt a burning in his throat and feared his eyes might tear. He muttered, "And me, head over heels for war. Fool."

When the song ended, she saw Uncle Joshua nod his head toward the musicians. As Senator of the Twenty-Fourth District of South Missouri, he stood among his constituency gathered at his home for news from Jefferson City. He stepped upon the porch, and raised his hand to settle the crowd. "Citizens and neighbors, Representative Deatherage, county judges, members of Father John Joseph Hogan's flock up from the wilderness, several of our reverends, family...ladies and gentlemen.

"During the last session of the Missouri Legislature, the temper of the times failed to allow calmness in deliberation and discussion, so very necessary to consider in matters of the state. While Gen. Sterling Price of the newly formed Missouri State Guard urged reason, General Lyon of the United States Army declared war on Missouri. Then, Missouri Governor Jackson 'seceded Missouri' from the Union. Neither Lyon nor Jackson is granted such authority. President Lincoln, of course, remanded the military order. The state legislature is up in arms with the governor's high-handed declarations and speeches betraying his campaign promises to keep Missouri neutral on the matter of secession.

"In St. Louis, General Fremont of the US Army abolished slavery in Missouri without authority. President Lincoln rescinded the order to abolish slavery. General Fremont is the son-in-law of our senator, Thomas Hart Benton, who formed an elite guard of German immigrants, well educated and battle honed for protection of Missouri borders. We pray public safety and the question of preservation of the union, states' rights, and slavery be discussed and decided without passion.

"In March of sixty-one, for the citizens of Missouri, the State Constitutional Convention voted overwhelmingly...ninety-eight to one, to remain neutral with regard to secession with the southern states. The legislature established a militia to protect our citizens and secure our neutral borders, ably led by our leading statesman, Sterling Price, under a Bears of Missouri flag. In mid-June, after the Camp Jackson affair and riots in St. Louis, General Lyon followed Jackson to Jefferson City, secured the capitol, and forced Gov. Jackson and his state government into exile in southwest Missouri. In July, the convention named Hamilton R.

Gamble provisional governor, dissolved the legislature, and set a date for elections. Governor Gamble is a slaveholder who opposes secession. A former chief justice of the Missouri Supreme Court, he favors the processes of civil law in matters of the state, rather than military action. He pressed President Lincoln to rescind martial law in our state. In doing so, Lincoln also removed General Fremont from command.

"I, as your senator, along with Representative Deatherage and all but two representatives of our twenty-fourth district, came home, rather than join the exiled state government. We must hold firm in our commitment to family, friend, and neighbor in these troubled times. May we all rise to greet each day on our own farms; to our favorite 'call to arms!'"

The whistled call of the quail, "Bob-bob-white," concluded his remarks.

Lizzie walked to Aunt Betsy's side. "My uncles are true orators! Never the mind, I seem to return to you like a pigeon. When Sam left for war, Uncle and all the boys rallied to our side to get in our crops and carry us here. I am forever thankful."

"My dear, you are like a daughter to me, and you look as much like my natural born as Susan. Speaking of natural born, what do you make of the advice Dr. Reed gave to his brother in a letter; this copy he sent me for doctoring?"

She took the letter and began to read.

"The flux this year in this country was connected with conjunctive or sinking chills—which made the flux so much worse than any flux we ever had in this country before. Thos. Chilton and family are well at present...as many as 7 in one family had Died with flux and Hundreds and Thousands in the State...gone to the good World.

Relative to your Disease—it is rather novel or new—still that does not disarm it of its fatality—nor reveal the secret of its cure. Of ... Tobacco-Tobacco mite have some effect in paralising the nerves of the lip. Tobacco you know is a narcotic poison that would dedon a nerve when applied it prudent of you to discontinue the use of the article for a

*while—or at any rate to keep the stuff on the underside of the Mouth—
and use as little as possable—there are many causes for palsy,...the only
prospect of cure is counter irritation on the part and around the part—
which can be done by blisters—to the part and blisters in the back of
the neck—cleansing of the Bowels with salts or if the discharges should
be fray some Calomel and if the system is full of Blood, bleeding will be
proper or abstemious living will be prudent. I would try Bleeding—if the
system is full—cleanse the Bowels, blister—then use the tartar emetic
ointment which is made mixing—say teaspoon of tarter Emetic in half
teacup of lard or Butter then rub the part 3 or 4 times per day—until
sores brake out then discontinue.*

*Be sure to pay strict attention to the Bowels keep them open and
discharges of a good Cholor and of the right consistancy—and if this all
failes it mite be proper to institute a drane in the back of the neck—and
keep sores in the temples by Blisters or ointment. the object of all this is
to guard the brane from inflammation ...."* [1.52]

Lizzie tossed the letter over her shoulder and watched it flutter to the
ground. "More likely kill the man than his disease. However, I do love
Doctor Reed and Aunt Polly so. We learned good medicine from him.
I apologize for my impertinence." Lizzie hurried to retrieve the letter,
which tumbled across the yard on the wind. With respect, she handed it
back to her aunt.

Aunt Betsy chuckled at her brash niece. "Apology accepted. Doctor
Reed saved many a patient with common sense, too. We pray to find
new medicine for the likes of Doctor Reed's brother. Thankfully, our
herbs give some comfort."

"Miz Patsy. Good day to you." Lizzie greeted Alexander's mother
with a kiss. "Will the Catholic flock hold discussions for all the redeemed
in the crowd, not just the Catholics? Reverend Reeves speaks hard against
the Church of Rome. The strong words of the Protestant circuit preachers
prompted Uncle Joshua to take a stand for calm in the Wilderness."

"A welcome stand, at that. We prepared for Father Hogan across
the river in our barn after the speeches, but he returned to his duties

in Chillicothe some months ago. I fear for his flock, but he trusts his absence contributes to calm. However, we Irish hold for the Union and such splits the people as sure as my own family. My husband insists the State Guard stands for neutrality. I maintain it will be in the Confederacy before the year ends."

Lizzie watched inquisitively as Aunt Betsy returned from the house with a large thick book. She reached for Lizzie's hand and pressed the book into her arms. "For you, my dear, the latest medical book all the way from St. Louis; Joshua brought it for you. Many new treatments therein." Aunt Betsy's eyes sparkled.

"Oh, my. Oh, my! Such a precious gift. I want to leave the dance to read and read. Miz Patsy, this is Volume I, A Treatise on Therapeutics, and Pharmacology or Materia Medica.[4.1] Are the words Latin?

"I believe it means medicines," Alexander's mother replied.

Lizzie returned her attention to the book. "By George B. Wood, published by J. B. Lippincott, Philadelphia, 1860. Oh, it is the newest of its kind."

"Volume II waits inside. Doctor Reed will be most happy to see us from time to time, especially when we bring our books. However, for now, guests await the lady of the house and all her daughters and sons. Shall we go while the politics and religions knit us together?"

Lizzie felt her blood leave her face as white as her tatted collar, and she whispered, "You gave me this book to better tend wounded soldiers."

Alexander stood with his father and Shadrach's brothers: Joshua, Thomas, William, James, Francis, Charles, John, and Andrew. He listened to the men talk politics.

Shadrach said, "Joshua came home, as did eight of the ten representatives in his twenty-fourth senatorial district. The other two, from Oregon and Howell counties, went to Neosho with exiled Governor Jackson and twenty-nine other representatives. Joshua doubts they make a quorum. But seeing as how they form the only duly elected representatives, he says we need to keep a cool head when they vote for secession and the Confederacy."

William said, "I fear most for our sons, to insure preservation of the Union."

John said, "If we can keep armies east of the Mississippi, a miracle resulted from fervent prayer, my brothers."

Shadrach answered, "If we can lead our sons in protection of our farms and neutral borders, perhaps all sons of Missouri will be saved from battles in the east. I answered the call of Price's passionate appeal with orders to report to the Springfield plains. We ride this week with Freeman and the companies of General McBride. For weeks, I carried a copy of Price's appeal for a Missouri Guard and now wait for the right time to read it to my wife. Such an appeal will surely carry weight with her."

Alexander felt sparks of shock and rising divisions between the brothers. Like Missouri, he realized his family swirled in mixed loyalties, confusion, and chaos. His own shock came, when he watched the brothers begin to embrace, their eyes filled with tears; every brother embraced the other, made their way to Joshua one at a time, and returned to their individual wives, sons, and daughters to enjoy the dance.

Alexander tucked his head close to his packhorse as he loaded cook and camp supplies. He listened to his father broach the subject of the Missouri Guard in late July 1861.

His mother turned on her heel and raised her arms in defeat, "Choose for themselves? God is my hope, keep them safe, and bring them back to me on the promised twelfth week."

Good-byes completed, he watched her faith wane as she followed at some distance behind the procession of men on the pasture trail. As if in pained desperation, she turned and ran toward the river, picked up a fallen branch, and waded knee-deep into the cold clear glassy current. She held the branch with both hands, and beat the water until no strength remained to raise her arms another time, nor breath for wails to the river whose riffles absorbed the energy of her suffering.

Alexander halted the column. "Shall I see to Mama?"

His father wiped his forehead and eyes with his shirtsleeve. "Not up to another good-bye. Move on."

Nobody moved.

Mesmerized, the men watched her return up the river trail to the house where beloved daughters, daughters-in-law, and grandchildren waited on the porch. They encircled her like a cloak against a violent storm.

Shadrach and his sons, Alexander, William, and John turned westward to war.

CHAPTER 3

BATTLE OF WILSON'S CREEK—1861

The incessant roll of musketry was deafening, and the balls fell
thick as hailstones, but still our gallant southerners pushed
onward, and with one wild yell broke upon the enemy, pushing
them back and strewing the ground with their dead.
—Ben. McCulloch, Brigadier-General, Commanding,
Confederate States of America [2.34]

Alexander pulled his raingear around him and cast a doubtful look at the dreary August dawn. "No battles today. One cannot keep the powder dry."

His father said, "Rain never stopped my boys rustling up breakfast."

Alexander dropped the tin cup in the water bucket. "Come, Pearl, set the hollers ringin'. Are you coming, William?"

He shifted his squirrel gun to his left shoulder, scratched his hound dog's ears, and he and his brother set out south beyond the cornfields and into the woods. He walked thankful for the bundle of stores set aside by his family, now packed in his saddlebags. Many of the men poached and feasted on green corn from the fields and then suffered the miserable consequences. [3.24]

The following day dawned with clearing skies. Alexander sat on the tongue of the supply wagon of another company of Oregon, Shannon, and Reynolds County boys and cleaned his gun. The mood of the camps in the Wilson's Creek valley was subdued.

He waited for the call to drill from Lt. John J. Bennett, from Oregon County. With his bent toward independence to a fault, Alexander grew impatient with the precision of march drills and turns and orders to fall into line, load guns, fire, reload, and fire imaginary powder and bullets. He shook his head and grimaced at the thought that less than half his company carried weapons, and the others marched and drilled with a wooden gun carved from a tree limb. Some army. No uniforms, no flash of saber, and less action than a fox hunt. He threw the rest of his sassafras tea into the sputtering fire.

"Gunshots! Take cover!" Alexander heard more shouts to the south, and then he saw horses bearing blue-suited soldiers far to his left. He dropped his tin cup, and wondered how so many soldiers came so close without detection. Surely the camp would not be overrun given the dense circles of wagons, campfires, pots, and pans. Nevertheless, he pulled his bullet bag over his shoulder, and ran low with his head ducked away from camp toward the high hill to the north. "William?"

"Here!" William ran parallel and just ahead of his younger brother. "Where's John?"

"Talking with the sergeant in the next camp." Alexander stopped. He saw a nest of gray-suited soldiers in the northwest, headed straight for the blues. "When will a line of battle start firing?" he asked his brother.

William shook his head and motioned northward toward his own captain of the William A. Farris Company, Missouri State Guard.

When hidden by trees on a rise, the two brothers stopped. Alexander, surrounded by other homespun-clad-soldiers, watched the two armies get closer.

"Rebels!" Alexander faintly heard the shout, and the blue army finally fired into the gray. He watched in dismay as the grays held back, and lines of toy-size men in the valley fell before his very eyes.

"They are falling back! William, the Rebels have the army overrun and in retreat!"

Cannon fire blasted from the North into the valley. In a delay of what seemed like minutes, balls of fire rolled beyond him. The valley lit up like a wildfire and Alexander ran toward the hill and the cannons in the distance. "Fool! What fool ran toward trouble?" he shouted to his brother.

No answer returned.

He saw hundreds of men moving in the same direction as him. "Safety on the river, in twos and threes," he said to the young man next to him.

"Guess the safety of rivers far from here," the reply.

Alexander heard the trees rustle like a hailstorm, yet he saw no enemy upon whom to set sights. He moved forward, until he reached a line of men who appeared to know where the enemy lay and what to do about it. He heard shouted orders and took them.

He watched a man fall; a mass of blood and matter defined the upper half of a human form. Fear encompassed him, and he took aim ahead, at no specific person. Reloaded and fired again.

He could barely make out several men and boys from Shannon County in the smoke that choked the engagement: James Kile, Jack Suggs to the right; John W. Adair, some of the Laxtons, and his cousin William Shakespeare Chilton to the left. He searched to no avail for his brothers and knew his father was far across the field with Freeman's Regiment.

He crept toward Jack Suggs and James Kile, who fought together in the battle and down in a ravine. They loaded their guns and slipped to where they could see the enemy and shoot.

He flinched when Kile shot at one and stood looking. "Did I get my man?"

Suggs shouted over the din, while he loaded his gun, "Come back out of sight!"

Alexander heard Kile say, "Lord, have mercy."

He ran toward the pair, but watched helplessly as Kile fell mortally wounded, a small red wound right between his eyes." [1.32]

When he saw an officer fall, another took his place in the battle line. The replacement shouted orders, "Move to the hill."

Alexander moved with the mass of men toward the hill. From the shouts, he assumed the officer to be a man named Coleman, one of the few who seemed to know exactly how to take charge of his men and move safely behind trees in an effective line.

He watched men fall with screams and with shouts, in what seemed a never-ending death song.

Then, silence. He whispered to the lad kneeled to his right. "Is it over?"

"I surely hope so," the reply.

Smoke filled the valley behind him and the hill ahead. It burned his eyes and filled his nostrils with sharp acrid smells of gunpowder. The sounds of a battlefield reached his ears. Screams of horse and man drifted endlessly. Would the fog ever lift?

He sat for what seemed an hour or more, then heard music to his ears: "Alexander, brother!" William and John ran unharmed to his side and took cover in the ravine folded safely into the hillside.

Then the order came to move again to the top of the hill and another wave of human carnage rose and fell as far as his eyes could see amid the smoke and chatter of leaves and limbs against bullets and cannon.

Alexander thrust pick and shovel until a six-by-four-foot grave took form. Uninvited scenes flashed into his stunned mind, and he brushed them aside with verses of poem or song.

As exhaustion increased, his ability to control his emotions decreased. Tears flowed as freely as the blood of the wounded on the prairie soil.

"Alexander, are you all right?" William walked to his younger brother's side. "August days in Missouri scorch man and beast."

"Yes, I could use some water, though.

"Cold water sounds good. But somebody said the creek runs red."

When Alexander flinched, William dropped his shovel and embraced his brother. "When I saw you, John, Captain—uh—Papa, and James C., I felt more than all right, but I buried James Kile earlier in the day."

"Battle shakes a man to his boots."

Alexander knew his father a kind man, but his words and comfort to Mrs. Kile and the other women, come for their dead and wounded, surpassed all reckoning. "Alexander, go get your brothers. Mrs. Kile reports much trouble on the roads. Escort them home and travel with a group of refugees and mourners."

"Yes, sir, Captain Chilton." Alexander found William, and eventually located John, who refused to leave his burial duties. "OK, John. Finish your task here, then you better report to Captain."

"Fool. We report to Lt. Bennett and Captain Farris as soldiers now, not sons of Captain Chilton. Take your Pearl to Miz Kile, and give her a squirrel gun from out in the field there." John threw another shovelful of dirt on the mass grave.

"Yes, John." He dreaded another pass of the cornfield.

Alexander looked to the sky when he heard crows caw. "Look, crows and several eagles high above." He put his hand above his eyes against the hot sun to watch the circling eagles. Then he whispered, "No, turkey buzzards."

The realization struck his stomach like a fist, and he ran into the weeds to vomit the terror out of his being. The smell of man and beast melting in the August sun assailed his senses. "Deus spes mea! God is my hope." He fell to his knees and held his head in his hands as if it would take flight if he did otherwise.

He heard his older brother, John, bark orders to the supply wagon drivers, then to him. "Alexander, you take to the center and manage additions of our men to fill openings in the line as we pass along the trail."

He saw William gallop to the back of the long train of soldiers and the few wagons with each company headed northwest. He then realized his assignment to the center gave added protection from enemy soldiers. *Enemy? Never had enemies before.* He looked to the east and then the west. As his mother taught him, he made the sign of the cross for his beloved brothers.

When a gap in the line appeared, he galloped to the slower wagon. "Can you keep pace or pull out for the end of the train?" Most flicked their reins and encouraged their mules or horses to move forward. A host of saddened souls moved like waves of heat in the sun.

He saw a wagon pull out of line. "Trouble? Can I help?"

"Can you raise the dead?"

He heard a faint shout from the end of the train, and saw William wave his hat. He waited until he could ride by his brother's side.

"Change horses with me. Mine is rested at this pace, while yours works the wagons and the long line of infantry." William stopped and led his mount toward his young brother. "I would take your position, but…"

"I know. John laid the plans. Take my position tomorrow when we are closer to the—the enemy." He saw the train slow and wagons pull into the welcome shade along a creek to take rest. Then the long line traveled late into the cooler night on the Springfield plain.

Rations shared in somber tone around campfires gave little comfort.

Alexander heard someone say, "Private Chilton." He turned to look at his brothers and snickered.

"Attention." A soldier walked in front of the gathering of men. "Do you find something funny about a command, Private Chilton?"

Alexander stood to attention and nodded to the sergeant stripes on his gray uniform. "No, Sergeant. There are three of us by that name, brothers."

"Privates Chilton, then, which of you managed the supply train to Springfield?"

His brother John stood. "Pvt. John Chilton."

"Chilton, report to the rear and the supply officer in charge."

"Yes, Sergeant. Any notion of destination?"

"Set to invade Kansas and capture us a Union fort. Dismissed." The sergeant pivoted and returned to the neighboring camp toward the supply wagons.

Alexander said to his brother William, "I thought we signed on to protect Missouri from invaders into the borders. Now we invade Kansas. Probably see Kansas easy from here, if you look west."

"See clear to the ocean from here, if not for the wind and head-high grasses. I never knew flat country could be so beautiful, as if the ground itself rolls and weaves from horizon to horizon." William stood to gather his pack into a knapsack "borrowed" from a soldier who no longer made use of it. "Prepare to march, little brother. Our horses along with about four hundred others are to be confiscated and sent south with the Confederates to Arkansas."

"Union soldiers! Take cover!" Captain Farris fell to the ground beside Alexander and fired at the rush of five hundred or more cavalry in blue who galloped toward the Confederates near a ravine at Dry Wood Creek, some twelve miles from Fort Scott, Kansas.

Alexander fell to his belly. He heard gunfire to his right, and prepared his own gun for battle.

"Hold your fire," his captain ordered. "We can overwhelm this small bunch of Union Jayhawkers with sheer numbers. Steady now."

"Small bunch with superior fire power, sir." Alexander kept his opinion to a murmur. Just prior, he sat with his captain and lieutenant who planned a scout assignment. He realized the Union soldiers were a scout detachment from the fort who sought the Confederates. However, he vowed to volunteer for scout duty every chance, and to leave before daybreak like a squirrel hunter.

He saw the companies in the center of the five thousand Confederates begin to form the line of a crescent as if to encircle the approaching

Union scout detachment and squeeze them into retreat westward toward the fort. He reckoned if the fort commander could spare six hundred for a scout, taking a fort required a sizable trained army, and one with firepower and planners of experience. He considered firepower and experienced planners the missing factors of his own army.

Alexander sat next to his brother and breathed the dusty, hot air kicked up by the cavalry action and the wind. He pulled a square cotton scarf from his knapsack and folded it into a triangle. He tied it around his neck and turned it bandit style over his nose to cut the dust. When he heard Lt. Bennett call for inspection, he stood, thankful to stretch arms and legs after two hours of skirmish.

When the march resumed, it turned northeast toward the Missouri River.

Alexander marched beside his brothers and others of his company from his part of Missouri. "I'm proud to march for General McBride of Texas County. Papa called Captain Farris and Lt. Bennett a couple of fine lads after he heard they were from Reynolds and Oregon counties. Colonel Freeman, now, is he our blood cousin?"

John replied, "No, but his stepbrothers and stepsister are. Their mother was Grandmother Susannah's niece, but she died and Mr. Freeman married T. R.'s mother from Salem. Grandpa Boggs always treated him like his own nephew, in any case. I suppose that is why Freeman tapped Papa for one of his captains."

"I surely wish I could join Col. William Coleman's Fourth Cavalry. My boots wore clear through since the quartermaster appropriated our horses." Alexander marched awhile in silence. "Missouri River can't be far ahead. It must be September tenth or so. Do you think we march at the rear and eat dust because we are Price's Seventh Division, and the First to the Sixth march ahead?"

William spoke for the first time in hours. "These may be the finest fields of corn ever planted. I feel a touch of envy when I see rows stretching for miles around. Many trees ahead may signal a town."

"A heavy volley of musketry ahead. Ambush." Alexander pushed his brother toward the side of the road and sought cover.

Then he heard Lieutenant Bennett's command, "Forward march." He followed the crush of men across the road, and through an orchard and a corn patch into a cemetery. When they halted and formed a new line between the obstacles of trees and buildings at the edge of the town, the enemy opened fire from a hollow ahead. When his regiment returned fire, he shouted from behind a tree on a slight rise above the others, "The enemy fled like rats and didn't stop until they reached their entrenchments. They could hold us here for days from this vantage. Where do you think we are?"

Two blasts from a steamboat's horn answered his question. "Lexington, we made it to Lexington. I want to see the steamboat before some other regiment captures and burns it. I can't smell the river, though, so we must be a mile or more away."

John replied, "Captain Farris said Lexington boasts a ferry in addition to commercial boats. Capture this town and control the whole area for miles."

"Dig in, men. Forward companies hold the lines ahead. Eat before dark, and then assume routine watch. We have a town to capture tomorrow. We take the bluff to the left." Lieutenant Bennett summoned his sergeants and gestured assignments left and right, forward and back.

Alexander helped his brothers distribute supplies from the supply wagons for the following three days. He heard the lieutenant's orders to follow him to the high bluff overlooking the river and be alert for mines set by the enemy.

As the regiment pushed the enemy up the bluff and maintained steady fire, Alexander hit the ground after hearing two blasts he assumed were mines. The enemy held them at the summit until nightfall. He tried to sleep despite halting fire of musketry and the occasional discharge of grape shot. He saw none of his company injured but decided to look for Sam Nesbit's brother James come morning.

He found James without a search when several squads and companies combined for entrenchment duties. However, the men built entrenchments with hemp bales and pulled cannon up a newly constructed breastwork.

Under constant musketry fire, Alexander expected the whine of a bullet in his gut at any moment. As his squad moved forward against earnest enemy fire to gain the point, he understood the importance of the location. After hours of running battle, he saw a white flag rise high above the enemy's line along the bluffs above Missouri River's port at Lexington.

He saw Captain Farris make his way among his men, shaking hands and encouraging others, as was his custom. His heart filled with respect for his young leader. He stepped closer to hear Captain Farris read from the papers in his hands.

"September 20, 1861, Lexington, Missouri. To Major-General Sterling Price, Confederate Army of the West.

Of the officers and men under my command it is only necessary to say that on this, as on all former occasions, they have proved themselves equal to every emergency. The men who stole away from their homes in the presence of the enemy and marched 600 miles without tents, half-clad, and many of them unshod, can be safely relied on in the hour of danger. In the action of my command, 2 were killed upon the ground, 1 was mortally wounded, 4 severely wounded, and 7 slightly.

Respectfully, your obedient servant, J.H. McBride, Brigadier-General, Seventh Division, Missouri State Guards." [2.38]

Alexander asked his brothers, "Our three-month enlistment ends this month. Go or stay? Our family needs us. Crops to harvest, hay to put up. Captain says regiments arrived ahead of us at Stockton, Missouri, north of Springfield, to construct billets for those with six and twelve month enlistments.

John added, "Quartermaster says Price is determined to ravage and burn Kansas even if peace was declared tomorrow, and McCulloch is falling back to Arkansas. Rumors are five thousand Cherokees are rebels and moving north to join Price in Kansas. Chief John Ross agreed to remain neutral with the remainder of the tribe after three times hung from a tree.[2.40] Now, I am strong for protecting, but as to invading Kansas, I balk like a mule. I say, let's go home for the winter, and if hostilities are not at an end, we can decide for ourselves about reenlistment in the spring."

The group of young Shannon County men sat silent.

William stood, straightened, and reset his hat firmly on his head. "My hay needs put up." He leaned down, picked up his tattered knapsack, and walked slowly toward Lieutenant Bennett and Captain Farris, who sat at a small campfire about a hundred yards distant.

Alexander thought his brother looked as if the weight of the world crowded into the knapsack on his back. He followed suit, as did his brother John and friend, James Nesbit.

John raised his hand in salute to his officers. "Captain, Lieutenant, sirs."

Captain Farris saluted. "At ease, men. I sense the Shannon County boys stirred about something. Gentlemen?"

"Captain, Sir, our enrollments end, come November. Your thoughts are deemed welcome on the matter."

"Do you choose to travel home as five or as five hundred?"

"Five hundred into Union territory to the east, sounds the more favorable, sir." John turned to his brothers and friends for agreement.

"I thank you for your discretion. Many simply pick up and leave without a word. You know we will likely fight and dodge our way back to Thomasville?"

After a long silence, Alexander stepped forward and extended his hand to his captain. "The Chiltons favor a march with you all the way to Current River and the Reynolds County line, Captain Farris."

"Shadrach? James C.?" Alexander heard his mother's cry and litany of questions, and dreaded his answers; he watched her run the length of their long lane toward her sons.

"We came through sound. Of James C. and Papa, we haven't heard."
He dismounted and embraced her. "Lordy, home never looked so good."
He removed his hat and wiped his forehead with his bloodstained shirtsleeve. "I can water the horses." True meaning, "*I must get to the river.*"
　He watched his brothers greet and embrace their mother, then turn to
their own homes. Then he secured the remaining horses to a root wad,
waded in deep, and sat in the clear spring-fed waters, boots and all. He
leaned back, extended his arms, eyes all the while on the blue sky of a
rare and warm sunny December afternoon; drifted under the cold water,
drowned the sounds, and cleansed the soul.

CHAPTER 4

BATTLE OF PEA RIDGE — 1862

The left wing, advancing rapidly soon began to ascend the mountain cliff, from which the artillery had driven most of the rebel force. The upward movement of the gallant Thirty-sixth Illinois, with its dark-blue line of men and its gleaming bayonets, steadily rose from base to summit, when it dashed forward into the forest, driving and scattering the rebels from these commanding heights.
—Samuel L. Curtis, Major-General, US Army [2.45]

A lexander sensed the change his three-month enlistment wrought as he observed his mother busy about her kitchen. He noticed she quickly corrected reference to "the captain" with "your father" and spoke as if his father simply left on a fall deer hunt.

Rut season arrived, and venison lay in smoke most every week for winter stores, and still no word on Shadrach. Alexander field dressed a small doe at a fold in the ridge above the river. His family farm lay on high ground in fine Jacks Fork river bottomland. He heard what seemed to be two or three horses on the trail off the ridge to the ford, so he took his gun from its scabbard tied to the saddle and ran through the trees to investigate.

Just before he called halt, two riders appeared over the rise. He shouted, "Papa!" He approached the two riders, and shook each man's hand until he was sure he pried their arms from their sockets. "I killed a deer a hundred yards down the ridge. Help me wrap and load it. Then watch the happiest women in the world cross our pasture."

Alexander, his father, and his cousin galloped up the river trail toward home. Knowing his father well, he prepared for what came next. The horses took the bit and headed for the barn in a run. The men grabbed their hats, flagged the horse's flanks, and whooped for joy, his father in the lead.

Alexander slowed when he saw his mother at the river. She sat on a half-buried log and swayed a small branch this way and that way in the water. He knew when she saw Shadrach's horse canter toward her on the far bank because she ran into water up to her chest and kept on wading, despite the cold. She failed to get very far because Shadrach jumped from his horse and met her midstream. The swift current caught them, swept gravel from under their feet, and they came up sputtering. Still in a clinch, they whooped and hollered between kisses.

"We're too old for such goings on!" Patsy joyfully shouted and flailed water in every direction.

"Darlin', we are never too old for such goings on." Water swept him under and he came up sputtering yet again.

The current carried them past the ford at the upper end of the pasture, past the high red clay bank, to the second shoal near his brother William's house. Alexander doubted his parents minded the long walk despite the cold.

By nightfall, the sad stories told, anger vented, tears dried, Alexander played host as his father told how he came to be home. Family and a few brave nephews gathered round for the first time since mid-July.

"Colonel Freeman gave leave after the raid on Salem the first of the month. I think the vittles ran short!"

Alexander resumed time spent with Uncle Joshua and became the family reporter in Shadrach's absence. "Uncle Joshua said the Rebel legislature at Neosho adopted the Acts of Secession, and the Confederacy admitted Missouri as the twelfth secessionist state. However, the Jefferson City Convention voted against secession. He said the Union holds North Missouri, and the Confederates hold the South."

Alexander's sister, Mary Louisa, covered the home front. "It feels like a noose tightened around Missouri right across Shannon County. Not even a dance anymore, and me now old enough to go. Mama says the boys may be gone to war, but they only enlisted for three or six months. Too long for me. Uncle Joshua says hard feelings already exist between the local factions of North and South sympathies so strong they may carry it to their graves."

"Eat your supper, Mary Louisa. You became a beautiful woman. No war is mean enough to rob you of a feller." Alexander noticed Mary Louisa wound her braids into a grown-up bun at the back of her neck. He teased her to the edge of their mother's patience. "Shall we make some music with Lizzie after supper? You can play my guitar, if you give no sass on the way."

"I favor sass and my own violin!" Mary Louisa replied.

Without answer, Alexander continued news of war. "Colonel Freeman's company grew to a regiment. He attacked Union Major Bowen's First Battalion Missouri Cavalry on December 3 at Salem. The Rebels found themselves routed and melted into the Current River hills, but Major Bowen pursued for two days until he ran out of supplies. Colonel Freeman and his Rebels continued to harass the troops at Salem for two months. Some say Colonel Freeman plans to join General Price's Missouri State Guard's winter quarters in Springfield.

"Missouri finds herself in dire straits, Mama. Union General Curtis prepares his army at Rolla to push General Price out of Missouri. Colonel Coleman's men, at least several companies, billet in West Plains, with others scattered along the south border."

His mother rose from her chair and reached for Alexander's plate. "I suggest you play music and stop this talk of joining either army. Missouri is not in dire straits because she rightly refuses to secede.

Colonel Freeman and your Papa will see the light when he meets with the general's nonsense in Springfield."

Alexander nodded ascent to peace in his home, rose to get his guitar, and motioned to Mary Louisa to follow with her fiddle. "You come along, too, Elizabeth. Let us gallop to Lizzie's house. We best bundle warmly against the winter wind. Good night, Papa. Mama." He knew an infrequently empty house would find silence welcomed by Capt. Shadrach Chilton of Company B, Freeman Regiment and his wife.

As he forded the river on horseback, thoughts of war splashed downstream, and he and his sisters sang their way westward one mile along the river trail.

The following February, Alexander threw open the door to Lizzie's cabin, yet again, without knocking. "My darling cousin, let's make some music."

"Well, I declare. Alexander, come in. Mary Louisa and little Elizabeth, come in from the cold. Shut that drafty door. A communiqué from Colonel Freeman and your father came this week." Lizzie took a small glass jar from her apron pocket, lifted the lid, removed a piece of paper covered in tiny scrawls, and began to read aloud.

"16 Feb '62 AD Honorable Senator Joshua T. Chilton, Shannon County.

We abandoned Springfield, having failed to dig fortifications, and the Union marched in without a fight. If McCulloch's Rebels will not join us in Missouri, we march to join him in Arkansas. General Price' pride must smart on that matter. We fight with the rear guard and tramp south on the Wire Road. The snow and sleet froze our clothes to our bodies. We passed broken wagons, dead horses, and ransacked supplies of chairs, pans, bedding and clothes, some of which we made good use.

"On 14 Feb AD '62, a sharp engagement flared with the Union vanguard at Crane Creek. Colonel Freeman, Capt. Shade Chilton, and more than fifty of our men disappeared behind the line of blue uniforms of Maj. William D. Bowen's cavalry battalion. Insult added

to injury when a cheer resounded at the capture, Bowen and Freeman being such archenemies since the start of hostilities in and around Salem. Wounded lay freezing where they fell. Soldiers straggled along, half-starved toward the Confederate's winter quarters and ample supply.

"I write close to a fire built of abandoned wooden chairs and desks and thankful for it. We crossed the state line into Arkansas; crossed with a sad heart, for I fear we suffered an irreversible defeat when we abandoned Missouri today.

"Rumors report Gen. James McBride's capture today by Union soldiers. The scout carries this missive to Senator Chilton posthaste to recruit reinforcements for Missouri's state's rights. Respectfully, Lt. J. L. Campbell, Co B, Freeman Regiment." [2.42]

Alexander pushed aside the thought his father might be dead. "I am confident the Union will release Papa, Freeman, and McBride in a prisoner exchange. Often enlisted men enjoy no such advantage. Colonel Freeman's brother serves in his Rebel company and another brother chose Union. Meet Susannah's William, Louisa's Benjamin, or Thomas Davis on the battlefield? I can't imagine."

Lizzie fell on her knees at his side. "Your Papa, captured and freezing. I can't bear the thought."

Alexander patted then kissed the top of her head. He had no heart to tell her that he and John reenlisted into the Missouri State Guard at Birch Tree on February 15, 1862, for the largest battle yet planned west of the Mississippi. Price's Missouri Guard added to Confederates in Arkansas aimed for sixteen thousand men and sixty-five cannon. He heard reports that the Union General's force numbered ten thousand men and fifty cannon, but balanced by superior personal weapons and military training.

"I delivered some horses to Colonel Coleman's men at West Plains last week. Union calls him South Missouri's chief guerilla. Word of mountain howitzer movement from the north to Salem best scatters the guerillas into the swamps and mountains, if you ask me."

Lizzie sat up, instantly alert. "What is a mountain howitzer, pray tell?"

"Like a twelve-pound cannon only lighter. It can launch various kinds of trouble. Get up now; enjoy a fine waltz with me."

The tune of a slow waltz drifted from the two dancers' lips and served to lift the mood in Lizzie's cabin. He held the woman of any sane man's dream, so he drew her close and waltzed his finest good-bye steps.

"Fall in."

Alexander heard the call and took a place beside his brother John on February 25, 1862. His mother called them Rebels. Never mind her resistance; he looked thankfully at the large pack of supplies behind his saddle. One thing he learned at Wilson's Creek; the Guard provided little provision. A private best prepare, and pray for an officer to see to his men. He left his family in the care of his brother William. Since General Price folded the Missouri State Guard into the Confederate Army, many hoped for warm, gray-wool uniforms and military weaponry.

The man behind him made his mark and stepped back from the enrollment table to fall in at Birch Tree, Shannon County, Missouri. "We welcome a February thaw today. Bright and sunny, a good day to march to war."

Alexander replied, "A fine day at that. However, I double-checked my pack for rain and cold. Winter can turn mean, and I know little about the prairie ahead." Alexander gathered his reins, reached for his saddle horn with one hand and the stirrup with his other.

The man beside him said, "Don't you know you signed for infantry?"

"A mounted infantry for me. I aim for scout." Alexander rode a mare he bought cheap. Another lesson from his father: do not bring the colt you trained into battle. He remembered his father's exact words, "We can set a broken leg, but a broken heart heals of its own accord; sometimes crooked, sometimes straight, and sometimes an open wound forever."

His heart skipped a beat, and he calculated the odds of his father surviving a February prisoner's march to St. Louis or Illinois prisons. He simply refused to think about survival in prison. He kicked his mare into a gentle trot to the back of the small gathering of new recruits where two other men on horseback welcomed him three abreast.

Lieutenant Bennett rode at the front of the column of infantry. After five miles, the lieutenant showed no sign of rest. Alexander and his brother John served with Lt. John J. Bennett during their three-month enlistment in Capt. William Farris's company of partisans and fought with him at Wilson's Creek, Dry Wood, Lexington, and numerous skirmishes.

County after county across South Missouri passed behind them; more men joined the column. Rest came with each acquisition. He worried that men did not come with provisions or guns. Their leaders assured the men that the Confederacy provided guns and proper gray uniforms in Arkansas. A small supply wagon followed Alexander and the mounted infantry to the rear.

The column turned southward into rougher mountainous terrain as they approached Springfield. Marching all day and half the night, they traveled a brutal one hundred and twenty miles in about six days. On the following day, evidence of a large army on the march began to appear.

He heard a call from the middle of the column and saw a mounted man gallop toward him.

"Chiltons, follow me." The lieutenant pointed at Alexander and his brother John. "Scout ahead. Look out for Union pickets." He pointed at two other mounted men. "I will send these two men over the next hours to relay periodic reports. Dismissed."

When the two scouts came to a small creek, Alexander stopped on the far bank, dismounted, and took rest. The crossing broke the ice for the horses, and he filled canteens. As darkness fell, the temperature plummeted. "I will rest a bit, return to report, and pray the relay is a good tracker. We pushed the lieutenant's orders close to insubordination already. From my map, we approach Bentonville by morning unless we meet Union pickets."

"Let's go on, meet the pickets, and find something to report. What say ye?" John grinned at Alexander and gathered his horse's reins, prepared to mount.

"To the pickets, then hightail it back to our company. Scout duty suits me, but it may prove a short assignment." He swung into the saddle.

"Who goes there?"

"Bob-bob-white," Alexander replied with a whistle to a man dressed similarly to him. Brownish gray trousers, homespun wool topcoat, and a wool scarf tied over his head and wrapped around his neck against the pelting snow. A brown felted-wool hat brim protected his face from the weather.

"Bob-bob-white," whistled the man in reply.

"Fourth Missouri Confederate scout coming in." Alexander dismounted, led his horse forward, and turned to see John follow suit.

"Any sustenance?" The soldier asked. "We left camp with only three days rations and are about starved." The Rebel picket kept his weapon at the ready, and his eye on the large pack behind Alexander's saddle.

"Jerky and whiskey acceptable?" Alexander gave the gloved hand jerky from one pocket and a small glass bottle from the other.

"The good Lord blessed me today." The picket took the frozen jerky, drained the small bottle, and then turned to cough and recover from the strong spirits. "Good 'shine. You a mountain man?"

"The very same. Where are we? We expected a Union picket." Alexander nodded toward his brother. "Private Chilton and I are a day late with reports."

"Price's army. We aimed to circle round the Union in a brutal march out of the Boston Mountains. Generals split the forces to pass on either side of the Big Mountain. We surely count on an element of surprise." The picket paused. "I'm reaching for a limb, now." The picket was cautious with two men bearing guns and pistols.

He drew lines in the snow as he spoke. "Big Mountain here. Little Mountain here. Telegraph Road here to Elkhorn Tavern. Cross Timber Hollow here, just south of us. We move south on Telegraph Road tonight.

The picket summarized General Van Dorn's Rebel army locations. Price's Division of Confederate units located to the south. "McCullough's Confederate Division and sixty-five cannon located to the north. Generals push us without food or drink. Whole companies fall exhausted by the wayside. Pickets have the best of it. I am thinking we find a Union supply train somewhere before we find the army. About all my mind can conjure—supply train. Some say our generals are so confident of quick victory they left supply far behind. Ammunition and all. Fools."

"For you and your partner. A refill of the bottle, and we will see you on the morrow with fresh recruits for Company I." Alexander handed the man two small pieces of deer jerky and took the empty bottle. He handed the bottle to his brother to refill, mounted his horse, and turned northeast.

After an hour up Telegraph Road toward his company, confident of Price's securing points north of Elkhorn, he saw his brother stop ahead and begin to walk toward a small fire. He heard someone say, "Fourth Missouri Confederate, coming in."

Then a reply, "Confederate picket. Come on."

He dismounted and walked his horse a ways to give some pitiful measure of relief. The snow stopped, but the temperature seemed much colder. He saw a large burned out black circle with a fire in the center. A full company of men lay on the black ground in close groups, most with one blanket and others shivering near the fire where pots sat on stones. Men added snow repeatedly to pots for water. He noticed the burned-out ground was decidedly warmer than the snow-covered road.

He retrieved his own pan from his pack, dropped the reins and walked to scoop up snow to melt for water for himself and his horse. He thought about fodder for his horse, and decided to wait until later for either to feed. Selfish, but essential for scouts among famished men. He sat to rest by the welcome fire and then looked about for John.

When he saw John circle the group and head north on the road, he gathered another pan of snow water and followed afoot. He stopped at John's pack and poured water for man, then beast.

"Thank you. And my horse thanks you." John patted his mount and retrieved fodder and bread frozen hard as tack. He handed Alexander a stick, one end glowing. "I will walk, you ride. Rest the horses and proceed back north to meet our company."

"How do you know so much about winter marches?" Alexander rode beside his walking partner.

"Deer woods." John pulled his wool scarf above his nose and walked a faster pace, head-down into the brutal north wind toward their company to report.

Alexander slid to the frozen ground to walk and rest his horse. The physical movement warmed him. His breath and that of his horse collected as ice crystals around their nose and eyes. Never a raccoon or possum hunt proved as miserable as did this army on the march. He wondered if he could hold out until morning. At times, he felt certain he would die on Telegraph Road.

Without a word, he watched John roll into the saddle and lay his head on his horse's mane, arms around the horse's neck for warmth.

He took John's reins and led the horses forward.

After what seemed hours, his horse whinnied, and another answered in the distance. He put John's reins over the horse's head, swung into his own saddle, and kicked his horse forward. He tried to shout, "Fourth Missouri Confederate," but his voice shied to a croak. He removed his hat and waved it in large high circles. If it proved other than his company, he felt ready to meet his maker.

"Fourth Missouri Infantry Confederate. Welcome home, scout." The soldier reached for Alexander's outreached arm and stepped forward to embrace him with the other.

"Price's army, an hour's ride south on the road. Stragglers built a welcome fire about halfway." Alexander walked past the Rebel picket some quarter mile to the slow-moving column.

"Private Chilton. And Private Chilton." The lieutenant met Alexander and his brother with a sharp salute.

"Lieutenant Bennett, sir. A straggler fire ahead about one hour. Price's army continues a slow march behind Union lines."

"Price's entire army north of the Union line?" The lieutenant asked with obvious surprise and disbelief.

John stepped closer. "Price and Van Dorn moved eastward around the Union encampment on a high limestone bluff. Picket reports a morning surprise attack to their rear guard with cannons most likely pointed opposite our line. McCullough moved westward to meet at the junction at an inn on the ridge called Elkhorn Tavern. I believe we have time to rest the men, build what fire we can muster, and join our company about dawn."

Alexander spoke after a pause. "Did you give us up for lost? We considered the thought from time to time ourselves, sir."

"No. Everything about you and your brother said 'scouts.' But another voice said, 'independent cusses.'" The lieutenant extended his hand in thanks and then turned to the soldier far to his left. "Sergeant, break column. We rest and build small fires if combustibles can be found."

Somewhere in the dark, a voice croaked. "Been collecting combustibles for hours now, sir."

Alexander heard what sounded like chairs tossed into piles. He thought Company I proved itself resourceful.

He and his brother tended to their horses, and joined the other mounted infantry around multiple fires. He heard one of the privates assume charge and assign two men, then saw nods to pairs of others to stand watch from their fire to the woods. He fell into a deep sleep, thankful for the warmth of the blankets woven by his sisters and mother, and the smells of home that warmed his heart.

At dawn, Alexander felt someone kick the bottom of his near-frozen booted foot. He opened his eyes to see his brother, towering above him.

"Time to join the Confederates and shoot some Yankees." John kicked the other foot, and set a water pan filled with bread and jerky floating in the steaming liquid. "A spot of the picket's bottle will do for thanks."

"Small thanks to break the fast with such well-prepared food." Alexander chuckled at his own sarcasm, raised himself to his elbow, and rubbed his hands along his stiff limbs and back, certain of no response.

He turned to the private who took charge in the night. "No roust for watch? I thank you. Tonight, I will take the first."

The private said, "No man on the march envied your scout assignment."

"Hope to rescue a captain from a Union stronghold on our victory march back to Missouri. My father. Best fighter in Missouri. Whipped a bear once. Saw it myself. Bear brought first blood, however. Come on, 'Bears of Missouri.' We let first blood on Yankees today then hightail it back to Missouri where we belong."

He saw the private smile and nod.

"Missouri Bears, one and all. A warm fire awaits us to the south." Alexander raised his hat to the men around the waning fire, stopped to pick up several smoking limbs, and carefully tied them to the saddle. "Learned that from my brother. Carry fire to the next meal." He and his brother rode to the front of the column to await orders for the day.

Lieutenant Bennett greeted his scouts with a casual salute. "Scout ahead until you reach Price's pickets. One mounted infantryman will serve as relay, then another, and give the captain of Company I the news of fresh recruits on the way. Capt. Matthew Norman out of Oregon County most likely leads our new company as Fourth Missouri Infantry, Confederate States Army. News came that Union army captured Capt. William Farris and marched him to the Alton, Illinois prison. Select your own men. Until a drink at the tavern, then. Dismissed." He paused for the scouts' salutes and turned a soldier's crisp about-face to his infantrymen by the waning fire.

John said, "Sorry about Farris. I will choose our relay and catch up before dawn breaks over the hill."

Alexander nodded, mounted his horse, and turned south toward the tavern on the top of the mountain. About the time he reached the burned circle, he turned to watch John and the relay man join him. When they reached the north watch, he identified himself and proceeded without delay until the trio reached Price's army in a valley east of Telegraph Road. After identification, he bid the relay man Godspeed. He motioned to John toward the ridge ahead, but waited to move forward until he saw John's nod of agreement. It was too cold to move his scarf from his face for conversation. He was glad his brother kept his own counsel.

He dismounted and trudged uphill at a snail's pace behind a long irregular line of battle across the series of steep ridges and narrow valleys. He handed his reins to John and climbed to the top of a large oak tree. "I see movement over the next ridge directly west. This is one powerful Rebel force, if indeed ours. Never saw so many men. Another force, most likely the Union, moves at the top of a high ridge to the south southwest, to the east of what yesterday's picket drew as Big Mountain. Looks as if we may need to take the valley after we secure the tavern on the mountain."

John replied, "Yes, first secure the tavern. Perhaps the generals will seek strong spirits with the same fervor as do we."

"Union movements into the hollow, Cross Timber, as I recall." Alexander stepped down limb-by-limb and dropped to the ground next to John. Then he heard the Union army open fire on the Confederates and the battle lines stopped and exchanged constant fire.

By sound, he identified more Confederate batteries join the fight. "That will be a mix of solid shot, grape shot, case shot, shell, splinters, and rocks raining down on the Union in the valley. Their caissons are exploding, and many guns are disabled. Price holds back in the valley. The Union pulls back to the ridge. Let's get closer to the front and then report."

Alexander mounted his horse and the scouts moved down into the smoky valley. "It's solid haze. Sounds indicate a Union push down to the valley. Union or Rebel ahead? Let's ride to the enemy's left flank and beyond, then report." He saw John fall in beside him, and they backtracked and made for the left.

When the scouts reached the last of the sound of fire, it seemed the enemy drew toward Telegraph Road rather than extending their flank. Alexander whirled his mount and the scouts galloped back to report to the nearest Rebel company.

"Fourth Missouri Confederate scouts reporting, sir." Alexander saluted the officer. "Enemy's left flank consolidating toward the road. Shells cleared the path behind their retreat. Not open, mind you, but sprouts fell."

"Thank you, Privates." The officer saluted the scouts and whirled his horse toward the back of the line.

John said, "Let us lead the line to the tavern. I feel powerful thirsty."

Alexander whooped, and the scouts made a line drive toward the enemy's left flank and up the ridge. He could hear friendly fire and infantry crashing behind them up the ridge and either side of Telegraph Road. The last few hours of daylight remained.

A small company of cavalry caught up with the scouts who hid in a grove of trees until fellow Rebels of the Missouri Third Infantry surrounded them in the haze. "Fourth Missouri Confederate scouts. Hold fire." He saw the closest cavalryman turn and press up the hill. The small infantry groups that followed grew less and less aggressive as fatigue overcame the soldiers, and they fell on their faces to rest and revive. He could discern no consistent line of fire. Each company sought their own pace and path.

When the scouts reached level ground, they emerged from the haze in the hollow only to see the enemy not more than a hundred yards away. Alexander shouted, "To the tavern, men!" Despite his rank as private, he and his brother plunged forward in musketry more abundant than either experienced before. Leaves and twigs took on a life of their own in rhythm with the concussion of the guns. In the clearing, Alexander could see hundreds of men fall. Staggered by enemy fire, the Missouri regiments lost ground back to the crest.

"The whole world is filled with Rebs," shouted John as he pressed forward again. "The enemy broke on the west."

Behind them, the Confederates reformed their line.

Although Alexander could see many men crumbled from fatigue, they rose to stumble forward with a bloodcurdling Rebel shriek. He felt every hair on his head stand to attention. He joined the yelling throng.

He saw the Union fall back to their battery. Instead of firing, as he feared, the Union infantry assisted the frantic limbering of guns to escape behind the newly formed line of infantry fire. The few big guns that fired silenced dozens of Confederates and deafened most all with the concussions. He saw Confederates swarm the tavern in massed confusion. "Let's fall back and find our company to the east. Might even capture us a supply train." He and his brother retreated around the ridge and into the haze below.

As the scouts made their way around the ridge, they could see Confederates below in an open field; Union troops moved between the trees and made a stand against overwhelming numbers. Just as he thought the Confederates would overcome the line, artillery sounded behind the blue line. He and his brother raced to the front, reloading as they rode, and fired at blue uniforms behind trees.

Darkness approached as the Union pulled back. The artillery mowed Confederates down until the field looked like rows of gray and butternut cornstalks. Without food or sufficient ammunition, and mowed thin, the Confederate attack slowed. He rode forward with wonder that the frozen army moved at all.

Alexander felt his mount give way. He heard a Union cheer, as if it roared for his fall alone. On March 7, 1862, he looked for John, but found a black wall as he crashed and felt his boot protected by the stirrup under the belly of his mount.

When he awoke, he felt shards of ice cut at his wrists and shoulder. He lay with his back to his near-dead steed, one boot still in the stirrup, the other frozen to the ground. His groggy mind struggled to grasp his location. He could make out hundreds of mounds on the ground:

frozen bodies surrounded him. He gave thanks for life, and for some hasty soul who pushed him close to his horse's warm body for the night, wrapped his face and head with the plaid linsey-woolsey scarf of home, and pressed his wool hat firmly on top, however askew. The silence was deafening.

He pulled his free leg's boot from the frozen ground and began to push and rock his horse until he felt it make a valiant lunge to roll to a stance. He felt the stirrup give and he pulled his foot free before the horse fell back with a pitiful moan. "You saved my life, old mare, and hastened your death to set me free." He patted her neck, and watched her eyes close. She continued an ever-weakening moan. He dared a shot to end her misery.

He removed his pack from the saddle, crawled low on his elbows, and inched himself closer to the tree line to the north. He closed his eyes against the sight of shattered bodies of frost-covered men and horses. He prayed his near-frozen leg was not broken and gave thanks he had no feeling in it. He drew courage to check bodies for ammunition or pistols and found little or none of either.

He heard deafening cannonade whose thunder stretched for more than a mile either side of him. It lasted two hours as he crawled through the shattered mountain forest. The only direction open: retreat north. He figured the sound must reach fifty or more miles in every direction. To the east, a mountain roared back in response. Despite the devastation it surely wrought, blasting the mountain's limestone into shards like a million arrows into man and beast, he thought it the most exhilarating sound he would hear in his lifetime.

"A—tten—tion!"

Alexander Chilton stood straighter and joined fifty or more men who followed a Confederate officer to the edge of the makeshift camp. Many of the men wore homespun coats and pants, rustic boots, and felted-wool hats with wide brims. The colorful assortment of calico shirt collars aptly identified the exhausted-looking men as farmers. Others were clad in gray, butternut, or white wool, a feeble attempt to match Confederate Army uniforms.

He listened to an injured Confederate major's story as the group of stragglers sat around the campfire. "We never stood a chance the second morning. First, Union artillery softened our line, and then their infantry filled with smoke from their guns. When our infantry fell back and held our line, Union cavalry filled our retreating footprints. Their cavalry pushed us back, and when we held the line, Union artillery moved forward to blast our Confederate lines yet again. The Union strategy was to smash our lines backward, again and again, into broken and scattered masses of blood." The Confederate major paused. "I never knew of such strategy used in battle before now."

Alexander heard only silence. The weight of the loss devastated his meager reserves. He gathered his pack and retreated a few yards into the dark, pulling his single blanket about him.

The next morning Alexander packed his bedding and looked left and right, yet undecided whether to search for his company in Arkansas, head eastward toward Shannon County and Jacks Fork River with other men separated from their companies; or closer at hand, walk to his oldest sister's house at Granby in Newton County. He knew she lived near Springfield, at the Granby lead mines, from the letters she wrote to her family.

Alexander, age twenty years, chose to find a way south to Arkansas, back to Price's Confederate Army. However, at every trail south, patrols on the roads of Arkansas forced him to take cover and travel northwest. After a two-day walk to the Missouri state line, the appeal of a relatively nearby sister's house replaced cold determination.

"Do you know where William Orchard's house stands?" Alexander handed his last coins hidden in his boots to the merchant for a small sack of cornmeal. He stamped his feet and rubbed his near-frozen hands to warm himself.

"The Granby lead mines attracted a boomtown. Two turns that way. Fail to know the exact house, though. Lucky you stopped here because eight thousand people cramped into a section; 640 acres of pitiful humanity. Good for business, though."

"Thank you, sir." He stepped into the winter sun, made the two turns, and selected the second house on the right from the multitude of rough wooden structures surrounded by bare ground. Susannah always kept a tidy space, and the porch floor of the chosen house looked clean enough to take a meal. He removed his hat and knocked on the door.

"God is my hope. Alexander!" Susannah moved the small lad in her arms to one hip, and embraced her youngest brother with her free arm. Tears ran down her cheeks as she pushed him away, studied his face, and embraced him again.

"I guess you know I lost my best defenses when you up and married. I decided to come rescue you when your letter said W. T. joined the Union Army in Springfield."

"Your antics deserved punishment, but who could switch such a fine lad as you? Come in. Come into the kitchen. Lift the towel on the leftovers and I will find the molasses. Yes, William T. Orchard swept me off my feet, what with being an older and wiser man with those fine Kentucky manners. He went for the Union, though. You would think he owned the mine and smelter, but he does show a head for business."

"I brought you a sack of meal." He handed the gift to his sister. He saw as many Union soldiers fall as Confederate. What if William did not survive the onslaught? He tossed the thought aside. "Now whom do you carry there? I think I see a finger about to pull a smile as wide as a river."

The lad of about two years cautiously smiled and turned his head into his mother's collar, then risked one peek at the stranger.

"James Shadrach Orchard, the finest lad in town. We call him Jess. Can you say 'Uncle'?" She stretched her armful of boy toward Alexander, stepped back, and beamed at the pair.

After chucking his nephew's cheeks, he sat at the table with his nephew on his knee and forced himself to eat slowly, embarrassed to let her know he sat half starved. After pleasantries, he tackled the purpose of his visit. "Let me pack you and the boys for travel. What with the war all around you, and the smelter destroyed by the Confederates before the capture, Shannon County bodes a safe site for you. Besides, I will be Mama's favorite if I bring her grandson to her house to stay forever."

"Forever? Oh, forever? No. I studied whether and how to visit. I'm highly agreeable, if we travel safe."

"War doesn't like winter, and both armies are nursing their wounds for a spell. We will cook on the road about a week. I still have my guns for game."

"Pea Ridge? God is my hope. You deserted!"

"No, just on the march, Price's army spread all over South Missouri and North Arkansas, and the Union is everywhere in between. I'm more than thankful for it, since a lady needs escort."

Alexander finished his meal, braced himself for the prairie wind, and brought the horse and wagon from the barn to the back step. Without a word, he scanned the few possessions in the barn, roped the cow to the wagon, and loaded what little grain she owned under the wagon seat in case of inclement weather. Then he fashioned a makeshift hitch to turn the doubletree into a single. One scrawny horse and more than a hundred miles lay eastward. March could be mean in the Ozarks.

"A puppy?" Alexander's tone alerted Jess to trouble.

"Mine."

"Sure enough. Black-and-tan furry mutt might make a fine bear dog."

Susannah said, "Now, enough play. We need neither tears nor tantrums. W. T.'s nephew, James, comes home from school after sweep-up for the teacher. My, how he has grown and almost as tall as you. Holds sweet on the teacher. When he puts up resistance, talk to him about mines and smelters. W. T. made good at it. We own our house outright. Lock up tight and I will come back home in no time. No talk of war. He is only fourteen, but threatens to enlist. No war talks."

"Yes, sister."

Susannah pressed her lips and shook her finger. "I'm serious."

"Yes, sister."

After enduring the loud discussion in the back room between James and Susannah, Alexander gave James the handshake of a man.

James politely nodded, donned his coat and hat, and nearly slammed the door off its hinges.

"I guess we aim to travel." Alexander picked up Jess, put an arm around his sister, and guided her away from her home and possessions into an uncertain wartime world.

Alexander stepped to the porch of home and opened the door.

"Alexander, sakes alive. Where are John and your father? Son, come in." His mother embraced him and stepped inside the house.

"We marched to Pea Ridge, Arkansas, and arrived the first week of March. A genuine war battle, for sure, and the same as Wilson's Creek, except the South retreated and scattered all over Arkansas and Missouri. I heard nothing of John since, but he serves most likely with Captain Norman safe in central Arkansas. I am strong, Mama. It serves me well. But I must learn to run faster."

Alexander swung his mother around the kitchen. "I bring a surprise. To the barn, after you, Mama dear."

"Mama!" Susannah walked behind her nephew but ran past to greet her mother.

"Susannah! James, you grew so tall! Where is little Jess?" Martha hugged her daughter and young James Orchard.

"On a blanket in the wagon."

"Oh, my. Our beautiful Jess. God is my hope." She picked up her skirts, ran to the wagon, and lifted her firstborn grandson, wrapped against the cold. She pressed her face deep into the colorful quilt.

Alexander rallied the rest of his family from the warmth of the kitchen stove into a brisk March day. Homecoming.

The men called him Pvt. Alex Chilton in Company I, Fourth Missouri Infantry. In spite of it all, he wanted to resume his love to fight and wrestle. A family reputation to keep; sisters and a farm required protection from the invaders.

Life on the river seemed as in the days before the battles at Wilson's Creek and Pea Ridge—except for the harrowing nightmares. The disturbed calm lasted about three days.

Alexander woke with a start, terrified, and then lay back on the pillow when he recognized home. He felt shame, anger, and resolve as he accounted for his brother and father. He dreaded to face his brother John and prayed he was alive and with Price's army, who marched southeast to Tennessee or Alabama or Mississippi. Capt. Shadrach Chilton signed many a man's paper as enrolling officer. However, if he truly lay injured in a Union prison with others of Freeman's Regiment, Alexander knew the situation grave.

John and James Nesbit reportedly avoided capture at Pea Ridge and soldiered on with Price and Capt. Matthew Norman in Company I, Fourth Missouri Infantry, CSA, unless the Union captured him. He felt ashamed to be safe and well at home. He owed James Nesbit's family that news, at least.

From his brother William, who remained with wife, baby, and the family farms after his three-month enlistment, Alexander drew some peace. He rolled from his bed and dressed for a hot breakfast with William and the hired men. "It sounded like a hailstorm, but it didn't take long to tell the difference between a March hailstorm and a barrage of bullets from a thousand guns lined up shoulder to shoulder. Men left and right, shoulders and knees shattered. Fortunately, Northwest Arkansas's heavy forest and limestone bluffs proved friendly to hill-country men who knew how to use the cover, unlike fools who preferred open pasture. Confusion and a rare regroup prevailed when officers fell. Some officers led us right into trouble and capture behind the Union lines." Alexander stopped tales of war, finished his breakfast, kissed his mother and sisters, and grabbed his hat. "Thank you."

"Well, I declare. What came over Alexander? Thank you and kisses?" Martha "Patsy" Chilton chuckled with pride and pleasure at her youngest son's changed attitude since his return from war. "It will be over soon, in time for your father and brother to be home at Christmas."

The following morning, Alexander forded the river and rode his brother's horse up the familiar trail to Uncle Joshua and Aunt Betsy's farm. He patted the thick pack of supply behind the saddle. He heard the click of a gun. "Alexander Chilton, here." He raised his hands high and his horse continued to walk toward the gun peeking out from a tree on his left.

John Story stepped from behind the tree. "Dang, Alexander. Last person on earth I expected this morning. Go on in. Union Army is all over the border counties. Union General Curtis's army marches on his way back to the Mississippi River, some say to West Plains."

Alexander nodded, dismounted, and led the horse to the front hitching rail. "Favorite nephew home from the wars," he shouted.

He did not expect so many welcoming hands to greet him and pull him into the warm kitchen and to a table laden with bounty. "Don't tell Mama, but I can take you up on that offer of a plate overflowing."

He felt Aunt Betsy pat his back every time she passed behind him as she busied herself about the kitchen. He strongly felt the need to talk with his uncle and cousins. "Can I help you with barn chores this morning?"

"Chores long done, but the wood box needs a fill." Uncle Joshua donned his hat and coat and led the way to the barn. "You will find other stragglers from the battle at Elkhorn Tavern camped in Thomasville. Curtis's supply line requires attention, and the sooner he takes note that Confederates cut it, the sooner his army leaves for lack of resources. Can you stay a few days?"

"I'm bound for Thomasville within the hour. All seems well at home. And you?"

"We stand alert, of course, but no activity this far back in the hills in winter. Curtis seems the only man bent on winter battle. What about John?"

"We traveled together, fought together, and battle separated us the first night at Elkhorn Tavern. I pray he found our unit and marches safely on his way southeast with the Confederate Army. And no word of Papa?"

"None, my lad. None." Uncle Joshua rubbed his hands and stomped his feet as if the barn dust carried good news.

Alexander rode across the ford above Uncle Joshua's field and crossed Jacks Fork headed due south. Thomasville promised to be a day's hard ride. Before he reached the Eleven Point watershed, he heard the hoofbeats of several horses coming fast behind him. He spurred his horse off the trail and slid to the forest floor knee deep in pine needles. He covered the horse's nose with his hat and calmed himself and his horse with gentle rubs along the bridle.

He recognized the friendly faces, removed his hat from the horse's nose, and waved it from behind the tree.

"Halt. Who goes there?" The leader skidded his mount to a stop and pulled both pistols.

"Alexander Chilton. On my way to Thomasville to join supply cutters." Alexander stepped cautiously from his protection.

"Then join up. We are bound more westward, to West Plains Courthouse." The leader kicked his horse into a slow gallop and continued his journey.

Alexander swung into the saddle without so much as a stirrup up, waved his hat with a soft Rebel yell, and joined the back of the group of some fifty men dressed in homespun.

The group rode hard, taking rest only at creeks for water. Then they slowed and took the main trail to the courthouse. Alexander could see fresh wagon tracks ahead.

"Take your places, men." The leader slid off his horse while it still moved, dropped the reins, and slapped its rump to send it farther into the woods where it stopped.

Alexander followed suit with the others. He checked both pistols and his gun and eased forward down the edge of the trail. Soon, he could hear the sounds of wagon wheels crunching the rocky road and bumping into deep tracks where the ground thawed and mudded and then refroze in the night.

He saw the leader motion with his gun to return down the trail, and then a man on horseback came out of the woods, waved his hat, and made silent motions indicating the numbers five and zero. Fifty guards accompanied the wagons.

He joined the band back in the woods for the horses, mounted, and waited for orders.

"Five and fifty, a fair amount of lead on alert. Same drivers as before. The rest of you kill or maim every Union you can and protect the retreat. Go." The leader turned and led at a full run.

Alexander stayed in line, readied his weapons, and fired when ordered. He laid his head on his horse's heaving neck and fired with both pistols toward the blue blur ahead. He saw the Rebels jump from their horses into the open supply wagons and battle for the reins.

He realized the leader knew the road well. An open field lay ahead with room to turn stolen wagons. He fired and reloaded. Then he swung around to protect the next wagon overcome.

He felt a bee sting his left thigh and his horse stumbled, but caught stride. Then he spied the source of enemy fire: three groups of ten soldiers on horseback bore down on both sides of the field and out of the woods in front of the first wagon.

He heard a shout, "Ride!" and saw his companions turn two wagons and horses and run northward.

When he shifted his weight in the saddle, pressed his knee hard against his horses ribs, and kicked the opposite flank to turn, his horse stumbled and fell, and he with it.

He recovered his fall to the ground, and ran for the east woods, but five horses soon surrounded him despite possible loaded pistols. His clicked empty. He stopped, dropped his weapons, and raised his hands. He knew a man bested.

A soldier caught the riderless horse and brought it to his side, while another pulled his hands behind his back and bound them with strips of leather. "Get him up."

He felt two sets of hands push him toward his mount and rough him up into the saddle. It was then he noticed a small hole in his trousers and felt a sticky liquid in his boot. A nick in the leather of his saddle told the story of a bullet clean through to knick the saddle and take a thin slice of the horse's front shoulder. Man and beast would live to fight another day.

Alexander saw the West Plains Courthouse just ahead. Bullet holes covered the entire front as if a howitzer recently opened fire upon the building. A large wooden stockade arose to the west since his last visit. When a double door swung open, he saw some fifteen or twenty prisoners tied to metal rings stapled into the main support posts. Five wooden buckets set in the center.

"Dismount and move into the stockade." An officer in blue uniform slapped a quirt in rhythm against his leg. "Move."

Alexander and fully half the men in his group fell into line and marched into the stockade.

He heard one soldier ask, "Did we get Bose?"

Then the reply, "Not today. Next trap."

He vowed never again to follow. He vowed to lead the next gang. He wondered when and how he became so trusting. He knew soldiering rules fail for woodsmen, and he kicked a clot of what he hoped was mud into the rough round posts of the stockade.

Immediately, two soldiers with paper and pen followed him and the other men into the stockade and began to ask questions and write answers.

"Name?"

"Alexander Chilton."

"County of Residence?"

"Shannon."

"Rank?"

Alexander paused. He started to say citizen, and then realized rules of war were the safer bet. "Private."

"Unit?"

"Company I, Fourth Missouri, Infantry, CSA."

"Another Elkhorn straggler, sir. Back to the wall, secesh."

Alexander felt his face redden, but he suppressed his denial and his tongue. He knew he was no secessionist, so what was he? He owned no slaves. His family owned no slaves. He just wanted the invaders out of his part of the country, out of Missouri.

"Your Missouri Guard just disloyaled itself into the Confederate Army. I understand your plight. I joined the Union and my brother joined the Guard to 'protect,' he claimed." The soldier paused and spit the ground. "Back closer to the wall. You can sit later." The young soldier tied the leather strips to the iron circle and stepped to the "secesh" to Alexander's left.

Alexander prepared to spend another cold night on the cold wet ground. His body screamed for the indignity of the bucket, and he finally responded after nightfall. Shortly thereafter, the gates opened again, and five soldiers brought various packs to the prisoners. He recognized his own. He muttered, "Thank you. The blankets prove most welcome." He wondered if he would ever fall asleep.

The following morning he found himself roused, untied, and brought before a long table in the West Plains Courthouse, the interior walls badly damaged by perhaps an exploded howitzer shell. He looked into the eyes of an officer he deemed intelligent. [2.43]

The officer said, "Alexander Chilton, do you take an oath of loyalty to never again take up arms against your country, reside within your home county for the duration, and so sign or make your mark? If you fail to do so, expect transfer forthwith to Union prison. So recorded, thief. Your mark or signature confirms your guilt. March 31, 1862."

"Yes, sir." Alexander reached for the pen offered, signed his name, thankful for the hours when his mama taught him his letters and numbers. However, he could not muster gratitude toward his old schoolmaster he saw escorted out of the county, whose northern ways just became abundantly clear. Thief. *Thief.* The words rang repeatedly in his head as if a school bell called him to task. His cheeks burned with humiliation. *Chiltons pay for their stock,* he recalled admonishing David Smith.

He lowered his head for a moment, then straightened his shoulders, stood tall, looked the officer directly in the eye, and took his punishment like a man. He resisted the impulse to bust the man's nose. However, he knew when he lost a battle.

He felt another soldier press his shoulder, then push him toward the courthouse steps. The soldier escorted him to the edge of the encampment and said, "Dismissed. Go home. Plow your fields, Rebel." [2.45]

CHAPTER 5

TRAGEDY OF ELEVEN—1862

Lieutenant-Colonel Weydemeyer, Commanding Post at Salem, SIR:...I shall have to investigate the killing of those prisoners by Lieutenant Lacy. The more I hear of it the more aggravated the case seems. I hope you will counteract every impression that seems to indicate that we murder prisoners or indulge those who do. We may make a very favorable impression upon such men as those in question who have turned the other side and have returned to us for forgiveness and protection.
—Colonel J. M. Glover, Missouri Volunteers, US Army [2.51]

W hen Alexander arrived at the house, he found his horse saddled and supplies packed.

Fifteen-year-old Shade removed his hat. "The Federal soldiers crossed the river at the county foad the day before yesterday. Father sent me to warn the men to take to the woods. Father set up camp, and I am to lead the way. None of the children or women can know where, so to avoid torture to tell. Take a message to your uncles to prepare a camp in the woods. Your oath papers in hand?"

Alexander only nodded and swung into the saddle.

Mary Louisa led Shade's horse to the hitching rail. "When we saw Little Shade, we knew something must be amiss with Uncle John and Aunt Sophia, what with his horse all lathered and all."

She told Shade, "Help yourself to the table. Mama's tea towel always covers a good taste."

Alexander rode to the iron bell and rang a signal to William. *"No trouble, come home."* Then, he galloped to the ford toward Uncle Joshua's home.

Message well along the family relay to ten uncles, Alexander turned back southeast to retrieve Shade and his rested horse. The two came next to Uncle Andrew Jackson Chilton's farm with the warning and then hastened to Uncle Francis Marion at Powder Mill, watered and rested the horses, then moved quickly downriver where Uncle John's camp lay hidden in the Current River woods.

Uncle John farmed at Henpeck, south of the Shannon-Carter county line, some thirty-five miles downriver from his brothers. John, Joshua, and Thomas married sisters, Sophia, Betsy, and Mary Josephine. The neighbors failed to keep the Chilton clan straight. They lumped the Chiltons into one bunch—respected or otherwise.

The news of soldiers, of either faith, at the county ford found no welcome. Where one army crossed the Current River, the other crossed in due time to provision man, beast, and crops.

Alexander watched Lizzie Davis Nesbit, his beloved fifth cousin, as she carried water in one hand and led toddler, William, with the other. Her faded dress showed four dark streaks of let-out darts.

Lizzie set her bucket on the ground and tipped her bonnet with the back of her hand. "Alexander! Just like you to show up without a sound."

"I know how to travel through woods." Alexander relieved her of both bucket and son. The trio walked inside the rustic log cabin and sat by the kitchen table. "I went to the camps for a few days until things quieted down along the rivers. I am back—for a time."

"And you brought news of the war?"

"Yes, and of family, too." He sat on the porch step. "Early in April 1862, Federal Captain McCameron with a company of sixty soldiers entered the north part of Carter County, on the State Road and came west to Current River at Uncle John's farm. The children planted corn near the river at the County Road Ford. Shade took charge well for a lad only 15 years old.

"The people of the community expected the soldiers, and when they rode into the river, Shade started to warn the next farm up the river. He ran about sixty rods through plowed ground when soldiers rode out of the river and up to the fence.

"Shade's little brother J.J. chimed, 'Their blue uniforms and weapons flashed in the sun, and their fine horses glistened as they ran through the field.' Guess such a sight made an exciting impression on the lad.

"Shade thought the soldiers much closer upon him than they actually were, so he crawled under a log where one of the pursuers discovered him. Bringing him out from his hiding place, they forced him to guide them to the next farm. Sam Hanger and Baty Chitwood worked in another part of the field, but discovered the raiders in time to slip away.

"The Federals returned to Uncle's home, released Shade, and asked Aunt Sophia numerous questions, but got little true information.

"They went down river to the next farm at Woods Mill and camped. After dark, some of the soldiers saddled up to ride around some that night. When one of the men, thus engaged, discovered a man nearby, he asked, 'Who comes there?' The man replied with a shot, which took effect in the soldier's wrist. We heard it caused his death four days later at Greenville.

"Believing they were being attacked by an enemy in the dark, the soldiers stampeded and fled about a half mile down the river to the Brokaw farm where they formed a line of battle and remained in line until near daybreak. Confederate Capt. Owen Hawkins and Captain Ponder, with a band of Rebels, located the Federals and sent them scurrying back to Greenville.

"The local citizens, who first fired on the band, left the scene in an opposite direction from their homes, rode a mile or so and left the road one at a time, so that the enemy could not track them, and returned home in time to get some sleep before daylight."[1.13]

Lizzie gave Alexander a quizzical grin. "I want to know the names of the local citizens who make it so hard on the Federals."

"Nobody says. The Federals rove Shannon and Oregon Counties, and Colonel Coleman gives chase now and again. Nevertheless, how about Lizzie and little William? How do you do?"

After a long silence, Lizzie answered more seriously than the tone of the question. "We do just fine. I thought I preferred you wild and charming types, but Sam suits me. Keeps me settled. I expect another child the end of August. If a boy, I aim to call him George, after Grandpapa Davis. When Sam joined the Third Missouri with Lt. Seth Farris in Reynolds County, my temper burned hotter than the July day. He came home after his six-month enlistment only to provision up and return to the Confederates. Lot of good it did me." Lizzie patted her waist and laughed.

Alexander sat at her side, uncomfortable at the revelation of her delicate state.

Finally, she stood and faced him, her hands on her hips and a smile so wide her cheeks disappeared. "I wrote a new song. I call it 'Tale of Current River.' Lizzie tuned up her banjo and motioned four-year-old William to Alexander's knee.

> *Traveling North by Northwest, we came upon a ledge.*
> *Shrouded there in misty blue, just like the old man said.*
> *We stood and wondered what lie beneath the morning fog.*
> *What mysteries would we find? Oh, we knew it all along.*
> *Treasures hidden in the heart of God,*
> *So hard to find by man.*
> *Secrets of the mountains stirring deep,*
> *Wind, water, and land.*

Climbing down the precipice, holding on to ice and rock.
Finally made it down safely, with pine trees green and soft.
Made our way through hill and dale, by waterfalls and streams.
It all looks familiar, but things are not as they seem.
Treasures hidden in the heart of God,
So hard to find by man.
Secrets of the mountains stirring deep,
Wind, water, and land.
Sitting by the bright flames, a proverb in our minds.
We realized in an instant, these are the best of times.
Then the rain came suddenly, underneath the granite peaks.
A rainbow brought the answer to the questions that we seek.
Treasures hidden in the heart of God,
So hard to find by man.
Secrets of the mountains stirring deep,
Wind, water, and land. [7.4]

Alexander felt touched by the floating melody and Lizzie's mellow voice. "Very nice. We need more rainbows right now."

"Thank you, kind sir. It lifts my spirits."

"You said you hated Sam's long hunting trips, but his woods knowledge saves his life and the lives of many others who are less seasoned. Soldiers cross our rivers and keep everyone on alert. You keep a pistol. You and your herbs make fine tea, but the chicory—brrrr."

"The chicory bush they call 'bushwhackers'? Yes, unpredictable—strong and bitter." She laughed for the upper hand in the banter.

"Any fool knows the folly to line men up on either side of a pasture to shoot at each other. That is, unless they shoot old flintlocks that ignite another's powder. Captain Farris led us like bushwhackers at Wilson's Creek, as did Captain Norman at Pea Ridge. Saved our lives, the bushwhacker way. Failed to sit well with the generals, though. War proves a bad lot, Lizzie, a bad lot."

When Lizzie began to tear up, he asked, "Why the tears?"

She laid her needlework in the basket, and on it, her little silver thimble. "I received no word from Sam with the Rebels; nor Thomas who took the oath for the Union. Like most others with mixed sympathies, what would happen if our family met on a battlefield somewhere? Oh, I always stay close to tears when I am with child. Ignore me."

He comforted her with an embrace and encouragement. "Sam and Thomas may march home this very day." He stood, cupped his fingers under her chin, and wiped the tears from her cheeks with his thumbs. "Be back tomorrow."

Then he strode to the gate, swung into the saddle, lifted his hat toward her like a gentleman, placed her thimble in his vest pocket, and rode until the trail began to curve. He reached into his pocket and withdrew the thimble. He moved his hand side to side and watched the silver flash in the sun. He whispered, "For where your treasure is, there will your heart be also."

He turned to see Lizzie pull little William to her. However, William pushed away, ran to the gate, and his sweet melodic voice drifted upriver on the afternoon breeze. "Bye-bye. Come back tomorrow!"

"The Federals camped at Eminence Courthouse and all along the river at Round Spring. Federals ordered a West Point man, General Davidson, and his engineers to build supply roads and bridges to support the war effort and secure Missouri for the North." Alexander could see worry in his uncle's eyes, but he continued when Joshua motioned a hand.

"A skirmish erupted at Eminence on June seventh. Ten days later, Rebels fired volleys into the Federal camp, but few wounds bled. The Courthouse and jail survived the encampment.

"Federals ransacked Thomas T.'s farmhouse and confiscated the livestock and food stores for the soldiers. The women and children escaped to Doctor Reed and Aunt Polly downriver. They arrived several days later in bad shape. The girls stand bound to secrecy. God is my hope. Surely they escaped a molesting."

He stopped, twirled his hat in his hands, and then continued. "During the fracas, a soldier hit George F. in the head with the butt of a rifle. George F. failed to listen when we told him his Round Spring farm lay too close to the enemy at Salem. His neighbors are a bunch of Northern sympathizers who killed his father. George said he believed his father's death an accident, but we all know better." Alexander stopped abruptly. "What happened to our family?"

Joshua replied, "War, Alexander, a bona fide war."

The July sun scalded man and beast at high noon. "Race you to Hole-in-the-Wall!" Alexander's long stride and head start put him a wagon's length ahead of William in a foot race to the river.

One splash, two splashes, and a volley of whoops echoed against the limestone bluff. A large measure of "boy" filled the souls of Shadrach's sons. "Lunch calls my name. We can finish the rest of the hay before dark." Alexander swam to the gravel bar, donned his clothes and boots, and waited.

William dived from a giant rock pried from the side of the mountain some eons past by tree roots and winter ice, and waded ashore. "Seems small groups gather near Inman Hollow. Shall we ride to Montauk Spring and sell the boys a horse or two?"

"We may find some Independence Day celebration upon arrival. I say we leave today. We best stay alert. Colonel Glover sends Federal sorties out of Rolla right along. Add Colonel Weydemeyer's bunch and a fellow must be careful nearing Salem." Alexander walked to the house, packed for a few days' journey, and met William at the ford.

Twilight streamed through the pine and oak trunks when he neared the home of David Smith, north of Round Spring. He decided he could add insult to injury. "David Smith accused me of stealing his horse. We might as well make him an honest man."

Alexander spied the horses in question grazing on a rise in a large pasture west of the house. He whispered, "Swing east and stay low." He lay as far down his horse's side as he dared, eased the rail from its wooden notch, and let it fall. He circled the horses and gently eased them out of the gate into open woods.

He motioned to William to draw alongside the two young mares, and the four horses silently disappeared into the evening breeze. At a safe distance, he fashioned lead ropes for the two and handed one to William. "We best camp in a deep draw and venture on to Coleman's camps at dawn. No reason to invite friendly fire."

At sunrise, the four horses and two Chilton riders stopped when they smelled campfires. "Shannon County boys coming in," Alexander said quietly. He whistled, "bob-bob-white!"

"Bob-bob-white," came the answer.

"Horses for the quartermaster."

"Straight on and to your left by the wagons." The picket returned to vigilance.

Alexander poured himself the motley hot drink at the campfire nearest the woods, rather than at the quartermaster's fire. He felt the hair stand at the back of his neck from the smell of the brew or perhaps fear of Federals nearby. He feigned a sip and tossed the remainder in the fire where sizzle and sparks flew. "Federals!" he shouted.

He swung into the saddle as more than a hundred Federals in blue charged the camp at full speed. "William?"

"Here, scatter south!"

He caught a glimpse of William ahead. He dodged a scramble of man, mule, and horse toward the hills on either side of Inman Hollow. He saw several men fall empty handed. The element of surprise stranded clothes, guns, and supplies by the campfires.

He decided to avoid the route to the bridge where he reckoned soldiers likely awaited those in flight. He melted into the woods, and sounds of gunfire faded and slowed to silence.

When he reached the river, he rested his lathered horse and let him drink. He was not familiar with landmarks this far up Current River.

"Alexander!" He heard his name called and saw William some ways downriver.

"We were lucky today, brother. Serious firepower and numbers routed the Rebels today." Alexander fell in beside his brother, and they crossed at the ford and followed the trail between the rivers toward home.

William asked, "Do you think John and Papa will come home by Christmas?"

"I pray they come home."

As the Federal presence grew, southern sympathies roused where neutral sympathies once prevailed. Depriving cavalry of horses exacted maximum disruption of battle and forage plans. Southern-sympathy citizens provided such disruptions the better part of many a summer night in sixty-two, to the frustration of Col. Joseph Weydemeyer and his principal scout, William Monks.

William Monks removed his hat and stepped into the colonel's quarters. "Scout report, sir."

"At ease, Monks. How many men in the Coleman regiment? Name the locations of the companies."

"Surveillance and prisoner interrogation indicate as many as four hundred men in our area. Their scarcity of ammunition and arms saves us from embarrassment and losses. Our sources report many men from the Current River valley furloughed from the Coleman Regiment and scattered to harvest crops; then return with much needed supplies to their companies posted in Thomasville, West Plains, Doniphan, and across the Arkansas line near Mammoth Springs. There could be as many as a thousand Rebels in neighboring counties right now. My written report, sir." Monks placed the report on the colonel's table and stepped back to wait for further questions or orders.

"Tell me more about Lieutenant Boyd's contacts in Shannon and Dent."

"Well, sir, Lt. John Boyd grew up in Northern Shannon County and knows the whereabouts and sympathies of the citizens. Boyd's former neighbors in Newton Township wait outside with certain information on a nest of secesh on Jacks Fork and Big Creek. He names Senator Chilton the most successful recruiter for the Rebs in the county.

"Boyd highly recommends John Worthington and David Smith, settlers from Pennsylvania and Maine, educated miners and solid Unionists. John Worthington became an enemy of Senator Joshua Chilton over an imagined political wrong. In addition, Chilton hired the man who killed Worthington's brother in sixty-one, named Henry Smith, no kin to the other scout.

"David Smith holds low regard for the senator's nephews, Alexander and William. He claims them responsible for Smith's missing horses and other wrongs against the citizenry too numerous to mention. Says they ride with Coleman. Smith says their uncle, the senator, thinks he's the 'King of Shannon County,' and says he recruits with sizable influence for the Confederacy in all of Southeast Missouri."

"What do you say, Monks?"

"Sir, the record shows when the legislature disbanded in February of sixty-one, Senator Chilton and eight of the ten representatives from the Twenty-Fourth District came home. I am ashamed to say, Howell and Oregon county representatives voted for secession with Jackson in Neosho. Some say the senator advocates 'reason with the pen.' Since 1818, the Chiltons grew to number more than a hundred souls from Round Spring to below Van Buren. Most sons ride with Coleman and Freeman or with Price in the Confederacy. Some remain neutral."

"What dispatch, the senator's sons? Or perhaps he lost 'reason' in his own house?"

"No, sir, his sons remain neutral, with neither army. When conscription comes, they must choose sides. Most of the neutrals take to the woods with the guerrillas, so I find it hard to say. Worthington and Smith call the Chiltons a nest of copperheads, whose capture would ensure Union control in the Twenty-Fourth District."

"You entertain political ambitions, Monks?" Colonel Weydemeyer enjoyed a chuckle at Monks' expense and then praised him for a balanced report. "Bring in Worthington and Smith and summon Lieutenant

93

Boyd and the paymaster. We move against the Current and Jacks Fork
Valley with reinforcements from Salem and Rolla, Captain Bradway
commanding."

Monks took the special orders in hand and began to read:

Special Order No. 11.
U.S. Military Post Salem MO
August 23d 62

Capt. Bradway Commanding Co E 3d MO Cavalry is hereby direct-
ed to detail 50 men and one Command Officer to proceed tomorrow with
daybreak in a southern direction to the valley of the Current River and
of Jack's Fork to carry out as far as possible the following instructions.

The first object of the expedition is to surprise partisan settlements
where it is supposed that members of Coleman's Command are hid-
ing. Two faithful guides will be added to the Command to prevent that
previous information may reach the Rebels the Command will leave the
post in another than the finally intended direction and take to the woods
*when advised by the guides. **Armed men have not to be made prison-***
ers but to be shot on the spot every man in whose possession is found
***property.** Horses etc. Should be found, has to be arrested and sending*
them to be tried by the Provost Marshal. All suspicious Houses have to
be thoroughly searched for weapons of any kind. And such weapons to
be confiscated buildings known to be harboring places for Rebels have
to be destroyed the furniture being removed previously if possible.

The 2nd object is to confiscate from secessionists and rebel sym-
pathizers, such property as May be turned over to the use of the U.S.
as Cattle Forage Horses etc. if it is possible wheat will be thrashed
and ground at the nearest mill. Transportation has to be furnished by
rebel sympathizers. it is sufficient to leave a family one milk cow so
much provision as is necessary for their support through the year. Of
all confiscated property a correct list has to be kept by the Commanding
Officer to be delivered to the Provo Marshal of this Post after return,
The Command will provide themselves with five days rations of Sugar

and salt. All other subsistence has to be drawn through the country. They will return as soon or before the before mentioned objects are accomplished as far as it is in their power not before.

To Capt. Bradway   J Weydemeyer
Comg Co. "E" 3rd Cav   Lt Col Comg Post [6.1]

In the last dark hours before dawn, Alexander lay sound asleep. He woke with a start, raised to his elbow, and listened intently. He bolted out of bed about the time someone kicked in a door and tromped in heavy boots up the stairs. The glow of a torch below outlined a man and a long gun with bayonet.

"Dress quietly so no harm comes to you or your family." The soldier kept the gun pressed tight against Alexander's belly.

He dressed, pulled on his boots, and started down the steep steps.

He heard the two young hired men behind him. Henry Smith, age twenty, and James Gallion, age nineteen, received similar treatment. He knew James's broken leg, not quite healed, slowed progress.

When he reached the last step, he saw his mother and sisters in the front room where they shivered in spite of the blankets around their shoulders.

"Outside, secesh." A second soldier pushed Alexander, James, and Henry through the door and into the dark yard.

"Oh, no. There's no cause." Alexander moaned when he saw his brother, William, in the faint glow of the newly lit torch. Little Paulina, clad in her nightgown, broke from her mother's hands, and toddled to the porch steps and into her grandmother's arms.

"We march to Salem. Sergeant, take charge of the prisoners. Move out." The officer turned toward the unmounted soldiers. "Search the house and barn for contraband and weapons." The leader of the group of fifty or so men gave firm orders in a subdued tone.

Alexander failed to recognize anyone in the party within range of the torch light. He knew something organized and dangerous descended on the peaceful river. He feared for himself, his family, and his neighbors.

Alexander and the other prisoners waded into the swift shoal. Water rose to just above their knees. When the gravel shifted, the horses' shoulders and rope tethers kept the prisoners vertical to press forward. The splash from the horses drenched him, and water ran down his face and dripped from his chin. The farm of Alexander's uncle, Senator Joshua and Aunt Betsy Chilton, lay around the next bend.

Fog hung over the river and drifted along the narrow valley. Despite the cool August night air, and wet clothes, sweat beaded along Alexander's hairline.

Within sight of the house, the soldiers stopped, bound the four prisoners to a tree, and gagged them with their own kerchiefs. Four soldiers guarded the prisoners. The others rode forward, guns drawn.

Joshua's house lay in a rich, wide river-bottom valley. The unpainted two-story structure held four large rooms, two down, two up, with a staircase in the expansive center hall that most folks called a dogtrot. Wide porches ran the length of the building, both front and back. A light shone from every room. Several people moved about the kitchen.

Dawn broke fast.

Alexander could see the outlines of soldiers surround the house. When a soldier kicked in one front door, three men bolted from the second front door, and one from the back door, south into the river bottom pasture planted high with corn.

A shot rang from inside the house, and soldiers returned fire into the dogtrot. "Halt!"

The four men ran.

"Fire at will!"

Alexander saw sixteen-year-old Perry run across the road, flinch, fall to his knees, rise, run, and disappear out of sight into the woods up the north hillside.

Soldiers spurred their horses in hot pursuit but turned to find a less steep path.

Another group of soldiers ran to the back of the house, and the leader motioned with both arms. "Spread out! Get the horses and any contraband."

Another man from inside the house almost made it into the south woods when he fell about a hundred yards from Alexander and William. Alexander could not make out whether it was Jesse or Louis Conway. Jesse lived in the household, and Louis helped with the extra August farm work and fall harvest.

The leader galloped his horse toward the river and shouted, "Man in the river! You two in, two cross, two of you search downriver." The clink, scrunch, and splash of horses on the gravel road and in the river began to fade as the soldiers followed orders downriver.

The wrist and chest bindings cut into Alexander's flesh. His gag dripped spit. Pain assaulted his heart and mind.

Sun rose over the eastern woods and burned the fog. Sounds of horses and men carried up the river road, and then Alexander recognized the man, hands tied in front of him, who walked in front of six cavalry guards. Uncle Joshua.

It pained him when Joshua stumbled and moaned as he met Alexander's gaze and saw his nephews and hired men bound to the trees. His uncle righted himself and stood tall and proud despite the circumstances, every inch the senator. The long swim downriver left him soaked from head to toe in clothes suited for a day's work on the farm or in the mill. With his fingers, hands tied, he slicked wet black hair from his wide forehead. The straight Chilton nose and square jaw of the proud man rose slightly in confidence and a certain air of defiance.

When Alexander saw David Smith on Joshua's fine sorrel, he pulled at his bindings to no avail. The gag suppressed the curses on his tongue and saved him from certain death.

Smith's smile reeked with disgust. "Democrats." He spurred the sorrel and galloped to the front of the raiders.

August 25, 1862. One sorry day. Alexander lowered his chin to his chest at the thought.

The fifty soldiers rode. The five prisoners walked. The raiding expedition followed the Jacks Fork River northward on the Story's Creek road, crossed the small creek several times, and came to a fork. The westerly road to the left continued up Jacks Fork River to Alley Spring. The northerly road followed Story's Creek toward Current River and the town of Salem.

Alexander met his Uncle Joshua's gaze and glanced to the left upriver. He knew by the nod of Joshua's head that he also thought Perry, Nelson, or someone passed word of the raid to Uncle Thomas J. and Aunt Mary Josephine. Ten guards galloped past Alexander and the other prisoners. He could not hear the voices, but by the motion of hands, the soldiers confirmed the house abandoned and horses gone.

He listened to the conversation of the nearby guards for any word of his fourth uncle, who lived downriver and likely the first ambushed. Uncle Andrew or his hired hands' absence from the march could mean death or, at best, passed over.

The expedition followed the creek and stopped to rest. They watered their horses at a spring at the foot of Lawson's Hill, before the steep climb out of the valley into the Flatwoods.

The expedition marched north between the rivers without incident to David Smith's farm on Current River, a distance of fifteen or more miles. Here they camped until morning when the expedition split. Some twenty soldiers guarded the prisoners and thirty or so others followed orders to search Big Creek, which lay in a northeasterly direction.

Alexander heard voices behind him. Discussion of the raid commenced.

One guard walked behind the prisoners and checked each set of bound hands. "You be the lucky ones." He sat by the other guards but knew himself within prisoners' hearing and bragged. "Old man West talked Lieutenant Reed down and turned to leave when the son opened fire. One dumb move. When the wife ran into the line of fire and pushed her husband toward the door, she took a load of lead in the back. Doubt she makes it."

"What about the old man and son?" another guard asked.

"Dead, I figure. Chilton escaped out the back of the main house. I wandered in his sheep paddock, barn, and pasture to no avail. Escaped on hands and knees through the sheep, sure as shootin'."

A third guard tossed his cup of water into the weeds. "Good-looking woman in the Chilton house with a passel of kids. Unharmed from the looks of her. I do not abide killing women and children. This war? Tearing me up, and I am not too proud to admit it."

Alexander breathed a low groan of thanks; saw his brother William's shoulder droop, but Uncle Joshua's shoulders squared in anger.

Then he saw the cause. John Worthington, private citizen and paid guide, walked past the prisoners, and Alexander heard a hiss from fellow prisoner Henry Smith. "Worthington, you are a dead man. I got your brother in sixty-one, and I will get you."

Alexander kicked at Smith's foot and whispered. "You want to get us killed on the spot?"

On the morning of the twenty-seventh, Lt. Herbert Reed, "appropriated" the wagon and oxen of Shannon County Representative Alfred Deatherage to transport the families of David Smith and his brother, Dan. The expedition continued toward the military outpost at Salem.

When the expedition reached the residence of Joseph Conway, it encamped for the night. Returning from Big Creek, the balance of the command herded several horses and one prisoner, Jackson Herrin.

"Jackson, what of your brothers?" Joshua scooted sideways to make room for the new prisoner. Joshua knew every family in a six-county area and beyond because of campaigning for public service and his Masonic affiliation.

"Away, thank God, away." Jackson sat by Joshua and the other four exhausted prisoners.

August 28, five p.m., the expedition reported to the outpost at Salem, prisoners and contraband property dutifully noted and delivered.

Confident of survival, Alexander and William gave assist to James Gallion whose broken leg worsened every mile of the forty marched. He then attended to Uncle Joshua, a strong man at age forty-four and father of nine children, the youngest a newborn baby, Martha Belle. Alexander saw the weight of the world lying on his beloved uncle's countenance and frame. Worry for home and avowed responsibility for the prisoners' safety.

Alexander took note of every soldier identified by name and the faces of the nameless.

The Third Missouri Cavalry, decisively commanded by Lt. Herbert Reed, led the march of more than forty miles, with fifty or more soldiers on horseback who guarded six prisoners on foot without incident from the remote hills in the Jacks Fork and Current River Valley to the Ozark Highlands of Salem. [3.25]

Alexander expected to see the lead scout for the Sixth Missouri Provisional Militia, William Monks, well known to Alexander. Lt. John Boyd, another of the Sixth Missouri, often joined Monks in unabashed coercion of local families in the name of peace for the citizenry. Nevertheless, the prisoners arrived safely at Salem, proof enough Monks and Boyd missed their chance to carry out Colonel Weydemeyer's special order, and the provost marshal's relentless efforts to find and capture the Chiltons, especially the senator, a Democrat.

Alexander knew from local men of Federal faith, who were nonetheless friends of the Chiltons, Colonel Weydemeyer believed all the Chiltons rode with his archenemies, Colonel Coleman and Colonel Freeman. None of the Chiltons rode with Coleman, but if he survived, Alexander was inclined to pack and join up. However, survival of another forty-mile march to Rolla lay ahead.

"*Death march*" kept invading his thoughts.

The guards held the six prisoners in an abandoned house on the edge of the Salem encampment. Well into the quiet night, James whispered to Alexander. "Not one more mile can I march on this leg. Let me knock out the guard with my boot, and the rest of you can escape."

"The Rolla officer, Capt. George S. Avery, reinforced Salem today with a hundred or more men. They must expect an attack by Coleman, or why else such heavy guard?" Alexander passed James's words and his own thoughts to Uncle Joshua.

"Under the influence of at least two Masons in the guards, I believe we can expect honorable treatment to Rolla. Escape attempts invite certain death or miserable conditions, at best. Heavy reinforcements may mean Avery expects a rescue attack from Coleman." Joshua looked to each man in the room for agreement or contrary opinion.

Nods all around fixed the plan to march on the morrow.

The guards awakened and unbound the prisoners then escorted all to the food line where Alexander recognized nary a man in the officer and soldier ranks. Lieutenant Reed and the Salem companies—gone.

Captain Avery rode his horse front and center. "Lieutenant Lacy commands the march from Salem to Rolla. Escape attempts invite certain death. Lieutenant, move out." Captain Avery saluted Lt. Alexander H. Lacy, turned, and set a fast pace northward toward Rolla.

"Move along there, secesh." The guard pushed Alexander with the toe of his boot, and the expedition marched about a mile from the encampment to the edge of a creek.

Alexander overheard two guards' conversation. "Orders named Captain Bradway for the raids, but Bradway checked into the infirmary and left the march to Lieutenant Reed. Good man, Reed. Captain Avery hightailed it back to Rolla at a run. Nevertheless, Lt. Lacy's inexperience arranged it for him. Lacy would not stretch past five and half foot tall and thin as a rail—doubt he controls this rough bunch. Prisoners will not last ten miles. Sergeant says one of the prisoners is a Senator. Likely too much politics for captains."

"Or honorable men," said the second guard.

"It is two in a hundred then, plus the haughty Masons." The first guard reined his horse sideways to bump James Gallion. "Move on there, cripple."

"My broken leg marched forty miles. I cannot go another mile without support on both sides."

"March."

James hobbled out of line, slid down the trunk of a tree to the ground, and brushed his hair back with his fingers. "Kill me and be damned."

The guard spurred his horse forward, took aim, and shot James between the eyes.

"James!" Alexander's first step toward James and the sound of the shot signaled immediate response from Lieutenant Lacy, who led the triple-wide column.

"Halt! Report!" Lieutenant Lacy reined in his horse with a flourish.

"Tried to escape, Lieutenant."

"Sergeant, return to Salem with two men and form a burial detail." Lieutenant Lacy galloped to the head of the column. "Forward, march."

Alexander quietly addressed his uncle. "Perhaps we erred about James' boot."

The march resumed, but two guards slowed and held William Chilton and Henry Smith behind the others, until a turn in the road put them out of sight.

"Eyes forward."

A shot rang back of the turn. Two more shots sent a wave of panic into horse and man alike.

"Keep moving!" The guards of the other three tightened their ring around their prisoners.

Shortly, the two soldiers who guarded William and Henry galloped past Alexander and the others to report to Lieutenant Lacy. "Prisoners tried to escape. We shot and killed them."

Lieutenant Lacy called a halt. "Prisoners, take off your boots. Attempt escapes under my command and meet certain death." He ordered the two guards to remain at the front of the column.

The prisoners sat and reluctantly reached for their boots, all except Joshua.

"Do you intend to shoot us down like brutes? I'm a Mason, an honorable man, held to my code of conduct as certain as some of you." Joshua nodded toward the large group of soldiers mounted at attention.

"When dead you can't tell an honorable man from a brute." Another guard, who wore neither Masonic Ring nor honorable bearing, pushed Joshua's shoulder backward with his boot. "Sit."

"I claim friends who can walk as deep in blood as any of you."

Alexander dropped flat to the ground and rolled when he saw the guard take aim for Joshua.

Guns fired. Powder floated.

Joshua fell across Jackson Herrin's legs.

Jackson slumped, and then fell backward from a blast at close range.

In the confusion, Alexander scooted unharmed into the brush, stood, and ran. His heart pounded. Terror and grief emboldened his pace. He was determined to find safety. He could hear shots and shouts. Horses crashed into the woods in fast pursuit. He made for a steep slope, found a limestone canyon on the other side, and slid farther and faster in a tumble toward a final drop of some ten feet. The fall knocked out his breath. Recovering, he rolled as close to the cliff as possible and listened for the buzz of the bullet sure to take his life.

Silence.

His chest heaved, and he gulped air. He fought for stillness. He finally gained control of his breath, felt for blood or broken bones and found no pain. Then he focused on the terrain ahead to plan an escape route.

He knew he needed to distance himself in the many hours before the safety of darkness. He knew how to move through woods. He rolled to his belly, raised to his knees, checked above and side to side, and then slipped as fast as he dared through the thick underbrush. When he found a stock path, he followed it a ways. Then he abruptly turned at a right angle and circled back toward the road where the others fell.

The soldiers gone, he breathed a sigh of relief, but asked himself what kind of fool risks a return to the scene of murderous slaughters? Alexander counted himself a determined fool.

He could make out that his brother William and Henry died where they fell. He began a careful search to the left of the road, then to the right, for others. He found Jackson on the right. Dead.

About two hundred yards farther, he found Joshua's body nearly hidden in the underbrush. "Oh, Uncle, you almost crawled to protection of the forest." Alexander immediately noticed the simply designed gold signet ring was gone from the center finger of Joshua's right hand.

"Steal a Masonic ring, punishable by death, you dishonorable brutes. I will hunt you down and hope a true Mason doesn't get you first." Anger, then pain, swept through his hissed oath.

He pulled his beloved uncle to his chest. He wanted to shout, but dared only a whisper into the blood-soaked hair. "I vow to find your ring and kill every man, if it takes a lifetime. I know their faces, and Lacy knows their names. I vow to protect our family without mercy. I…" The sound of hoofbeats and clank of metal on metal announced danger. Burial detail!

He slowly laid Joshua to the ground and crept deeper into the woods. He dared not trust himself to look back, but circled far west, then turned and made his way south. Move, listen, search, and plan. The rhythm began to soothe his anger and after four days led to familiar ground. Big Creek!

He saw a woman at the creek washing laundry but did not recognize her. He took a chance and approached her, arms raised in hopes of assurance. "I'm lost in the woods. Can you give me direction?"

"Big Creek lies a few miles above Eminence Courthouse at the Round Spring."

"I need to find Centerville."

"From Eminence, yes, take the Centerville Road. If you travel a more easterly direction and some south, you cross quicker than the creek trail."

"Thank you. I cannot stay lost forever, then."

"Centerville is a long walk and if you are short of food, these apples may see you through. Wish I had more."

He heard the faint crack of brush. "The clothes. Cover me quick"

Within minutes, soldiers in blue galloped toward the woman. "Did you see a man walking or riding this way the past hour or so?"

"Yes. Less than an hour ago, a man travelled afoot headed toward Centerville road. He seemed unsure of his destination."

Alexander heard the kick of a boot and hooves clink on the gravel. When all was silent, he said, "Can you hold those bed linens wide and carry them in front of me to a limb near the brush?"

Alexander nodded his thanks, and within sight and sound of the woman, he traveled east-southeast. He knew soldiers would soon return and search Big Creek.

Then he turned due south toward Sinking Creek to cross into the land between the rivers. He knew Lizzie's cabin to be empty, but Smith and Worthington would know the same and guess his destination. Several Chilton farms lay between Eminence Courthouse on the Current and his home on the Jacks Fork, but he knew his presence put all his family at risk; Lt. John Boyd could lead Monks to every farm of family and friend.

When he stopped to rest, he voiced regrets to the trees. "I sighted David Smith and John Worthington down my barrel multiple times and held fire."

Hungry. Hungry. Apples gone, blackberries finished, and persimmons would pucker until frost.

Alexander arrived home, late in the night of the eighth day, September 7, 1862. Fearing spies watched the doors; he crawled under the house to the trap door. He tapped the floor in a rhythm familiar to everyone in his home. He heard bare feet hit the floor in a run. The bed leg screeched across the trap door, and he saw the beautiful face of his mother appear inches from his own.

"God is my hope." Patsy bent into the dark opening, and drew her son's forehead to her lips. "Deus spes mea." She began to weep.

"William dead. Uncle dead. Why am I the one spared?" His pained voice broke in grief.

"Reports said they buried the three of you where you fell, at a site still unknown. The search for Jackson Herrin continues. Nobody searches for you."

Alexander pulled himself through the floor, on to the daybed by the cookstove, and watched his mother gather with one fell swoop the tea cloth and food left from supper.

"Cornbread and bacon never tasted so good. I lived eight days on three apples from a stranger."

His brother's wife, Mary, walked into the kitchen and sat in a chair, far away from the bed. "What about William? Is it true? Is he dead?"

He nodded. "More than a hundred soldiers guarded us after we reached Salem. Guards slowed William and Henry behind the rest of us. We heard shots, and the guards rode up to the lieutenant and said the prisoners tried to escape and they shot them dead. I escaped, and circled back around later that day and found their graves by the road where they fell. We can move him here, if you wish. Guards were all over me. I could not help him. I could not save him. I am so sorry, Mary." He waited for some response. "Mary?"

"Move him? Too many days passed. Too many days. Little Paulina cries for her father day and night. What am I to do?" Mary drifted to the back room like a spirit leaving the mortal world.

Guilt and grief tore at his heart. His mind scattered thoughts to the wind and called them back in a cyclone. He tried to substitute revenge for pain. It took all night.

Thankful the Federals failed to discover the guns, he packed several days of food and stowed his guns and ammunition in the leather sling.

"Say nothing to anyone. Be back tomorrow." He slipped out the door, hat drawn low, crossed the ford of the river to the familiar path to Aunt Betsy's house where he marched as prisoner only days before.

Alexander moved quietly, surprised to find the home uncharacteristically dark as dawn threatened the night sky. He tapped on the bedroom window.

"Joshua?" Aunt Betsy immediately sat up.

He watched her gently ease out of bed, slip to her first-floor window, and peer at the dark ground on either side.

She could make out the shadow of a large man against the house and pecked her window with her knuckle. "Alexander! Can it be?"

The shadow's hand pointed toward the back of the house.

"The report proved wrong. Maybe they all got away. Praise be." Aunt Betsy mumbled hope all the way down the dogtrot to the lock on the back door.

Alexander held the embrace of his aunt for several minutes as he tried to recall the planned words of comfort.

"Federals got us. All shot. I bolted just past Salem. Uncle Joshua, William, and the others, gone…removed Uncle's Masonic ring right off his dead body. I swear a solemn vow to hunt the guard down and bring you the ring—and the finger that wears it. Worthington and Smith, dead men. Dead men, I tell you." He shook his head in shame. What happened to the words of comfort?

As the Chilton women, girls, and little boys gathered around the stove and exchanged opinions whether to send for the older sons at camp in the woods, Aunt Betsy's newborn baby began to cry.

Alexander reached into the bentwood cradle by the daybed and drew ten-week-old Martha Belle to his chest. A painful sob escaped his breath, and he handed her to Aunt Betsy.

Martha Belle would never know her father, the "King of Shannon County," Senator Joshua T. Chilton. Alexander sat on the daybed and lowered his head to his hands. Devastation.

The kitchen door slammed against the wall with such force Alexander jumped and dodged the splash of cream Aunt Betsy poured into the butter churn placed on the floor at her knee. "Nelson, what on earth?"

"Alexander! Praise be!" Nelson embraced his cousin then turned to his family.

"Mother, news about Father and the others. Our men got word on the relay. Colonel Weydemeyer, the commander at Salem and Houston outposts, traveled this very day to investigate the matter in person, what with Father's stature and all. Perry is lucky the soldier's bullet only grazed his shoulder. His wound heals well. No other news."

"Lord, have mercy. Have mercy." Spill forgotten; Aunt Betsy leaned on her eldest son, Nelson, who led her to the daybed by the kitchen stove. She sat with her hands in her lap. Shivers assaulted her head, traveled down her spine, and shook her body as she suffered in silence.

Alexander leaned against the wall and watched silently as Aunt Betsy's other six youngsters gathered on the bed and the floor at her feet.

Martha Belle's cradle squeaked as it rocked to and fro, to and fro. Aunt Betsy pulled her toe from the cradle and finally broke the silence. "Nelson, take news to the camps. Be on the alert for trouble and keep to the woods."

Alexander saw his sister, Mary Louisa, who ran to the porch and entered the kitchen door from the dogtrot. "Mama sent me here to check on Perry. Nelson! You came! Oh, Nelson!"

Nelson met her midway into the room, just before she collapsed in his arms and sank to the floor with the others. "There now. There now." He stroked her back and kissed the top of her head.

Alexander, hat in hand, allowed the grief of his uncle's family to burrow into his bones. He looked among the large group of cousins, found Lizzie's little William, but did not see Lizzie. He glanced into the room across the dogtrot. When he saw the quilt move on the bed, he stepped inside.

Lizzie lay resting on Aunt Betsy's bed, a newborn baby in her arms. She stirred when the wide-planked pine floor creaked. "George Washington Nesbit, meet Cousin Alexander."

"He's a dandy."

Lizzie reached for Alexander's hand. "Can we bear this? Alexander, I cannot bear up. Aunt Betsy and the others need me." She lay silent. Words of anguish boiled up and spilled into a whisper. "When Sam deserted me for the Confederates, I drew up divorce papers." Sobs overtook her voice and her frame.

Alexander knelt on one knee, leaned over the bed, pressed his free hand behind her head. He gripped her hair in his fingers and drew her to his chest. "God is my hope, Lizzie, just hold treasures close and rest now."

He held her until her sobs calmed and then lowered her to the pillow. "I will protect you till my dying day." His gaze gripped her dark blue eyes, for what seemed eons of understanding. "Till my dying day."

Alexander rose, turned, and stepped into the dogtrot to gather his wits.

He motioned Nelson to the door. "Charles, Jack Smith, and I seek revenge at Worthington's, then on to find David Smith. Say nothing."

"But you are safe; we thought…I intend to come."

"No, stay, protect our family. He embraced Nelson and stepped out the door into the dawn. "Be back tomorrow."

Alexander walked to the farm of Charles T. Chilton.

Charles stood by his horse, packed and ready. "I knew they did not get you. Let us ride."

Alexander climbed behind Charles. The two men rode to the home of John "Jack" Smith, brother of the murdered Henry Smith.

Jack stepped to the porch and without a word, ran to the barn for his horse.

The three angry men kept a fast pace northward toward the Round Spring. Alexander said, "John Worthington stopped at his home near the Round Spring. He deserves his fate today. The coward, David Smith, loaded his family in a wagon and hides behind Federal skirts in Rolla. Federals made Alfred Deatherage provide the wagon. I will find David Smith. Federals paid Worthington and Smith cash money as guides. Partners in the mining business and now, partners in murder. Heaven above knows justice is deserved."

"Slow the pace until we find another horse. A brother's revenge knows no bounds of time."

Jack dismounted to walk a spell. "John Worthington celebrated his revenge when he reported my brother lived with the Chiltons and got Henry killed on the march. I know. I know." Jack raised his hands in dismay. "Henry killed Worthington's brother, Amos, in sixty-one. Yes, a brother's revenge knows no bounds, and I will take my revenge on John Worthington this very night, so help me God."

Charles thanked Jack for the turn on the horse and voiced his own thoughts. "Worthington and Smith must hate the Chiltons' politics and hate their persons with a vengeance. What earned you Smith's ire, Alexander?"

Alexander muffled a sarcastic laugh and savored the moment but hesitated to confess his sins to Charles. "I must admit I stole two of his horses. For a good cause, mind you. Colonel Coleman seemed mighty pleased. Shod, they were. Double value, given scarcity of shoes these days. The real injury? When his wife took a good look at my handsome countenance at music parties and dances, his face turned so red as to give steam out the ears. The sparks crackled like the air before the thunder, sparks of anger and perceived passion. 'Get to the house,' he said, and he ran for his weapons. I whooped louder than necessary to move out the horseflesh. Never enjoyed a whoop more, and he knew why. Do not get me wrong—I never touched her. Never."

The trio reached the Worthington farm after nightfall, east of Round Spring. Like the Federal raiders two weeks prior, they broke down the door without warning, guns drawn. John resisted and fell wounded. His wife helped him to their bed where they huddled and begged for mercy.

Alexander railed his accusations. "Our people didn't beg when you murdered them. Squat here from Pennsylvania and take power over others' lives for advantage and cash money? Turn us in to Federals for no just cause and go unpunished?"

Alexander, Charles, and Jack took their revenge, without regard to who dealt the fatal blow to John Worthington.

Alexander prepared for service with Colonel Coleman before the Federal spies knew he lived. It meant survival, revenge delayed.

He set about recruitment and attracted a full company of Shannon County men, some seasoned soldiers under oaths, some deserters, and others nigh on criminal. "We must protect the full length of the Current River valleys from Montauk to the Mississippi, from the Prongs to Two Rivers Junction, from the head of the Black to the Arkansas confluence with the White at Jacksonport. Coleman's Regiment rides bound to stop senseless killers and looters on our family farms. Disrupt the Federal supply lines, take horses to disrupt the cavalry, and borrow a few uniforms and weapons, all in the name of freedom. We are not free men. Federals disrupt our farms every hour."

"Cousin, you sound like a politician." David Clinton Reed rode into the clearing, flanked by his three brothers and a dozen or so Current River men from Shannon, Reynolds, and Carter Counties.

"Such runs in the family. What fails to come natural in the blood, beats into our ears from cradle to grave. How many are in your company, two hundred?"

"Sometimes more, mostly less. The generals back away from a hill-country skirmish. Guess the woods lend themselves mystery to West Point lines of doom. Federal General Grant marches down the Mississippi with pitiful resistance. Island Number Ten and New Madrid fell. Memphis fell, as did Fort Donelson and Fort Henry. Vicksburg must consider itself lucky when Grant turned up the Tennessee. Your brother, John, and the Fourth Missouri likely dig Vicksburg fortifications while you muster recruits.

"At the time, I did not put much store in the late Gov. Jackson's message to the Neosho legislature, but war certainly proved his accusations more than an embarrassment for the Camp Jackson Affair. Take a copy for your speeches." Clint handed Alexander a packet of papers bound with string.

"And we always count on you as a man of few words." Alexander chuckled, clasped his cousin's hand in affectionate greeting, then turned his horse west; Clint Reed turned his horse east; the raiding grounds of "no man's land" stretched across South Missouri to Little Rock, Arkansas. The citizens suffered the worst of it.

Alexander opened the folded, well-worn paper and read the exiled Missouri Gov. Jackson's speech to the October 28, 1861, Neosho legislative houses and one earlier in Richmond, Virginia. "The exiled governor gave inflammatory speeches from Richmond to Neosho in an attempt to rally the Confederate Army to enter Missouri, to no avail." Alexander paused and took notice of his men.

"My old schoolmaster would rap Jackson's knuckles for bad grammar. Perhaps such diminished his influence." Alexander raised his hand and motioned the company to follow. He rode for miles in silence. Then he stopped and started the politics anew. He knew his men struggled to size him up. "You know these truths, boys? No? Good thing you ride with me for instruction."

"'Tis real inner-stin, cap'n." The recruit slowed his horse to a walk. Somebody else earned a snooze beside the leader.

"I will be whatever you vote me, when we get to Colonel Coleman."

Joe Butler rode beside Alexander. "You ought to be governor, for all your high-toned talk. Guess you got a belly full of politics. Some Chilton or other always off to Jeff City or a county courthouse. I listened to your goings-on well into the night." Joe turned to the men nearest him. "I worked for the Chiltons, mostly the senator, but sometimes for Alexander's father. One daughter in the bunch makes a man forget all about Federals."

Alexander kept silent for a few miles and then burst forth in frustrated wisdom. "We need to understand for what we fight and die. Our state government in Jefferson City seeks to hold the state for the Union, until elections. We want the Federals out of our midst so we can plant crops. Colonel Coleman's priority lies with disruption of the spoils of harvest and ammunition stored in Federal General Curtis's supply wagons.

"Missouri Governor Gamble must balance the Unionist slave owner votes with the radical abolitionists. A former chief justice of Missouri Supreme Court, 'a man for these times,' my uncle said. He wrote the dissenting opinion when Dred Scott claimed 'once free always free' and courts ruled against it. Politics and liberty. Hard to figure." He shook his head and looked to the sky.

"Missouri may suffer civil disobedience and anarchy, but the government holds. We took oaths to protect the families under our charge, and protect them with our lives. No atrocities in this command. No trophies!" He knew he must settle his wits and frustrations.

With wounds too deep and guilt too pronounced, he counted his behavior the least honorable of his fallen family. Yet here he rode, alive, with men who looked up to him.

He sank into a deep chasm of grief and considered his twenty years a worthless life.

Under cloak of darkness, Alexander brought Colonel Coleman good news. Missouri newspapers further inflamed the politics swirling around Colonel Weydemeyer's headquarters. "Weydemeyer's dispatches described the Salem, Missouri outpost as fifty-four miles from civilization and complained of lassitude and incompetency of those under his command. Fremont's replacement injured his pride and sent him into the hinterlands."

Coleman remarked, "Weydemeyer's treatment of prisoners in the Chilton affair confirms no man of peaceful persuasion now dares surrender out of fear for his life at the hand of the very army heretofore their trusted protector or trusted foe. Every officer's tarnished honor escalates the war man by man, with sweeping consequences. The Coleman Regiment dominates his reports. If only we maintained his estimates, we could spare the lives of family and friends. Condolences to you and your family." Coleman asked Alexander to continue the assessment of Coleman's persistent enemy, Colonel Weydemeyer.

"Weydemeyer's military education includes all strategies, with the likely exception of guerilla warfare. Weydemeyer's battalion-sized post varies from eight hundred to fifteen hundred. One of his sorties became a massacre, an 'execution of a loyal Missouri legislator, Senator Joshua Chilton, captured for the purpose of questioning by Weydemeyer's superiors in Rolla; superiors now questioned Weydemeyer.' Newspapers all over the country picked up the story and cry out for retaliation."

Coleman added his knowledge of circumstances surrounding his regiment. "Federal command ordered all muster-out dates suspended for the duration of the war. Soldiers who enlisted for three or six months mutinied across Missouri, including Weydemeyer's companies. Word spread to his men that Weydemeyer assumed the post in political trouble, promoted to Lieutenant Colonel, and ousted downstate through no fault of his own. Weydemeyer crumbled and took to the hospital in St. Louis."

Rebel Colonel Coleman stood, shook Alexander's hand. "I fear the likes of Weydemeyer recovered and returned with ennobled vengeance. Good report, my man. I could use another lieutenant in my regiment."

"Thank you, Colonel. I bring men with me willing to fight to the death." Alexander saluted sharply, hand to wide-brimmed, well-worn brown felt hat, and then turned for the Chilton camp in the woods to provision and follow Coleman into Hades.

Alexander provisioned all he could pack from home and camped with his cousins in the woods. "Whatever the reason, 'tis a glad day to be in the turkey woods. A glad day. And what news of Colonel Freeman?" Alexander inquired.

"Federals returned him to Alton, Illinois from a prison back east. Most hope for a prisoner exchange. Pray he survives the deplorable prison conditions."

Alexander took another pull from the whiskey jug. "Perry, you boys make powerful good shine!"

Then he passed the jug to his young cousin who raised the jug to his shoulder. "Alexander, I shall entertain another story from you. I understand you rule in silent might. Only William played his cards closer to the chest."

The mention of Alexander's brother, William, silenced the group for quite some time, and then Alexander cleared his throat. He thought himself ready to speak. However, he took out his kerchief, blew his nose, and cleared his throat yet again. Words eluded him.

CHAPTER 6

DIABOLICAL CRIMES — 1862–63

*Now, in view of the recent assassinations, robberies, and murders com-
mitted in this military district by armed bands who in so doing assume
to be acting under authority derived from rebel sources, and who
are instigated thereto by the emissaries sent here by our enemies to
incite their adherents to the commission of the most diabolical crimes,
attended in some instances with acts of such savage cruelty and fiend-
ish atrocity that the history of the world can furnish no parallel for
them (the bodies of their victims are horribly mutilated; the bleeding,
quivering flesh is torn from the cheeks, as the face is stamped with the
boot-heels of the murderer; their ears are cut off; powder is poured
into their ears and exploded, and untold horrors fail to satiate the
malice of those who cause the fiends in hell to shudder by the enormity
of their crimes), it becomes an imperative duty to provide at once ade-
quate means to suppress these outranges and furnish full and ample
protection to loyal citizens against their recurrence.
—By order of Brigadier-General Loan: J. Rainsford,
Assistant Adjutant-General, US Army.* [2.52]

A lexander waited until after supper and until Lizzie's boys fell asleep to tell her the compelling reason he delayed in the woods longer than expected. "Aunt Sophia and the children suffer the grippe sweating sickness. The four older children came through, but the four little ones languish badly. Aunt Sophia sent word to the woods when she took to the bed and called for your help."

Lizzie said, "I cannot take William and baby George with me into the grippe or something worse. Aunt Betsy can wet-nurse George, but I must consider the additional work for her. I know you, Alexander. You always lead all the little boys and girls to the woods before nightfall, call hoot owls, and follow treed hounds."

"There's no grippe in the woods. No safer place in the country than with me."

"True. True. Do you say we both go to Uncle John's farm? You must stay with the older children at the barn and keep up chores."

"Well, I like the setup. We can be in the woods before dark after all." Alexander chuckled when he saw the lovely exasperated set of Lizzie's countenance. He took a basket from the wall peg and led her to her garden of herbs. She picked leaves enough for weeks of comfort and healing.

Before dawn the next morning, Lizzie packed for the sick and for the well. Into her basket went dried mints, sage, mullein, elder flowers and leaves, hyssop, goldenrod, butterfly weed, cardinal flower, Joe Pye weed, buckthorn jersey tea, wild bergamot, and black cohosh. Then she shut the door of the small hired hands' cabin east of Aunt Betsy's house. She could hardly bear to part from her boys—baby George for the first time and from young William for no more than a day or two as midwife to an expectant neighbor.

Aunt Betsy rocked her own baby, Martha Belle, in one arm and baby George in the other. "Our Lizzie? Take care of yourself as well as Sister Sophia, you hear?"

"Yes'm." She turned to embrace her young son. "Keep this good sweater of mine safe by your pillow until I return, darling William."

"Yes, Mama. Make J. J. and everybody well."

Aunt Sophia's eight children ranged from age seventeen to two. Uncle John was hiding in the woods away from the Federals. Lizzie wondered how they would manage, but manage they would. Everybody loved Alexander, especially the children. Lizzie knew his way with them would get the work done and set a happy playful scene in spite of sickness and the war. "It takes a man such as you to make a good life in times like these. And I love you for it."

Alexander and Lizzie clucked their horses into a trot; her packhorse followed, and they made their way downriver below Owls Bend to the county line. They arrived far into the night at the home of Uncle John and Aunt Sophia.

Lizzie expected the older children to be isolated in the haymow of the barn, as is custom at a sick house. The barn stood empty. "I best check on the family while you unpack provisions." Lizzie shouldered her herbal bag and walked toward the house. Slow heavy steps betrayed her optimistic tone of voice.

Candlelight shone through the window at the back of the house. Lizzie let herself inside. In the house, cold because windows were left open to 'let the sickness out,' she saw nine bodies of various lengths stretched on the floor around the fireplace. A large pitcher sat beside the oldest daughter who looked up and poured a cup of water for her sick two-year-old brother. He hardly sipped a thimbleful before ten or more coughs exhausted him.

Three little heads popped up and reached for Lizzie's hugs with almost desperate thankfulness. Lizzie sank among them and surveyed the other four. She saw Sophia stir. "Auntie, I am here. We will be fine."

"We will be fine. Thank you, Lizzie." Sophia rolled to her side and drew two young sons next to her in a strong one-armed embrace. With her other hand, she wiped the beads of sweat from her own brow with a wet rag and wiped their small foreheads with another. The family lay covered with quilts and fine woolen comforters held together with wool string at six-inch-squares, fashioned on warmer, happy days.

118

Lizzie set herself to the tasks of chest pouches, compresses, and boiling water to make teas and steam the vapors she fanned over her charges. A long week threatened.

Louisa, the oldest, woke. "I rested. You sleep for a while. You must be beat from the long ride downriver. I know to wake up the older boys in turn, some better, but still too weak to go to the barn for chores."

"Alexander sleeps in the barn hay, but even a hard floor looks welcome." Lizzie stirred as each shift of brothers cared for their family through the long night, and then she fell back to troubled sleep.

The younger children woke with sunup. Lizzie doctored them and then left the house with a cake of lye soap to launder compresses and bathe in the river. The gentle gurgles under the root wads and riffles around boulders washed away the sickness. Fear remained.

As she returned to the house, a welcome fire now burned in the outdoor kitchen pit, and hot water steamed beside the kitchen door where fresh warm milk and cornmeal gruel cooled on the wash bench. She passed the fire in a soaked shiver, on her way to the barn. She stepped into the blanket stretched between Alexander's arms and buried her head into his chest. "Thank you. Pray for a miracle."

She climbed into the loft, quickly changed into dry clothes, and sank to her knees in the sweet smelling hay. "How do I rescue you, my dear ones?" Lizzie prayed for her sons and for all the sick and war-stricken families up and down her beloved rivers. She even prayed for Sam, somewhere in the Deep South with General Price. She drifted into a fitful sleep.

Alexander lay stretched on the hay, with his head on his elbow, and studied her features. Her square-shaped face, blue eyes as dark as Fancher's spring, creamy white skin, and black wavy hair made for a strikingly beautiful woman. "No, stay still," he said to Lizzie. "Little Joshua died while you slept. I wrote in the Bible, November 21, 1862, only three weeks short of his tenth birthday."

"And Van Daemon?"

"It looks grim. He holds his chest as if it explodes."

Tears streamed down Lizzie's face. When he traced the path of her tears with his fingers and welcomed her embrace, she rose to kiss his lips.

She suddenly pushed back, wide eyed.

"It is all right, my dear Lizzie, a kiss of comfort from the tragedies, and I am glad for it.

"More than a year of life so cold and neglected. Uncle Joshua, William, your father, dead babies. I can't make it alone."

"You can. You know I love you, so hold firm."

Lizzie watched helplessly when Aunt Sophia held eight-year-old Van Daemon as he died the next day. The two youngest, J. J. and Thomas seemed stronger.

When Sophia rose from her illness, she breathed a determined breath. "I must somehow survive the loss of my sons, somehow. Praise be, you little ones are stronger." She drew them into her arms.

Alexander helped the four older children walk from house to barn. "Are you up for light chores? He gave them simple tasks, sent them to the hayloft with cobs and corn shellers, then walked to the back door of the house. "Lizzie?"

She stepped to the door. "Van Daemon died. Can you go for Uncle John?"

"Yes, however I leave for Coleman today."

"Go; keep us safe from Federals and the bushwhackers. We can manage here." Lizzie lost her courage. "No, stay! Stay here with me." She clung to Alexander and sobbed.

He drew her near. "Lizzie." He paused. "Just cry it out. My heart breaks in our loss. But your tears pull me asunder." Compassion, love, loss, and confusion assailed him from all sides.

When her sobs subsided, he found his voice. "I dug the graves. Uncle John came in for a few hours and wants to bury little Joshua and Van Daemon himself. Tell Aunt Sophia. Be back tomorrow." Alexander took her hands from the embrace, kissed each one, found the stirrup to the saddle packed for war, turned his horse into the Current River at Henpeck, and never looked back.

Lizzie did her best to raise Aunt Sophia's spirits, but circumstances of war pressed the family harder than ever. When she and the older children finished the supper dishes, they sat by the fireplace, hot water in the iron teakettle swung over the fire. She dropped a handful of herbs into the water, and led song after song between cups of the comforting brew.

Sophia set aside her knitting. "What in this world? Such a ruckus."

A few seconds later, Young J.J. bolted into the room. He gasped for his breath. "The Federal soldiers are here! The most ever! Hundreds and hundreds. Will they relieve us of our surplus as Papa said? Soldiers pitched camp all over the south pasture; probably clear to the fort at Van Buren.

Lizzie intervened. "Lad, slow down. Go rest by your mother." She nodded to her aunt and stepped out the door to assess the ruckus toward the river.

She saw ten or fifteen wagons accompanied by fifty to a hundred soldiers in the upper pasture near the corncrib. Three logs removed from the crib lay on the ground. Soldiers helped themselves to the precious flow of yellow kernels that spilled into greedy shovels.

She ran past the smokehouse toward the barn. She saw a sea of soldiers spread across the bountiful farm where several soldiers herded cows toward the wagons. One lone cow stood at the high rail fence. The moos joined the pitiful sounds of calves lost from their mothers.

Another group of soldiers chased the cacophony of ducks, geese, and chickens.

She nearly fell when a soldier's horse bumped her shoulder. "No!" She screamed when she saw his men stream into the house and out again with linens from the bedsteads. She turned, ran to the porch and into the front room where others of his men searched every box, chest, and trunk, took a sidesaddle and some books. When she elbowed her way to her aunt's side, an officer's gold stripes slashed across the uniform's blue sleeves onto her face.

"Foraging need not find danger. Cease resistance. Do you want to be arrested and sent to prison in St. Louis?

Shocked, Lizzie responded with calm indignation. "My *good* sir, we have a house full of sick children. My aunt mourns the death of her two youngest sons laid out on a stone fence, graves awaiting in yonder yard. Your cruelty more slavishly rendered than death, I fail to imagine. Depart at once!" She felt her calm erode, so she pulled her shawl over her hair and stomped to the open door. "After you, Captain!" She assumed a regal stance and thrust her open palm toward the gray limestone cliff. Starved trees cast long shadows on the devastation.

She rallied the next day when news of Gen. Jeff Thompson's Rebels reached her aunt's kitchen table.

The neighbor took off his hat and sat at the table. He reported: "four hundred men came along the Pilot Knob and Pocahontas Road to the road that goes uphill out of Pike Creek Valley. At a point where a cyclone had blown down a lot of timber, the Rebels took their horses on a safe distance, dismounted, and took up a position among the logs. When the pursuing party came within gunshot, the Rebels opened fire. The two armies swapped lead for about thirty minutes, but the Federals failed to dislodge them. When they turned back, the Federals who rode the fastest horses got to Van Buren first. Jeff Thompson went his way having taken the pleasure out of the foraging and put some Rebel caution in it." [1.16]

Lizzie rose from the table. "Thank you for news. Sadly, the Federals and the grim reaper took their pleasure at John Chilton's farm without caution."

The neighbor removed his hat and turned to the proud stolid woman seated at the end of the table. "I am very sorry for your loss, Miz Sophia. I must continue the relay upriver." He backed out the door, hat in hand.

After two weeks, Lizzie returned on a warm winter day to Aunt Betsy's home where she saw Aunt Betsy and her daughters sitting on the porch in the shade cast by the oak trees east of the house. Her peace restored at the clink of black walnut nutmeats into the tin pans held in the women's laps and the creak of the bentwood oak cradle on unpainted porch boards. Such gentle motion gave as much comfort to mothers as to colicky babies.

She leaned over the cradle where Martha Belle and George lay asleep, side-by-side.

When she saw her William come running, she caught him under the arms and lifted him high into the air.

"Mama. Mama!" he shouted. "Come with us. Come see our new kittens in the barn. I named mine Scottrompus."

"William, dear, your shining face lights my path and lifts my spirits to the treetops." She scampered after the children toward joy of new life.

When the sounds of her own newborn reached her ears, Lizzie returned to the house. She leaned to hug her aunt on the way to the noisy cradle.

Aunt Betsy smoothed Lizzie's hair with both hands and whispered her thanks. "My dear orphaned niece bears her own grief with dignity. How could I fathom to do otherwise?"

"What's that you say, Mother?" asked one of her daughters.

"I count our blessings but find it more difficult than one might hope."

Lizzie told them the local news of the war near Aunt Sophia at Henpeck, while a batch of persimmon seeds clinked in the pans. The late frost meant sweet golden persimmon sauce.

"Sy Moore was found dead. He claimed the Federal faith and died somewhat outspoken. He was in possession of Woods Mill property northwest of Van Buren. He scouted out somewhere and came home riding a fine saddle horse that belonged to a Rebel captain. The captain sent Alexander, Joe Butler, George H. Davis, and some others, to get the animal and, incidentally, to bring Mr. Moore along."

"Federals call any animal outside their possession 'contraband,'" another of Aunt Betsy's daughters added with a tone near fury.

"They found him at the home of his father-in-law. Mrs. Moore got her father to go with them, and they went east about five miles to Samuel Hanger's farm. There they sent her father back home. A little farther on, Moore and Alexander got into a hot argument, and Moore gave Alexander the slip. However, sometime later, someone found Moore dead near the place where the argument took place. The Rebel captain got his horse back." [1.19]

All remained silent except for the creak of the rockers under the cradle. Lizzie's shoulders sagged, and tears washed her cheeks.

One of the daughters cleared her throat, "On a lighter note, an old farmer in Wayne County planted corn. Not caring to be bothered, he played the ignoramus on some Federal soldiers when they called him from his work and asked him several questions. One asked, 'Are there any Rebels about here?'

"He said, 'Not on this creek, but over on Rung's Creek they have plenty of it, and when I get my corn planted I aim to go over and get a jug full.'

"They passed him up as hopeless." [1.31]

Aunt Betsy chuckled and eased her baby out of the cradle. "All my girls. I am so thankful for each one of you. Lizzie, you gave me a real scare birthing William.

"Lizzie stood by me at your birth, Anne, when she was only fourteen. She helped me midwife several babies by then, so we did fine. Then we brought Rebecca, James, Francis Marion, and Thomas into the world. Our Martha Belle probably thinks she has four mamas. Many loving hands build confidence in a child."

Lizzie knew, truth be told, forty-year-old Aunt Betsy experienced a hard time with the birth of her ninth and last child.

"I can be of more help—starting tomorrow. I just love little George." Twelve-year-old Anne sounded determined.

Lizzie surveyed the stair steps of little boys who played in the yard, each a year's growth taller than the next. "When Nelson and

Perry come in from camp, we will have ourselves a feast." She thought of Aunt Betsy's older sons: Nelson, age twenty, Perry, age eighteen. Joshua's neutral influence kept them from the armies, but living at the Chilton camp, and often with Alexander, they might as well be on the Confederate muster rolls. "Ladies, we boast a houseful."

The spring of 1863 saw war, but it also saw peace. Lizzie stirred diapers in the iron kettle over a fire near Aunt Betsy's kitchen porch. She waved at Nelson and Mary Louisa, who walked up the hill with buckets of water from the river and placed them on the wash bench beside the kitchen door. "Hello, Nelson, Mary Louisa. Something serious?" asked Lizzie.

Nelson nodded to Lizzie and then turned to greet his mother, hat in one hand and Mary Louisa's hand in his other. "Mother, I love Mary Louisa. We want to be married."

"Oh, Nelson," Aunt Betsy sighed. "Mary Louisa, close cousins, too dangerous."

"We love each other. We are not double cousins. We want to marry."

Nelson put his arm around Mary Louisa's waist and spoke softly. "I will probably die in the war anyway, so we want to marry now."

The family gathered for the marriage on a sunny and warm day. Mary Louisa chose her sister, Susannah Chilton Orchard, as her witness. She and her four-year-old son James Shadrach found happiness as special ones in the marriage preparations.

Nelson chose his brother, Perry, as witness. The two hid in the woods as neutrals, most hated by both Federal and Rebel.

In the weeks after Mary Louisa moved to Spring Valley, Nelson soon ran out of different unbeaten paths from camp to home and Mary Louisa.

Lizzie received word of her Uncle Truman's family. Doctor Reed and Aunt Polly, died within days of each other. Lizzie joined the large extended Chilton family, a somber group, who gathered on a cold winter day at the Reed settlement across from Rocky Creek. Someone swept the barn floor clean and tossed hay in piles for comfortable seating on quilts. Sympathies mixed with fear. Chilton farms lay along both rivers, surrounded by Federals. Confederate companies rode in friendly territory, but the raids veiled as "foraging trips" punished the citizens just as soundly. Both armies searched for the neutrals, forcing them to "join or die."

She knew Clint placed guards at the road into the settlement and atop every ridge hollow to the river. The sad event of his parents' wake included an exchange of war news, both far and near. She drew closer when Clint stood to speak.

"More than 3,000 Federal soldiers moved from Pilot Knob to Van Buren where they encamped to stay for some time. Camp Lincoln. In order to keep in touch with all the movements of the war, they put up a telegraph line from Pilot Knob to within five or six miles of Van Buren, and in some way the builders found menace until they quit. Others tried to finish the line, but without success.

"Finally, Mr. Crow said he would finish and operate the line. James Mayberry and Martin MacLemurry seemed to be the hindrance to place insulators, nailed to trees, along the Pilot Knob and Pocahontas Road over which the soldiers moved supplies to Van Buren and to points south.

"Mr. Crow started his work and set a long ladder against a tree, climbed to the top and nailed an insulator to the tree when a shot fired from nearby. Mr. Crow dropped from the ladder. We buried him across the river on the west side of the Chilton farm, and hid the grave. The work stopped completely. The citizens took the wire down and found many uses for it. Uncle John Chilton got enough of it to trellis fifty grapevines, used it in place of hickory withes and papaw bark around the farm and feed lots." [1.102]

Nelson refilled his dinner plate and shared news of the west and north townships where he farmed in Spring Valley. "Federal General Davidson left West Plains with about ten thousand soldiers, encamped at the Round Spring, and entrenched in Eminence Courthouse. In mid-February, a skirmish erupted and the courthouse burned. If the Federals have their way, no home or courthouse in the entire country stands before they move out. Some say the bushwhackers burned the courthouse, but of southern or northern faith, none voiced claim.

"Uncle Truman's son, Thomas T. failed to survive the first occupation in February sixty-one, and several neighbors exited this world upon the second. One wonders the terrible reasons for the silence our women adopt and find comfort within their circle to protect their honor. Silence certainly broke when the Federals turned their cannons on the timber for transport across Current River. Turkeys lost their caulk and gobble for a season, from fright no doubt.

"Since Mary Louisa and I moved to Spring Valley and set up housekeeping, we better know and love Uncle Truman's progeny, who wrapped their cousins in welcome arms. Today we gather to bury his beloved daughter, Mary "Polly" Chilton Reed. May she rest in peace. The families gathered here today share your loss of father and mother within a fortnight. Dr. Thomas Reed, valued by the community and a much-loved member of our family, may he rest in peace beside loving wife, mother, sister, and aunt, Miz Polly."

Clint coughed and gathered his resources and shifted his sorrow to words of war. "Federals pay for their war with the whiskey tax, as you know. At the outbreak of the war, the United States counted less than $4 million in the Treasury. Therefore, President Lincoln and his cabinet soon guessed how they might get money to carry on the war: tax whiskey, wine, and beer. Therefore, a tax of twenty cents per gallon on distilled spirits went into effect the first day of September, 1862. Why, the tax must extract $5 million a year or more from the citizens. [1.95]

"What does the Confederacy have? Nothing, boys. Nothing but grit and determination—and a fair amount of lead. We hear the Confederates march, bound for Vicksburg. Our own Fifteenth Missouri companies march, bound for Tennessee and Kentucky, much to the chagrin of the sergeants who argue their men enrolled for service within Missouri boundaries. Their absence is a dangerous loss to our counties.

"At this time, Union forces press the undisciplined central Missouri guerrilla-militia units southward into our counties. Captain Reeves believes Centerville within our control could bring peace to our farms for a time. We pray for a peace, knowing until such time, the day of rest comes all too often to family, friend, and foe."

On February 7, 1863, Alexander, Jack Smith, and Thomas J. Thorpe stopped at the Leavitt's store for supplies. The trio dismounted, and Alexander took the reins of all three horses. "What are you thinking, Jack? No need to shoot our way in when a simple knock on the door suffices!"

Alexander ran with Thorpe to the back and kicked in the door. Alexander saw Leavitt grab a gun and run to the front of the store toward Jack. Alexander and Thorpe shot toward Leavitt, but he did not fall.

Before Alexander could capture Levitt, he ran into his bedroom on the left, and locked the door. "We have a shotgun aimed at the door. Leave my wife and me alone!"

Alexander tried to coax Mrs. Leavitt out of the room. "Miz Nancy, come on out now. Tend to your husband's wounds. We shot to save our ill-advised friend at the front door."

The answer came as a blast from her gun. "My husband lies safe in his bed and there he will stay. Get on out of here. I recognized all three of you but promise to not report you."

Thorpe said, "Your husband reported us to the Federals; named us disreputable bushwhackers and worse. Same as a bullet to our heads."

After an hour, Miz Nancy replied. "Alexander, you promise on the honor of both your grandfathers to not harm us? You promise to just buy groceries and not bother me or Obadiah or our critters?"

"Yes, I can only speak for myself. But I will take the horses." Alexander replied.

He saw the door to the bedroom open a crack and a gun barrel appeared. "That's right, now. Come on to the middle of the room with me. You can keep your gun."

He grabbed her around the shoulders and held her in the middle of the room, his hand over hers that still held the gun. "I promised to not hurt you."

"What do you claim he did bad enough to kill him?" she asked.

"We found enough to warrant his death, when he reported us to the Federals." Thorpe replied.

Alexander watched Jack go into the bedroom, pistol in hand, and point his gun at Leavitt's head. The first shot misfired. The second shot did not.

Alexander held Mrs. Leavitt when she struggled and screamed. "You promised!"

When Thorpe fully opened the door to the bedroom, Alexander could see Thorpe remove the dead man's boots, grab the man's hat and saddle from the bedstead, and make for the back door.

When Smith and Thorpe were out of sight, Alexander released Mrs. Levitt and ran outside. He swung into the saddle, joined the other two men, and galloped off with the three Leavitt horses.

"They will hang us for this one, more for manhandling the woman than the killing. Killing the Federals well understand, but most officers won't touch a woman." Alexander regretted his role in the incident as the three rode toward the Batesville, Arkansas horse market.

Thorpe added, "You can't say the same for the rank and file. I heard the tongue wagging about your sisters and cousins."

Alexander jumped from his horse, midair, and caught Thorpe by the belt. The momentum pulled both men off the horse to the ground. He kicked Thorpe and then pulled him up by the scruff of the neck to his feet, nose to nose. "Never—I say, never—bring my family into this madness. I will cut your tongue out." Alexander pulled his knife from the scabbard, just before Jack hit him from behind with the butt of his gun and knocked him out cold.

Jack helped Alexander to his feet but held a pistol toward his head. "Sorry, but at least I caught you some, to soften your fall. Been out awhile. You settled?"

"Settled." Alexander lifted his hand high in the air and pointed forward. "Go on."

The three guerilla partisans crossed the Arkansas line by midnight. [3.23]

Alexander loved to tease his cousins, especially about the horse trade. "Say, Josh, I hear you let Lieutenant Cotton of the Seventeenth Illinois capture that fine bay mare I brought you in early March. If your father's testimony could not save her, guess I must fetch her back."

Josh replied, "Named cousin to Alexander Chilton, noted guerilla, holds no positive evidence either. When any horse in five counties changes hands, you or Devil Dick Bose or George Crawford get the credit."

"The simple words 'Current River' strikes fear in the heart of the Federal cavalry. Then they draw up papers to fight the fight and name somebody or other. Provost Marshal spends most of his time sorting out horseflesh." Alexander chuckled and then turned to the matter now at hand. "In July, Dick Bose and I were in Ripley County and confiscated one bay mare and one gray mare from the farm of William Lowry. When Lowry objected, we took him prisoner, bound him, and left him near enough homes for discovery and release by a neighbor or a friendly sort. You hold on to this fine gray, you hear. I rather liked the bay for my brother John."

Alexander saw Anne step to the door. "You boys come for dinner, now."

He waved acknowledgement, but declined. "Please tell Anne there are Federal horses to drive to Coleman. Be back tomorrow."

Alexander readied his rifle, even though the rider gave the guerilla's day bird signal of a courier who crossed the spring branch and rode toward the cave, arms in the air. "Dismount, Private."

"Sir. Thank you, sir. Colonel Freeman sent me with two communi-qué's taken off a dead Federal scout. He said each was essential infor-mation for you." The soldier saluted and turned to remount.

"Stay for breakfast. Judging from the looks of you and your horse, you rode hard all night." Alexander handed the soldier a plate, took the cup hanging from the soldier's pack, and filled it with chicory coffee.

He retired to his tent, sat, opened the glass jar stuffed with torn pa-per, and began to read. The first brought a smile of fine remembrances, but the second pierced his heart with one word.

"29 April '63 I came on to the Chilton neighborhood and staid over-night at Chiltons where the party rang in frivolities but I took no part in it—there were quite a number of fine looking young ladies at the party & the men were Guerillas such men as Duckworth, Alex Chilton, Bill Kink, Joe Butler & Quigley all desperate characters & all armed with from two to four revolvers & in dancing kept their pistols belted around them...

"5 May '63 I came to Current river waded it deep wading rained on me all day I got a man to set me over Jacks Fork on a horse I stayed all night at the widow of Capt Shade Chilton I walked 32 miles today...

"8 May '63 I traveled in a South West direction aiming to reach Col Freemans Camp I took dinner 14 miles south of Thomasville While rest-ing Col Freeman came along & recognized me & talked some time with him & I went on to his camp at night walked 30 miles today." [6.4]

The word "widow" screamed from the page and settled into his bones; his father's widow! He recognized the handwriting of John James Sitton, his best recruiter from Oregon County, and prayed the notes fell from Sitton's journal rather than foul play. He served too many miles with Sitton in Lieutenant Bennett's company from Wilson's Creek to Lexington and home in 1861 to even dare consider his life lost in their own river country. He knew young Sitton to be a man of talent and pre-dicted a promising future when the cursed rebellion ended.

In the fall of 1863, Lizzie moved to the center of the barn at Alexander's family farm, spread a quilt on the hay, and settled William and George with a whisper. "Shush, now. Lie down and listen to a happy story."

Alexander's mother, Patsy, rose from her chair to address the Chilton family and neighbors. "I milked cows in the barn, and when I heard movement at the barn door, I froze. Expected the worst, I did. Then I slowly turned to face whatever darkened the door. My eldest son, John, stood tall, hardly recognizable in a full beard and hair to his shoulders. A ragged butternut gray uniform hung on his thin frame.

"'Elizabeth Francis!' I shouted. The sound of his wife's name may the sweetest sound John hears in a lifetime. To John, I said, 'Elizabeth and the children stay here. The Little Shawnee farm became too dangerous for a woman alone.'

"He told me, 'I received word of such and came here straightaway.' John caught Elizabeth midair on his way to the house. A host of little girls and boys surrounded him. The littlest ones knew without a doubt their mama thought the man special."

Lizzie nodded to her sons. "Homecoming. Joyous stories."

She and the others quieted as John laid his plate aside on the ground where he sat on a quilt surrounded by his wife and children.

John scratched the side of his chin, and chose his words carefully. "We surrendered at Vicksburg on July 4, 1863. The Union took our oath and gave us release papers, but the Confederate army considers us all deserters. I joined up with several local boys, and we made our way home, mostly on foot. We hid from every man, woman, and child along the route north through Arkansas. I traveled with James Nesbit, Sam's brother, and with Captain Norman. Small groups could eat more easily and travel undetected. About a hundred local Missouri men took the oath and made their mark.

"The Vicksburg siege about starved us out. Missouri Union soldiers camped just across the river from Missouri Rebel camps inside the fortifications of Vicksburg. Missouri flags snapped high over each camp. When the rank and file Union men from Missouri knew our plight severe, they saved and gathered food, made the bobwhite call, and we sneaked them into our camp in the dead of night. After the feed, we whispered about home and exchanged news of the fate of Missouri. We knew peace for one night. In the first glow of dawn, they passed between our lines of guards, and safely crossed the river to give us fight the following day."

The group fell silent. Lizzie noticed Nelson and Perry exchange looks then shake their head from side to side, and look at the floor. *Was this the right time for John to hear bad news of home?* Lizzie stood and walked toward the table laden with food but stopped when she reached John and placed her hand on his forehead, playfully, as if to test his temperature.

"You're here and well, John; we celebrate tonight. We mourn loved ones tomorrow."

Lizzie sensed John's deep concern and fear, and his hope for strength enough to hear bad news tonight.

John leaned forward and crossed his arms. "What about William? And Captain?"

"Gone. We can tell you about it in the morning," Nelson offered.

"No, now." John gathered Elizabeth and his children around him and bore up to the details of the tragedy of eleven that included the death of his brother William and his uncle Joshua one year prior. Then, as if blow upon blow, he crumbled at the reported loss of his father, Capt. Shadrach Chilton.

In late August 1863, Lizzie scanned the communiqué handed to her by Joe Butler and John Story. The men brought the family gathered at Alexander's home the latest news of Alexander's company in Coleman's Regiment. She stood and read aloud the notes taken from a Federal report, hurriedly taken, if one considered the penmanship.

"Pilot Knob, MO

21 Aug '63 Livingston to Capt Finley, Centerville: 'Mr. James L. Stephens ten miles from Pilot Knob on Centerville road says 6 cavalrymen took a yellow girl from his house and also an old black horse. Examine your men who left here yesterday w/ supplies.'

"21 Livingston to Finley: 'Move a squad secretly to Three Forks about 6 miles from Centerville, and arrest—Wilson and any other bushwhackers who may be with him. Think he led party who robbed Stephens. Search for arms. Perhaps a little choking will force the truth out of him and he may tell who his accomplices are under promise of release. You will find Wilson at Ira Millers close of John Buffords. '[6.2]

"23 Aug '63 Livingston to Finley: 'Men supposed to have stolen Negro wench and horse at Belleview are Jo Butler, Alex Shelton and John Story living near Jacks Fork. Make Wilson take oath and require heavy bond.'" [6.3]

She shook her head and asked, "What on this good earth possessed you, a Reb, to rescue a slave. And why steal an old broken down horse?"

Joe twirled his wide brimmed hat in his hand. "Well, Lizzie, it happened this way. Alexander said your Aunt Louisa sent him a letter by way of her father, your Grandpa Coot. She figured Alexander the best person to rescue the girl she favored for some reason. Seeing as how we are the best horse suppliers in south Missouri, he chose John and me to ride guard. We parted from him and the girl when the trail forked east and south. We took the south fork. We expect his return within the month."

Lizzie crossed the room, gave the notes to Alexander's mother, and then watched her, precious notes in hand, make the sign of the cross. Lizzie knew Aunt Louisa and Alexander's mother shared her Unionist sympathies.

Alexander pulled his horse to a stop. He whispered, "Quiet, now."

"Yes, sir. Blessing on you, sir." The young slave rode behind Alexander and placed her head on his back, arms around his waist, and gripped the heavy gun belt as if there was no tomorrow. His rain cape covered her from head to bare toes, protection from prying eyes.

"Welcome rain. We go east. If we encounter trouble, hold tight because I aim to turn and run." His hat dripped a stream on his horse's mane, and his blue-and-white gingham shirt and leather vest were soon soaked to the skin.

"Tonight we find a barn or some shelter. Then we travel to cross the ferry near St. Genevieve and ride at night to the home of John Willis Menard near Kaskaskia in Illinois, fifteen or twenty miles from the ferry. Then we travel on to his abolitionist school in Sparta. Menard, a free man, knows what to do. Speaks at gatherings on his views, some disagreeable to the staunchest abolitionists. He risks his neck in some locales. Cairo crossing? Too dangerous. Like as not, my ignorance would land you in the so-called safe house of the reverse railroad and get you sold south. Menard and the school are our best bet."

"School. Oh, school?"

"You must find courage when mistrust wells up. I suspect you wonder whether you go to school or to molestation and death. We travel some sixty miles to the river through hard dangerous country for the likes of us. With provision, take heart, girl. This may be the only honorable deed I enact in my sorry life. What an adventure." Alexander gently spurred his horse, pointed the top of his hat into the driving cool rain, and prayed for deliverance.

Just before he reached the Mississippi River, he hid the girl deep in the fold of a forested valley.

He stopped at the corner of Third and Market in St. Genevieve. He asked directions to the ferry. He bought a sorry-looking packhorse.

Ticket and supplies purchased, he returned to the valley before darkness fell. "What is your name, girl? Here, jerky and bread, not too stale. My name is, well, let's just say James Alexander for now."

"My brother, he took the name Chilton, Francis Marion Chilton, and joined the Union over in Washington County. I's just plain Arminta."

"It's Chilton, then. Arminta Chilton. Nothing plain about you. A fine-looking woman hides behind your trail clothes, what with the combs and skirts my sisters fashion. Before all that, however, wrapped in the cape and tent bindings, you look like the provisions of a young man bent for muster in the Illinois Union Infantry. You cannot move or make a sound. Understand?"

"Like a deer carcass, smoked and bound for the quartermaster." Arminta showed spunk.

Evening fell, and fog descended on the mountains and steamed up from the valley. Alexander wrapped Arminta, placed her belly-down on the horse, his supply of jerky along her back near the splice rope, and walked the horses toward the ferry.

The ferryman motioned Alexander aboard and to the right side of the ferry. "Last ferry of the day. Steady there, young man. Horse a bit skittish?"

"Yes, sir, skittish." Alexander handed the ferryboat captain the fare and moved the mounts forward. While not his first encounter with the Mississippi, the power and danger of the rolling coffee swirls gave him pause. "Skittish, just like you, mares." He stroked and patted his horses' necks and calmed his own racing heart.

The Illinois road, away from the river, mired and clung to hoof and foot. Going was slow across the flood plain, no doubt to the thankfulness of Arminta. After five miles, the road gave way to forested hills, and he chose a smooth path into the switchback of a narrow game trail. Well hidden, he opened the pack and helped Arminta roll to the ground with a moan.

"You hurt?"

"No, stiff as a carcass, mind you. Bruised my chin a bit." She rubbed her ribs, stretched her back, reached for the sky and breathed gulps of air. "The sweet air of freedom!"

He remained quiet for some time. He had no notion of the depth of the young woman's feelings. "We have a ways to go. Pray for rain, and put the cape back around you and over your head. One never knows who hides in the bush all around. Since the road is well used, we best take the time required through the hills. I know how to travel through woods. Eat up, now. Ten miles or more ahead."

Well into the dark of earliest morning, Alexander inquired with a knock at the barn door of a prosperous looking farm. "Anybody up milking cows?"

"Who wants to know?" A young man opened the top half of the door and lifted his lantern aside to view the stranger.

"James Alexander crossed over from Missouri to enlist in the Union at Kaskaskia. Am I closing the gap?"

"Yes, this is the Menard farm. Follow this road to the town square. Soldiers everywhere."

"John Menard, the abolitionist?"

"No, the Pierre Menard farm, old family around here. President Lincoln called the abolitionist to Washington not long ago. Good day to you, now."

Alexander followed the road a short distance and then turned into the woods along a small stream. He stopped and considered the next step.

"We take a risk, any way we go."

"I can put away slave words and speak like a proper lady, a young lady on her way to school. I read and write. Mama taught us under threat of death."

"You stay with the horses. I will venture to the square; ask assistance for the dressmakers for my 'sister' a new dress and practical shoes, perhaps ladies' boots?"

"I can wait a long time, right here. Yes, sir. New dress and ladies' boots. Someday, I will find you, and repay your kindness tenfold."

Alexander nodded, and made for the town square. Kindness the furthest thing from his mind; he pictured two long ropes thrown over a high limb and trembled at the thought.

Alexander turned into the woods where he left his charge. He jumped off his horse, pulled his rifle to his shoulder at one pass, and stepped toward the sound of voices just ahead. He saw two men hovered over a small cook fire; their persons appeared rough and mean. Alexander softly stepped backward, took his horse's reins, and backed her to the open road.

He wondered whether Arminta hid left or right. He took in the lay of the land and chose right. He picked his way around the other side of the hill and sat for a time. His horse whinnied a soft greeting to the pack-horse. Then he saw Arminta step from behind a tree. He dismounted, untied the saddle bindings, and handed her a large package wrapped in brown paper and tied with hemp twine.

She ducked her head in embarrassment. "A Missouri bushwhacker done me a good deed. I thought myself from bad to worse circumstances." She slipped back behind the tree and reappeared minutes later, a proper young woman dressed for travel. "Ribbons. Never such finery passed through my fingers. What possessed you to steal me from slavery? How do you know about the school?

"Uncle was a Missouri state senator and read about Menard in the Saint Louis newspapers. I spent many hours with my uncle. Now, don your cape. We are many miles from the school in Sparta—about thirty or forty miles, that way." He pointed to the road in a northeasterly direction. "My cousin and her husband are staunch Unionists and kindness is her middle name. Despite my affiliations, she said my soldiering reputation proved me the right man to rescue you from a bad master. She wrote me a letter from Middle Brook in Iron County and asked me to find you and take you to freedom. She also knew of your brother, attached to the Union Army's Sixty-Eighth Colored Troops."

"But you could be hanged!"

"There is that, there is." Alexander pressed his knees to his horse to set a smooth single-foot on the dangerous path, come what may.

He rode side by side with Arminta and delivered her safely to the abolitionist school after two long days of travel. He signed her "indentured servant" release papers as James Alexander, Springfield, Illinois.

"Best regards, Miss Chilton." He tipped his hat to the schoolmaster, then to Miss Chilton.

She said, "Give my best to Miz Louisa."

He coughed in surprise. He had not fooled Arminta for one second about his identity. He stepped out the door and into a world free of care. The condition lasted nine days.

He crossed the river at Cape Girardeau, certain he could locate Louisa Chilton Sinclair. Her husband, Benjamin, fought with the Union and was bound for battle in Tennessee. Per her last letter to her family, she aimed for the Cape. Then Alexander thought better of it. She was right friendly to their old schoolmaster, a staunch abolitionist, Capt. James M. L. Jamison at the Knob. *"Like as not,"* he thought, *"her righteous indignation could get my ankles and wrists cooled by iron, until my latest sins reach her ears in due course."*

Alexander turned west toward Current River and that dreadful communiqué regarding "Shade Chilton's widow," his mother. The implication that his father was dead brought a stinging lump to his throat that seemed more than he could bear; whether she already knew or whether he bore the news contained in the report, the words burned a hole in his pocket, clear through his heart.

Alexander made his way across Current River and directly toward Lizzie's house. He feared for her safety even though she doctored wounded Federals. Harboring guerillas and southern sympathizers stood as insufferable crime. He folded the fist of stolen papers, a mixture of love and hate on his countenance, and stepped decisively into the warm herb-filled cabin. "You look like a woman with something on her mind."

"Alexander!" Lizzie could hardly breathe at the sight of him after months of worry and wonder. She pointed to a chair and shifted her thoughts to her fears. "The armies raid like crazed men, and the citizens get the worst of it! Since the autumn of 1863, the war in Current River country escalated to a fever pitch. We hear reports of large numbers of Federals moving into our area and points south: Captain Monks, Major Wilson, Captain Leeper. Our neighbor west of Sinking Creek, Lieutenant Boyd, burned 20 or more houses and killed 10 men on one raid! Moreover, the riffraff pushed southward from northern counties stop at our farms daily; some say they commit unspeakable atrocities upon their captives. We fear for our children as never before. How could you safely travel to me? I must confess, I am happy beyond words that you came. Sit. Sit. Food? Um, tea?" [2.58-62]

When he drank his tea without a word, she sat silent for a time and then blurted it out. "The judge sentenced Thorpe to be hanged at the April trial. Nancy Leavitt's testimony implicated you and Jack Smith. She talked hard against you but did not claim molestation."

"No, I did not molest her, but her husband—we..." He stopped. "Yes, times are bad. Both sides press for victory in new ways with new recruitment."

Lizzie looked up, her face a mask of fear. However, she chose to remain silent. She took a drink of her calming tea and nodded for him to continue.

"I am for Arkansas, come morning. But, for now, stitch me up and bring me another cup of that strong mysterious tea I smell brewing."

"Stitch you up? God is my hope, Alexander!" Lizzie took him by the shoulders, turned him around, and directed him to a chair closer to the candle lamp on the table. She ladled tea in his cup and poured a shot of whiskey in it for good measure. After removing his torn shirt, she began cleaning a deep cut on his shoulder. "I suppose it's futile to ask how you obtained such a nasty wound." She began stitching. "Sorry. I know this hurts."

She felt the urge to ask him to stay, and then something unfathomable stopped her words. The long months of war and loss made her want to throw all caution to the wind and live for a moment of warmth and genuine affection. A nagging sense of lust pushed its way out of her mind, but not her body.

"Lizzie?" He paused...then tossed the question aside.

She wiped the wound with a whiskey-soaked cloth. She felt her throat burn as if she could cry. "Yes?" she whispered.

He wrapped his arms around her, buried his head in the soft folds of yards of muslin, and held her tight. When he heard a soft "oh", he stood to look into blue eyes filled with tears and longing. Her kiss tasted of mint tea and the fresh musky air of her herb-filled cabin. "My Lizzie."

When he pulled her to his chest, she responded with desperate passion.

CHAPTER 7

PRICE'S LAST RAID—1864

...a march through enemy territory of nearly 1,500 miles; 43 battles and skirmishes; capture and parole of 3,000 Federal prisoners; capture of large quantities of arms and ammunition; and destruction of property estimated to be worth nearly $10,000,000.
—Sterling Price, Major General, Confederate States of America. [2.69]

Alexander sat on the campstool and briefed his sergeants. "General Price prepares to capture Missouri for the Confederacy. We start the invasion tomorrow morning. Many on half rations and dying horses will find the news welcome, in hopes of less-gleaned fields of Missouri.

"All three divisions enter Missouri through Ripley County: General Shelby on the west, to cross Current River at Doniphan; General Fagan in the middle to cross Current River at Trail of Tears Ford; General Marmaduke, on the east, from Pocahontas to Poplar Bluff.

"Coleman's Regiment rides unattached to any brigade, on the west with General Shelby. Current River Country, boys. Pray we travel due north and not westward through the fields of home. Federals destroy every farm they reach. Prepare for the chase. Dismissed."

Alexander and his men rode the better part of the day at the west edge of Shelby's main force. Smoke billowed into the sky above the next set of mountains. "Doniphan burns. Expect Colonel Coleman within the hour."

Before the hour passed, Colonel Coleman and two other officers rode up beside Lt. Alexander Chilton. "Colonel Johnson needs a hundred fifty men familiar with the area to hunt down the Federals responsible for burning Doniphan. My guerilla companies move more decisively than regulars do, so Johnson best move or find himself run down by my outfit!"

"Yes, sir, Colonel." Alexander steered his fifty-plus company to Johnson, and fell in beside the colonel.

"Lieutenant Chilton, Coleman's Regiment. Reporting, sir. I understand arsonists and murderers await punishment."

Colonel Johnson replied, "Yes, I believe we chase Federal Lieutenant Pape. He often receives orders to scout for Maj. James Wilson because Pape will carry out the illegal orders of the butcher. Pape no doubt burned Doniphan. Scouts report the Federals routed the Rebels of Missouri Fifteenth under Colonel Reeves, who held Doniphan for a time; and then Federals chased him into Arkansas, returned, and burned the town. Their advantage? Federals came armed with repeating rifles."

"Pompous Pape won't ride through the night. Likely camped on the Little Black before hightailing it to Fort Davidson." Alexander knew Pape's movements well.

"Thank you, Lieutenant."

"Colonel." Alexander saluted and dispersed his men across the Courtois Hills, in twos and threes, confident to attack at dawn somewhere north.

He heard his main scout give the password to the pickets and watched him walk into camp. "For what location do we ride?"

"Colonel Johnson's men circled east of Pape's Federal camp at Ponder's Mill. We have the west."

"First blood for Price's Missouri raid drawn September 20, 1864. Remember the date. Fire and hold 'em." Alexander led the wide line of Company H into position and half-circled the camp.

"Report." Colonel Johnson took measure of the three lieutenants, who chose one representative to report their chase and skirmish win.

Alexander began. "We buried Confederate men on the south side of the Military Road, and Federals on the north side. We estimate fifty or more enemy wounded and escaped along with Pape. He burned every farm still standing between Doniphan and Pilot Knob. Price sent us reinforcements from Trail of Tears Ford, who joined us when they heard gunfire. Reinforcements. A word welcome to my ears, unspoken since 1862."

He paused to give way for the colonel. When the colonel was silent, he continued. "Colonel Reeves held Doniphan as long as he could before the burning. Says Pape took reprisal on citizens, as ordered by Major Wilson. A colonel on parole from Little Rock requested reprisal for ill-treated Fifty-Fourth Illinois Union men in sixty-three. In addition, a request came from a regiment poisoned with food served at the hotel. A surgeon accompanied them and saved their sorry lives from certain death."

"And Colonel Reeves?" Colonel Johnson inquired.

"Chased into Arkansas unharmed."

"Thank you, gentlemen. Lieutenant Pape and Major Wilson stand in our path—to be captured and stand trial another day. Dismissed." [3.26]

Alexander returned to General Shelby's main forces, already on the march toward St. Louis. He was but one lieutenant in the Coleman Regiment recently reorganized as the Arkansas Forty-Sixth Mounted Infantry. Price insisted every soldier rode a horse. Coleman fought with Price's large army at Pea Ridge. Perhaps Price learned a thing or two since. "Gentlemen, let us specu—"

"So now we're *gentlemen*?" One soldier interrupted and joked. "Excuse me, sir. This here almost-peaceful campfire made me lose my manners."

"Yes. As I was saying, before properly addressed, let us speculate on the generals' conversations this night."

"First, sir, they ask for second helpings!" The soldiers burst into laughter at the solid truth of the matter, voiced by one of their own.

"Shall we reconnoiter seconds when we pull even with Shannon County, Sergeant?"

"Excellent idea, sir."

Alexander paused and looked at the fine men seated around the campfire. "General Price has too few men to prevail over the multiple forts around Saint Louis. I propose he wants Federal scouts to report our large numbers, to force the St. Louis command to pull reinforcements from the smaller forts, such as Jefferson City. Then, we swing west, move ahead of Rosecrans's strength, and take the capital. If the capitol is not his primary destination, it ought to be."

One of the men said, "Could be, sir, Price wants to punish every small fort from Pilot Knob to the capital, and down to Springfield. We pull punishing firepower. However, such a drain on ammunition and men gives Rosecrans time to organize. Time. Our guerilla units attack and melt into the woods and keep up a constant fight. Dissolve their time."

Alexander nodded his head in agreement. "Private Butler?"

"Give our so-called unassigned units free reign, and Federals will chase us all over Missouri. Then Price's men can wrap up Saint Louis, the capital, and Westport to boot. We are bushwhackers, strong and bitter as chicory. Unassigned units sipping coffee is plumb prissy. Sure tastes good, though." Pvt. Joe Butler knew bushwhacking and its high value.

Alexander gave thanks that Joe Butler rode with him and others of Coleman's old Missouri Regiment; they kept the Federals in South Missouri at chase since Pea Ridge. Coleman's new Forty-Sixth Arkansas Mounted Infantry, formed from a few old regiments and a host of new Arkansas men, boasted seasoned soldiers all.

Another soldier contributed his observations. "Supply. Federals raided for three long years. Missouri farms starved. Empty wagons

145

best fill with food and grain soon, as I see it. A hundred empty wagons or more of an army on the march gathers like a lodestone. Attracts iron, not grain. Ill-advised supply hindered many a retreat in Mississippi and Tennessee. General Price never failed to confiscate cannonade. I reckon he did so against the advice of every major in the Army of the West."

"Gentlemen, I will be sure to pass along our considerable collective wisdom to the general," said Alexander.

Private Butler ventured to cajole his leader and best friend. "No doubt, a conversation at the morning breakfast, sir?"

Alexander tossed the remainder of his chicory coffee into the camp-fire. "No doubt." He laughed with his men and found his way to his bed-roll. Although he made light of the discussion and never met a general face-to-face, he would inform the colonel. He knew his men identified the weaknesses and their own value as sure as the dawn.

The next morning, Alexander listened to orders from his colonel to send his scouting party as advance, northward to the fort at Patterson.

Headquarters Shelby's Division:
...Remaining three days at Fredericktown, I started early on the morning of the 26th for the Iron Mountain Railroad, the heavy clouds overhead dark and portentous with impending destruction and encamped five miles from the doomed track, the whistle of the familiar locomotives sounding merrily and shrill on the air as if no enemy were watching and waiting for the coming daylight.
—JO. O. SHELBY, Brigadier-General, Commanding [2.72]

Colonel Coleman continued, "On September 27, while we were burning bridges and iron rails to cut Federal supply lines and reinforce-ments from St. Louis, General Price thought he won Ft. Davidson at Pilot Knob. He suffered considerable loss of men in the early hours of the charges upon the fort. Federal General Ewing set slow fuses, escaped from the fort in the night, assumed by our pickets as a Confederate unit changing position. The fort blew about three a.m. and Price assumed an accident occurred within the fort. Instead, he captured an empty crater.

Tomorrow we again ride to the front of General Shelby's division to assess pursuit of Ewing and then join General Price's main forces, which move to the west instead of St Louis. Our job, well done. Dismissed."

Alexander and his men saw battle day and night. Time and again, General Shelby's forces battled at the front. During the month of October, the Army of Missouri experienced brutal wins at every town on Price's expedition along the Missouri River.

The Confederacy hungered for victories and counted on the Army of Missouri to embarrass the Union and influence Lincoln's bid for reelection. Federal General Grant's armies marched relentlessly into the South and the East. The mayor of Atlanta surrendered the city to General Sherman on Sept 2, 1864. General Sheridan defeated the Confederates in the Shenandoah Valley on Sept 22, 1864. Grant could consolidate forces on Richmond, Virginia.

Then came the resounding Confederate loss at Westport, Missouri; Price retreated south-southwest from Marais des Cygnes, Mine Creek, Marmiton River, to Newtonia near the Arkansas and Indian Territory borders on the Springfield plain.

On October 28, 1864, Price's army stopped to rest about two miles south of Newtonia, Missouri. Rebel Gen. Jo Shelby's Iron Brigade engaged the Union forces and overlapped the flanks.

Alexander's company led the outside left flank. "Push them hard toward the cornfield and open ground. It will be a turkey shoot." Alexander found protection in a draw, lined with trees and undergrowth, so he determined to hold and fire.

"Fine house back of the field. Shame to let the Federals burn 'em out." Joe Butler slipped to Alexander's left and leaned against a large oak tree.

"Hey, Joe." Alexander surveyed his friend and found him sound. "First sign of torch, we will knock it down. If cannon, we will pull back, invite cannon fire our way and save a family."

"Pull way back, I opine," said Pvt. Joe Butler.

Fighting raged until Federal cannon drew within range. "Fall back. Keep cover until nightfall." Alexander heard similar commands to his right, and battle cries drifted farther and farther to his left. Night fell and Company H moved southeast to await orders.

Alexander walked to a campfire and kicked the last burning limb into the low flame. "Assemble the men, Sergeant."

When assembled, Alexander addressed Company H. "Our mission at Newtonia held the Federals until Major General Price's main army could retreat toward the Indian Territory. Our own General Shelby's Iron Brigade lost two hundred fifty men. Under Shelby with Gen. M. Jeff Thompson, the enemy experienced maximum losses, perhaps as many as four hundred men. Our company suffered no losses.

"Our orders from Colonel Coleman give furlough to return to our homes. We are to forage and regroup at Searcy, Arkansas, by December 1. The overall engagement to secure Missouri for the Confederacy was a striking loss, but also a frustration to Federal generals in the East by troops denied. The war is not over. I stand here, proud of every man in Company H. Dismissed."

Alexander left members of his company and turned up Current River to Uncle John and Aunt Sophia's farm at Henpeck.

"Mother, Cousin Alexander came to see us! Back from the war!" Young J. J. shouted and galloped for joy. Cousin Alexander was the eight-year-old's hero.

Sophia ran to the hitching rail and embraced her nephew. "Best stay with us and not go home just now. Shannon County is badly infested with raiders."

"Shannon County is always infested with raiders. What's for supper?"

"Chicken, dumplings, and grits. I will make persimmon pudding for this special thanksgiving."

Alexander ruffled J. J.'s hair. "Let us find the lye soap and scrub down at the river. I'm a man for a bath before supper."

"We got lots of soap." J. J. found the soap, and his brothers, Shade and Zimri, who joined the trek to the river. "Papa hides at his camp in the woods."

Alexander sat with his youngest cousins at his side and asked, "Does anyone know a good story about the John Chilton bunch at Henpeck?"

"I do, I do, I do!" Replies rang from the youngsters.

"To make it fair, you boys take turns. Start with the youngest and work your way around until Aunt Sophia calls a halt."

J. J. said, "You go first, big brother. I always find favor because I am so young."

Shadrach "Shade" Chilton, age seventeen, said, "We see the war from our local sufferings, but Papa brought us a stack of newspapers I read page by page and start anew. While Missouri argued about slavery since statehood, emancipation of slaves is now the Union cause, befitting moral outrage. At the first of the war, the Union cause sought to preserve the Republic. Whatever the many differences between our North and South regions regarding a strong federal government or strong state governments, states' rights now becomes synonymous with racism. Words like "antiwar Democrats" imply meaning beyond my understanding. The danged war interrupted my education. I developed great admiration for Union General Grant, but dare not say it beyond the walls of my home. I surely wish Uncle Joshua was here to help me sort this out, in the detail."

Alexander said, "Well stated, and well on your way as the next family orator. You stand for state representative when age qualified. You hear?" He saw his cousin blush and knew the courage it took to express views contrary to the majority of regional sympathies on middle Current River and some in his own family. He liked the way Shade challenged a man's way of thinking in his search for understanding. Rare occurrence these days.

He considered his own choices in light of Shade's wish that Uncle Joshua lived to pass the torch of wisdom and believed himself sorely misdirected on several counts.

When he saw Zimri stand, Alexander nodded to the lad and flashed an encouraging smile.

Zimri cleared his throat. "I committed to memory a poem by Cousin Robert from Washington and the Congress."

THE CRISIS

The cannon's thunders jar the air,
While, mingled with the battle-cry,
Swells the blown bugle's ringing blare;
But over all I hear the prayer
Breathed by our sires in days gone by.

'Twas theirs to win: 'tis ours to guard;
They faltered not when faint and few;
And shall we deem the service hard
Who bear the banner many-starred,
O'er which their victor eagle flew?

Oh, not in vain their memoires plead
That we should walk the narrow way,
Content to scorn each selfish creed,
And in our father's valor read
The noble lesson of To-day.
—R. S. Chilton
Washington, Sept. 1862 [2.32]

When silence fell upon the room, J. J. stood as if to tell a story. "You done good, Zimri. I pass my turn to Alexander. Tell us how your papa fought a bear."

Alexander felt his cheeks burn. He wondered how two young cousins understood the war better than most grown men did. He knew the foundation for his choice of a side sat on sand, but his ruthless fight sat on rock solid revenge. He breathed deeply and began the scary story, a favorite told over and again around Chilton family tables.

"One fine early spring day when I was just a lad, my large black-and-tan bear dog, Rascal, stopped and sniffed a fresh print pressed in the sandy creek bank. 'Ah, just a half-grown cub, ol' boy.' I scratched my dog's ears, raised my hand high in the air, and pointed forward. 'Go on.'

"By 1860, my family farmed six hundred acres, as far as the eye can see. The bulk of our land lay along the Jacks Fork River a few miles above Shawnee Creek in Shannon County Missouri. Tall shortleaf pines towered on the steep hills, and protected drifts of pure white dogwood blossoms pierced by redbud limbs like bloody sabers. I tracked a young bear way past Rowlett Gap, but the scent ran cold, so I called my dog and turned to a long trek home.

"I said, 'Let us track him tomorrow.' One tempts Shadrach's work brittle when a bear hunt beckoned.

"Shadrach said, 'We best wait until after Sunday dinner at your grandpa's. Maybe catch scent of a big one.' Shadrach's eyes glistened. 'Or, perhaps we should start early Saturday. Get to your chores now, son.'

"Grandpa Thomas Boggs Chilton lived downriver on the Owls Bend Farm on Current River, seven miles below Two Rivers Junction. Add five miles of Jacks Fork, a full day's journey lay ahead.

"Late Saturday afternoon, I sat at the end of the lower front porch of the two-story home of Grandfather Boggs. Grandfather, Father, and the older brothers passed the jug to and fro. I could always tell when my father, Shadrach, felt his liquor. Extravagant estimates of his physical powers rolled as smooth as the 'shine.

"Shadrach said, 'I can whip any man in the county.'

"'Now, Shaddie, that is true,' Boggs agreed. 'You proved the best fighter I ever knew anywhere.'

"'I thought about it a good deal, and I decided I can whip a bear.'

"'Enjoy this extra good feeling right now and stop talking such foolishness.'

"'Talking foolish, am I? Call the dogs, Alexander.'

"'Hold on, there,' Boggs said, 'I do know where a bear comes usin'. Better to let the dogs do the taming. A bear chaws and claws a man all to pieces.'"

J. J. filled the pause, "Tell about the Grrrrr, part! Are you sad, Alexander?"

Alexander realized he told the story for himself as much as for the youngsters, but knew they would get the gist and full appreciation over time. He continued.

"I whistled for the bear dogs and joined the other men. We crossed the river and rode up Big Bloom Creek. The dogs struck a trail, ran a bear up the hill on the ridge between Big and Little Bloom, and treed him at the head of a steep draw.

"'Alexander, catch and hold the dogs.' Boggs directed. 'Now, Shaddie, if you get to needing help, just holler. Tell us to turn the dogs loose. You just say the word.'

"'Oh no, whatever you do, hold the dogs. If I fail to whip such a little feller, I am ashamed to live. Let it kill me. Load my gun for bear, Alexander.' Shadrach walked over to the small shagbark hickory and motioned his father and sons to help shake the bear down. When the bear reached the ground, Shadrach swung a haymaker punch into the side of the bear's head and a tangle of arms, legs, and bear paws flailed. Growls and grunts mixed with shouts and curses as man and bear rolled and tumbled down the rough hillside.

"Soon Shadrach called in a muffled tone, 'Turn the dogs loose, boys; turn the dogs loose. Bear's eatin' me up.'

"Boggs replied, 'Oh no, Shaddie. You just stick and stay. I promised to hold the dogs. Hold 'em boys.'

"Shadrach somehow laid hold of a pine knot and struck the bear a fatal blow in the head. Almost naked and bloody all over, he won the battle. He ran to his rifle and aimed it at Boggs. He snapped the trigger twice before he realized that Boggs earlier removed the cap lock.

"Boggs knew his son well and foresaw Shadrach might shoot him in a blind rage.

"The sports of the Chiltons ran rugged, and I stood witness to many instances of proof. My brothers, William and John, and I washed and bound our father's wounds as best we could. We loaded him in a wagon and made the fifteen-mile trip upriver.

"I recognized my mother's frustration and fury as she muttered and prepared a place on her bed for the wounded wrestler. 'He requires no more liquor. Strong drink obviously addled his mind. What kind of fool fights a bear?'

"'Shall I go for Aunt Betsy? His flesh tore something awful.'

"'Yes, we need a practiced hand to stitch the torn flesh. Go.'

"I covered the one-mile trip in record time, and Aunt Betsy sent Shadrach's little ones out of earshot.

"'Bring the whiskey,' she told his grown sons. 'Hold him still.'

"Aunt Betsy washed sand, fur, and blood from the wounds and stitched flesh. 'Chaw and claw. Chaw and claw.' The cadence focused her mind on the stitches and strengthened her ability to ignore her patient's blue streak of curses. She sighed as she made the final stitch. 'Shadrach. Such a poor sufferer.' In pity for his family, she gave Shadrach the last of the whiskey and stayed until he fell into a fitful sleep." [1.51]

Early the following morning, Alexander gently offered the bit to his horse, dropped the reins, tied his cleaned bedroll and guitar behind the saddle, and swung up. Dawn threatened behind the eastern woods. He breathed the clean familiar smell of the river, spread his arms wide, and threw back his head in joyful thanks at the wonder. "I live to cross Current River on a crisp fall morning. Deus spes mea!"

He planned a stop at the Reeds at Rocky Creek on his journey home. Clint and his three brothers knew the Federal situation better than most. Uncle Francis Marion, Uncle Andrew, home, Aunt Betsy, and Uncle T.

J.'s farm—yes, with route planned, he rode into the thick fog not yet lifted off the swift current at the County Road Ford.

A few days later, in October 1864, Alexander sat with Aunt Betsy and her daughters and sons in the south room. Before anyone was aware of their presence, Federal soldiers appeared at the gate on the west side of the yard. Alexander sprang into the hall. Though they fired several shots through the hall, they missed. Bullets lodged in the wall.

Alexander escaped through a wooded pasture into a cornfield of fifty acres and ran near the east end of the field. One of the soldiers overtook him and shouted back, "Come on boys, I got him."

Alexander attempted to shoot, but his pistol failed.

He saw the soldier drop as low as he could on the opposite side of his horse.

Alexander slipped along the south side by the river, then across to the west end of the field and into the wooded pasture. He climbed a big white-oak tree. A cluster of grape vines grew about twenty-five feet from the ground. In the thick cluster, he hid completely from view of the men who searched for him.

He held his back tighter against the trunk when he saw two soldiers pass under the tree. One soldier remarked, "I would like to know how that danged Rebel got away."

Alexander caught his breath and waited. He remained in the tree until he was sure they were clear gone before climbing down.

He crossed the pasture to Aunt Betsy's house.

His young cousin James ran to greet him. "I cried when you failed to show, but Mother said you must be safe, or we would hear the Federals cheer. She says we must preserve the tree as a monument. Never cut our tree down in a million years."

Alexander ruffled James' hair. "That is a fine idea, seeing as how I am the hero of Shannon County, come home alive from the Civil War. Let us find the kitchen table. I am hungry as a bear."

When he finished his meal, he continued teasing the table full of young cousins. "The Federals arrested me three different times and attempted to kill me; but each time I escaped. Correction, once paroled under oath.

"I stand six feet tall, weigh 215 pounds. I am remarkably active, a fast runner, and of great strength and courage equal to my physical prowess. If not thus qualified, the soldiers would have caught me in the cornfield." [1.26]

Hardly a week passed in the fall of 1864 when one Chilton or another avoided capture. Alexander settled in his mother's keeping room by the cook stove and listened to his brother, John, relate the latest event.

"Federals caught Nelson. Well, they up and took Nelson into the woods to kill him. He rode Joe Butler's saddle horse, a good one and a fast runner. One of the Federals aimed to shoot Nelson in the back, but he watched the soldier closely and just as the soldier shot, Nelson spurred his horse and it jumped forward. The shot missed. The soldier shot again when Nelson was about eighty yards away and hit him in the arm, but the speed of Joe's horse carried him to safety. [1.29]

"He went to Lizzie's cabin, and she removed the bullet and applied some healing herbs. He is fine now. Right, Mother? Good thing, too. Mary Louisa let out one dart already."

Patsy intervened. "Yes, dear. Time for supper. Children, bring in your stick horses so the hounds won't carry them off."

"I intend to recruit Sam Nesbit into Coleman's Regiment. Be like old times. Joe Butler, William Mahan, James Mahan, J. T. Apsley, Jesse Huddleston, Jefferson Chalk, and a fine bunch from Northeast Arkansas earlier recruited for General Price's recent raid around Missouri."

"Supper, Alexander."

"Yes, Mama." Alexander looked at each treasured face around the table and quietly murmured each name: "Mama, young Elizabeth, Little Paulina. Does she remember her grandfather, her father, or her mother? Shadrach dead, William dead, and Mary expired from grief. John and

Elizabeth Francis and their four children." Alexander ducked his head and pulled aside his kerchief as if wiping sweat to hide his tears of remorse and guilt, anything to avoid spoiling his mother's fine meal.

His mother said, "What did you say, son?"

"Pray for our loved ones, every day, by name."

Lizzie watched her sons bring the smaller pieces of wood and stack it close to the house for the fireplace. "Fine sons, have I," she called. After placing her laundry on the rail fence, she grasped the large grapevine basket, and carried it to the bench on the porch at the front door.

Melodious voices drifted into the tiny house near Aunt Betsy, so she stepped outside onto the porch and watched her two sons, well down the road in a run to meet a lone rider.

Sam. She watched him very slowly dismount and kneel to one knee and gather his sons into his arms; press his face into the neck of first one son and then the other. Tears ran down her face and her throat ached. She wondered how the boys could possibly recognize the gaunt man as their father after years of absence. She stepped off the porch and hastened her walk into a run to greet her husband with whom she lived such short months compared to years without him.

"Husband." She embraced Sam and remembered the way he held her, first with his hands on her back, then fully engulfing her with his arms. She could not discern whether his sobs or hers sounded louder. She felt an arm of each young son, one around her skirt and another at her waist as they formed a weeping family circle.

Young George stepped back. "If we are so happy, why are we crying? Can I ride your horse to the house? Where is your saddle? What a pitiful steed. Did you borrow it?"

Sam answered, "One question at a time, lad. Your mother and brother can give you a foot up to ride this pitiful steed to the house, then help me drag this gimpy leg of mine to the kitchen that I know smells like horsemint and fallen leaves. Dreamed and longed for that kitchen lo these many months. And we will soon carry my family home to Sinking Creek."

Lizzie sat by her fireplace in her cabin at Sinking Creek, on the upper section of Current River and kissed the top of the head of her son William, who inherited the Chilton penchant for storytelling. She and George always provided a rapt audience. Tonight, she listened to the stories of his father, come home from war after the Battle of Franklin, Tennessee.

"Eighteen and sixty-four proved a difficult year for the Army of Tennessee and the Missouri Brigade. The hard fought battles of the Atlanta Campaign, Altoona, and finally the Battle of Franklin, Tennessee in November, nearly destroyed the Third Missouri and the brigade. At Franklin, Tennessee, alone, the brigade suffered over 60 percent casualties in a little over one hour of combat. Four thousand of us crossed the river in sixty-two. Lucky to see four hundred come home to Missouri."

Sam rubbed his bum leg and looked at nothing particular, with a motionless expression from eyes like cold lead bullets. "I'm one of the lucky ones. My wife can heal my wounds."

Lizzie changed the dressing and cursed all the sabers ever forged. She looked up, relieved that Sam's attention focused on his sons. She thought, "*I don't know the man who sits in my cabin.*"

She heard a hound jump from the porch. A rider dismounted and walked to the door. She recognized the familiar voice and stood by the window.

Alexander scratched the hound behind the ears. "Good girl. We will go hunting soon."

Sam sent George to open the door. "Alexander, come in."

"Lizzie. Sam." Alexander sat on the bench behind the table and placed young George on his knee. "William."

William scooted from the bench, sat on Sam's good knee, placed his arm protectively around his father's shoulders, and looked directly into Alexander's eyes. "Papa is a hero, home from the Tennessee wars. He told Mother he intended to join Coleman or Freeman. Put Mother in a dither, I can tell you."

"Ah, now, Lizzie. You know Coleman and I fight from a safe distance. Sam can be the cook and procurer of game."

"See, just like I told you, darling." Sam spoke with the first genuine light in his eyes since his return. "My brother, James, joined Colonel Freeman's regiment upon his return from Vicksburg."

Lizzie let well enough alone and continued her tasks by the fireplace in silence.

"Stay for supper?" Sam offered.

"Maybe next visit. Until next week, then, at Perry's camp." Alexander stood and took his hat from the peg by the door. "Lizzie."

"Alexander." She did not turn from the stove; the word hissed like ice water tossed on the fire.

Lizzie lay on her side, her back to Sam. Tears escaped their pool and slid down her temple and into her hair. "I fail to understand the local resistance to the Federal authorities. Hold to your family and take the oath while you can. Peace follows humility."

"Peace? Under my roof?" Sam chuckled. He put his arm over her shoulder and drew her closer.

She finally responded. "We hardly recognize each other after almost three years. And what of your sons?"

"I simply decided to die of old age to rear my sons, which kept me alive for four years. Give Price a few more months to regroup and then take Missouri into the Confederacy. He weakened and scattered General Rosecrans' Federal forces across Missouri." He waited in doubt for her response.

"You desert us, I leave—again."

"Generals Pap Price, Jo Shelby, Swamp Fox Thompson, and all other Confederate military finished for Missouri." Alexander paused a moment for the news to register with his men. "The guerilla forces and volunteer regiments continue the battle. Colonel Coleman's Forty-Sixth Arkansas numbers about three hundred men. However demoralized, the colonel kept his command intact.

"Confederate Captain Bolton and two men captured at Searcy Valley, two captured earlier, and our own Pvt. Harvey Blackburn sadly became the six men picked at random from the St. Louis prison at Lafayette Park to be executed. Federals tied them to an upright pole, informed them of their fate without a trial, and shot them by a firing squad of fifty-four Union soldiers. The murders occurred in retaliation for the execution of Federal Maj. James Wilson and five men of the Third Cavalry MSM. Confederate Col. Tim Reeves held Wilson and his men responsible for the burning of Doniphan."

A cheer resounded for the execution of Wilson. Then a quiet moment swept over Lt. Alexander Chilton's Company H, for the loss of Blackburn and the others.

He raised his head and continued. "Now, if all the generals were as crafty as "Swamp Fox," a different outcome loomed possible because after he captured Sedalia and Lexington, he saved Colonel Gordon's regiments from serious Federal efforts to reclaim the huge howitzer. To the Swamp Fox!" Alexander raised his cup of moonshine whiskey made by his brother John in Shannon County especially for Company H.

"Swamp Fox!" The men joined Alexander in the camp song, but with less enthusiasm than ever before.

Alexander started to set aside his guitar, but the men started up another song, "...Abe was a fool and hadn't halter strong enough to hold Jo Shelby's Mule." He shouted, "Singing and 'shine! Mighty good for a man!" His guitar found the key, and the rhythms rumbled well into the night.

On November 8, 1864, voters reelected President Lincoln in a tremendous victory. The annihilation of Missouri loomed incomplete.

CHAPTER 8

REIGN OF TERROR—1865

I have the honor to report that Capt. William Monks, Sixteenth Missouri Cavalry, had several skirmishes with Yeates' band of guerrillas in Texas County on the 9th, 10th, and 11th instant, in which he killed 9 and wounded 1. The wounded guerrilla escaped. Captain Monks' men must be good marksmen, as it is seldom so large a proportion of hits prove fatal.
—E. B. BROWN, Brigadier-General, Commanding, US Army. [2.74]

Lizzie Davis Nesbit and her two sons visited at the home of Aunt Sophia, at Henpeck on the Current River above Van Buren. She crossed the threshold for the first time since November 1862 when she cared for the whole family down with the grippe.

Lizzie returned as the one in need, sick to heart. When she heard part of the Coleman Regiment took on the middle Current near Chilton Creek, she decided to throw herself into the fray of cuts, gunshots, and broken bones that followed, sure as night followed day. She almost forgot her own troubles.

She asked, "J. J., do you know some stories for us tonight?" Lizzie and her sons, William and George, loved their visit, in no small part due to J. J.'s stories. Also born in 1858 and six years old, wartime made youngsters like J. J. older than their years.

"Why, yes I do. Not whoppers, true as I live. Right, Mama?"

Sophia nodded and kept to her knitting. "One story and then hop to it and off to bed." Sophia often said she never tired of her son's innocent view of times more brutal than she cared to tell. She patted J. J.'s head with affection, but he emphatically shrugged off such baby-type attention and pushed away her hand.

"Capt. Lucian Farris and a large band of the Rebel faith paid us a visit," J. J. said, "and this is what happened. They came to Mark Moore's home in search of a suitable campsite. Mr. Moore and a neighbor, Robert Bolton, fell out a short time before, so Mr. Moore piloted them up to the Bolton place. Farris found it unsuitable, so they circled back to our home and pitched camp by a twelve-acre field of yellow corn and orange pumpkins. When the soldiers used the pumpkins, cut in halves, for bread trays, Mother's fury knew no bounds. Then of course, the corn disappeared to feed their animals. A herd of Robert Taylor's cattle fed nearby, and they selected two fat heifers and butchered them. They stayed three days. The soldiers and horses numbered four hundred. [1.31]

"Mother, accustomed to the Federal's rude foraging, expected more from the Grays who crossed Current River at the ford. When the Rebels took her pumpkins, she walked right up to Colonel Farris. 'Lucian, as friends for many years, you know me a generous soul, but I entreat you to harness your men.'

"'Miz Sophia, what needs correction?'

"'Gather the pumpkins the men split and wasted as platters; order the men to clean the pieces in the river, and deliver same to my maple sugar kettles and any kettles you carry. Build fires with just enough water to render the pumpkin pulp.'

"'Madam, we are at your service.' He took a slight bow and motioned to his men.

"'Private Rayfield, see to the request. Tell your sergeant to send any laggards to me.' Colonel Farris knew better than risk even a smile. When he saw the stunned look on her face, he reconsidered his own attitude.

"'In times of peace, pumpkin and squash are a delicacy, a side dish. This is war, gentlemen, and by the time this particular campaign ends, pumpkin may be the only remaining sustenance for women, children, and armies. We are but guests of Mrs. Chilton. Please afford her and her property every thanks and respect.'

"Mother filled every jar and crock on the place in one day, with spares for neighbors. Colonel Farris travelled on with a good measure of pumpkin."

Young George said, "One more, please? A very short story?"

Sophia nodded her permission. "Very short story. You hear, J. J.?"

"Yes, Mother," J. J. responded and began the last story of the evening. "Back in the days when game was very plentiful in this section, before the Federals harvested it all, hunters invented what they called a fire pan, which consisted of a vessel to contain live fire coals of short bits of rich pine laid to make a bright light. The pan attached to a handle about six feet long, and the hunter carried it on his shoulder with the light behind him. Hunters used such pans to hunt deer in the night. With such a light behind a person and a deer in front, the animal's eyes would look like balls of fire." J. J. stood on his feet by the end of the story, eyes as wide as the deer, and his hands threw balls of fire far into the heavens. [1.54]

J.J. said, "William, tomorrow you can commit to memory a poem, 'The Crisis.' Seeing as how your mother is a Unionist and all, she will burst with pride at your accomplishment."

"Good story, son. Off to bed, everyone. Busy day ahead and we pray no one needs Lizzie's doctoring skills. God above, spare my family. The Federals raid with a vengeance."

"What happened?" Lizzie ran to Aunt Sophia's front gate with her medicine bag in hand, black wool bonnet and cape drawn tight around her against the driving February rain.

Alexander tipped his hat and dismounted. "Come inside. Is Uncle John in from the woods?"

"No, but we can send word to him."

Wet coats and hats stowed, Alexander sat at the side of his Aunt Sophia and cast his gaze on each one of his Grandfather's legacy. "Our beloved Grandfather Boggs passed easily into angelic arms on the thirteenth day of this month in the year of our Lord, 1865. Blessings on us all as we grieve." He rose from his chair to regain his composure. His story of loss must continue in good time. He poured whatever hot liquid brewed over the fireplace, and motioned for the older boys to assist with something for each tortured soul in the room. Then he pulled the corncob from the jug by the window and poured a good measure to cool his drink and his mind. He sat for some time in the quiet room, and then spoke as if only Lizzie listened.

"Trouble at Shawnee Creek. Federal patrol caught my brother John. They told him, 'You are under arrest under special orders for the distillation and sale of whiskey.'

"John asked them, 'What evidence conceived such an illustrious order?'

"'We name witnesses from here to the Mississippi at Cape Girardeau. Your reputation precedes you far and wide. I must say, the evidence proved a well-practiced talent. Say your good-byes to your family, then march.'

"His Elizabeth said laughter never sounded so menacing. When he came out of the house with the guard, he realized their intention to kill him. He made a dash for liberty and ran upgrade through a lane about a hundred yards, when they shot and killed him. Elizabeth and the four children looked on." [1.29]

"Bring your medicine bag; it is too late for John, but not for others. Give my love to Aunt Sophia and come with me." Alexander ducked his head into his wool neckerchief, took his hat and coat off the pegs, and walked out the door. He swung into the saddle and turned the horses' tails into the wind.

"Lord have mercy," Lizzie murmured. She returned with a blanket fully stuffed, tied it to the packhorse, and leaped from the porch step into her saddle, already soaked with icy rain.

"Travel safe, you hear?" Aunt Sophia called from the doorway. Lizzie waved to her sons who stood on either side of Aunt Sophia. "Be back tomorrow."

Alexander and Lizzie rode all night and arrived at his home early in the day. They saw a wagon draw up from the opposite direction. Nelson and Mary Louisa, heavy with child, traveled from Spring Valley to his farm for bereavement with her family for her brother John and her grandfather. The men unloaded items from the wagon, and the women walked safely inside the house.

Revenge hung unspoken in the air.

Alexander and Nelson left before noon and joined their cousin, Joshua Chilton, brother of Aunt Betsy and Sophia. They came down Blair Creek in Shannon County past Joshua's home with his aging father, Coot. His sister, Anne, waved from the yard where sap of sugar maple trees bubbled gently in a large black open kettle hung over a fire. "Take a cake of sugar and keep away from all roads. The danger of Federals anywhere looms ominous."

Ignoring her advice, the trio traveled the road to Big Shawnee Creek. About half a mile up the creek, Alexander heard the sound of several horses, most likely the "local patrol band."

Alexander knew raiders came hard and fast when they smelled blood. He saw Nelson and Joshua whirl their horses at a flat-out run toward the safety of the river.

Alexander rode parallel in the woods, yet undetected. Shots rang out over their heads. He saw one shot catch Joshua in the shoulder.

"I'm hit...go on." Leaning down to his horse's shoulder, Joshua's saddle gave in to his weight. The girth broke.

Nelson immediately turned around and headed at a full gallop toward the fallen Joshua. "Go on, I will get him."

Joshua stood, swung up behind Nelson, and called, "Get them in a cross fire."

"We got 'em." Alexander shouted and shot into the raiders' midst, but the soldiers ignored the ploy and bore down on the two, undeterred.

He watched bullets riddle the two men's backs and legs; watched Nelson and Joshua fall to the ground and the horses flee toward their respective barns up and downriver.

Alexander emptied his three guns, but the patrol disappeared into the safety of the trees and left the young men in the mud where they fell.

Alexander ran first to Joshua and found a pulse. "Hold tight, boys."

"Nelson?"

"I'm hit but breathing." [1.29]

Nelson's horse reached his mother's home on Jacks Fork. Blood on the saddle told Lizzie more than she could bear. She said to Aunt Betsy and her cousins, "You stay inside; I will tie up the horse."

Lizzie returned, made herb tea, and comforted her family as best she knew. She and Aunt Betsy's daughters cooked and paced the floor; Aunt Betsy's young sons fed the wood stove.

In a few hours, she heard a wagon crunch down the road. She saw Nelson's horse break the reins free of the hitch and gallop to the wagon where Nelson, Joshua, and John lay covered with quilts. The horse followed the wagon down the lane and nudged, then sniffed Nelson's still body. "Start more water to boil." Lizzie shouted and suppressed a scream.

She knew Alexander risked his life when he delivered the wagon to the front gate with a small contingent of his men to protect his cousins. Then she saw John's wife and children, who hovered in the wagon under blankets protected by the wagon seat.

"We sent summons to camp for Perry to come quick." Lizzie brought Alexander's horse, tied at the back of the wagon, to the hitching rail but dropped the reins. She left Nelson's horse at the side but fashioned a rope halter, shimmied it over its nose, and tied it to the wagon.

"Bad business. So sorry. Maybe you can save Nelson." Alexander gathered the horses' reins and swung into the saddle. "We will escort Mama and Mary Louisa."

She knew Alexander and his men would again give chase to the raiders, and it took her breath away.

Lizzie quickly checked the jugulars of the three men. John, dead. Joshua, dead. Nelson, near gone. "Take Nelson's boots off while I reapply the tourniquet to the leg. Get him inside first!"

She followed Aunt Betsy and the two men who carried Nelson from the wagon to the porch and into the house. She made a pillow from her cape, helped them lay Nelson on the floor of the dogtrot, the wide center hall of the house, and motioned Aunt Betsy to stay."

She saw another wagon pull next to the one with the bodies of the other two men. Alexander's mother, Patsy, helped the very pregnant Mary Louisa from the wagon. Mary Louisa sank into the frosty February grass when she recognized Nelson's boots and the bodies of her brother and her cousin in the wagon.

Lizzie ran outside and knelt at Mary Louisa's side." You must gather your strength, now. Nelson needs you. He's inside."

"Alive! Oh, Nelson. But Alexander? Joshua?"

"Joshua died. Alexander left for the woods. Bear up, girl."

Lizzie lifted and half carried her pregnant cousin and followed the procession of women, men, and children who carried the other two bodies to the dogtrot. "Miz Patsy, take this chair, you look faint."

Miz Patsy sank to the floor by her dead son, John, pulled him into her arms, and rocked and moaned in quiet, bone-crushing grief.

Then Lizzie helped Elizabeth, John's wife, to his side. Having said her good-byes at the scene of the crime, she stroked his hair and held the hand of his mother, soon surrounded by John's four children.

Nelson's wounds looked substantial. Lizzie and Aunt Betsy cleansed the wounds and began the painful process to remove the bullets sunk deep into Nelson's back and leg. Lizzie absentmindedly hummed the Scottish tune "The Flowers of the Forest" as she probed for the sound of metal upon metal. She caught herself and chose silence over the tune of the sad burial song.

She motioned to Mary Louisa to get a better hold on Nelson's arms. Lizzie felt the probe scrape on the bullet. She widened the pincer and with a swift, smooth pull, the bullet appeared.

Blood sprayed Mary Louisa's apron, and Lizzie grabbed a strip of cloth to tie off the bleeding until it clotted.

Now for the bullet wound on his shoulder where Aunt Betsy kept vigil. Lizzie passed Aunt Betsy the probe and completed her work on Nelson's arm.

"The bullet passed through the shoulder, I can patch it. Turn him on his side." Aunt Betsy waited for Lizzie to shift position, and then four practiced hands turned him swiftly and smoothly. "Hold him close, Mary Louisa, and pray for the healing touch."

Lizzie stepped to the door at the sound of horses and saw Perry and his cousins arrive in the dark of night. They added their reins to the ones still tethered to the wagons in the yard, and Perry motioned men to guard the road up and down river.

The glow of lamplights flickered in the wide central hallway window. Women and children sat on the floor in three groups.

"Mother." Perry knelt next to his mother, behind Nelson, and stroked Nelson's black hair. Tears rolled down his face as he opened his arms to his young brothers, Thomas and James, who began to cry like a beaver dam broken loose in a flash flood. "Can we move him to the daybed?"

"Best wait." Lizzie followed Perry's gaze to the blood-soaked wood floor. "We will tend to that later." She knew the bloodstain would never fully disappear.

She maintained vigilance over young Joshua, an uncle her same age, as she laid out his body for burial. The mere thought of her grandfather Coot's love for his youngest son tore at her last resources.

Lizzie fell into a half stupor and began washing and laying out the body of John. Then his wife nudged Lizzie aside, and his children filled the empty space left by Lizzie, to perform this last loving act for husband and father.

Lizzie stepped outside and ran to the river. The February wind whipped at her dress and petticoats. She dropped all on the gravel bar. Naked, she waded until the water rose to her waist. She splashed water on her face and reached for the heavens. "Oh, dear God. We can't bear this!" She screamed, cried, and beat her fists into the water until numb from shock and from frigid water. Panic passed. She dressed and returned to the house, ready for the inevitable.

At dawn, Lizzie sat on the floor of the dogtrot with the others, all eyes on Mary Louisa who gently caressed Nelson's face and arms, still propped on her bloodstained, apron-covered lap.

Nelson turned, pressed his cheek against his unborn child and voiced his last words, "Remember me forever."

Lizzie helped Perry and his sisters return the laid-out bodies of Nelson, John, and young Joshua to the wagon and walk to the Chilton Cemetery just northwest of Joshua and Betsy Chilton's house on Jacks Fork.

Mary Louisa!" Lizzie ran to her cousin who flung herself on the red gash of clay dug for Nelson's grave and then reached her hand leftward to touch the grave readied for her brother, John.

Mary Louisa refused comfort; refused to be moved from her disposition. "Alexander. Where is Alexander? We need Alexander."

Perry walked toward the two distraught cousins with Lizzie's sons in tow. He picked up George and held him tight. "A fine son."

Lizzie said, "I thought Sam one of the most caring and kind men I ever knew. Still do, for that matter. He shows up, claims ignorance of an event, and says he feels so bad about it. Typical Sam. Avoids responsibility and then begs genuine forgiveness."

"I am sorry."

"For our loss or for Sam?"

Perry stood silent a moment. "War, Lizzie. Sam seeks his responsibility somewhere with Coleman's Regiment."

"And you?"

"More involved than you ever imagined."

Lizzie gulped for air. Perry at risk, too? Then she caught sight of movement in the distance. The knowledge of guards posted on every ridge and hollow for funerals and wakes kept her from fainting.

"Boys, stay with Mary Louisa." She recognized Alexander and the Reeds. She picked up her skirts and ran toward them.

Alexander dismounted and caught her as she tripped on a rock and fell into his arms crying uncontrollably. "Mary Louisa is near crazy with grief; she calls and calls for you." She laid her head on his chest and gathered her resources. "Come, yonder near Nelson's grave. I will take your horse."

Alexander made a cursed vow of revenge for his second dead brother. "I will not let them get away with this." His words felt hollow as he stomped in slow anger to his mother's side and sat by John's grave. He raised himself to his knee and took his bereft sister into his arms. "I'm here, sweet sister, you need not fear."

"Where were you? Nobody but the women here. Federals and their bushwhackers ride everywhere along the river. Oh, Alexander, all three gone. They are going to kill us all before it's over."

"I'm here now. Hold tight." Alexander substituted anger for grief. Guilt swept over him as in the shadow of darkest evil. He could not move a muscle. Then, he said to his men, "Had Grandfather lived, this would surely stop his heartbeats. Let us tend to the burials."

Family and friends gathered for the wakes. The lower pasture filled with wagons, and if history predicted, would remain so for more than a week.

Alexander, Lizzie, and the other Chiltons, the Reeds, and their neighbors removed from the cemetery to Aunt Betsy's home thankful the February thaw allowed prompt burial. Plates filled with precious stores shared for the wake. Then the men adjourned to the barn to piece together events of the past days. Everything rode on anticipation of the Federals' next actions.

Clint Reed stepped forward first and led out with news of the Middle Current. "Robert Littral and William Ethridge live on Rodgers Creek about six miles west of Van Buren. They went into the Reed settlement. They killed six large hogs.

"Mr. Litteral spent a portion of his time in search of other people's property hidden from Federals. He resolved he would see all the Reeds, Chiltons, and several others, killed." [1.39]

Clint continued. "But I tell you true, more danger lingers than a seemingly greedy neighbor. Federal Lt. William Henry travels in these parts under orders from the governor himself and his men operate as trained assassins. Now, how can I say it more plainly? The whole of the Chilton and Reed clan are written on the eradication list, whether Federal, Rebel, or Homespun."

Perry took the floor and recited the situation in Jefferson City. "On January 6, 1865, our governor convened another Missouri constitutional convention. The radicals, bent on punishment, deny anyone considered a secesh to vote or hold office. On January 11, he and authorities abolished slavery in Missouri.

"The Federals prevail in every part of the nation, the Confederacy all but lost. The increased effectiveness of guerilla warfare and lawlessness across the state alarms both military and citizens alike, so the governor ordered a formal extension of the Missouri Militia. The incentive to enlist, a lifetime federal pension for both former Rebels and Union soldiers under an oath to serve Missouri. It replaces the 'provisional' Enrolled Missouri Militia, due to expire mid-March. Commanders named for the hundred-man units and the military men further enabled to execute its processes and judgments under their auspices to 'strengthen the hands of legal justice.' *Execute*—the operative word!"

"Our notorious 'friends,' Lieutenant Henry and Billy Monks..." Sounds of laughter and anger drowned Perry's next words of sarcastic humor. He continued with a slight shake of his head and a weak smile of acknowledgement. "Lt. Henry posts out of Pilot Knob with reinforcement from St. Louis. Dent County allowed Captain Kenamore a hundred militia. The ever-present Capt. William Monks leads the Howell County company. They call it a declaration of Missouri martial law. Some call it 'kill at will.'"

An anonymous voice shouted from the back of the barn, "Now that's something different from what's gone on around here for four years!"

After laughter at the irony died down, noise ceased. The neighbors of Federal sympathies in the barn, who came to pay respects to the Chiltons, rose and moved in a line to shake the hand of the seventy-two-year-old Chilton patriarch, Thomas Coot Chilton, and stood behind him as a group.

He broke the silence with his best wisdom to his large extended family and his neighbors. "My friends of all sympathies and creeds, as I see it, the time to set aside our differences marks this sad day. I commit my loyalty, and that of my family, to all my friends and neighbors of good faith. I fear a punishing reign of terror at hand."

Lizzie and her sons removed to Mary Louisa's home in Spring Valley to await the birth of the slain Nelson and Mary Louisa's unborn baby.

She helped William gather eggs in the chicken coop. "Papa! Mama, it is Papa." William dropped the basket and ran toward the horse and rider, still some ways from the house.

"Cracked eggs for dinner. Sam loves brains and eggs." Lizzie rushed to the house, placed the uncracked eggs in a bowl, and broke the cracked ones into a skillet by the stove.

"Georgie, look out the door. Company for dinner today." Lizzie stood at the door and watched George run to greet the "guest," and waited for his shouts when he recognized his father. "Amazing if George remembers his father."

She saw Sam jump from the horse and untie a group of packages. Each son proudly reached for a package or two. Sam scooped George into his arms and walked to the door with William's head under one guiding hand. "Oh, my Lizzie." He took her into his arms. He stood a moment, and then moved to kiss and envelop her as was his custom. When she did not respond, he stepped back.

"Hello, Sam. Welcome to yet another's home. We seem vagabonds from one family to another."

"Miz Betsy told me you were here for Mary Louisa's confinement. It is good to see you."

Mary Louisa came from the side room. "Sam, welcome home. Take a chair. I think tea brews on the hearth."

"Thank you, yes. You look well."

"Lizzie and I wait and wait. She says it could be any day now." Mary Louisa poured everyone a cup of the warm dark liquid and sat at the table across from Sam. "Tell us your adventures. We love stories."

"J. J. saw Quantrill, the James brothers, and all the heroes of the burning of Lawrence, Kansas."

William climbed on his father's knee. "Your leg good now?"

"Fine, just fine. Now let's hear about Quantrill's gang." Sam smiled when he saw Lizzie roll her eyes and turn to start dinner.

"The winter of 1864-65 was cold with much snow and all was very quiet. However, early in 1865, J.J. went one day to the field with his older brothers to haul some fodder, and while two of the boys loaded the fodder, one chopped some fish out of the ice on a pond frozen several inches deep and J.J. strung the fish.

"About the time the boys drove up to the gate with the fodder, they looked up the road and saw many Federals, as the boys thought, coming. They wore Federal uniforms, but treated the boys in a friendly way. Some asked questions about the fish. To the boys' surprise, they were not harsh. They left the boys guessing as to why they were so different to other Federals.

"We learned afterwards that it was Quantrill and his band, consisting of the James brothers, Frank and Jesse, Cole, James and Bob Younger, and 66 others, 72 in all. They came down Current River from its headwaters and disturbed nobody. They went on down through Southeast Missouri and over into Tennessee and stayed there and in Kentucky." [1.33]

"Lizzie! It's started." Mary Louisa stood in the kitchen, the back of her dress wet with birth's beginnings.

"No rush or fears, Mary Louisa. Today is a fine day for a birthing. Just add water to the kettle."

Sam stepped forward, took Mary Louisa's arm, and led her to her bed in the back room. "Fine day."

Lizzie helped her out of her dress and undergarments and into a white nightdress with handmade lace around the neckline and sleeves. "You look radiant. Now lay back. Gentle-like, I will check your progress." Lizzie washed her patient with soap and warm water from waist to toes. "Fresh and clean. You will be a mother before the cock crows."

Sam stepped back into the room. "Can I be of any help?"

"You and the boys sit with her and talk of crops and love and beauty while I make last preparations. The baby is on the small side, I think. All seems well. There may be no time to fetch her mother as we hoped."

Lizzie listened to Sam and the boys tease and encourage Mary Louisa. A pang of jealousy swept her when she noticed Sam's easy ways emerge with Mary Louisa and his sons. When the pains of birth grew closer, she sent Sam and the boys out of the room.

"It's a boy. Sam, come help, it's a boy." Lizzie handed the slippery baby to his mother. She wrapped him in a swaddling cloth and waited. "Push a bit when the urge comes for the afterbirth. Good." Lizzie checked the list of requirements and found all well with patient and son. After clearing the birthing supplies and cloths into a basket, she thought she would help with the baby's first acts of life but saw that Sam helped Mary Louisa with the baby to her breast.

She took the basket outside and cried tears of relief and grief. "We will see to it your son remembers you forever, dear Nelson."

Lizzie finished her tasks and guided the inquisitive William and George to the bedroom door.

Mary Louisa's tired happy voice greeted them. "He's beautiful. Thank you, oh, thank you for my healthy son. Invite the boys in before I fall totally sound asleep. Francis Marion Chilton, meet your cousins George and William. You will be great friends till the end of your days." Mary Louisa beamed.

"Can we hold him?" William asked.
"Soon. Soon, my dears."

The week of March 26, 1865, Alexander received disturbing news via the bushwhacker relay. The notorious Federal Lieutenant Henry of the Seventh Kansas and the Seventeenth Illinois camped near his Uncle John and Aunt Sophia's home. He rode directly to their farm.

As he drew near, Alexander saw Pad Reed walk toward him with somber steps. The two men knocked at the door.

"Come in. News can end our long hours of worry and wonder." Sophia pulled another chair close to the fireplace. "Sit my dear ones. Tell us true, however fearful."

Pad sipped chicory coffee and then began his terrifying news. "The night after the rain began, ten men were dispatched to get the Reeds and Isaac and George Baker. Mrs. Betsy Moore, who is of the Federal faith, but a friend of the Chiltons, Reeds, and Bakers, sent warnings that Mr. Litteral went for a mob to kill all of them.

"The Chiltons and Bakers heeded the warnings, but we Reeds did not and were all at home that day.

"They caught my brother Tom first and ordered him to bring his ox team and wagon down to your home, and went on and arrested me and brought me on down to your home to join up with Tom.

"Meantime, five of the band went up to the home of my brothers, George and Charles. They arrested them both and brought them down to the ford at the junction of Carr Creek and Current River. There they shot and killed George. He fell near enough to the water's edge and next morning when I found his body, his feet and legs barely held him from floating away.

"The red-haired fiend that shot him galloped up by Charles, after catching up with the band half a mile down the road, and shot him in the side of the head, letting him fall by the roadside, and then led both their horses with blood on the saddles for Tom and me to see. He said he enjoyed shooting prisoners to watch them kick." [1.41]

Pad paused, gathered his wits, wiped his tears, and accepted more food and coffee.

"Come morning, orders were given to three guards to take me and Tom down to a stack of fodder...and make us carry some of it to camp. The creek was flush and they walked across the end of the field that extends down from the house to the end of the bottom. Tom saw a place to cross the creek and mentioned it.

"One of the guards said, 'Along this side will do you all right.'

"One of the guards was walking by the side of us prisoners. One of the two guards behind said, 'Step out from that man a little,' and at the same time the two following aimed to shoot us prisoners in the back, but the guns failed to fire. Maybe the rain fouled the powder.

"I succeeded in taking the gun away from my guard and knocked him down with the butt of it. I dropped the gun and ran away into the woods.

"Tom was unable to take the gun from his assailant and the third guard struck him with his gun. Then he shot him. [1.44]

"I ran over the point of the hill southward until out of sight, and then turned up the ridge, northwest. I passed a Federal who, instead of shooting or stopping me, whistled at me to make me run faster. I ran nearly two miles and came to Jack Tinker's farm...asked if any of the Federals were around there.

"Mr. Tinker told me no.

"I started along a path up the hill and was soon out of sight and out of danger.

"My clothing was rain soaked. I wore a heavy overcoat, but made fairly good time just the same. I went on over the hill keeping near the river. When I reached Bolton Bluff, I noticed smoke rising, and at the brow of the hill, I slipped to the edge and peeped over. John L. Smith and his sons, Bailey and Dan, hid under the bluff. They were not aware of my presence until I asked, 'What are you doing down there?' It nearly stampeded the Smiths.

"I made my way home that day and told my sister-in-law what happened; Tom's wife, Tennessee Fancher, you know. That night she started for the scene of the killing, and reached the Coleman home early next morning, a distance of about twelve miles.

"The Federals advised Mr. Coleman to remove to Pilot Knob. Fearing to refuse, he went with them and left his boys to get the ox team and load in household goods and the family, and come on.

"They were ready to start when Tom's wife arrived. Mrs. Coleman told her they feared to stay to render assistance, but bade her welcome to the house and such conveniences as she could find about the place, and drove away.

"I do not know who assisted her to bury her husband Tom, but it was mostly women who dug the grave. There are very few citizens here at this time and what men there are here, are afraid to come out in the open in daytime. [1.45]

"Clint barely escaped the same fate. On the day following the killing of our three brothers, Devil "Dick" Bose came to Clint's home, no doubt thinking Clint stashed some of Father's money in the house. Clint and his three grown sons; John, Bailey and Dan Smith; and Robert Fancher were well armed, so Bose passed on without disclosing his mission." [1.75]

The family sat in stunned silence.

"A refill of this bitter chicory girds my strength. Thank you, Miz Sophia. Proceed."

Sophia sat in her chair and told the Chilton events. "Early on the same morning when your brothers were murdered, a detachment of ten men took our son Zimri and began to prowl. We heard the guns fired that killed your brothers, the shots being about twenty minutes apart.

"Soldiers came on to the house and brought something they took from their search. They sat down and began to talk about it.

"I looked on awhile, and asked them if they killed anyone down at the river.

"'Of course we did,' was the cruel reply.[1.42] 'As we came down Dry Valley, I shot James Edgar. Edgar would not face me and turned his side to me, and I shot a hole in him as big as my fist.' The small, red haired freckled-faced fiend that shot most of the prisoners...talked loudly so the children could all hear him and be terrified, of course.[1.41]

"The band came back through the upper part of the farm and killed a nice young deer, then went up a hollow half a mile to one of John's camps to his wood shop. There was a grindstone and tools for working in wood. They broke the grindstone, piled the other stuff together, and burned it. Then they went to where the meat was stored. They carried the hams and middlings to camp, but the shoulders were not good enough for these warriors to eat, so they burned them.

"There was a large box near the bin where the meat was stored and in it were some bedclothes and other articles including a quantity of thread.

"The sheep and cotton, we raised, processed the fibers, and planned to weave cloth for everyday wear. When we spun the supply for the year 1864, there was a surplus of both cotton and wool thread.

"The soldiers took the thread out and burned the box with the rest of the contents.

"Two of them took an armload each of thread, carried it to the house, walked in with an air and dignity of brave soldiers fighting to save the Union, and laid the thread on the fire one hank at a time in the presence of my daughters and me.

"The first soldier laid his supply on the fire and stepped back. Then the other one laid his supply in the same way. The girls wept inconsolably.

"Mr. Litteral located everything we owned. What he failed to find, his large red dog located for him. He destroyed about everything that people put away for miles around.

"We grew a crop of tobacco in 1864, and cured about 3,000 pounds worth about $1,500. Mr. Litteral showed the soldiers the tobacco. They tore the shed and the rain spoiled it. Next, they found our guns.[1.43]

Alexander wasted no time after the death of his brother and five cousins. On April 3, 1865, he gathered four of his command: Sam Nesbit, George H. Davis, Joe Butler, and Charles Chilton. He contacted

177

Lt. William Chronister, whose company included the notorious George Crawford and others returned from the South.

He chose a half-moon night for the raid. The State Militia of Lieutenant Henry and the Illinois Seventeenth camped on upper Logan's Creek at the Hugh Chitwood farm in Reynolds County.

The house sat on an elevation between the creek and the road. A small hollow ran across the road, six feet lower than the house. A wagon sat in the hollow.

The militia slept in the house and on the porch. Alexander and twelve others slipped into the militia's camp and led away twenty-four good horses to a safe distance.

Alexander whispered, "I resolve to go back and kill some of the militia who murdered my Reed cousins and perhaps my brother John and two Chilton cousins. My main target is their red-haired butcher, a short pasty-looking feller, who will be with the supply wagon. Joe, follow me."

He motioned to Chronister and nine others to make their way to the porch floor to open fire.

Alexander and Joe Butler bent low, guns drawn, and crept behind the wagon in the hollow. Alexander stepped over the wagon tongue and accidentally tapped it with his heel. He knew the heeltap on the tongue could mean trouble. The red-haired, freckle-faced butcher—the one who bragged he shot the Reed brothers down to see them kick—lay either asleep under the wagon or stood watch.

The butcher crawled from under the wagon and asked, "Who comes there?"

Alexander turned, but Joe Butler replied with the first shot, and the butcher fell.

"Fire!" Alexander shouted as he put a pistol round of his own into the butcher. He stepped behind the wagon for protection. Lead shot cracked in all directions. He saw Chronister and the other men reach the desired position, but after several rounds, the bushwhackers fled and melted into the night woods.

Alexander and his men rendezvoused at the Current River. "Joe Butler robbed me of the pleasure and shot the red-haired butcher. My mission completed with satisfaction. [2.23] Thanks to each of you, we can also deliver twenty-four good horses to the profitable Southern Missouri horse market. Dismissed." [1.46]

CHAPTER 9

SURRENDER IN THE WEST—1865

In compliance with instructions from the Secretary of War a salute of 200 guns will be fired at every post and arsenal in this department at meridian on the day of the receipt of this order in commemoration of the surrender of General Lee and the Army of Northern Virginia to Lieutenant-General Grant and the army under his command.
By order of Major-General Dodge:
—J.W.BARNES, Assistant Adjutant-General, US Army [2.77]

We have nothing here to fire with; nothing in the capital of the State to sound forth the joyful news.
—Thomas C. Fletcher, Governor, State of Missouri [2.78]

That there will be some disturbances and much lawlessness in the counties of the border cannot be doubted.
—Clinton B. Fisk, Brigadier-General, U.S. Volunteers. [2.79]

In early May 1865, Lizzie and her sons resided at the home of Uncle John and Aunt Sophia. About one o'clock in the afternoon, she wiped George's tears with a white linen handkerchief her sister made for her before the war: the cursive letter "E" set in the corner, embroidered in three pink strands of thread surrounded by two swirls of soft green. "Your Aunt Caroline fashioned this kerchief as a gift before you were born. Perhaps she foretold the birth of such a fine son as you."

"But I want to play with William and J. J.! They ran off to their secret hidey-hole and left me here. Called me a baby."

"Climb up here on my lap and choose a story."

"Tell me about the king in Scotland where they named a town after us, and his castle of gray stones, just like these holding up the porch."

She lifted George into her lap and began a naptime story. "Once upon a time, King George led his army to his castle in Scotland. The village of Nesbit set in the king's woods near the castle, for protection from invaders."

"Look, Mama, invaders gallop across Uncle John's pasture."

Lizzie jumped up so quickly she toppled George to the floor. "William! J. J.!" she shouted. "Georgie, ring the dinner bell, loud and fast."

She felt a hand slip into hers and saw it was her aunt. "Lt. Joseph Norris with his Federals. Thank goodness, John left the house a few minutes ago on an errand to a neighbor's house, five miles away. He rode safely out of their reach."

Moments later, the officer stopped his horse near the porch rail. "Missus Chilton, we are here to persuade your husband to come in and surrender; go to Pilot Knob and take the oath of allegiance." Lieutenant Norris continued his "persuading" for about an hour.

"Shade, carry the message to Father, if you can find him. In addition, send J. J. and William home. Like as not, they are in their secret hidey hole at the bluff."

"Yes, Mama."

Lizzie said, "George, stay with Aunt Sophia while I help Shade find the boys."

Lizzie and Shade walked past the barn toward the bluff. Lizzie said, "Go on to your father and stay there."

When she saw two soldiers ride toward the bluff ahead of her, she repeated, "Shade, go on to your father." She quickened her step in abject fear. Then she ran toward the soldiers who held J. J. on the rise west of the house and out of sight of his mother.

One of them took a belt from around his pants and buckled it around J. J.'s neck, then bent a small sapling over, tied the end of the belt around it, and hung him up for a minute or so. Then he let him down. "Where's your father?"

"I do not know."

Lizzie ran nearer behind a tree. When they let J. J. down a second time, she heard him say, "Papa worked down in the field."

"Oh, J. J., don't lie. The soldiers came by the field," she whispered and watched helplessly as they hung him up again.

Then she saw movement on the bluff above.

A man stepped into view, gun at the ready. He made himself known with a calm order. "Let the boy down. Now."

As one soldier turned to release the lad from the sapling, the other opened fire on the man who stood on the bluff above.

"Fool!" The man fell forward off the bluff and landed at J. J.'s feet.

Lizzie knew her uncle's words affirmed his concern his young nephew would catch a bullet in the fracas if he fired. She ran toward the soldiers and gathered J. J. into her arms.

"Uncle saved me. Did he die, Lizzie?"

"Can we see to the man?" Lizzie spoke to the soldiers but moved without waiting for permission. She knelt at the body of her uncle, young Thomas Coot Chilton, Jr. She found him dead.

"Where's William?" She took J. J. by the shoulders, looked directly into his eyes, and then held him to her.

J. J. whispered into Lizzie's ear. "He hid safe in our secret hidey hole."

"Show me." She followed J. J. to a small opening on the backside of the bluff. "William, it is mother and J. J." She helped her son out of the opening in the gray limestone bluff about five feet above the ground.

William said, "We hide all our secret finds in our hidey hole. You mustn't tell George or anyone."

She drew William into her arms and held him so long and so tight, he finally pushed her away. [1.47]

Lizzie and Aunt Sophia waited while the Federal soldiers' campfires glowed in the pasture nearby. About midnight, the hounds made such a friendly ruckus she knew Uncle John must be about the place. She walked toward the campfire where several soldiers moved about.

The dogs greeted their owner, and he responded with hands raised. "Here is John Chilton; you chased me for four years, and I came to see what it is for."

The soldier replied, "I want you to go to Pilot Knob and take the oath of allegiance to the United States." [1.46]

"I will go. However, I must return my wife's brother to his home for burial.

"My men can assist you." The lieutenant summoned three soldiers.

"Assist? My old bones appreciate assists. Bet you thought me a young man by the looks of my children. Second family. First family all passed."

"Mr. Chilton, are you aware the war ended? Gen. M. Jeff Thompson signed surrender papers in May. Gen. Robert E. Lee surrendered some weeks prior."

"Why, no. Best reason I know for Federals camped in my river bottom. Excuse me; I have family duties to attend."

Lizzie met Uncle John with a smile. "I heard. The war ended. Praise be. Come on to the house." She took his hand and kissed it.

When Lizzie heard that a group of men intended to help John carry the body of her young uncle on his final journey upriver, she packed her belongings, intent on a return home to Sinking Creek.

The small group grew to fifteen before it reached her young uncle's home. Lizzie went into the house first and then returned. "I need to stay here a few days. Aunt Jane crumbled at the news of her husband's death."

"Fine, girl. We will get you home upon my return from the fort at the Knob," John said.

Lizzie returned to the modest home to care for yet another casualty of war.

"Aunt Jane, you must take sustenance. Your five children need you."

"Take my children, you know about orphans' needs. I will love you forever." Jane died—whether of a broken heart or a bad heart, Lizzie could not say.

She moved the children of her Uncle Thomas Coot Chilton, Jr. and Aunt Jane to her cabin at Sinking Creek. She knew orphaned siblings needed each other. It meant everything. She took her chance to give back the gift given her.

The Chiltons, with the help of their Deatherage neighbors, cleaned the long-neglected home and added a wide dogtrot and a second room for Mary, age sixteen, Sarah Jane, fifteen, Elizabeth, twelve, John Coot, nine, and Martha, eight.

"Mama, Sarah Jane and young Jasper Deatherage like each other. We can tell." William nodded to Martha, who affirmed young William's proclamation.

Lizzie and youngsters William, George, John Coot, and Martha packed a cotton poke for a picnic and a swim in Current River where the creek joined. She recognized Sam's countenance a quarter mile away but waited to let the boys greet him first.

"Mama. William. It's Papa!" George took off in a footrace with his brother.

Lizzie saw Sam grab each boy's hands, pull one to the front and the other to the back of the saddle, and ride slowly toward her.

"Well, what have we here?" Sam lowered first William, then George, to the ground and dismounted.

"Federals shot Uncle, and Aunt Jane died of a broken heart. All the kids are ours now." George walked over to Martha, took her by the hand, and pulled her forward. "This is Papa. Sam Nesbit."

"And you are a pretty one, Martha." Sam looked over the heads of the children at Lizzie and whispered, "What have you done?"

"What needed doing. Let us gather up this picnic."

"You are something, Lizzie. Really something." Sam put all four children on his horse, placed his gun and knapsack over his shoulder, and walked beside Lizzie toward the house.

"I can see and feel something very wrong between us." Sam sat in the yard at nightfall and watched the children chase the fireflies whose tiny blinking lights rose from the grass and into the trees.

Lizzie looked down at her clasped hands for a time. "Yes. When you left with Alexander for Colonel Coleman's Regiment, I signed papers for a divorce decree. You are a kind and good man, Sam. I am truly sorry. I am. Perhaps the war hardened me, or I took to extreme the views in Garrison's *Liberator* newspapers. I do not know. In any event, the year ends soon, and I plan to be at the judge's bench to see the decree finalized on the grounds you allied yourself with a band of horse thieves and abandoned your wife and two children." Her lips closed straight and firm. Her arms crossed against her chest.

"Such a sad day. You gave us no chance. I claim rights to my sons." Sam picked up his gun and walked into the woods.

"Miz Nesbit. We have a wounded man here. George Crawford." The stranger twirled his hat between his fingers.

"I know the name. Bushwhacking horse thief, as I recall."

"The one and the same. Claims he and Preston Edgar bought some horses over in Reynolds County from a man named Carson and then encountered some trouble with the Counts brothers."

"Take him into the cabin, yonder. My aunt and I will be there directly." Lizzie tied back her hair, placed the basket of wet laundry on the porch, and called to William. "Go for Aunt Betsy. Tell her we have a wounded man here."

She watched William run as fast as he could down the road the short distance to Aunt Betsy's house from his own, their home again in the hired hands' cabin. George ran his best but could not catch up, so he sat at the side of the road to pout and wait. After a short time he, William, and Aunt Betsy came into view.

"You boys will be doctors or never want to see another drop of blood. Only the Lord knows which. Hand me another compress, Georgie. Thank you, son."

"He's got a good chance." Aunt Betsy washed her hands in the tin wash pan and wielded bullet pincers toward the wounded man full of small shot. "Good thing the Counts brothers are loaded for small game instead of a Minie ball. Stole their horses, did you?"

Her patient gave a painful reply. "No. I bought horses at Mr. Carson's near Sinking Creek at Current River. He hired the Counts brothers to track the so-called thieves and return his two gray mares." [1.56]

She asked Aunt Betsy, "You want to keep him here or at your house?" Lizzie finished the stitches in the ripped flesh and turned to face her aunt. "There will be talk if he stays. I ignore talk. They say he is mean, but he would not be full of lead if angelic." Lizzie laughed at her own sayings as she washed and stowed her medical instruments.

"You stay close, then, my dear. We heard a ghost in the green room. Wanders down the stairs in a Confederate uniform, real slow like, and his saber clinks on the steps. Of course, the steps squeak, too." Aunt Betsy teased Lizzie and her sons, then laughed her full hearty chuckle.

"Thomas and James claim he wears a Federal's blue uniform." Lizzie confirmed the story already marched down the path. She led her aunt outside under the large welcoming elm.

Aunt Betsy said, "Could be either blue or gray, as only you and I know. A hundred years from now, my house will burn and Confederate buttons and Federal belt buckles will rise from the ashes and search for the spirits of the men we buried to save our own lives and those of our children. Mark my word. We will be found out."

"Perhaps. We did no wrong. However, in a hundred years, Georgie or Martha Belle's grandchildren will share our medical book. Someday we should tell them. For now, let William carry your basket. I added a bit of supper for you."

As she watched her aunt and son walk down the road, young Georgie climbed into her lap and pulled her face to look directly into his eyes. "Mama, do you know the good story about the ghost? Can we live here forever? But I miss Papa and our house on Sinking Creek."

Lizzie leaned her head back to watch the white puffy clouds drift overhead. "Shall we locate a blanket and find all kinds of cloud animals? Perhaps you can tell me a story about a cloud animal."

When the Union Army's strategy in the West rode the rivers and landed the final blows of war, Gen. M. Jeff "Swamp Fox" Thompson surrendered six thousand men at Jacksonport, Arkansas.

Alexander listened with great interest to General Thompson's remarks when he stepped forward to address his army. At what seemed the end of his speech, Alexander saw one of the brigade leaders whisper to the general.

General Thompson's eyes scanned the hundreds of men in gray and homespun who sat and stood as far as he could see from the knoll, which slanted down the land between the rivers to the Mississippi. Tattered and worn gray uniforms covered hosts of men, most with gaunt faces and dark sunken eyes, somewhere beyond saddened. Thompson pointed to the sad skeleton of a man to his right. "When the guerilla brigades cast their eyes on brave men in gray, they see a real soldier! Sacrifice, like this soldier with one arm and one leg!"

Alexander heard the Swamp Fox, known for his flamboyance and hot temper, but did not quite catch the meaning at first. He scanned those gathered. The guerilla bunch at the surrender, in fact, looked a sorry lot: ragged homespun shirts and trousers, barefooted—or same-as, from the looks of their boots—unkempt about their person, all wild haired and bearded, but not starved. The men in Colonel Coleman and General Freeman's Confederate regiments, diehard partisans all, knew how to live off the woods. The Swamp Fox's insult stung like a hornet.[2.80]

Alexander stayed to speak to Brig. Gen. Thomas R. Freeman, the last to surrender. Alexander removed his hat, stowed it under his arm, and saluted the fearless General. "General Freeman, my father fought with you since Wilson's Creek. Capt. Shadrach Chilton."

The General pointed northwest. "Your father was a fine man who loved a good fistfight, and won most of them, too. His Company B camps up the valley yonder. Colonel Coleman speaks well of his Shannon County men, as do I. You grew a spell since I last visited the family. Godspeed."

Alexander made his way northwest through the throng of surrendered men to find his deceased father's company. It did not take long to find Company B from the sounds of a friendly brouhaha, as if his fighting father were alive to captain it. Alexander walked to the edge of the ring of men who surrounded two men poised with fists and smiles, hankering to wrestle.

One man paused, stepped toward Alexander, extended his right hand, and embraced Alexander with his left. "Lieutenant Chilton. I rode with your father in the early days." The man turned to his leader. "Captain Chilton's son rides with Coleman. His father claimed him the fastest man in the country, especially through the woods!"

His father's replacement turned to the circle of men. He clutched a fistful of papers. "Reports arrived that surrenders are enacted by generals all across the South. Gen. Robert E. Lee surrendered the Army of North Virginia to General Grant; gets all the notoriety…and likely most of the reconstruction compensations. Dad-gum radical corruption everywhere, it is. Texas did not surrender. Many of our Missouri boys left for Texas with General Price or with General Shelby who refused to surrender. Confederate President Davis traveled to Cuba with his cabinet to regroup and return. Dismissed." Captain Cook stepped back.

Alexander tipped his hat to the captain and then to the captain's men. He stepped back instinctively when every man in the company rose to attention and snapped and held a salute in memory of a fallen leader, Capt. Shadrach Chilton. One man stepped forward and extended a gun with its scabbard. "I believe this rightly belongs to you. Nobody here knows how your father met his maker. Condolences."

Alexander instantly recognized the carving in the wooden gunstock. "My father's," he whispered. Tears welled up in his eyes, and his throat burned such that he could not speak. In a daze, he returned the salute with equal respect and shook the captain's hand. At first, his feet would not move, and then he gathered his wits. With a crisp turn, he walked alone, away from a handful of the remaining men who marched at his father's side and fought in battle at the foot of Bloody Hill at Wilson's Creek in Prairie Grove.

CHAPTER 10

BUSHWHACKERS—1866

And better I like to see her sit
alone in her easy chair
Her mein more pensive her cheek more pale
Busied with work that was telling a tale
Of a new-known pleasure and care. [2.31]

L izzie now lived alone in the cabin at Sinking Creek. She pulled the angle iron away from the fire and lifted the lid from the hot Dutch oven. She felt the steam cross her hands, and she dropped a handful of dried leaves into the hot water to steep.

Instantly alert when the barnyard gate slammed against its post, she dropped the lid, grabbed her gun, and blew out the lamp. She watched a man stomp across her porch and into the house. Recognizing the intruder, she un-cocked the gun. "Alexander, what in the world?"

Without a word, Alexander slung a newspaper across the table toward her. "*George Crawford*? *George Crawford*! What were you thinking?"

"The war ended over a year ago. We heard nothing from you since. What were *you* thinking?"

He stood his ground with a fixed stare and revealed little.

She yielded. "All right, George and Preston Edgar stole some horses and were shot. Edgar died and George lay badly wounded. The owners brought George to Aunt Betsy's for healing. We cut out the bullets, and he lived. I guess he sort of fell in love with me during his confinement."

"Your patients always fall in love with you. What about you? Did you love him?"

She looked around the room, thankful to spy the newspaper that probably reported George's death and his sins; that Sam claimed rights to her boys. She relit the lamp, set it on the table by her chair, and silently began to read. Shivers coursed through her frame, and the violent memories seared her forehead. In print forever, low life, lower than her mind could grip! Humiliation fueled the force of her hands that ripped and smashed the newspaper and hurled it into the fireplace. The fire caught, and the sheets of black crinkled ash floated briefly upward, then settled into the flames.

She turned to face her agitated guest. Pain dissolved and reality settled like the ashes. The man she treasured stood just across the room. Safe. Her breath slowed, her fists opened. The soft white palms of a healer lifted toward Alexander. "I declare. Gone for more than a year, you can at least sit down and drink some tea."

"Did you love him, a bushwhacker and a known horse thief?"

"I hear you turned bushwhacker and horse thief yourself!" Her anger refueled.

"True and not true, but I expect better for you."

She felt her defenses begin to crumble, so she walked to the stove, ladled wild and tame herb tea into two cups, calmly sat down at the table, and waited for him to take the chair across from her.

Silence fell heavy between them.

He sat his large frame in the smallish wooden chair and picked up the steaming cup. "Whew, strong leaf." The rich aroma filled his nostrils. He took a careful drink of the hot liquid.

"For the wounded." She twisted the cup in her hands, intent on the swirl of leaves. "George and I married and moved to Oregon County." Lizzie motioned to the fireplace. "You know I traveled with him when Mr. Young shot and killed him." She stopped, unable to confess the mistake of marriage for security. "For goodness' sake, we were married for only a couple of months." Her dark eyes flashed, but her shoulders sagged. "Where did you go?" A sob caught in Lizzie's throat. "When did you return?"

"Not soon enough." He stood with such force that the chair overturned and crashed against the wall. Four steps took him around the table to her side. His large hands covered her shoulders. He lifted her from the chair and into his arms. "Not soon enough."

The violence of his kiss cut her lip. His grip strengthened when she tried to pull away.

She pressed her hand along the outside of his arm, gently touched his face, and then yielded to the confusion and passion of the moment. "What happens here?"

No answer shouted every answer. Lizzie gasped when Alexander leaned slightly to the side, placed his arm under her knees, and swept her up and into the room across the dogtrot.

Alexander sat in the yard above Current River and waited for Lizzie to stir. He heard a soft step behind him and raised his hand high and back in the air.

She placed her hand in his, squeezed, and whirled around him and into his lap.

Alexander said, "I want to hear your side of the story of how George Crawford met his maker."

"Oh, for goodness sake. Let it be."

"I want to hear. The newspapers are unkind. I just need to know the truth."

She sought a more comfortable position and laid her head on his shoulder. She set her sights far into the morning forest as row after row of blue mountains pulled her into their distance. Fog nestled on the river. She began.

"A Mr. Young from Tennessee moved to a neighboring farm in Oregon County and pastured superior horses. George and I left one morning with a small herd toward the Arkansas market. We camped that night. He left the next morning before I woke, and I assumed he was buying more stock for the drive. He appeared at midday with Young's two mares, and we pressed on.

"Late that afternoon, Young stepped out of the woods into our path. 'Nothing in the world lower than a horse thief,' he said. He drew his pistol and pointed it toward George. Then he threw ropes at me, told me to catch and halter his horses and to make it quick.

"I caught his horses, twisted halters over their heads, and then tied the two lead ropes to a sapling. I searched out a fallen log for a boost and stalled to gather my thoughts. The leather squeaked like a hundred lashes as I pulled into the saddle.

"Bullets started to fly. George dropped to the ground, lifeless. Intent on the cash money it would bring to my sorry life, I suppose I brushed away the thought that George backtracked the night before and stole the horses.

"When Mr. Young tried to manhandle me, I kicked free, whirled my horse's hindquarters in his face, and nearly knocked him down. When he forced his way around, he made for my reins. I told him to keep his murdering hands off my Morgan. Furthermore, since he killed George, he could bury him.

"I turned with such flourish, it skittered his horses. I expected a shot in my back, but he howled with laughter. I grabbed one rein of George's horse, whistled the herd to get on, hightailed it north to Shannon County, and never looked back." [1.56]

Alexander twirled one black curl of her hair and then another. He knew she awaited his reaction because she sat warm, soft, and unmoving.

"Lizzie, you are something. Really something. And I am no damn good."

The following days, Alexander rode beside Lizzie on trails along the Current River and up Sinking Creek. Beautiful valleys awaited the farmer's plow. Springs trickled where new cabins could rise and restore community in the ravaged Current River valley. As lovers do, their hands stroked soft faces.

After bathing at the river one evening, they lay bare on a quilt spread on soft sand. Lizzie asked, "Where did you go the summer the war ended?"

"Many would brand me a traitor, but I did what I thought right for me and for Missouri. I signed into the newly formed 1865 Enrolled Missouri Militia. My service papers described me as six feet tall, two hundred pounds, fair complexion, brown hair and gray eyes. Fine specimen of a man." He paused. "I rode in troubled southwest bald knob country. Lord knows I spent many military days on the prairie and felt a draw to the troubled citizens there who kept stragglers alive. In the expanse of sky, one finds room to stretch the imagination."

"I do believe you because I love you. I knew your gentle ways, my dear, before the war. However, I also believe something more draws you to the southwest. The governor issued a warrant for your arrest, you know."

"So be it." He remained silent for a long time. "Many of the Union men signed for duty in the west; the likes of Federal General Davidson, to name one. I hold my vow to my fallen family as sacred. I killed two Federals in Indian Territory. One could call it brutal revenge. I confess my emotions cross that same fine line on sleepless nights."

"Or after terrifying nightmares interrupt sweet dreams?"

"There lays open my most private being."

Lizzie embraced him, wiped his eyes with her damp hair, and laid her head on his shoulder until the sun set behind the blue foggy mountains.

Alexander gave no ground when it came to the governor's new orders for a re-formed enrolled Missouri Militia to run him and his kind out of the border counties or "meet their fate."

Christmas night fell dark and stormy. Alexander and Joe Butler rode into crossfire just below Mahan's Creek. Bullets whizzed around them and riddled flesh. Since they rode the fastest horses in the county, they escaped to Aunt Betsy's kitchen. Alexander sent Perry to Joe's cabin to fetch Mary Louisa and hide the horses.

Perry left no more than five minutes with the lathered steeds before six militiamen rode into the yard; broke the hitching rail in their race to surprise and catch their prey. Alexander heard Aunt Betsy cover the secret trap with a rag rug after he and his wounded brother-in-law crawled into the hidey-hole under the kitchen floor.

He heard the soldiers force their way into the dogtrot from the front and the back doors.

From the click, click, click of her shoes, Alexander knew she marched with indignation and met them in the wide hallway. "When a gentleman comes to my home, I hear a knock at the door and entertain a semblance of decorum. Families celebrate the birth of our Savior. Sakes alive, why are you not in prayer? You dare frighten our children on Christmas Day!"

"Known to doctor both friend and foe, but every reason points to you harboring Alexander Chilton and Joe Butler. And search we shall, under the hands of martial law and justice, search for bushwhackers and thieves."

"In the name of common decency, come into my home with respect given to my neutral hands in their attempt to heal. I never turn their ministration to improve one's injured state over to your 'brand of justice.'"

"Mrs. Chilton, one of my men took shot during the chase. We request he stay with you to remove the bullets and stay until he heals. He speaks broken English. Does anyone in the house speak German? A fine officer, he schooled and trained in Berlin, similar to our own West Point."

"No. Only English spoken here, but as some would say, not the King's English. Place him in the room to the right. He will leave here under his own energy. You shot and killed all the men folk of this house who might bring you word of his recovery, so leave his horse for such purposes."

"Leave his horse unattended? It would be the last time the militia set eyes on it."

"In that case, take your man with you and pray he survives the journey."

Undeterred by Aunt Betsy, he said, "Speaking of folk, Private, bring the lieutenant's pack, including his volkszither."

Alexander heard the militiamen's boots tromp into her bedroom and begin a search of the house room by room, but evidently, they found no sign of the two men on notice. The exit of boots and sound of horse hooves on the move indicated they soon gave chase down the river road.

Aunt Betsy and the others worked as quickly as possible to bring Alexander and Joe from under the shallow dusty space under the house. "Shush," Aunt Betsy whispered and pointed to the room across the hall.

Alexander nodded. He and his cousins half pulled and half-lifted Joe to the kitchen floor. It would be touch and go even if Aunt Betsy's experienced hands found Joe's pulse.

Alexander stumbled with help to the all-too-familiar daybed by the stove. After two hours or more, he seemed saved. Five bullets lay in the pan. Bandages covered his arms, legs, and shoulders; the critical belly and chest spared.

He caught a glimpse of his aunt as she carried hot water and medical bag to her bedroom across the hall to tend to the wounded soldier.

Perry whispered, "When sounds of soldiers on patrol faded, I carefully recrossed the river to deliver Mary Louisa to Joe's bedside. It took more than an hour because Mary Louisa soon expects Joe's child." Joe Butler, sweet on Mary Louisa long before he came calling in the summer of 1866, married her with Alexander's blessing.

From the familiar daybed by Aunt Betsy's stove, Alexander watched his friend, comrade-in-arms, and brother-in-law, Joe Butler, die in his wife's arms on Christmas Day, 1866. Alexander wept for his friend, his sister, and their unborn child.

After the wake for Joe Butler, the family gathered at the home of Aunt Betsy. She walked to Lizzie's side. "The soldier's wounds need extra care. Can you stay for a time?"

Lizzie tended the wounded Federal soldier who lay dying in the bedroom across the hall from the large kitchen. She said, "Please drink the broth. You need strength and many liquids to wash away the swelling."

In broken English, he said, "I lie dying. This I know. Please accept my volkszither. Your singing and its strings you play so beautifully gave ease to my painful days. Join your family in mourning Herr Butler. Your secret dies with me."

"You rest now and take sips as you can. We will sing together again on a happier day." She patted the soldiers shoulder and walked across the hall into the kitchen. When she met Aunt Betsy's gaze, she shook her head side to side as if to say, "No hope."

She filled a plate of food and returned to sit with the soldier. "Nobody should die alone. Nobody," she whispered.

She sat the night with the soldier, who died before dawn. While all were asleep, she removed his Union Army uniform and placed it on his boots. She covered him with a sheet for burial in a grave dug during the January thaw between the house and the barn, beside two others.

Aunt Betsy tiptoed into the room, nodded at the uniform, and whispered, "Between the walls." She knelt beside Lizzie and said a bedside prayer for his soul's journey to his maker and for wisdom as to the best story to tell, should his captain return.

The two widows, Lizzie and Mary Louisa, awaited the birth of Mary Louisa's baby daughter, Perneice Josephine Butler, born May 1867.

Lizzie heard steps on the porch and familiar little voices. "Mama, Mary Louisa. We came to see the baby and Francis Marion, too."

"George! William!" She embraced her sons with the fervor of joy.

"Good day, Lizzie. I thought it a good time for a visit." Sam stood on the porch, a bit unsure of his welcome.

"Oh, for goodness' sake, Sam, come in." Lizzie led Sam and their sons across the dogtrot where Mary Louisa and her young son, Francis, sat beside a cradle.

Mary Louisa lay radiant, all propped comfortably with pillows. "She came easy—healthy and beautiful. I named her Perneice Josephine after Joe and his mother."

"Hold her. Hold her." Francis asked, and patted the baby, protective and proud.

Sam sat on the bed beside Mary Louisa and lifted the blanket to touch the tiny toes. "A fine girl. Favors Joe, some."

"Mama says to watch the soft spot." William moved closer to his father to see the baby.

"Can we be next, Papa?" George seemed quite taken with the infant and looked up at Lizzie for help on his behalf.

Sam answered, "Surely and soon. You go visit with William and your mother. I will be in shortly."

Lizzie turned from the sweet scene, smiled a knowing smile, and murmured, "Kind Sam, and needy widow."

She called everyone to the kitchen to take a meal. She noticed Sam set the baby by his chair and help Mary Louisa into hers.

Sam brought news of family from the Jacks Fork community where he settled on a farm up Shawnee Creek. "All healthy and busy. As to local news, word passed around over the county for a mass meeting of all voters for selecting county officers to serve until elections. On the day set for the meeting, a large majority of the men in Shannon County reported. Someone called the meeting to order and selected officials to preside. The chairman rose to outline the purpose and the procedure to follow and to offer some suggestions as to how the county government financed until assessments and taxes collected.

"The chairman said, 'Owing to the destruction and disastrous results of the war, and the fact Shannon County suffered from bands of robbers to such an extent, no one has money enough to finance any sort of business. Even the consideration of securing a loan for temporary operations would be useless.'

"As the discussion went on, someone asked, 'Where is Alex Deatherage? He told me he wanted to be here for sure.'

"About that time, Alex Deatherage rode up, dismounted, tied his horse, and entered the meeting. He walked over to the chairman and laid the treasurer's book on the table, set a sack on top of it, and remarked, 'Here's the book and gold coin just as they were when I left here four years ago. I beg you appoint a committee to audit same.'

"In the selections of officers, Alex Deatherage again served as county treasurer. Just where he stashed the book and money during the war, no one but Alex Deatherage knows. [1.134]

"Someone said, 'We need to rebuild the courthouse and the jail, but I propose we select a more central location in the county than the Round Spring burned-out valley. Trouble is, very few properties claim clear title.'

"Thomas J. Chilton spoke up. 'I own clear title to my land. If the citizens so vote, I could deed forty or fifty acres for a new town fronting Jacks Fork, if we can find a judge and a courthouse still standing in the state to record it.' Well, after a good laugh, people took the opportunity and voted for the Chilton site; voted to keep the name of the town as Eminence even though it would lie in a valley.

"Alexander Chilton suggested we needed a general store and a saloon, and offered to pursue funds."

"Now that would be like a chicken guarding the corn," Lizzie said. "You boys get your bedrolls and spread them before dark. You might find eggs in the chicken coop. Here's a basket."

She noticed Sam's gaze at the grapevine basket he fashioned for her before the war, then the shake of his head and his turn toward Mary Louisa to help her lift the baby to her lap. She wondered at the warm feelings between her, Sam, and Mary Louisa. Most people would conjure anger, jealousy, or remorse. Lizzie considered her sons lucky if Mary Louisa married Sam. Lucky indeed.

Alexander listened to stories and told a few of his own on the newly built porch of Freeman's store, saloon, and law office in the new Eminence on Jacks Fork River. Although most called him Colonel

Freeman, he attained the rank of General by war's close. More than a year passed since the surrender and the only talk: war stories and politics.

Shannon County, among others in south Missouri, went unrepresented in the legislature due to lack of voting processes and qualified northern-sympathy voters; accusations swelled of voter registration manipulation by the radicals.

Alexander set the evening jug on the porch floor of the new Eminence saloon. "When General Freeman moved his field of battle from North Arkansas to Shannon County Courtroom, he determined his young adult children soon join him. A. J. P. Deatherage served with him since sixty-one. Both lawyers, they argued their points well into the battlefield nights. They now share a legal shingle, a general store, and a saloon. Alfred, his partner in war and partner in peace."

Alexander liked General Freeman's saloon duties, and the rewards were of no complaint. His friend and new brother-in-law, George Davis, who married Susannah Chilton Orchard, kept the Freeman store in the next room. The war claimed her first husband.

Standing in the doorway between the two rooms, George started the ongoing verbal spar. "You need to learn storekeeper duties. I can keep the saloon from time to time."

"Keep talking, George. It might happen someday." Alexander paused. "When I lose my taste for whiskey." He burst into laughter and slapped George's back.

In the quiet moments that followed, Alexander wondered why the peace of an early evening porch left him with such anxious emptiness. It always begged the same answer. "All gone, all of them gone."

He picked up the jug to fill the space. "Colonel Coleman commanded our regiment until the close. We all miss the colonel. But then, we do claim a general!

"Monks, a major now. Politics got him assigned by the governor to clean 'em out. Raids general stores, appropriates the land and the houses of helpless women and children. We stand in his path, boys. Vigilance,

George. Monks needs provisions and we are a long ride from Howell County. Claims bushwhacker gangs ride about worse than horse thieves; vows to run us out of Shannon and Oregon County." Alexander chuckled.

"Monks avoided the march of the eleven to Salem in sixty-two, and saved his sorry self from me till now. Monks' new braggarts raise the ire to such levels, he may never leave Oregon County alive. I feel better already." Alexander took another draw from the jug, stepped off the porch, and nearly stumbled. "Plan Monks' humiliation someday soon. Someday soon. How about it, George?"

"I expect more gentlemanly talk from you, Alexander. A businessman must mind his manners." Alexander's mother walked from behind her wagon and linked her arm through that of her son.

"Hello, Mama, I'm no businessman. I'm a barkeep!" Alexander picked up his mother and spun her around.

"Alexander. Put me down and do not sip the profits. Colonel Freeman and I insist!" His mother's eyes snapped, then she laughed and chided, just like old times.

He knew he talked too much with the drink. However, when his mind stayed active, it did not punish him so. General Freeman chided him lately for the drink. Said he saw survivor's guilt in many a man caught in circumstances no human could control.

He felt hopelessly tangled in the names and relationships of family and friends, of traumatic events of the past six years; he felt he was losing his mind in all the details that swept over his thinking that made no sense whatsoever to others who listened to his diatribes. He could not stop the onslaught in his mind.

"William was the best of us," he uttered before he passed out cold.

In 1867, with the first dry goods store and saloon in Eminence, Saturdays marked an exciting occasion for the town and surroundings. Alexander caught a glimpse of Aunt Betsy and Anne walk into the store from his vantage point in the saloon.

"Missus Chilton, how may I help you? Anne? Here, bolt goods, just arrived." Colonel Freeman's son, Marion, reached for a soft blue-and-white striped fabric and laid it on the counter between him and Aunt Betsy Chilton and her daughter, Anne, age sixteen. "And this one?"

Aunt Betsy ran her hand over the blue-striped fabric. "Oh, my. So fine and smooth. This dark purple, almost as lovely a color as the plums at my back fence. Show me the black one on the left." Aunt Betsy exclaimed, "I do believe these the finest spun yarns I ever swept my hand across. Anne?"

"The blue for a skirt would be very nice, Mother. It may be the finest in the store." She turned to the young store clerk. "Thank you, Marion. Your artistic eye for my first-ever England-weave fabric proves welcome."

"Come around the counter and see the other selections."

Alexander thought Marion smitten by Anne. He walked through the door between the two establishments. "Annie, are you old enough to start sparking in a store-bought dress?"

"With someone Mother approves, perhaps I am. But she offers no approval for scallywags the likes of you, cousin." Anne skipped to Alexander's side and kissed him on the cheek. "I can load the sugar, Mother. Thank you, Marion. Thank you for the kiss, Alexander."

Alexander heard Marion mutter under his breath, "Lucky devil."

"My mail, please, Mr. Freeman," said Aunt Betsy. She winked at Alexander.

Perry Chilton stepped into the store with Emmaline Freeman's hand in the crook of his arm. "Hey, cousin," he said to Alexander.

"Good morning, Emmaline. Perry," said Alexander. He winked back at Aunt Betsy. "Out for a stroll in the growing village of Eminence?"

Before anyone could answer, Alexander heard a ruckus outside and stepped to the porch with Marion and George to check the matter.

"Soldiers, and both of Colonel Freeman's offspring in the store," he muttered. "Get inside Marion, now! Keep the women inside."

Alexander recognized Maj. "Billy" Monks and some of the fifteen soldiers. He knew their mission: pursue, arrest, and drive out known bushwhackers. He also knew Monks and his men brought in few prisoners, a formal accusation by Confederate Colonel Freeman and rebuffed by Federal Colonel Livingston during the war.

"Alexander Chilton. George Davis. We are here to take your test oath."

Alexander walked from the porch onto the wood plank walk and pulled papers from his pants pocket. "I took the oath. Here are my papers."

"Sergeant, examine the papers. George Davis failed to take the oath."

George came at a run from the store. "I will take your oath. I will sign, and so will all the other people in town, so your return to our town proves unnecessary for all time."

The sergeant said, "Cool down, lad. Bring a table for the signing."

George went into the store for a table and a chair for the soldier.

Major Monks led the townspeople in the Ironclad Oath and took the chair opposite the citizens to make their marks or signatures. Then he stood and shouted, "We confiscate the goods of rebels and bushwhackers. Seize the goods! Arrest Chilton, and take Davis for questioning!"

Alexander bolted and moved through the crowd in a run. Protected from soldiers' view by the citizens, he escaped into the woods behind the store, passed the general's home in a run, crossed the creek, and followed the valley's creek to the river.

He knew George remained inside the store while soldiers carried off the goods. Monks used the excuse of two bushwhackers he vowed to run out of Shannon County to punish his old archenemy who owned the Eminence store and saloon.

Alexander heard horses ahead of him on the trail downriver. As he topped the last ridge, he saw smoke and flames engulf his childhood home, one mile or so south of the new Eminence.

"The war ended, Monks. Your treason? Crimes against humanity!" Alexander did not care whether his shouts carried to the valley. All he could imagine was the sound of cheering soldiers and the sight of his mother, sisters, nieces and nephews standing in the yard as they held each other and wept, all possessions and provisions destroyed by flames that scorched the skies above.

After he waited for the soldiers to leave, and dusk to approach, Alexander helped his distraught family take refuge at the neighboring farm of Aunt Betsy. He hid in the woods nearby. Father and brothers dead, he must stay alive.

When the house quieted, Lizzie wiped her forehead with her apron and settled in a chair in the yard where she lived alone at Sinking Creek. "Alexander, come in. What news of home?"

"Colonel Monks, now appointed major, says the governor sent him to Shannon, Oregon, and Dent counties with orders to be rid of bushwhackers. I must leave here. My presence brings certain danger to my family and my friends. He burned us out."

"Where do you plan to go? How far must you go to avoid recognition? Get tracked down?"

"Little Dixie. General Freeman gave me a letter of introduction. Come with me, Lizzie. I loved you the first time I saw you twirl in a yellow birthday dress, hardly more than thirteen, when you came here from Tennessee.

"Mother, Elizabeth, Paulina, Mary Louisa, Perneice, Francis Marion, Sam, and your boys must leave with us. We make a confused family to others, but we know our places; learned to dance long ago as friends and family. If you agree, we can marry up north because Monks cannot know about the marriage and hold you responsible for me. I need you. You can live with your sons, at last."

CHAPTER 11

NORTH TO LITTLE DIXIE—1867

In the fall of 1867, the counties of Oregon and Shannon were still controlled by those roving bands of outlaws who ruled the counties with an iron hand. A despotism, unequalled at any stage of the war, existed there. During my march and stay...I had driven out the worst set of bushwhackers, thieves and murderers that ever lived.
—William Monks, Major, Missouri State Militia [1.4]

The Chilton-Nesbit families settled in Little Dixie, north of the Missouri River in Concordia, Lafayette County, west of Boonville. One day, Lizzie heard a knock at the door. She assessed the scruffy citizen on the other side and said "Good afternoon."

"Hello, ma'am. Is Lieutenant Chilton here?"

"No. May I help you?"

"Yes, you give him this letter. Cap'm said it was highly confra... confra —denchial, ma'am."

"I will see he reads it forthwith."

The man in the bushwhacker relay left the porch. She locked the door, flung herself on the bed, and cried herself into a desperate state.

"Lizzie, what goes on here?" Alexander entered Lizzie's small bedroom.

"I am going with you. I can ride and shoot. Moreover, if you are shot, I can see you do not die. The letter no doubt tells you what direction we take, come morning."

Alexander slowly opened the letter, hesitated, and looked at her a long sad time. Then he read the letter. The next morning, he closed his affairs, bade family Godspeed, packed provisions and bedrolls, and headed east-northeast. Lizzie rode by his side.

Lizzie returned without Alexander some months later. She related the details of their journey to her family in Concordia. "We travelled up the Mississippi and stopped at Illinois River towns. Then we headed back on inland trails. I never knew whether we were the hunter or the hunted. I spent hours in the woods along the Illinois River, alone with my music, the wind, water, and land as flat as a millpond. He tracked his quarry but lost the trail in mid-Illinois.

When we reached the confluence of the Illinois and Mississippi above St. Louis, I knew. Living on the run took its toll on me, and Alexander wanted to travel fast. He turned east from Boonville. I came west and home to Concordia and all of you."

Lizzie waited.

Alexander knocked on the door of the dilapidated house on Biddle Street, between Seventeenth and Eighteenth in the Ninth Ward of St. Louis. "Is Mr. Smith home?"

A woman opened the door a mere crack. "Sorry, sir, Mr. Smith and his family moved out some time ago."

"Any word of his destination, since this letter concerns him?" Alexander removed a letter from his vest pocket.

"Upriver to the rapids or down to Memphis, most likely. He works the riverboats, you know."

"Thank you, madam. I will try the freight companies at the landing."

Alexander picked his way through the mud and mire to firm ground where flies swarmed the putrid air and dodged his horse's tail for a time. If meager funds allowed, comforts of a riverboat passage would be welcome change from the trail. In the spring of 1868, St. Louis streets to the river held more beings than a horse could safely push along.

He dismounted, tied his horse to a crowded hitching rail, and walked down the steep cobblestone-lined banks of the Mississippi. The first steam wheeler scheduled up the Mississippi left the following week. One downriver left two weeks hence. Passage took nearly every coin in his pocket, so he sold his horse for a good price. He worked wharfer duties prior to departure and signed on as dishwasher and cook in the galley to defray expenses.

"I will take the large poster you refer to as an Illuminated Roster of Glover's Cavalry, Third Regiment Missouri Volunteers. Union, yes, that one, 1860–62." He quickly spotted the names of Captain Bradway, Lt. Herbert Reed, and the soldiers in the command. He paid the vendor, rolled the large poster like a scroll, and tucked it under his arm. Then he added, "By any chance did you print Captain Avery's Third Regiment Roster from 1862?" [3.25]

The vendor replied, "Not today, but if available, can you come back tomorrow? Wonderful celebration of the Grand Army veterans, no?"

"Grand celebration. I appreciate your kind services. On the morrow, then." Alexander tipped his hat and moved down the busy walkway. With the Glover and Avery rosters, the revenge list was complete.

Unused to crowded spaces, he welcomed late-night trips to the top deck. The lonely troubled sound of water cut and splashed by the big wheeler matched his mood. He rolled a smoke and took in the expanse of a midnight sky that stretched from horizon to horizon of flat prairie land. Although muddy and wide, the familiar smells of a river tapped thoughts of home. He disembarked at Quincy, Illinois, and made his way to the local newspaper office.

"Can I help you, sir?" The newspaperman wiped ink from his hands and laid the stained cloth on the counter.

"I want to talk to your editor, Mr. Lacy."

"Not here. Sold the paper and headed west."

"Do you know his destination?"

"Not for the likes of you. Now please excuse me and move along."

Alexander reached across the counter and grabbed the newspaperman's shirt in a twisted wad. He lifted him so they were nose to nose. "I asked you politely, and now I am telling you. Give me Lacy's destination. I traveled many days and mean the man no harm. But I must talk with him."

"I don't know the exact city, but Colorado. That is the truth of it. Please put me down, now."

Alexander let the man go and gave him a push backward, fully confident the man lied. Further inquiries around the town square gave even less satisfaction, so he turned his horse northeast toward Chicago. David Smith and Captain Avery reportedly removed to Illinois. The Seventeenth Illinois and Illinois members of Seventh Kansas most likely returned to Winnetka, the rough and tumble home of their youth. Alexander knew the faces of the other two men who shot down his Reed cousins; each would answer for his deeds.

He pressed his horse on the trail. Unlike Alexander, a man of means could travel by rail.

"Captain Avery, madam." Alexander stood with respect, hat in hand, at the home of a man he saw many times at a distance, but never met.

"May I give your name, sir?"

"Alexander Chilton, Lt. Alexander Chilton."

"Wait here, please."

Alexander stepped into the hallway of the clean modest home of a man he resented less and less since August 1862. Capt. William S. Avery led the Third Missouri Cavalry, USA, on sortie after sortie into the Current River valleys with orders to arrest and kill southern sympathizers and known bushwhackers such as himself.

"Mr. Chilton, we chased the likes of you for the better part of four years."

"I mean you no harm, Captain. I aim to square the damage done my family in ways fair to all concerned."

"Step to the porch and take a chair." Avery motioned to a chair near the end rail and took the one most near the door.

"What is your story, son?"

"In 1862, you handed command to Lieutenant Lacy at Salem for transport of six prisoners to Rolla for questioning. Senator Joshua Chilton and events surrounding his death likely stand out in your memory."

"Yes, I remember the case; regrettable affair. Perhaps you hold judgment for my decision?"

"For a year or more, I took a shot at every blue coat that moved across my sights. Four years of war gave me a more logical mind. I need to hear your regrets and perhaps find some semblance of peace to give the widows. More than half the men in my family are dead, none at the hand of battle but of senseless bushwhackers, uniformed all. Uncle Joshua recognized you and three guards as Masons, and he believed that under your honor-bound authority we could reach Rolla for fair judgment. More than a hundred men stood guard over us." Alexander took a deep breath and calmed himself.

"Alexander Chilton, yes. Your brother was also killed while attempting escape, as I recall."

"Not so, Captain. Two guards held him behind the main column and shot him dead at close range. I alone escaped. A tragedy for the eleven killed."

"What do you want from me? Apology? True, a Mason vows honor to kill a fellow Mason only at direct order. I passed authority to Lieutenant Lacy, an honorable man well known to me. Apology may be due if Lacy, a recently promoted lieutenant, lost influence with the guards. Now, I do not say that is the case, but if so in any small measure, I offer my apology. War's a bad business. Bad business. The sooner we put it behind us, the better for all concerned." Avery paused for several minutes. "Names of the guards and whereabouts of Lacy are unknown to me. Lt. Herbert Reed met his maker in the Battle of Little Rock. Now, I bid you good day and Godspeed." The captain stood and offered a handshake.

Alexander sat for what seemed a lifetime and twirled his hat in his hands. He rose from his chair, stood tall, and reached for the offered hand. He met the gaze of the captain. Surprise and sadness swept his heart when he saw the captain's face awash in tears. "Godspeed, sir. Thank you for your time."

He made a solemn vow to Aunt Betsy, and he determined to stick with it. Captain Avery was not the man responsible. Avery same as confessed he turned over command because he was a Mason and refused to follow ill-advised orders to kill a fellow Mason in cold blood.

Alexander gave no such latitude to David Smith. *"David Smith, doom gathers in a race to your miserable cowardice, and vengeance is mine."* He removed the mysterious letter from his vest pocket. It read, *"David Smith. Rock River Freight Company. Rockford, Illinois."* Alexander referenced his map and headed his horse westward from Chicago for a drink of Rock River.

Alexander rode into the small river town of Rockford, Illinois. He signed the hotel register "James Alexander."

The following morning he sought and found work as a stevedore. Hard work—good work for a tormented soul. He fell into a rented bed at the back of the warehouse, exhausted. Soon might come the day to avenge his brother and uncle. Kill David Smith.

Late one afternoon, boat loaded, Alexander walked the decks of the riverboat and the ferry nearby, eyes peeled for Smith. He stopped, took two steps back, and saw a heavily bearded man wearing glasses and a wide-brimmed hat. David Smith! Alexander crept down the deck, head ducked to avoid recognition himself. He followed the bearded man into the passageway to the engine room. He heard running steps behind him.

"Hey, you, there. No passengers below decks." A sweaty, grime-covered man motioned him out.

"Yes, sir." Alexander turned and ran up the steep stairs into the passageway and onto the deck. He looked left and right. Nothing. Water lapped against the boat. When he scanned the crowded landing, people were hurrying this way and that, climbing into buggies and wagons.

"BLAAAAAT." The steam whistle jarred the air. "All ashore that's going ashore."

Alexander ran down the plank and pushed his way toward the main avenue to the rocky landing, Smith nowhere in sight.

Then he realized where he earlier saw the bearded man several times—the Rockford ferry.

He went to the warehouse, gathered his belongings and pay due him, and chose one of two roads out of Rockford. His vigil proved in vain, so he returned to the town and slowly traveled each street until he reached the edge. He saw a woman sweep the porch of an empty house. "Howdy, ma'am. This house for rent?"

"Yes, sirree, lad. Family just vacated bound for who knows where."

"If they left remainder rent, I would sure appreciate the offer."

"Rent? People left owing, said they would make it right by mail. You a bounty hunter, mister?"

"Not exactly, but people make interesting study. No?" Without further word, he turned his mount around and searched each main road at an easy gallop. Nothing. He next checked steamers with passengers embarking since Smith's disappearance: two small steamers, one freight-only; the other with passengers two hours later, bound for points southwest. Alexander noted the route posted at the ticket office and began the long journey down the Rock River in pursuit.

He traveled the length of the Rock River to the Mississippi. Along the way, he found traces of three wagons hired within reasonable days from river and land travel to the Illinois River. He chose to travel westward to ports on the Mississippi River. He sold his horse, stowed his tack, and waited for a steamer to St. Louis scheduled within the week.

Occasionally people would gather on the deck and listen to his guitar. He did not consider himself much of a singer, but with a whiskey or two, he judged his talents improved considerably. The stars blinked appreciation.

From St. Louis, Alexander took passage up the Missouri to Concordia, Lafayette County, and returned to his Lizzie, mother, and sisters in the home of Sam Nesbit.

Lizzie and little Clementine sauntered down the dusty path to the shed that served as a barn for the milk cow and two horses. She helped her daughter to the board fence and removed her mittens. "Hold the apple and then make your hand very flat like a johnnycake. We don't want Nonie to eat fingers for supper."

"Nonie, Nonie. Apple." Clementine delighted in the horse she claimed as her own. She squealed when the young horse tickled her palm with his lips in pursuit of apple slices.

"More. More."

"One for Clementine, one for Nonie." Lizzie sliced the apple and tossed the core to the garden.

"Whoa!" Lizzie felt arms encircle her, lift her into the air, and swing her high in a circle. "Alexander! God is my hope! Alexander!"

When he set her down, she turned in his arms and cried tears of joy that salted their kisses. "Home, home to me at long last." She gasped when he swept her into his arms and kissed her with unbridled passion.

After her feet touched the ground, she straightened her skirt and tucked her hair back into the snood. She said, "Here stands a young lady I want you to meet. Clementine."

Alexander squatted to study the tiny girl, the very image of Lizzie. Brown curls, dark blue eyes, and a creamy complexion peeked out of her knitted wool hat. From her sleeves emerged tiny, dimpled hands.

"Papa home?" Clementine studied the man's face and then looked at her mother for direction.

"Papa came home. He likes big hugs." Lizzie leaned to touch Clementine's shoulders and urged her toward Alexander.

"Big hugs, Clementine." Alexander picked up his daughter and tossed her curls from her face. "My Clementine?" he inquired of her mother.

"Your Clementine."

Arm in arm, Alexander and Lizzie walked the half mile to the Missouri River and sat on the bank high above the brown boiling swirls of the Big Muddy.

"Fro wocks in ribber." Clementine threw stones and grass into the wind and water, while her parents enjoyed the silence and warmth of her father's homecoming.

"And what of your trip?" Lizzie ventured into troubled waters.

"I truly regret I was not here for the birth. Left you to the tongue-waggers. I stand shamed. What do you say?"

"I introduce myself as Elizabeth Clementine Chilton. 'My husband,' I say, 'is away at this time.' You once proposed marriage and I missed my chance. No blame falls upon you. I feel no regret for our precious baby girl. Now, what of your trip?"

"Smith worked on the ferryboat in Rockford, Illinois. He disguised himself with a beard and glasses but spotted me before I saw him. I suppose he knew I was about and packed his family ready for a quick getaway. He disappeared and I tracked him to St. Louis where the trail went cold. I found clues. Most likely he traveled on a steamer bound for New Orleans."

"But you came home. I'm so happy you came home to me."

"Come with me to New Orleans. You love riverboats. I can work at the docks or the harvest and save enough for the boys, too. Marry me."

"Wife and children with a man hunter to New Orleans on a, um, an adventure?"

"Start packing for an adventure, woman. Bring your banjo. Singers on the big steamers below St. Louis wear red satin dresses and put feathers in their hair."

"Would we make a sight? William and George play a little banjo, and Clementine sings her heart out. Not a word or tune you ever heard. Now, seriously, Alexander."

"Seriously. Marry me. Come with me. You travel safe with me."

Alexander and Lizzie married on December 28, 1868 in Lafayette County. [2.22]

Alexander watched his mother's face turn from joy to fear as she read a letter from her eldest daughter, Susannah Orchard Davis, and laid the letter on the table. "Susannah and George buried a stillborn daughter two months ago. She finds herself with child again and asks me to come home to Shannon County."

Alexander said, "You are too fragile for travel, but I hold no doubts regarding her delicate condition."

His mother turned her gaze on her daughter, Mary Louisa, who responded, "I will go. Elizabeth can stay and help Mother. Lizzie?"

Lizzie thought for a moment then said, "Of course we must go. Ready my packhorse."

Alexander led Lizzie, young George, and Mary Louisa to Shannon County. He kept to the old trails in fear of discovery because anarchy prevailed in the border counties as 1869 radical politics further stirred troubled waters. After seeing them settled, he embraced his wife and sisters and left his beloved Jack Fork river valley for parts best left unspoken.

In the summer of 1870, he galloped the familiar trail to his home-place to carry Lizzie, George, Mary Louisa, and James Shadrach "Jess" Orchard back to Lafayette County. He found himself unprepared to deliver his mother news of home when they arrived in Little Dixie.

He set the brake on the wagon and helped the women to the ground. "George, fine lad, secure the horses to the rail."

"Yes, sir, Alexander. Then I will bring the family to the porch to hear the devastating news."

Lizzie sighed, "Oh, Georgie." She squeezed Mary Louisa's hand and made her way toward the chairs on the porch. Before she reached the steps, the entire family poured from the house with noisy greetings.

Alexander led his mother up the steps and to a chair on the porch.

His mother drew her grandson close. "Jess, you came for a visit—such makes me more than happy! And what news of Susannah, the baby, and George Davis?"

Mary Louisa quickly sat at her mother's feet and spoke softly. "Susannah and the baby died at the birth. Aunt Betsy said it was too near the loss of the last baby. Lizzie says her blood likely does not mix with George's and it poisoned her and both babies. George is inconsolable."

"What more grief must we bear before broken asunder? Come, Jess." Patsy rose from her chair and led her orphaned grandson into the house.

When Alexander heard the soft sounds of his mother's voice float through the doorway, he remembered and spoke from her store of wisdom. "Grief is best borne in service to others."

Lizzie found Mary Louisa and Sam on the porch. She never argued with Sam because he refused to fight. A trip to New Orleans with Alexander was another matter.

No fight, Sam simply refused. "The boys stay with me. You and Alexander are unpredictable as individuals and nigh on dangerous together." Sam turned to his task to carve a twisted limb into a walking stick.

Lizzie retorted, "You decide before you hear any detail of the plans, the education, and the adventure? New Orleans? The ocean?"

Silence.

She turned to her cousin. "Mary Louisa?"

"The boys love the river here. We can catch a riverboat to Jefferson City. Education, adventure, and no gu...no cooped-up hours in a boat cabin." Mary Louisa leaned toward Sam's view in this matter.

Lizzie often depended on Mary Louisa to see the situation from a woman's point of view, and the two of them to persuade Sam toward compromise. Compromise, the art of this deal played in Sam's favor.

Sam said, "I know the advantages, but travel for a year or more? Too long from a father's influence. Too long. The boys stay here with me and Mary Louisa in a loving, peaceful home."

CHAPTER 12

INTO THE DEEP
SOUTH—1871

Or work forgotten —her dark eyes closed—
Her fancy with sweet dreams rife,
Of a tiny form by her arm caressed,
A baby face to her bosom pressed—
The mother, as well as the wife. [2.31]

In 1871, Alexander purchased passage for three, and prepared to board a steamboat for St. Louis.

"I love you, William. I love you, George. Goodbye and Godspeed." Lizzie expected William to pull away and turn around without a word or sign of his feelings, but six-year-old George's response floored her.

"Goodbye, Mother. Our boat trip to Jefferson City comes soon with no worry of bullet shots from the viper, David Smith, or the guards." George turned to rebuff Lizzie's kiss, only to plant one on Clementine's cheek. "Godspeed, sweet sister, and mind Mama. You hear?"

"Bye-bye, Geo, bye-bye, Will." Clementine covered her ears at the sound of the riverboat's whistle and then scrambled up the plank with glee, nearly lost in the skirts of other passengers. "Tina gone!"

Lizzie watched Patsy's face lose all its color.

Alexander settled himself, a bit uncomfortable at a bona fide poker table with a dealer. He looked to his left, then to his right, wondering if either man was a professional gambler. Each certainly looked downright dapper. He knew firsthand how gamblers frequented riverboats and separated a poker player from his money. This trip would be different. He stacked his chips on the table.

"Five Card Stud. Place your bets." The dealer dealt everyone a down card. Then an up card.

The betting started with the best hand showing. Alexander, with an ace, bet ten dollars.

The betting continued until the last card fell.

Alexander drew a pair of aces and a pair of queens showing. "Raise you a hundred dollars."

Everyone folded except a man with an eight, nine, ten, and a jack of diamonds showing.

"Raise fifty."

"I call," Alexander said.

The man turned over the seven of diamonds and tucked it under the eight. "Straight flush."

Alexander pushed away from the table and turned over his seven of diamonds.

"Barker." The dealer stood. "To the back room. No trouble here."

Alexander felt his elbows pulled to his back, saw a man disable "the winning hand" in the same way. Then Alexander, "the winning hand," and their escorts followed the dealer and the barker to a room at the back. He watched the dealer hand the game's deck, the winning cards, and Alexander's cards to a fleshy man who smoked a cigar.

The man laid his cigar in a fancy ashtray. Smoke circled to the ceiling. "Both of you prepare to disembark at the next dock. Meanwhile, the chips on the table are frozen. Most times, both players remain dockside. This matter is closed. Any further action or discussion on your part will be pursued with diligence by this line and proper authorities."

Alexander looked into the eyes of "the winning hand," and held an emotionless gaze until the man looked at the dealer, nodded his head, and exited. Alexander walked out the door and found himself escorted to his room.

"My, my. Back so soon?" Lizzie teased her sober husband.

"Met a winning hand. Shall we sing a song and tell a story?" He looked at Clementine who lay sound asleep on the small trundle.

"Or something?" He flashed Lizzie his sideways grin, pulled her from her chair, and leaned her back with a passionate kiss.

Near dawn, Alexander heard a knock at the door. "Breakfast, sir."

"One moment." Alexander pulled on his pants, tucked a pistol in his belt at his back, and opened the door.

"On the table here?"

"Yes. And thank you." Alexander tipped the steward and closed the door behind him.

A small envelope lay beside one of three covered plates on the service platter. He opened it and the note inside.

"Please find your winnings at the bursar's office. We trust your trip onward to New Orleans will be a pleasant one. Please join your wife, daughter, and me for dinner at the captain's table this evening. Captain Armitage."

"You must use your best manners when you wear ribbons and dine with adults." Lizzie tied Clementine's curls with a deep blue satin ribbon.

"I know. Papa explained."

"Then, of course, we worry not. I brought a few morsels for now." As Lizzie prepared for the dining room, she turned her attention to her husband. "I must confess that jealousy burns my cheeks when we walk the decks and greet the ladies. Surrounded by family my entire life in remote country, I am ill prepared for the expansive public thoroughfare beyond the hills."

"I understand. My life spent among men at war and family leaves me in dire straits. I rather like the opportunities, my dear."

"My dear, is it now? Fortunately, Uncle Joshua instilled fine table manners and formal language at his table. We should follow his example. In all things, really. In many ways, we lived a protected, elegant life. We see each other in new ways as well. I love you even more from every angle."

"My two beautiful ladies, shall we depart?" Alexander lifted Clementine into his left arm and offered Lizzie his right.

Alexander both dreaded and welcomed the stop at Vicksburg. The reality of war laid bare in battlements, devastation, and refugees. He sought the site where his brother, John, described the Missouri regiments dug in for the siege of 1863. He walked the length of the riverfront, returned a sobered and more humble man. No trace of David Smith surfaced.

Alexander boarded the steamer and walked to the upper deck where Lizzie and Clementine often sat singing high above the coffee swirls of the Mississippi. He heard Lizzie's voice and banjo before he saw her. He also heard the discord of Clementine's volkszither, and caught a glimpse of her as she strummed like crazy and sang no melody in particular. He stood at the back of the crowd gathered on the upper deck and sang when other brave souls so ventured. With the next song, he stepped behind mother and daughter, and caught up his guitar to join in his favorite, a real whopper of a ballad based on the tall tales of the biggest steamboat on the river, "The Hurricano."

When the song ended, Clementine drew the felted wool pick across the zither strings, nodded her head at her father, mimicking him exactly, and said, "Pearly Mae." [7.2]

Alexander picked up the melody on guitar strings and sang with his daughter, while Lizzie strummed softly on her banjo.

"Anybody for a scary story?"

"A scary story!" Clementine ran half the length of the boat and returned to her father's strong hands for a toss in the air. "Wheeee! More!"

He tossed her twice more into the air. "Story time." Alexander pulled a large chair beside his wife. "I named this story 'Shadrach Fights a Bear.'"

Lizzie set her volkszither on Clementine's lap. "Perhaps a funny story near bedtime works better. What about the beautiful princess and the new kitchen stove?" Lizzie tickled her daughter's ribs and laughed. She told the kitchen stove story many times before.

Clementine pulled a long strum of discord across the zither's strings.

On cue, Alexander began. "Once upon a time, a handsome prince rode his trusty steed and splashed across a big, clear, and cold river, through the soft-green piney woods to the castle of his beloved princess. There she lived with Uncle Joshua, Aunt Betsy, and ten children."

"You are the handsome prince, Papa."

"Yes, and who is the beautiful princess?"

"Mama, Mama is the princess. Someday I shall be the beautiful princess and live with Uncle Joshua and Aunt Betsy."

"Yes, the beautiful princess." Alexander held Lizzie's gaze and returned her smile.

"The children caught lightning bugs that rose from the grass in the yard and up into the trees. Blink, blink, blink, shone their tails. The children played tag until bedtime. After Aunt Betsy heard their prayers, she tucked them in for the night. The children heard her steps go 'tap, tap, tap' down the wooden stairs to the dogtrot and into her room. The house fell silent for a good night's sleep."

Clementine pressed her fingers to her father's face so he would look directly into her eyes. "Did the boys fight with pillows and get in big trouble? Geo and Will always fight and get into big trouble."

"Usually we stirred up some kind of mischief, but not this night." Alexander continued the story. "Aunt Betsy awoke and sat up in the bed. She smelled smoke. 'Wake up, everyone, wake up! Come downstairs and out the front door.'

"The older girls helped the little girls wake up. They checked the boys' room and found it stood empty. They followed the little girls down the stairs to the dogtrot and out the front door. Aunt Betsy counted the girls to be sure everyone was out of the house and asked, 'Where are the boys?'

"She shouted, 'Boys, where are you?'

"The boys ran around the house from the backyard to the front yard. 'Here we are. The smoke won't go up the kitchen chimney.'

"The boys ran back around the house to the back yard, now followed by the girls and Aunt Betsy. 'Stop, we must stay outside.'

"Aunt Betsy soon saw Uncle Joshua come outside through the kitchen door with the metal ash bucket full of smoking fiery pieces of wood. Uncle Joshua laughed so hard, he could hardly speak. Tears ran down his cheeks from smoke and laughter. 'Betsy, darling.'

"Aunt Betsy said, 'Do not Betsy darling me. We almost burned up.'

"When Uncle Joshua finally caught his breath, he said, 'The boys built the fire in the oven instead of the firebox.'

"'Boys, open the upstairs windows to let the smoke away.' He began laughing again.

"'The oven? What oven?' asked Aunt Betsy.

"Uncle Joshua took his wife's hand and led her into the smoky kitchen.

"'Oh, my,' she exclaimed. 'A cast iron cook stove! Thank you, thank you. We shall use it well.' Aunt Betsy's fears drifted away with the smoke. She and her loved ones were safe. The oven cooked many a fine biscuit, to this very day.

"And that's the story of the new kitchen stove, the first in Shannon County."

He looked at his daughter, lulled to sleep by the gentle roll of a boat in deep waters. He said to his wife, "I didn't notice when we left the shore."

"You got lost in the telling, too." Lizzie knew the story brought sweet memories of beloved men in his life, now lost until the end of his days on this earth. "Shall we take the daughter of the prince to our cabin so he can sit with his princess on the deck, and sit very near the cabin door, in the event the cook builds a fire in the oven instead of the fire-box?" She took her handkerchief tucked inside her sleeve and dabbed his tears, and then her own.

Alexander found work at the wharfs. Prosperity and misery sat side by side in New Orleans. His wife and daughter delighted in the multitude of cultures in civilized and uncivilized society. Large elegant homes lined the streets, some built around a central court for protection from criminals, beggars, knowing eyes of the righteous, and the dreaded yellow fever, which swamped New Orleans in epidemic after epidemic.

Alexander and Lizzie lived with no such protection. Their front room opened onto the brick walkway of Rue Dauphine. The one-story house held two families, side by side. A central double chimney rose through the roof, to accommodate two tiny, black iron cookstoves on either side of the wall. Stucco covered the exterior brick walls. Slate tiles covered the roof, and large thick walls rose a foot or more above the roof at each end. Heavy indoor louvered shutters covered each of four doors, front and back. The cross-ventilation with doors open and shutters closed, allowed sunlight, safety and comfort because there were no windows—only the high French doors. The building stood lovely in its ancient simplicity.

Lizzie guarded against the plague of crawling and flying insects with bergamot and yards of scrim draped over doors and beds. In the Ozarks, lowlands meant chills and fever, and New Orleans fully qualified.

When Alexander came down with a mild fever, headache, chills, back pain, loss of appetite, nausea, and vomiting, she gave thanks when her ministrations were unnecessary after four or five days.

"You are quiet tonight. What needs telling?" Lizzie sat next to Alexander in their tiny rented two rooms and put her hand on his knee.

He took a letter from his vest pocket and handed it to her. "Arrived in Concordia just before we left. I'm for Texas in the morning."

"I knew the day would come, but somehow the thrill of New Orleans set it aside. Do what you must and come home to us soon."

A month after Alexander left for Texas, Lizzie put her cheek to Clementine's and found her burning with fever. She suffered discomforts similar to her father's and symptoms began to fade. However, after a few days of comfort, she entered a mean phase. Fever recurred, and her skin turned the color of her yellow silk dress.

"Hurt. Hurt." Clementine sobbed and lay on her side, bent double with belly pain.

Lizzie sent for the doctor. "My herbs and liquids give her no comfort. I prepared black cohosh for dock fever, just in case, and it helps her respiration some."

"Continue your ways, but if bleeding occurs under the skin, the mouth, or the eyes, or if her vomitus contains blood, summon me immediately. Continue to bathe her in cool water."

"What diseases cause such bleeding?"

"I believe you diagnosed the most likely. Yellow fever, some call it dock or stranger fever. Isolate her and insure her blood does not mix with yours. Many people survive, given the care you provide, and never suffer the disease again in their lifetime. For others, damage to internal organs brings certain death. You know your treatments well, Mrs. Chilton, so the child stands in better stead than most. Few cases appeared this season; thank the heavens. I will send our cook around with food until the contagion passes."

Blood crept under Clementine's skin and in the whites of her eyes, and on his next visit, the doctor gave no hope. "Prepare yourself for the worst. Does your family live nearby?"

"No, my husband left for some time. As a midwife and healer, I know many days alone, but this hour breaks me asunder."

"May my priest visit? Whatever your faith, he ministers to the young as a calling."

"Yes, thank you. I believe in the laying-on of hands, whether papist or preacher."

The doctor placed his hand on top of Lizzie's hand. "Perhaps hope remains justified; more than half survive the fever."

She sat a week of evenings with the priest. He baptized the beautiful Clementine into the faith. Then late one fateful night, he performed last rites.

Lizzie thought she grieved her daughter over the past days of lost hope. She was wrong.

Alexander returned from Texas and walked into a soundless house, unkept for days. "Clementine? Is Clementine with neighbors while you recover from illness?" He tenderly wiped Lizzie's wild dark hair away from her face.

"Clementine died from yellow fever some weeks after you left on your trip to Texas. She suffered so."

"Are you ill?"

"No. Yes, sick with grief."

Alexander lay beside Lizzie on the bed, pulled her close, and wept. He felt grief for loss of father, uncle, brother, cousin, friend; but his teardrops for Clementine became a flood.

Lizzie sat in the tidied keeping room, two herbal teas ready with healing vapors. "Perhaps if I assist the good doctor, compassionate work may ease my troubled mind."

Alexander sat silent and swirled the tealeaves in his cup. "I owe you some explanation about what happened in Texas. Are you up to the story?"

"I can stop you if I find myself ajar."

"David Smith took his family to a small town outside Dallas in Central Texas—Garden Valley, a new railhead for cotton and other crops. No family deserves to suffer the sight of their loved one killed, so I waited and followed him to a saloon. I stood on the plank walk in front of the saloon, and held back the swinging doors and shouted. 'David Smith, come outside, or I will shoot you where you stand. Save the barkeep trouble. Come out! You hear?'

"The barkeep came around the counter and cocked both barrels of his shotgun. 'Outside, Smith.'

"I moved back from the doors, and down two steps to the ground below. 'Come into the street.'

"Smith stepped into the street. 'I carry no gun.'

"When I raised my pistols to aim, he sank to his knees and begged for mercy, rightly reminding me of the eight years that passed. I must admit, he was no coward and seemed genuinely sorry for his sins, in general. He begged no forgiveness for his role in the Tragedy of Eleven. Eleven deaths, Lizzie.

"The weight of it all rekindled my resolve, and I said, 'I confess I delivered your horses to Colonel Coleman. However, you showed no mercy to my brother, uncle, and nine others.'

"I left David Smith in the dust, one bullet to his head and two in his chest. I outran the law and came home to you."

Lizzie stood, walked to Alexander's side, and drew his head to her chest. "Then he lies dead; your revenge complete?"

She saw his eyes close and felt his breath deepen. Suddenly she knew his love for her kept him silent. Lieutenant Lacy and two guards remained alive—his vow to Aunt Betsy unfulfilled.

Lizzie respected his silence for the next two weeks, and then invited him into her steps toward peace. "Write a verse of song, play a tune with me."

"Lizzie, dang it all, give me time. We both know time softens the blows of life. You said your good-byes, while I chased a vow."

"The beautiful cemetery gives comfort." Lizzie picked up her parasol. "Walk with me."

"I always come with you because I love you. I find no comfort at the above-ground stone tombs where six months of blistering southern sun consecrates dust to dust." Alexander picked up his hat, took Lizzie's hand into the crook of his arm, and led her from Dauphine to Canal Street and into the soft early evening light of New Orleans.

Water lapped the banks of Memphis, followed by the rush of the wake the large boat raised as it approached the pier. The ponderous trip upriver rocked peace into the two heartbroken lovers, Alexander and Lizzie. The year 1873 gave way to a slow peacetime recovery of land and society along the Mississippi. Could Missouri rancor hold up inevitable healing?

Lizzie sat on the Concordia, Lafayette County porch with her sons, William and George, cousin Jess Orchard, and little cousins Francis and Perneice. Patsy and her youngest daughter Elizabeth waited at a table for Mary Louisa to return from the kitchen with tea.

Lizzie said, "Back in late 1869, when Mary Louisa and I went to Shannon County, Jess' mother was very ill, as were two other family members. We left you with your grandmother and Sam because we did not want you to get sick.

George climbed into her lap. "We understand, Mama. You left to rescue Jess when Aunt Susannah died and made him an orphan like you."

Lizzie sighed and said "That is correct, Georgie. Susannah loved Jess with every power of the universe."

Then she turned to her other son, William, and pushed his damp hair from his face. "I know you may never forgive my absence. Please try very hard to believe I love you dearly. I hope you also understand that Alexander rides to who knows where, in part, for his vow to revenge the murders of our family. However, he also carries Clementine's ashes in a leather case. I believe he runs from guilt that he survives. I pray Clementine's ashes will rise, visit Alexander, and say, 'I forgive you, Papa, for being gone when my spirit passed to the happy place beyond the veil.'

"I envision a most beautiful rose bush against a high brick wall. One sprig grows through a crack in the wall to the opposite side where a silver-pink rose blooms eternal. Our Clementine."

Lizzie awoke from a short reverie when William sat at her feet, arms around her knees, and sobbed mournful tears that melted into her skirt. He looked up at her with the saddest of eyes and blotched red cheeks. "Oh, Mother, I do miss her so."

Lizzie heard the door click and saw Mary Louisa who carried the tea tray to the porch to five weeping children who surrounded Lizzie.

Mary Louisa asked, "What in this world made everyone cry?"

Lizzie replied, "Our sad stories. Aunt Betsy claims stories about our loved ones speed healing of the heart."

Late one afternoon in the winter of 1873, two riders on horseback cantered down the lane toward the Joshua Chilton farm. Alexander saw Aunt Betsy first, and he let out his signature yell and raced Lizzie to the gate.

Aunt Betsy called, "Oh, I am glad to see you. You stayed away so long we gave you up for dead."

"First, I went to Rockford, Illinois. Found David Smith on a ferryboat. The murderer got away from me—disguised himself and slipped away. However, I found him in Texas. The last time I saw David Smith, he lay in the dust near the door of a saloon with a bullet in his head and two in his breast. The law in Texas ran fast, but I ran faster." [1.5]

Aunt Betsy gasped, crossed her arms as if chilled by more than the sharp evening breeze, and gazed at the sky ablaze with dying embers. "Alexander and Lizzie, my prayers are answered. You are safe again by my hearth." She stepped off the porch into grass, on which past feet stepped with the greatest of joy and the saddest of grief.

Lizzie nearly crumbled from fury at the violence of Alexander's words. Aunt Betsy deserved more compassionate handling. She did not argue when he insisted she tell nobody but Aunt Betsy of Smith's fate. He refused to let anyone speak of Clementine in his presence.

She quietly joined Aunt Betsy in the yard and put her arm around her dear aunt's shoulder. "I am sorry for Alexander's brutal words. Friends from childhood, bound by family ties, we loved each other for a very long time...troubled times. I fail to understand what happened to the young boy I loved. What happened to me?"

"War, my dear, war happened to us all."

Lizzie helped Aunt Betsy to a chair on the back porch, brought two hot cups of tea, sat a lamp and chair beside her, and began the story of baby Clementine.

Alexander and Perry offered to accompany Perry's grandfather home the day after the welcoming dance held in Aunt Betsy's barn. Thomas Coot Chilton accepted. Blair Creek lay a good twenty miles downriver from the new Eminence site on Jacks Fork. Coot's saddlebred gelding stepped out with the gait of a rocking chair. They made good time. With Perry and Alexander, time was his friend. Coot could still set a fast pace for a man in his eighth decade.

"Remember when you were lads, and Perry caught the biggest fish? I suppose we will never be free of the story with Perry in the room!" Coot still remembered everything of long ago. "And look at him now, eyeing General Freeman's daughter. The lad always fishes for the catch of the day."

Alexander teased. "Yes, if he tangles up with Freeman, he will end up a lawyer in the legislature."

"Perry, you watch General Freeman's ways and remember your father's. Big shoes to fill. Big shoes to fill. Perry is the leader, that one. Betsy bore fine sons. I am proud of every last one of you." Coot saw all his grandchildren and young kin as one rollicking group and proffered equal affection.

"Now, you boys should know about the ruckus the last time Eminence was sited. Bunch of Reynolds and Shannon County folks pooled our resources and bought land, forty or eighty acres—can't rightly recall—on top of the mountain where the trail goes down to Logyard. Named it Eminence, a high lofty place. Well, the disagreements between the parties reached such a fever pitch that Pat Buford and some others took their shares and went home.

"So Eminence found itself sited at a wooly place below the Round Spring." Coot rubbed his beard. "Took a war to get it moved again. Two steep hills on either side of the valley out of the river bottom on T. J.'s offering. Be interesting on which high place they build the courthouse.

Strong feelings it should be on a high and lofty site, and there are several on the property. I passed the reins of leadership to the lads this go-around. Rather go fishing."

Alexander helped Perry settle his grandfather on the bank by a deep hole at the end of the blue channel below the entry of the creek. Blair Creek could really roll in heavy rains. The root wad washed parallel to the cut bank would slow and hold bait, whether on or off a hook. The fish waited, ready, long about sundown.

He led the horses up the slope, brushed down Coot's horse, and caught up the fishing poles and an old bowl for bait. Coot grew worms behind the abandoned barn at the creek in soil so loose a china bowl dipped a daylong batch of wigglers with ease.

Alexander whistled on his way back to the fishing hole. One look at the slope of Perry's embrace of the sleeping old man told the story.

Perry said, "Grandpa Coot dreamed of the big catch for the last time today on the Current River banks."

Alexander knelt by his cousin and supported his shoulders while both wept woeful tears of loss. He and Perry then fashioned a litter behind Coot's horse to carry him to the Blair Creek farm for burial, funeral, and wake of the last founding father of the three: Boggs, Coot, Truman.

Alexander and Lizzie set about construction of a small home on the site of the burned-out Shadrach Chilton farmhouse of his childhood and wrote to his mother and the Nesbits with the sad news of the patriarch's passing and a bit of good news. *"Safe to return home to Shannon County. Await your presence with joy and celebration. Our love to William, George, and all."*

Alexander resumed his position at the rebuilt Freeman store and saloon. It took many days to catch up on the events and society of Shannon County family and friends. He and Lizzie gave general answers regarding the children. All could wait until the Nesbit-Chilton families returned to Shannon County in the coming weeks.

Lizzie rejoiced with Mary Eliza on her news of a coming birth. With the birth of a baby in their home, she prayed that George and William could gradually offer forgiveness to Alexander and her for the death of their beloved sister, Clementine.

She heard the anticipated words soon after the birth of Martha Elizabeth Nesbit. "Tell us about the riverboat and how Clementine sang with you and Cousin Alexander on the top deck."

Sharing the stories with her sons saved Lizzie. Allowing none in his hearing, Alexander suffered.

Then the stone began to crumble because the children persisted. "Take us fishing. Our worm bed behind the barn already wriggles." George, William, Jess, Francis, and Perneice grabbed their cane poles, scooped a jar of worms and leaves, haltered Nonie, and waited for Alexander to set them on the horse for a ride across the pasture to Jacks Fork River.

"When your mothers and I came here fishing, we brought our guitar, fiddle, and banjo. Sang us some tunes. Listen to this tune about an honorable man and a scallywag."

"Is the woman the scallywag?" Perneice asked.

"No. The song of beautiful honorable women comes next. Listen now. I expect you boys to take after our grandfathers and Uncle Joshua, fine honorable men. I remain the only scallywag in the family."

"Aw, Alexander, you are no scallywag. Are you sort of our father, now that Clementine lives with Jesus?" George chimed.

William elbowed his brother. "Dang it, George."

"We frown on cussin', now, lads. Fish are hungry. Get at it." Alexander thought his throat would burst from pain. He swallowed his suffering and vowed to enjoy his time with other men's children as if they were his own. "The good book of Proverbs says, 'A cheerful heart fills the day with song.'"

Perneice added, "We know the fishing proverb. 'The one who knows much, says little; an understanding person remains calm—and catches more fish.'"

Alexander and Lizzie visited Aunt Betsy's home. He loved to tell stories, and events in the winter of 1874 gave ample supply.

"Five mysterious travelers rode through Arkansas into South Missouri. On January 31, the five heavily armed men robbed the Little Rock Express on its way from St. Louis, at a little southeast Missouri town called Gads Hill, near Piedmont.

"Remote Shannon County lay on the gang's escape route. They crossed the lower Current River and followed the river north to the Jacks Fork. Cousin George F. Chilton, the sheriff of Eminence on the Jacks Fork, got word the James Gang rode for town. He cleared the streets, cleared the saloon, and cleared the hotel and general store for as long as the gang stayed in town. Sherriff Chilton greeted the gang and invited them to the saloon where I served up plentiful food and beverage. The gang rested themselves and their horses for a few hours; then they peacefully went on their way up the Current. Looked like the James Gang to me!" [1.5]

Alexander paused. He heard a horse stop at the gate and saw a rider dismount, walk to the front door, and knock.

He opened the door, stepped onto the porch, and accepted a letter from the hand of the rider. He shook the rider's hand, and they exchanged silent nods, full of complete understanding.

Lizzie stood up, smoothed her skirt, and waited beside the table. She fully understood what the letter meant.

Alexander returned to the kitchen, and took Lizzie's hands into his. "Colorado."

Then he walked into the dogtrot and looked at the bloodstains in the floorboards. He looked at the bullets in the wall.

Stunned by the power of remembrance when she followed his gaze, Lizzie ran to him and held him by his shoulders. "No. Please. Stay with us. End this with your word." She took the Bible from the hall table and pushed it under his hand.

Alexander spoke in his quiet way, "I vowed to avenge the needless cold-blooded murders of my family. I give you my word; it will end when I return Uncle Joshua's Masonic ring to Aunt Betsy."

"I cannot bear life without you," she pleaded. "If you leave again, I may not be here when you return."

He kissed her hands that still gripped the Bible. "Then do not be here." His whole frame shook. He put on his hat and nodded to Aunt Betsy. "Be back tomorrow."

He walked out the door, placed his rifle in the saddle scabbard and rode upriver, turned to the left, and lifted his hand to tip his hat…toward the Chilton cemetery.

A bobwhite called in the distance.

CHAPTER 13

REVENGE
IN THE WEST—1874

Love came around.
I was nowhere to be found.
Be back tomorrow,
Or maybe not at all, child.
Another day,
Another time, another life.
It's your mistake, got nothing left inside now. [7.3]

Alexander rode horseback to familiar ground in Little Dixie. From there, he boarded the new train through Kansas to Denver, Colorado. He took the Denver to Santa Fe stagecoach due south through Colorado Springs to Pueblo and decided to ride horseback through the foothills of the Rocky Mountains to Silver Cliff. Hundreds of people crowded the area, en route to the silver mines. The letter said, *"Editor Alexander H. Lacy runs the Silver Cliff newspaper."*

The terrain lay dry and flat. In the distance, mountains covered with evergreen trees scraped skies. Then he caught a glimpse through the evergreens—snow-covered peaks of the Rockies. The sight left him breathless in the rugged country a man could learn to love in an instant.

Silver Cliff was a boomtown. He opted to first take his meal in the thriving hotel and locate the newspaper after warm food filled his belly and a hot bath restored his mind and spirits. Look, plan, move. Some things never changed.

"Good afternoon. May I speak with your editor?"

"Yes, sir. Please follow me." A young man of about twelve years motioned Alexander to follow to the back of the small wooden building where tangy sharp metallic smells of ink and paper permeated the room. "Father, a man to see you. I forgot to ask his name and his business."

"My name is Alexander Chilton. I mean you no harm, but my business involves the painful past of war events."

"Pardon me if I show distrust of your motives, but I do remember your face and recall the incident as if yesterday. It was devastating to many involved. I prefer to talk with you after we close for the day, as perhaps you suspected. I can see you are a serious man with serious things on your mind. May I suggest six o'clock at the hotel lobby where we can take a small repast?"

"In one hour, then." Alexander nodded to the boy and tipped his hat to Lacy. Memories boiled up inside him and threatened civility. He turned with an urge to run out the door in escape.

He took time to move his horse to the hitching rail at the side of the newspaper office. He passed a rancid-looking water trough, but decided to go for fresher water for his horse. The dry air begged relentless thirst. Words, crafted and replayed over the past eleven years, filled his mind and heart. Choices loomed.

A gun stayed with a man, and he intended to keep his holstered. He saw Alexander H. Lacy, the man of small stature with sandy hair and blue eyes, the lieutenant assigned responsibility for the 1862 death march from Salem to Rolla. He entered the lobby and chose to sit at Alexander's right hand.

Smart move, Alexander thought.

"Mr. Chilton, shall we begin with a drink and discussion?"

Alexander nodded and motioned for the server. Then he began. "My pain and suffering behind me, I seek to find peace and perhaps words of revenge, but no actions. You may recall reports of the dead, but they named the wrong man. I saw a report that named you the man who killed the prisoners. However, I knew who drew guns. As a lieutenant myself, I know the official record most generally names the officer in charge responsible for the deaths."

"No, sir, I did not peruse reports. I thought you dead and I considered the distant past behind me. Named an officer days before the 1862 raid, I considered myself up to the task of protecting a senator among six prisoners, given one hundred twenty-five men. However, the outcome proved me wrong or ill advised, a question I put to rest when I resigned my commission shortly thereafter, following the Battle of Hartville, January 11, 1863.

"Condolences are due, but as one eloquent officer wrote, '...the dangers of being hurt which every brave man runs when facing the glorious music of war—Colonel Livingston to your Colonel Freeman, as I recall." [2.68]

"Glorious music of war. Some days the strains play long into the darkest of nights. Anger wells up in me, past reason. My visit with your Captain Avery tempered my resolve, but retribution stands high, yet today. Please tell your story. You know mine—brother and uncle slain."

Lacy began. "For some years, replaying events in my mind, I moved the prisoners closer to the front of the column and envisioned my calming influence more effective with the guards and, perhaps, with the prisoners. As the war progressed and further tested my mettle—injury and danger the rule, not the exception—I hardened. Determined to find my way back to civilization, I moved here to its edge. The unconquerable mountains humble me. Reminders abound that 'God won't starve an honest soul, but he frustrates the appetites of the wicked.' To that end, I tell you honestly, I know not the names of the guards. Neither did I seek identification. Perhaps generals assign revolving companies of men to total more than one hundred, in order to prolong the stability of their lieutenants. With such hindsight and insight, I rest my case. I returned to the war of words." Lacy waved his hand toward his newspaper's signage and to the bustling audience in the street, many of whom likely could neither read nor write.

Alexander sat for some time and savored the burning amber liquid. Then he ordered a platter of bread and meat for two. "Newspapers dubbed the incident 'Tragedy of Eleven.' My youthful vow to avenge their death lies strong in my heart. More than half the men in my family are dead, none at the hand of battle, but of guerilla tactics or army hospital infections, more than twenty-five all told. Those of dishonorable hands met their maker by me or by one of our own. Two remain. Your Captain Avery rightly said, 'War's a bad business.'"

"And you make your way to California before the snow closes the rails? Yes. I am thirty-five years old, my wife five years younger, and children eleven, nine, and one. I seek adventure with a mix of security and love; pursue it with all my being. I advise you to consider its worth, turn around a wiser man for having visited the mountains that divide a continent." Lieutenant Lacy rose from his repast, turned, and walked out the lobby.

Whether Lacy fully expected a bullet in his back, Alexander could argue both yea and nay.

He paid his due and continued his journey to the edge of the continent at the Pacific Ocean.

Alexander bought pistols and rifles with the new repeating and accurate action and a large knife in a scabbard. He savored the thought of two guards' deaths and the fulfillment of his vow. San Francisco lay crowded and menacing below the fog. He removed from his vest pocket the addresses and names beaten from other soldiers on the list, gathered by numerous fellow partisans over the twelve years past. Honor—swift and certain. Such lay foremost in his mind.

He knocked at a door in the wharf district. Night fell as watery and cold as the grave. The door opened. He found his man. The sound of one shot and one stab of the knife on bone split the air. He checked for a pulse, waited until none presented, and walked casually around the corner into the foggy night.

The months he took to find and understand the routines of the marked men proved well spent. The last guard on his revenge list walked down the dark alley, stumbled a bit, and asked, "Got a light?"

Alexander snapped a match and held it near the man's face. "When dead, you can't tell the difference in an honorable man and a brute."

He waited to enjoy the look of recognition and terror that engulfed the marked man's face.

Then, a shot rattled the alley walls. The man screamed his last insult when the knife cut off the offending finger as a trophy, and then pierced his heart.

Alexander wrapped Uncle Joshua's Masonic ring in a soft cloth and placed it in a silk drawstring bag; packed the trophy in a salt-filled wooden box; stowed bag, box, and weapons in a leather saddlebag thrown over his shoulder; breathed the wet droplets of predawn air he deemed freedom.

Then he prayed for absolution.

Lizzie waited and waited for word from Alexander. She filed for divorce in May 1875. [2.1] She traveled to her people in Tennessee. [1.56]

Then the much-anticipated letter came from Aunt Betsy. *"My Dearest Lizzie. Alexander returned. Please come home. Thomas, Martha Belle, and Alexander live with me and prove great help. Alexander sits saddened and closes the saloon far later than necessary. I worry and believe you the best tonic.*

Everyone here is mostly well. Your Aunt Louisa Sinclair recovered from the County Farm and lives with her eldest. Your Aunt Anne and Aunt Melvina farm alone and well. Perry and Emmaline's Mary Elizabeth is two and new baby Russia Belle favors Perry. James C. and Elizabeth's William, Martha, Rebecca and Mary Issabella want you to live with them again until your troubles sort themselves out. Margaret,

still alone, has Elizabeth, Wesley, Robert and Evaline to keep her com-
pany. She thinks of your brother as a son, and word came from Thomas
Davis in Washington and Oregon, of late. Young James married Mary
Elizabeth at last and newborn, Charles O., thrives. Andrew Jackson's
wife Elizabeth passed at the birth of Rosa Belle. He suffers remorse. He
offers to bring you home when he comes to Tennessee for Susan Chilton,
a young distant cousin he spoke for, and a recent widow herself.

"As to your own Nesbit sons, I send good news. William lives in Salem
and works at the hardware. Your George proves a good farmhand, ram-
bunctious as ever, and plays banjo like a wild man. Sam and Mary Louisa
still farm on Shawnee Creek, with their Martha, Marshall, Charles, and
newborn Arthur, plus Thomas Stelfox from England who now boards with
the Nesbit family. Her Perneice Butler is lovely and all mourn the loss of
our Francis Marion something fierce. When Francis died, the last trace of
Nelson went to the grave. My heart is heavy. I pray for the recovery of the
joyful countenance time affords, and your presence with me would sooner
lay painful memories to rest in peace. Set aside your stubborn pride and
hurt, if your visit with your Davis family in Tennessee draws to a close.
Give my love to Caroline. Forever, Aunt Betsy."

Lizzie stayed put.

She sent a letter from the Davis family addressed to Aunt Betsy, which offered Alexander a good position and land in Tennessee. [1.56]

Alexander tended the saloon and farmed the Jacks Fork river bottom.

One beautiful autumn morning in 1876, Lizzie hummed a sad tune and dried the dishes. She felt arms encircle her, lift her into the air, and swing her high in a circle. "Alexander! God is my hope! Alexander!"

When he set her down, she turned in his arms and cried tears of joy. "You came for me at long last."

"When I received word the courts dismissed the divorce interlocu-tory decree in November, I packed for travel and left before I could think about anything but almost losing you." [2.1]

"And if another letter arrives?" She kept her gaze directly into his eyes when he picked her up, carried her outside, and set her in the wagon at the front entrance to the tiny house. "Alexander?"

"Aunt Betsy holds Uncle Joshua's ring."

"And?"

"I think you want to see New York." Alexander clucked to the horse, flicked the reins, and delivered Lizzie and her traveling trunk alongside his to the railroad station in Knoxville, Tennessee. "Your grandmother Davis sent you on an errand and packed your bags the morning of my arrival."

"Conspiracy!" She attempted to maintain an angry look on her face, but her joy evaporated all else.

Lizzie's eyes sparkled and her mood soared. Whether from love or train travel, she cared not a whit.

When the train drew into the station, Alexander flagged the porter for assistance with their two bags and hired a carriage for transport to the nearest inn.

She stood in the bedroom of the inn, her nightclothes amiss, stretched hands overhead, twirled, and curtsied low like a princess. "I own no dresses for the likes of New York."

"Well, then, we shall keep to the countryside until we remedy the matter. This country is a sight to behold, and I intend to embrace the continent."

Alexander saw to their trunks and helped Lizzie re-board the train. "Next, I want to take you into the West. The mountains soar to the heavens, much higher than these." He watched the heavily wooded eastern mountains that rose sharply on either side of the train. He heard the steam whistle blow and felt the train slowly move forward.

"What are we doing here?"

"Reconstruction, my dear, reconstruction. Cincinnati, Cleveland, Buffalo, Rochester, Albany, and New York City."

"Who are we chasing this trip?" Lizzie felt tired and mildly annoyed.

Alexander took her hand. "I saw Kansas, Colorado, the desert, San Francisco, the ocean. I want you to see this country with me. My past fades in new places. I chase the unknown."

"Alexander, I try to believe you. My trust in life itself is shattered. Perhaps in your unknown I can find life again. Like your mother, my father kept his motto close at hand. 'When you have nothing, God is enough.' Nothing terrifies me more because time and again I fail to thrive in his motto."

He put his arm around her shoulders and drew her close. "We strong."

"We strong." Lizzie smiled at the remembrance of her son, William, when he was a small lad, and men left for war.

She felt the click-clack of heavy metal wheels on the rails lull her toward welcome sleep.

A fellow traveler spoke to Lizzie across the railcar aisle. "Your words indicate a southern disposition."

"Missouri. Not so southern, not so northern. A middle place."

"Did you suffer during the war?"

"War touches all, sir. What special sights can we expect on this part of our journey? I enjoyed your knowledge of Ohio."

"The lakes are so large as to be oceans. The fish of the lakes, you must try those new to your taste."

"That I shall, thank you." Lizzie turned back to the papers collected at the last stop. She looked at her dress in comparison to the drawings and those worn by a few ladies on the train. She found her fashion hopelessly lacking. She knew the best dressmakers sewed twenty stitches per thumb-width. Perhaps in Buffalo, New York, she could find work with a dressmaker. She determined to discuss a stop there with Alexander when he returned from the card parlor.

"A stop in Buffalo sets well with me." Alexander took his father's watch from his vest pocket. "We should arrive before sunset."

Lizzie rose with the sun, dressed, and made her way down the stairs to the dining room of the inn in Rochester, New York. "Good morning. Might there be a dressmaker nearby?"

The innkeeper said, "Some ten streets east you will find ladies and gentlemen's finery. My daughter can assist you, if you so desire."

"Thank you. If my husband is otherwise engaged, she would be a welcome companion."

"She attends school to become a teacher. Her mother and I are very proud. We fear the lure of independence out West may take her far away from us. Can you tell her about the West?"

"When she returns from school, we can order tea and share our experiences. I find the East much a mystery. Life proves much less genteel in the West. Our schoolmaster was from Ohio and possessed a sense of elegance I see in the men and women here. Sadly, he died from war injuries. Lizzie paused when she saw pain in the man's eyes. "I apologize; I see you flinched at my rude mention of the past."

"Yes, two sons lost for the Union. All the more reason to hold fast to a daughter." He turned to accept a plate from the kitchen and set it at Lizzie's place. "A fine morning to you. If not to your taste, please advise. Excuse me, now."

She finished her breakfast and returned to her room to wait for Alexander.

She heard him bound up the stairs. "I found work at the docks. The ships, the men, the cargo, all seem larger than life. I see you already dined, as did I. Fish, everywhere the smell of fish. Where do you want to go this morning? I start work come Monday. We can explore the town."

"With a twirl of my umbrella, we shall hasten to the dress shops."

"I apologize. Dresses require cash money. Perhaps after a few weeks?" Alexander felt embarrassed. Poker on the train unexpectedly depleted his funds.

"Oh, I mean to find work as an assistant dressmaker or milliner. Midwifery would keep us in food but hardly pay for a new dress." Lizzie picked up her umbrella and placed her hand on his arm. She decided his coat and vest were due a cleaning when he set them aside for work clothes. She thought of her sons and wondered whether they were hunting with their father or working on the farm in homespun. Lonesomeness welled up in her throat at the thought.

"Mary Louisa will find herself in finely woven cloth for her love and care of my sons. What a strange family we make." She laid her head against his shoulder and held his arm like a buoy. She found the large lake and town frightening. The air blew fresh and cool off the lake. In the winter, it no doubt cut like ice.

When Alexander returned from work, he tried his new coat, vest, shirt, and string tie. "Thank you. I believe we should sit for our pictures. What do you think?"

"Oh, not for me. When I can wear a new dress, then I will take my turn. But you must go."

"I have something of yours, I believe. Brought me unspeakable luck. Now you are mine, it can be our good luck charm." He reached into his vest pocket and placed a tiny silver thimble on the third finger of her right hand.

"Oh, I thought I lost Mama's thimble forever. She gave it to me on my thirteenth birthday. You remember."

"I well remember. I took it from your sewing basket when I left for war. A silly thing to do, I suppose. It meant everything to me. A symbol I loved you first and forever, come what may."

She reached for him and tasted his kisses…salty from tears. "Thank you," she whispered.

Embarrassed, he turned to the mirror, brushed his unruly brown hair, but curls escaped in spite of his efforts. "Now this rascal almost appears honorable."

When his picture returned from the photographer, she placed it in a frame on the chest of drawers in their rented room. Life seemed as fragile and unreal as a photograph.

One Sunday, she decided to attend the church on the corner. It was a new experience, and the organ music lifted her spirits to the rafters. Her banjo seemed quaint by comparison, but still she missed playing and singing at play parties.

When she returned, she saw Alexander's profile in the window of their room, and tripped lightly up the stairs. "We must attend the concert in the town square. Who knows, perhaps we will be invited to play banjo and guitar."

"I would welcome a waltz played by any string." He swung her around the room in a waltz and found her smile as entrancing as ever. "I love you, Lizzie."

"Well, you seem so serious. However, serious or playful, I cherish those words, 'I love you.'" She loosened his tie, unbuttoned his new coat and shirt, and laid her head on his chest. "It's a very nice day to love."

The idea of the concert faded. There would be other concerts.

"I'm going to Lockport again today. Therefore, my return could be tomorrow. Will you miss me?" Alexander pulled on his work boots and took a heavier coat, should the evening turn cold.

"I always miss you, especially at mealtime. Be safe." She kissed him soundly but noticed that certain sadness in the way he looked at her. In an instant it passed.

He nodded and was gone.

When he did not return the next evening, she walked to the docks to inquire about his expected return. The clerk at the shipping company assured her that his delay was temporary. She waited.

Alexander was worried about her well-being and returned directly from the shipping office. "I am sorry about the delay. The weather, the shipment, all worked against the schedule."

"Do you think we should pack for winter inland? If we do not leave now, we spend a winter in snow deeper than ever imagined in Missouri. Sometimes twenty feet. Just imagine." She wanted to leave before the cold set in.

"Then we shall go inland. Unaccustomed to the conditions, we could unknowingly put ourselves in grave danger, from what the townspeople say. We bought our clothes, fabric for family, presents for all."

Two weeks later, Lizzie packed their trunks and scheduled the livery to the railroad station. She posted a letter to her sons and to Aunt Betsy.

She and her husband boarded the train for the East Coast—New York City.

"No jobs again today? Perhaps we should use our savings for rail tickets back to Missouri instead of an ocean journey around the coast to Mobile or New Orleans." She grew lonely and bored because Alexander spent more and more time away from their rented rooms. With winter coming on, a decision stood imminent for comfortable travel.

"Not until your photo lies safely in my pocket."

"A photo today then. Do you think the camera steals your soul?" She teased while she put on her black silk blouse, her mother's brooch at the lace-trimmed military collar, the black-and-white plaid skirt, and black string belt that held a tie for her matching reticule. A black crocheted snood completed her attire. She only wished her stitches were as fine as those of a real dressmaker.

She and her husband left Hudson, New York, for Albany and the long trip to Saint Louis, Missouri. She finally gathered the courage to ask him about the letter she found in his work pants one laundry day. Not that she feared him; rather, she feared the contents of the letter.

He handed her the envelope. "You must not worry. A wartime acquaintance believed he saw David Smith working the canal near Buffalo. While I believe him dead and buried, it troubled me. My resolve remains no less than years past."

"I found the letter but could not bear to open it. Besides, it was addressed to you. Your joy in travel with me seemed sincere."

"Indeed, sincere and remains so this very day. What an adventure, a grand eastern tour. I am satisfied the man mistook another for Smith. I booked passage on the southernmost routes. Continue our 'reconstruction,'" Alexander reassured her with a fine embrace and kiss for good measure.

A kernel of emptiness settled deep as the miles of parallel track led westward, back to a future that already felt like his past.

Lizzie shook the dust and cinders from her skirt and reboarded the train. "Thank you for routing through Tennessee. Granny Davis was so fragile when we left, I feared for her. I don't plan to see Tennessee again, so I want to say my good-byes."

"We possess all the time in the world, but not all the funds. I can replenish my funds on some cousin or other's Tennessee farm." Alexander savored his last cigar and smiled at the thought of cash money enough to fill his treasured cedar cigar box, which kept beetles at bay.

Knoxville to Chattanooga rails sped by, and soon their hired livery arrived at the Davis farm. Lizzie saw Granny Davis on the porch and began to cry. "Praise be, she lives." She jumped from the wagon and ran up the porch steps into her grandmother's arms.

Granny Davis said, "A letter arrived addressed to Alexander." She removed it from the stack on the porch table and handed it to Lizzie.

Lizzie felt her face flush with quick temper. "Oh, Uncle Andrew wrote the letter. I can hold it for later." She placed the letter in her reticule and helped with the bags packed with gifts.

When settled in her room, she remembered the letter. "I slept in this room alone, and tonight I share it with you, my husband. I rest very happy. Uncle Andrew addressed a letter to you. Shall I read it aloud?"

Alexander said, "Relations between Uncle and me frayed after our escape in the sixty-two raids and unraveled thereafter. On one thing, we could agree. The worst of the eleven survived."

"Alexander! What a statement!"

"William and Uncle Joshua were the best of us. Now, is that better?"

Lizzie opened the letter and then said, "Aunt Elizabeth died in childbirth some time ago. Uncle Andrew contacted a distant cousin in Tennessee, a widow, and she agreed to marry him. He requests she travel with you upon your return to Missouri. I suppose he assumed we would not reunite. Never the mind, we can travel with her by rail, if the bridges and railroad to Rolla or Pilot Knob are now restored."

"A good plan, it is. Come here, woman, and reunite."

"Alexander, for goodness' sake, she can't be much older than twenty and Uncle twice that at least. However, I like her. She is friendly, educated, well dressed, and beautiful. We hit it off from the start. What do you think of Susan?"

"I would say 'beautiful and we hit it off from the start.' I travel surrounded by beauty, one raven-haired and one golden." Alexander chuckled and kissed Lizzie's hand. They walked the length of the street to hire livery and passage for three to the rail station, bound for St. Louis and Rolla, Missouri.

"Come, Miz Susan. Up you go." Alexander helped his distant cousin into the saddle on the calmest mare of the three. You will become one with the stride and handling before we reach Shannon County. Guaranteed."

"I always preferred books to horses. I am afraid you find me ill equipped for the trail, and for farm life, for that matter. I worry more and more whether my decision to marry and run a large family overreaches my abilities."

Lizzie said, "Your astute assessment of our encounters on our trip shows me you can handle all challenges. You will find the Missouri Chilton family accomplished, but as rugged as our surroundings, a wilderness compared to Chattanooga. Uncle has children much your age to join you in the tasks of the home. Henry already runs the farm quite well. In any event, it is a short gallop to any number of aunts, uncles, and cousins. You may chafe from too many guests rather than absences."

Susan replied, "Thank you. I believe you and your husband will enjoy our travel with a group of wagons, so I can visit with others in addition to yourselves. At times, I believe you and Alexander are thirteen years old without a care in the world. Such energy for life. Such playfulness. You lifted my spirits and ended my mourning, to start life afresh and leave the war behind me."

Lizzie decided to save talk of war for another day; another year. "When I say one, two, three, go, you hold your reins tight because Alexander is under the delusion he can best me in a horse race."

"And indeed, I hear a challenge, but I deem it best to wait for a smooth soft pasture on which to land your derriere when you are unseated." Alexander liked his own wife immensely, her independence, her spirit. He feared Uncle Andrew would balk when he met his match in a woman of similar character to Lizzie. When Uncle Andrew's future wife, Susan, became resolved in a matter, sparks would fly. He smiled at the thought of Uncle challenged by the young woman half his age. He was curious why she did not inquire about the man. She inquired about each of his children.

"We will miss you, Susan. You make a fine traveling companion." Alexander turned from the golden lass to the raven one and shouted, "One, two, three, go!"

"Cheater!" Lizzie believed the two of them raced halfway to Salem before Alexander slowed to a trot.

When she drew alongside him, breathless and invigorated, she asked, "Why did you slow before we finished the race?"

"I slowed out of consideration for your fine derriere, my love. The others are miles behind us." He raised his eyebrows like a question, not a statement, and smiled his wicked sideways grin.

CHAPTER 14

LOVE CAME AROUND—1876

How do you get something from nothing, like stars in the evening sky.
A life so cold and neglected, a second chance to make it right.
Then it happened out of nothing, stars began to shine.
When they circled round each other, I realized true love was mine. [7.3]

Lizzie and Mary Louisa placed supplies from the Nesbit farm into the cupboards of Alexander's saloon in Eminence, Missouri. Lizzie mused, "I love the emotions in the faces when I sing for folks. Why, they sometimes seem enthralled with my songs, as if emotion seats memories forever. Just a few sprigs of melody recall a scene and the emotion of the moment or an emotion affected by the passage of time and events. Perhaps the secret to healing Alexander's suffering is to place another emotion to dissolve the sound of bullets and groans, the smell of blood, and the feel of heat off houses in flames. Or find some way to make the memory less—potent."

Mary Louisa said, "He thought revenge the answer and perhaps found some compensation for the disturbing memories. Mama always said to replace bad times of the past with service to others in the present. Perhaps he just needs a reminder. Come for supper and a sing." Mary

Louisa hugged her cousin, took up her baskets, and loaded them in her wagon. "Send Sam around back, and thank you. Cash money goes a long way these days. But I tend babies more than pluck violin strings lately."

Lizzie walked from the back room to the bar of Alexander's saloon to clear away the pan of empties. "Sam, Mary Louisa awaits you in the back for the drive to Little Shawnee."

Sam tipped his hat and said his good-byes.

Alexander recognized the old codger who made his way slowly from door to bar, laid his cane on top, and said, "Whiskey. Strong whiskey."

"We stock no other, Sir."

"You need to know that the Chiltons hanged my grandfather."

Alexander instinctively placed his hand on his pistol. "I cannot attest to whether we did or whether we did not. However, if we did, he needed it."

The old codger slapped the bar and howled with laughter. "Wise response, lad. Wise response. Pour me another."

Conversation from the end of the bar drifted Lizzie's way. "Son, you should see the woman's...the, uh, woman."

"Why your pause, Jake? See a lady and clean up your words? I like a man of such good judgment." Lizzie chuckled, wiped up the spills, and noticed the buzz of laughter and masculine conversation resume.

It came into her like a flash. "I well remember events and adventures with Alexander. The emotion surrounding Papa's death the week of my thirteenth birthday set the stage, and I knew the lad was for me. Alexander claims little recall of the details of our courtship." She tossed her long single braid over her shoulder and chuckled. "What makes you remember every detail of the 'uh-woman'?"

"Compassion, my dear. Compassion."

"More like pure passion, sounds to me." She tried to keep a straight face but finally grinned, and the man broke into laughter and slid his glass toward Lizzie.

"Nope. Nothing pure about the 'uh-woman.' Pour me another and one for yourself, my lady."

Lizzie picked up the full dishpan with a zestful flourish. "Alexander pours the drinks around here, and you can drink mine on this fine day!"

She was surprised when the old codger hobbled toward her and placed his hand on top of her wrist. "Now, Alexander is a fine lad. Nevertheless, you should know that all the Chiltons have a mean streak."

"I ought to know. My mama was a Chilton and I married one." She laughed all the way to the back room. "A mean streak indeed," she muttered to herself. "Alexander pours the drinks all right, too many for himself. At least he gets temporary peace in addition to the hangover, but whiskey is no good for either of us. Then she spoke aloud. "'Milady,' yes, and a lady I'm determined to stay!"

"You are my lady." Alexander stepped into the kitchen.

She grabbed a thick tea towel, folded it over the handle of the hot teakettle on the small cast-iron wood stove, and poured boiling water over the glasses in the rinse pan. "Jake remembers every detail of the 'uh-woman'! If impure passion sets a man's memory, your inattention almost makes me wish I was a hussy."

Lizzie burst into tears and dropped the kettle. Hot water spread over the floor and splashed like red coals on her feet and ankles. Stark realization of Alexander's past, her past, and their losses tore at her insides.

She raced out the back door of the saloon, ran down the town branch to where it met Jacks Fork, waded into the river, and sloshed and drifted downstream the mile toward home. When she reached the deep pool where a path led from the ford past the high red-clay bank to the house, she stripped the weight of her petticoats and dress, dropped them on the gravel, and dived into the deep. She floated on her back, let the current catch her cares and wash her clean.

"My lady. Ma'lady, a man stops yearning and remembering the uh-woman when he claims the heart of the likes of you." Alexander flipped the reins of his horse over a limb, pulled off his shirt, boots, and all, then dived into the swimming hole and swam straight for Lizzie.

The next thing Lizzie knew, he pulled her underwater. Pressed to the rocky ledge where she floated breathless.

Alexander kissed her and swam to the surface. "You take off at the most surprising times!"

Lizzie stiffened her arms, placed her hands on Alexander's shoulders, pushed high in the air, and shoved Alexander underwater for another round. Just like old times.

She rubbed her hair with a dry section of her petticoat, and lay back on the sandbar, which floods swept up in the watery edge of the gravel expanse. "How did you know where to find me?"

"I heard a duck splash in my swimming hole."

"Did you want to peek at the duck?"

Alexander leaned over Lizzie, laced his fingers through hers. He gently pushed her hands above her head and lowered himself to the sand. "Do not fly away anytime soon."

At Alexander's home, the front porch overlooked a dark river-bottom forest. The house set on a high bank above the Jack Fork where the river rushed gurgles and splashes of peace into hearts and minds. During floods channels changed, cut on one side and deposited on the other. Giant sycamores toppled when angry waters washed the soil from their roots. The land gently rolled. Pastures nestled against steep hillsides covered with pine and hardwoods, which prevented erosion of the deep humus of the forest floor. Mountains encircled the pastures and protected the wide expanse. Alexander breathed the wind in the pines and the smells of spring-fed waters.

"A man and his wife take pride in such a place." He repeated the chorus:

"Love came around; I was nowhere to be found.

"The dark minor chord and words ring true, deep in my chest somewhere." He closed his eyes where sparks and artillery flashed on a high ridge above him; flashed him back to Wilson's Creek on the distant prairie of the Springfield plain at the foot of Bloody Hill. His hands began to shake, and he voiced a sad mournful groan, stood, and walked with a jerk and a limp a few steps into the night.

"Alexander, wait for me." She ran to his side and put her arm around his waist. "Let's walk to the barn and check the horses. I will sing you the entire song along on the way. William and Georgie could say this song is about me, too. I like songs with happy endings."

"Then it happened out of nothing, stars began to shine.
When they circled round each other, I realized your love was mine.
Love came around..."

Alexander answered very softly, *"I was nowhere to be found."* [7.3]

Alexander tossed the letters on the table and hung his jacket and hat on the pegs by the door. Letter from someone you hold dear."

"The 'someone I hold dear' walked into my kitchen." Lizzie teased but rushed to open the letter. "Thomas Davis! Did you hold his letter the entire day? You kept a letter from my brother, all the while?" She did not wait for an answer and tore open the well-traveled envelope.

"He is well. Restless. Misses home. Sweet on a woman somewhat older. His work takes him up the coast of Oregon and Washington. Ummm." She stopped dead in her tracks.

Silently she read Thomas's terrifying words. *"I send you these words in confidence. On my last trip to Mehama in Marion County, Oregon, I saw a man who favored David Smith. Believing him dead, I followed the man to his home and saw his wife, Lucinda. No mistake. Daniel Alonzo—he goes by Alonzo now; his family lives in the same house on the large farm. Smith seems frail, perhaps some disabled. I saw no evidence of wounds, but he still boasts a thick shock of hair and clothing covered him elsewhere. Whether you tell Alexander he did not get his man, I leave up to you. I encourage you to let the matter lay silent. Those troubled times are past, and Smith seems to be a calm, compassionate old man now."* [2.24]

Lizzie decided to let the matter lie silent, for a time. Then after some thought, she determined, *"I must tell the truth. It is Alexander's decision, not mine."* She crossed the room to Alexander's side. "Brrrr. April tries to break into spring, but winter hates to go. Soup and cornbread. Come, my dear." She could not utter her brother's words.

Alexander took notice of Lizzie as they ate supper in silence. He started to ask if she felt troubled. He sensed something amiss but knew she would say so in her own good time.

Little did he know how terror crept into her very soul.

This particular beautiful day in May in 1879, Lizzie wondered whether today was the time to tell him David Smith lived. Tell him the Texas bullets betrayed their purpose. Remind him how his revenge trip kept him from his dearest Clementine the week she died calling his name. Lizzie decided, maybe tomorrow. She could not reopen healed wounds of her beloved. She could not bear for him to leave her on a revenge trip, ever again. "I'm ready for the party!" She placed her hat on her head, skipped to the barn, looped her ever-present medicine bag over the saddle horn, and tied a large loaf of bread behind the saddle. She held up a heavy sack for his pack. "Herbs for Emmaline's garden."

Alexander walked under her horse's neck, took the sack, set it on the ground, and held out his hands, fingers entwined. "How about a boost?"

Alexander and Lizzie rode their horses downriver four miles to the family gathering at Perry's farm for the celebration of the birth of Ora Ann.

Alexander said, "When Uncle Andrew asked me to bring his child-bride-to-be to Missouri from Tennessee, I deemed it a nuisance. Nevertheless, I decided—him with five children, one an infant—if I brought her, it might become my good deed of the year. It gave you and me time to reacquaint and put a damper on uncivilized discourse along the way. I must confess happiness when she befriended others in our wagon line. I say you and I 'acquainted' rather well that trip."

"Rather well, I say," Lizzie responded. "One, two, three, go!" The race was on, across the flats to Perry's barn and the party. She spurned a ladies' sidesaddle. While others chided, she knew Alexander loved a good chase. It made him smile to see her rebel and ride her horse just like a man.

Alexander returned to Perry's yard with the men after he helped Lizzie inside with the food. He raised the parcel of herbs she dug for Emmaline's garden. "Perry, did the senator ever go anywhere without a poke of freshly dug herbs?"

"I see she brought a start of every herb in her garden, but Emmaline made plenty of room last fall." Perry walked around his house with Alexander, retrieved a shovel, and proceeded to Emmaline's garden. "Lifetime of residence with 'yarb' women, one learns just where to plant what."

Alexander decided to hold the plants while Perry dug the holes. Early May ground was soft and moist, and Perry's farm lay in the rich river bottom of Jacks Fork about six miles below Eminence.

Alexander spoke without thinking. "Cousin Clint campaigns for representative. Seems like yesterday we went campaigning with the senator and the Reeds. Now they are all gone but us three." When he heard Perry take a deep breath, he realized his error. "I find it too painful to recall. Sorry."

Perry dug another hole. "I found my peace in your mother's way: replace pain with service. I plan to stand for representative when Clint calls a halt. Babies come so regular here at my house, I judge Jefferson City service best delayed. If Clint and I stand opposed, as with Father, we vowed no renewed family rancor over politics. Alexander's revenge sealed our loyalty. There, all done. Emmaline likes a tidy garden."

Inside, Lizzie took her chair beside Susan. She watched the distant cousin from Tennessee rock her four-year-old Edna and wondered how Susan held up under instant family, including a stepson about her own age.

As if she read Lizzie's thoughts, Susan said, "I refuse to give birth every year until I die of exhaustion and ruined health like Andrew's first wife. Say what you will, wisdom finds its way where cooperation rules. Makes for a somewhat jealous husband, however." She winked at Lizzie.

Aunt Betsy spoke with authority as the family matriarch with a jovial gleam in her eyes, far younger than her fifty-six years. "Jealousy, perhaps, but much pride for a beauty the likes of you. Not an easy life you assumed, my dear. We brought our Tennessee learning with us to Missouri, too. Chilton women circle our wagons when trouble brews. You stand firm on what you deem best for you and your family, Miz Susan."

"Thank you, Aunt Betsy. Can you keep an eye on Edna should she wake? I want to stretch a bit. You brought the herbs, Lizzie. I can fetch the water and puddle them in."

Lizzie noticed Andrew's eldest daughter, Sophia, kept her eyes on her needlework, lips thin and face motionless. Then she said, "The Chiltons aren't known for simple straightforward family ties, and none come more interesting than mine."

Lizzie laughed with the others. "And mine, Sophia, dear."

Henry, Uncle Andrew's twenty-two-year-old son, stepped inside the house. "Where did Susan go?"

"To the river or perhaps the spring for water. She took two buckets." Lizzie stood as she answered. She sensed the tension in the young man, so she followed him into the yard.

She saw Andrew and Henry run toward the river, and decided to follow. Andrew's heightened sensitivity regarding the activities of his young wife became a topic of interest in the conversations of the men at the saloon. She overheard many an off-color comment and laughter regarding Andrew's jealous behavior, and his son Henry's perceived boyish infatuation with his stepmother. As the barkeep's wife, Lizzie knew much more gossip about relationships than she cared to know. This time, however, she gave thanks for certain insight.

She looked for Alexander in the small crowd of men, all of whom watched the procession to the river. Lizzie thought Alexander must be with Susan, however guilty or innocent the tasks. Lizzie, Alexander, and Susan became true friends on the journey from Tennessee to Missouri. Nevertheless, trouble now brewed. She sensed emotions heavy in the air.

Lizzie ran toward the sound of shouts near the river. She stumbled to the top of the hill above the spring, dreading the scene just over the edge. She had no time to consider whether the gunshots, Susan's scream, or the hem of her skirt caused her to fall forward and roll a short way down the slope.

She did not notice the pain of deep scrapes on her hand and elbows as she pulled herself from the rocky ground, and limped toward the unfolding scene at the spring. The five-foot distance seemed like a five-mile walk in the slowest of fearful steps.

Susan beat her free hand against the chest of her husband who held the other hand at the wrist. "Turn me loose, you crazy old fool! It was not a romantic embrace but comfort for the tears of my plight! Now you have gone and killed your own nephew! God forgive us all!" Susan jerked her arm away, whirled and ran the short distance to the river's edge, and waded into the swift cold current at the ford.

A flash of hate engulfed Lizzie at the sight of Andrew's defiant stance, pistol in hand, over his nephew's body.

Andrew shouted, "Your behavior disrespects the Chilton name. You shall not extend dishonor into my own family! Make your apologies and mend your ways!"

She turned when she heard Henry stumble backward until he fell over a log. He rolled to his side and rose to his knees. In his sobs and moans, he sounded like a wounded animal, seeking refuge behind a sea of tears. He looked at the large rock he held in his left hand. With a look of terror, he flung it into the brush. He stared at his right hand as if it offended him, dropped to hands and knees, and then raised his head and two hands to the heavens.

Lizzie caught a glimpse of Susan as she reached the opposite river bank. The splashes ceased, replaced by the fading cries and screams of the hysterical woman who ran through the woods toward her home, more than two miles upriver.

Silence seemed eternal.

Her heart pounded in her ears at the sight of two ragged holes in Alexander's brown leather vest. Blood oozed from a long gash on his temple. The red stream from his chest slowly pooled around a large jagged rock near his head.

Pain shot through her dress and petticoats to her knees as she crashed to the ground and embraced Alexander's limp shoulders. She wailed the stifled cry of unbearable suffering. She tucked her lips into his neck and cried, "No. Live to see your thirty-eighth year. Nothing justifies this. Violence lay far behind and peace reigned in our home at long last. Darling, I am at one with you. Stay with me." She folded a handful of her dress and pressed it hard against the holes in his vest.

"Lizzie, my love." Alexander drew a raspy breath.

She cupped her hand under his head. "Have you prayed the sinner's prayer?"

Alexander closed his eyes and nodded his head, nearly imperceptible against her wrist.

She reached into the half-filled bucket beside his knee, cupped her hand, and poured a palmful of river water over his hair. She swept the sign of the cross above his chest, dipped her finger in his blood, and traced a "t" on his forehead. "What more can I do to spare your life?"

She swayed to and fro. She could not halt the flood of tears from her eyes as her dress stained crimson with his blood. Calmed by acceptance, she leaned closer, touched her lips to his, and breathed in his final whisper.

"Deus spes mea."

The Chilton Murder Trial

The case of State of Missouri vs. Andrew J. and Henry Chilton, which was tried last week, was watched with great interest by a large number of people, the court-room being crowded during the whole of its progress.

On the 20th of March, last, Andrew J. Chilton, Henry, his son, and Alexander Chilton had a fracas at the home of Perry Chilton, six miles down the river from town, during which Alexander Chilton met his death. The weapons used by Andy and Henry were a stone and a pistol. At the last May term of our circuit court Andy and Henry were indicted for murder in the first degree. It would not be policy for us to go into details further than to say that the friends of the defendants and also those of the deceased worked energetically for their respective objects. Seny, Wingo, and Woodside represented the defence, while Livingston and Evans prosecuted. The pleadings were logical and eloquent, and at about nine o'clock Saturday night the case was submitted to the "twelve good men and true." Nearly all of that night men stood about the streets in groups discussing the evidence and the probable findings of the jury, but not until about seven o'clock Sunday morning did the result become known. The jury declared that they had failed to reach a verdict and stood six for acquittal and six for imprisonment in the penitentiary. The case was then continued and the jury dismissed. —Eminence Argus, 1879-11-22 [3.1]

Court reconvened the next session, and proclaimed yet another continuance. The next session, lawyers selected a new jury who acquitted Andrew and Henry on May 7, 1881 [1.6]

Andrew stood near his wagon at the courthouse, surrounded by his wife and six children and the large Chilton family. "We stand here penitent and beg your forgiveness, against which exists no law."

His nephew, Perry, stepped forward from the cluster of Chiltons gathered for the proceedings. "Your family extends forgiveness. Go in peace. However, be assured, we will shoot you on sight should you return to Shannon County. Godspeed, Uncle."

Andrew shook the hand offered but could not halt the tears that streamed down his face. Unashamed, he chose not to wipe them away. "Wife, children, take your places. Henry, follow my lead." He assisted Susan into the high seat of one of the two wagons packed for distant travel.

"Walk on, mare." He looked neither left nor right at the silent crowd that lined either side of the road for a quarter mile on the trail south of Eminence.

At the top of the ridge, he stopped the wagon. "Draw up alongside, Henry."

"My heart feels saddened by events forced upon you by my actions. I hope time and a new home in Arkansas will draw us into happiness once again. Turn now to overlook all we hold dear and say your good-byes." After some long moments, he flicked the reins. "Walk on, mare."

He spoke softly, so only his wife could hear his words. "Most important, I no longer accuse you of infidelity, for which my crime of passion dispensed. With all testimony laid bare, I now understand your deep affection for Lizzie and Alexander, from both your travels with them before you met me, and your travails since. If a natural attraction existed for one nearer your own age, it is understandable. Were my suspicions true, your honor kept you above reproach. I hope time softens your heart toward me and we find love and affection in coming years."

Susan reached across the wide expanse. "That is my aim, husband. I beg your patient understanding. There is much to accomplish for our own family in a new state, a new home, a new life. May we find ourselves strong for the challenges ahead." She patted his hand and resumed her stiff posture and resolve.

Three months later, seeking peace for himself with his brothers, Andrew traveled back to Shannon County alone. He knew the Chiltons received word of his approach many hours prior when he saw a dozen or so men canter through Rowlett Gap. Then he saw Lizzie.

From the looks of her and her horse, she hiked up her skirts and galloped full speed to the Gap.

She edged her lathered horse past the line of Chilton men and drew up beside Perry.

Perry dismounted and stepped forward, his shotgun pointed up and held close to his chest. "Uncle Andrew, we told you that if you set foot in Shannon County again, we would shoot you on sight. Leave now and return to your family in Arkansas. Chiltons do not kill their own. However, we vow 'an eye for an eye' after this reprieve, one far more generous than you deserve. Remember that your brothers expressed forgiveness. Forgive yourself and go in peace, if only for your children's sake. We welcome your wife's letters with news of you and your family. It brings us peace for our difficult stance—whether for or against you, one can hardly differentiate."

Andrew bowed his head. His shoulders drooped as a pine bough piled high with snow. "Maybe someday. Perhaps one pays a lifetime for mistakes." He slowly turned his horse and then cantered south toward Arkansas. Somehow, he previously failed to understand his family's additional pain of parting from him and his children. Their affection for his wife expressed the true measure of their honor.

He murmured aloud to the heavens above, "For this alone, my trip was not in vain; prayers are answered in unexpected ways."

Lizzie followed the road north toward Eminence. She rode side by side with Perry. "Life must move on, but how?"

Perry replied, "I promise you to never revisit the pain of the murder ever again. Go forward and marry James Mahan. I know him. Although twenty-five years your senior, 'Uncle Jimmie' is a good man. You well deserve happiness. While beholden to you for his life, he also appears quite smitten. But, then, your patients always fall in love with you."

Lizzie breathed deeply and then responded, "Shadrach's sizeable estate passed to his surviving daughters and William's Paulina upon Alexander's death in May 1879. Alexander provided well for me. A home stands open to me at the welcome of Paulina who understands the isolation deep inside of orphans first hand, living with first one aunt, then another. But foremost on my mind, I must share a confidence with you, a guilt beyond human understanding."

She saw him shake his head side to side and meet her gaze with inquisitive interest.

She explained, "My brother sent me a letter a month before Alexander died. Thomas saw David Smith alive and well in Oregon. Selfishly, I chose to delay the news. Had I told Alexander his bullets missed their mark, he would be the one alive today. I could not bear to see him leave me again. Instead, he left me forever."

Perry leaned in the saddle and reached his hand to press his beloved cousin's shoulder. "We fail to know the future or a journey untraveled. I understand your pain. However, I would make the same choice. Alexander would know no peace while Smith lived. Smith did not order the raid on Chilton farms; he served as guide, however opportunistic or passionate his beliefs. Some take the war to the grave, but the peace of forgiveness often comes with time."

"Deus spes mea; God is my hope."

The gentle James Mahan reached for Lizzie's hand as their wagon forded Mahan's Creek. "I am an old man, and can't meet all the needs of a young woman."

"James, dear James. At age forty-three, I am no longer a young woman. I need your love."

James turned the wagon team along the creek bed toward his farm where the spring fed stream met Jacks Fork.

Lizzie twisted her new gold band, fully enjoying the moment. "Mrs. James Mahan. Lizzie Mahan. I like the sound. It will be about noon when we get to your place—our place. We will take a nice cool dip in the river." [1.3]

Summer turned to fall, then winter on Mahan's Creek. Lizzie pulled her wool shawl tighter around her shoulders, reset the cedar shawl pin deep into the warm yellow folds, and reached for the poker to stir the logs in the fireplace. "Brrrr, it is cold for November." She patted James's knee, settled back in her chair, and drifted into a light sleep.

His hand lay on her stomach, in hopes of a kick of his unborn baby. Lizzie was midway with child.

The sound of alert-barks startled Lizzie awake. She saw James step to the door and onto the porch. "It is OK, hounds. Come on in, Perry."

Lizzie was up in an instant. Emmaline was due any day.

Without a word, Perry tipped his hat to James, helped Lizzie into the wagon, and set her doctoring basket in a thick blanket under the wagon seat. A sharp wind carried rain and a bit of ice into their faces as they turned east toward Perry's farm some seven miles down Jacks Fork. "This could be a doozy. We will catch our death out here tonight. Emmaline's labor just began, but I came for you early when this weather threatened. Here, take another blanket for our knees."

Lizzie threw her head back and whooped as the rain spattered her smile and her face. "Alexander and I knew many nights like this in our chase up the Illinois and back. Missouri woods do not know the meaning of cold wind compared to the Illinois prairie where the rain blows sideways. Maybe these are Illinois raindrops just now reaching the ground."

Sleet and distance dampened Lizzie's spirits a bit by the time the wagon stopped as close to the front stoop as Perry could manage. Perry set the brake and helped her from the wagon. "I will see to the horses."

"I will see to the lady of the house." Lizzie carefully negotiated the slick steps and entered the warm welcoming room rich with memories, both sweet and sorrowful.

"And do we have time for a cup of mint tea before our work begins, Emmaline dear?"

Emmaline sat in a chair pulled close to the black cast iron stove where a kettle steamed and gurgled. "The kettle boils for tea and for our work, as you so joyfully call my 'labors.'"

Lizzie gave Emmaline an encouraging embrace. "How are we progressing?"

"I am glad you came early. No urge to push yet. Maybe by sunrise." Emmaline took Lizzie's hands in her own. "Are you with child? I believe I see one dart let out."

Lizzie rubbed her stomach and beamed. "Yes, I do believe I am. James is quite pleased and surprised. Like you, Emmaline dear, this must be my last child. We entered the dangerous years for mother and babe."

Just before sunrise on November 21, 1882, Leon O. Chilton wailed his first hearty breath. "Lee will be a teacher. He can already call the children to task." Perry chuckled and held Emmaline close. "I will bring the children to visit the two of you when dawn breaks. Shall we enjoy celebratory tea?"

Lizzie followed Perry into the kitchen and turned to the stove to steep another cotton bag of mint, bergamot, and lemon balm. "She suffered a difficult labor, and it needs to be her last."

"Yes, she endured much discomfort for this child. The death of young Marion, then tiny Ora Ann, makes this last baby doubly cherished. Emmaline can't survive another loss." Perry cleared his throat. "I will sit with her while you sleep. Rest well, dear cousin. I will bring Mother with me tomorrow, or as soon as the weather breaks."

"I see she sent the daybed ahead for a good long stay with her grandchildren."

Lizzie sank into the deep feathers on the bed by the stove and fell asleep recounting the many men, women, and children who found comfort by Aunt Betsy's stove.

Dawn broke sunny. Light streamed into Perry and Emmaline's room. Their children, Mary Elizabeth, nearly nine years old, Russia, age eight, and Thomas Joshua, age seven, giggled and tiptoed into the arms of their father who closed the bedroom door.

Lizzie set the table for breakfast. She warmed at the sounds of soft loving voices from the adjoining room. New life. A special day. "*What a privileged life a midwife leads.*" She absentmindedly touched her forehead, then her cheeks. She felt flushed and her heart raced. She gathered her cloak and basket by the door for the long trip home to Mahan's Creek.

As December beckoned, Lizzie felt faint and her heart palpitations lasted for hours before subsiding. Her feet and legs swelled. "Perhaps we should send for the doctor. No need to worry Aunt Betsy unnecessarily, now that we have a doctor."

From her window, she watched James ride east to Eminence and soon return with Dr. W. H. Crandall. [1.5]

The doctor closed his leather instrument case and then placed a comforting hand on Lizzie's shoulder.

Lizzie spoke before he shared his diagnosis. "The fainting and the heart troubles occurred for years. Many of the Chilton family have the palpitations. Could it be the Chilton heart?"

"I fear it complicates your situation. However, your recent headaches, flushing, vomitus, swelling, and heartburn are signs of the toxemia. You need to set your affairs in order, should there be a crisis."

Lizzie pulled her banjo across the bed, lay slightly on her side to strum and hum a few bars of nothing particular. She sang the chorus of an ancient ballad.

> *I'll dye my petticoats, I'll dye them red,*
> *And through the streets I'll beg for bread,*
> *For the lad I love from me has fled,*
> *Johnny has gone for a soldier.*

> *Oh my baby, oh my love,*
> *Gone the rainbow, gone the dove.*
> *Your father was my one true love;*
> *Johnny has gone for a soldier.* [7.1]

She stopped, then softly half spoke, half sang, "Now, I am the one gone; gone Home to you, Alexander and my Clementine." Her voice broke, and she laid her banjo aside. She cried tears for her unborn child, for herself, for her family, and for James. "Why, Lord? What medicine can save us to sing another day?"

Lizzie took note of Aunt Betsy's every move to assist the doctor in delivery of a pre-mature stillborn baby in the early hours of the morning. Then she fell into a deep sleep until late afternoon.

When she stirred, Aunt Betsy's loving hands held her niece close. "My dear, I cherish you so."

Lizzie nodded and tears seeped from the corners of her closed eyes.

She heard her son William enter the room and greet his brother and the others. He stood by the window, leaned on the sill, and focused his gaze on the December skiff of snow that lay on the pines like a shroud.

"William, dear, come sit awhile with me. Was the road from Salem slippery?"

"Very, but no falls. My young horse, while inexperienced, proved surefooted. I named him Jet, as black and shiny as your cameo. Moreover, before you ask, I claim no sweetheart to date. I just turned twenty-five, so there remains hope, perhaps next year, in eighty-three?" William paused and shook his head. "Mother, I am so very sorry for your loss." He rose from the chair, brushed his mother's hair back from her face, stroked her cheek with the back of his hand, and returned to stand by the window.

George took the chair at the side of Lizzie's bed. "Now, I am just a lad, at age twenty, hardly ready for a wife and family. I want to see the West before I settle down. Papa says I inherited wanderlust from you." George glanced at his father and Mary Louisa, who stood at the back of the room with Lizzie's aunts and Cousin J. J. and others. He gathered his resources and continued. "William, always the serious one, directs my finances while I seek adventure. I took the steamboat from St. Louis to New Orleans, visited the sites and Dauphine Street. You must love us very much to take leave of New Orleans. How are you feeling, Mother?"

She answered in a soft voice, almost a whisper. "I feel like the song of a most fortunate woman. Fresh falling snow lifts ones spirits, promises a fast slide down the slope to the frozen creek and a skate. George, take my banjo. William, take my volkszither." Lizzie paused to give

George and William time to engage in the moment. "You are my joy. For your whole life through, know you are loved." She paused and cast her last gaze on her dear family gathered in the herb-filled kitchen.

"Be back tomorrow."

EPILOGUE

Twas thus I saw them—mother and babe—
but shrouded with floweret fair;
Unconscious both, as they calmly slept,
Of the bitter tears that he and I wept—
Of the long long vigils, we sadly kept—
Kept in our love and despair!

From the work her fingers would touch no more
I took that relic alone;
But your cheek is wet, and your lip is pale—
I should not have told this sorrowful tale—
Go, hide the relic, my own![2.31]

Christine dabbed her tears with her handkerchief and reached for John J.'s hand. "I shall treasure the thimble in my own sewing basket and give it to our daughter someday. May I write the closing words of your memoirs?"

He met her reach with his pen and read an epitaph aloud as she wrote:

Lizzie and Alexander died too
young – the river weeps.

APPENDIX 1. CHILTON FAMILY TREE. [2.2]
NOTE: THOSE KILLED AT THE HANDS OF WAR IN BOLD.

Column 1-Thomas Boggs Chilton descendants. Column 2-Thomas Coot Chilton descendants. Column 3-Charles Truman Chilton descendants. Brothers Thomas Coot and Charles Truman were first cousins to Thomas Boggs. Susannah Inman and Rachael Inman were sisters.

Thomas Boggs Chilton 1782-1865 1)Susannah (Inman) 1785-1831 2) Betsy (McCain) 1800-1846	Thomas Coot Chilton 1791-1872 Rebecca (Daniel) 1796-1859	Charles Truman Chilton 1780-1843 Rachael "Betsy" (Inman) 1784-1827
Joshua T. & Elizabeth "Betsy"(Chilton) **Chilton**	Elizabeth "Betsy" (Chilton) **& Joshua T. Chilton**	Mary "Polly" (Chilton) & Dr. Thomas Reed
- **Nelson** & Mary Louisa (Chilton) Chilton - Marion Chilton -Perry & Cynthia Emmaline (Freeman) Chilton -Anne (Chilton) & W. Marion Freeman -Rebecca (Chilton) & John Counts -Susan (Chilton) & Henry Jones -James & Mary (Depriest) 2) Anna (Griswold) Chilton -Thomas T. Chilton -Francis Marion & Louisa (Hammond) Chilton -Martha Belle (Chilton) & James Shadrach "Jess" Orchard		- **Rachael (Reed) & Henry Laughlin** - David Clinton & Emaline (Fancher), 2) Drawsilla (Baker) Reed - Patrick "Pad" & Martha (Ellington) Reed - Charles T. Reed - **George Reed** - Thomas Calvin & Tennessee (Fancher) Reed - Tennessee Jubeline (Reed) & Bailey Smith - Malinda (Reed) & Squire Ellis

Shadrach & Martha "Patsy" (Harvison) **Chilton**	Issabella (Chilton) & Samuel Davis	Charles T. & Nancy (Kelly) Chilton
- Alexander & Elizabeth "Lizzie" (Davis) Chilton 　- Clementine Chilton -Mary Louisa (Chilton) & **Nelson Chilton,** **2) Joseph Butler,** 3) Samuel Davis 　- Marion Chilton 　- Perniece Butler 　- Marshall T. Nesbit 　- Charles Nesbit 　- Martha E. Nesbit 　- Arthur C. Nesbit - **John** & Elizabeth (Frances) Chilton 　-Martha Ann 　-William Shadrach 　-Alexander 　-Mary 　-John M. - **William** & Mary (Holcom) Chilton 　- Paulina - Susannah (Chilton) & **William T. Orchard,** **2)** George W. Davis 　- James Shadrach "Jess" Orchard -Elizabeth (Chilton) & George Fetter	- Elizabeth "Lizzie" (Davis) & Samuel Nesbit, 　2) **George Davis,** 　3) **Alexander Chilton,** 　4) James Mahan 　- William Nesbit 　- George Nesbit 　- Clementine Chilton - Caroline Davis - Thomas Davis	- Clementine Chilton - Elizabeth Chilton - Susan Chilton - Mary Chilton - Thomas Chilton
John & Letitia (Carter) 2) Sophia (Chilton) Chilton	Sophia (Chilton) & John Chilton	**Thomas T.** & Sophia (Larew) Chilton
- John J. & Christine (Smith), 　2) Nancy (Hixon) Chilton 　- Zimri, 　- Shadrach "Shade", 　- Joshua, 　- Van Daemon		- George F. Chilton - Mary Chilton - James T. Chilton - Melinda Chilton

Thomas J. & Mary Josephine (Chilton) Chilton	Mary Josephine (Chilton) & Thomas J. Chilton	
Andrew J. & Elizabeth ( ) 2) Susan (Chilton) Chilton	- Charles T. & Josephine (Singleton) Chilton	
- Henry Chilton		
Charles T. & Nancy (Kelly) Chilton	Louisa (Chilton) & **Benjamin Sinclair**	
Clementine (Chilton) & Zimri Carter	John & Sarah (Sinclair) Chilton	
Francis Marion &Margaret (Fancher) Chilton	James C. & Charnelcy (Huddleston) Chilton	
- **Francis Marion Chilton**		
Mark & Betsy (Carter) Chilton	**Joshua C. Chilton**	
James & Esther (Alley) Chilton	Anne (Chilton) & John Wood	
Stephen Matthias Chilton	Melvinia Chilton	
Lucinda (Chilton) & James C. Carter	**Thomas Coot., Jr.** & Jane (Suggs) Chilton	
Susannah (Chilton) & William Hawkins		

APPENDIX 2. MAP – CENTRAL SHANNON COUNTY MISSOURI [5.2-5.3]

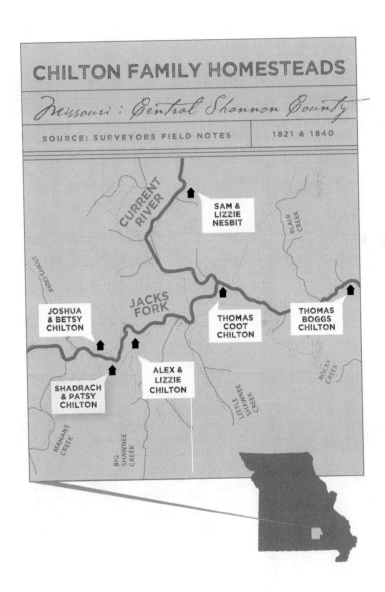

APPENDIX 3. PHOTOGRAPHS

SELECTED BIBLIOGRAPHY

We list here the memoirs, letters, genealogy, and official records used in the novel. This bibliography by no means reflects a complete record of all the works and sources we consulted. It indicates the substance upon which we present the historical events within the fictional framework of dialog and literary elements. We intend it to serve as a convenience for those who wish to pursue the study of Civil War in the Ozarks and the particular characters and subjects of our novel. Family stories, presented as fiction, afforded the most exciting moments in our research, when confirmed by official records.

. . . .

1. BOOKS AND NEWSPAPERS, by author and date:
1.1 Chilton, J. J., Eunice Pennington, David Lewis, Esau Huett, et al. *The Civil War in Carter and Shannon County Missouri.* Self-published by West Carter County Genealogy Society, P. O. Box 132, Van Buren, MO. 63965. [Secondary Source, reprinted newspaper series of articles by John J. Chilton.]
Chilton, John J. *True Ozark Tales From Bygone Days.* Van Buren, MO: The *Current Local* newspaper, September 10, 1931–December 7, 1933 [Primary Source]
1.11 Sept. 10, 1931. "Tragedy of Eleven." Reprint Book, p. 11.
1.13 Sept. 17, 1931. "First Visit of Soldiers to County Not Welcome." Reprint Book, p. 13.

1.16 Oct. 8, 1931. "Army Hearing of Fine Crops Moved in to Consume Surplus." Reprint Book, p. 16.
1.19 Oct. 15, 1931. "Life Was Held Cheap During Civil War Period." Reprint Book, p. 19.
1.20 Oct. 22, 1931. "Federals Make it Difficult For Rebels to Organize." Reprint Book, p. 20.
1.26 Nov. 26, 1931. "Alex Chilton Hides Safely in a Tree." Reprint Book, p. 26.
1.27 Dec. 3, 1931. "Many Narrow Escapes During Civil War Days." Reprint Book, p. 27.
1.29 Jan. 28, 1932. "John Chilton Shot Breaking For Liberty." Reprint Book, p. 29.
1.31 Dec. 31, 1931. "A Little Humor Mixed With Wars Grim Tales." Reprint Book, p. 31.
1.32 Jan. 7, 1932. "General Price's Raid Through This Section." Reprint Book, p. 32.
1.33 Jan. 14, 1932. "James Boys Made a Peaceful Visit Here." Reprint Book, p. 33.
1.39 March 10, 1932. "Patrol Squads Kept Citizens On Guard." Reprint Book, p. 39.
1.41 March 24, 1932. "Raiders Were Noted For Ruthless Killing." Reprint Book, p. 41.
1.42 March 31, 1932. "Chilton Too Wary For Federal Raiders." Reprint Book, p. 42.
1.43 April 7, 1932. "Soldiers Burn and Destroy Indiscriminately." Reprint Book, p. 43.
1.44 April 21, 1932. "Pad Reed Seized Guard and Makes His Escape." Reprint Book, p. 44.
1.45 April 28, 1932. "Federal's Whistle Puts Pep in Pad's Running." Reprint Book, p. 45.
1.46 May 12, 1932. "Federals Lose Butcher on Final Raid Here." Reprint Book, p. 46.

1.47 May 26, 1932. "Soldier Hangs Writer to Sapling With Belt." Reprint Book, p. 47.

1.54 Jul 28, 1932. "Sound of Deer Gun Spoils Fishing Party." Reprint Book, p. 54.

1.56 Aug. 18, 1932. "Stealing of Horses Cost Lives of Thieves." Reprint Book, p. 56.

1.60 Sept. 15, 1932. "Notorious Test Oath Causes Reign of Terror." Reprint Book, p. 60.

1.75 Jan. 26, 1933. "Four in One Family Meet Violent Deaths." Reprint Book, p. 75.

1.76 Feb. 2, 1933. "Kellys and Chiltons First Settlers in County." Reprint Book, p. 76.

1.77 Feb. 9, 1933. "Original Site of Van Buren West of River." Reprint Book, p. 77.

1.78 Feb. 16, 1933. "Early Day Settlers in Henpeck Valley." Reprint Book, p. 78.

1.79 Feb. 23, 1933. "Carters and Sniders Are Among Earliest Settlers." Reprint Book, p. 79.

1.80 March 3, 1933. "Earliest Settlers on Pike and Carter Creeks." Reprint Book, p. 80.

1.90 March 17, 1933. Earliest Settlers In East End Of Carter County. Page 81.

1.82 March 23, 1933. "Some of Earliest Settlers Along Current." Reprint Book, p. 82.

1.84 March 30, 1933. "Review of Settlements in Region of Eminence." Reprint Book, p. 84.

1.85 April 6, 1933. "Early Settlers in Black River Section." Reprint Book, p. 85.

1.90 May 11, 1933. "How Early Pioneers Made Their Own Clothes." Reprint Book, p. 90.

1.92 May 25, 1933. "Development of Society in Early Days of Ozarks." Reprint Book, p. 92.

1.93 June 8, 1933. Making Whiskey in The Ozarks in Early Days." Reprint Book, p. 93.

1.95 June 22, 1933. "History of the Early Taxation of Whiskey." Reprint Book, p. 95.

1.102 Sept. 14, 1933. "The Telegraph Line That Was Never Completed." Reprint Book, p. 102.

1.134 Weakley, Ray H., *Dark Clouds Over Shannon—Alex Deatherage,* Chapter II, Part 5, p. 134. Original Source: *The Ozarker,* May 1978, Part 2, June 1978. cont.

1.2 Denison, Edgar. "Missouri Wildflowers." Missouri Department of Conservation, Jefferson City, 2001.

1.3 Mahan, James "Uncle Jimmie." Obituary. January 1, 1895. *The Current Wave,* Eminence, MO. Courtesy of Genevieve Kile. Re: Marriage of James Mahan to Elizabeth Davis Nesbit [Chilton]. Note: 1880 census used to established marriage date.

1.4 Monks, William. *A History of Southern Missouri and Northern Arkansas.* Edited by John F. Bradbury, Jr. and Lou Wehmer. West Plains, MO: West Plains Journal Co., 1907.

Sutherland, Daniel E., ed. *The Civil War in the West.* Fayetteville, AR: The University of Arkansas Press, 2003.

1.5 Orchard, Charles L. and Marjory Orchard. *The Chiltons of Shannon, Carter and Reynolds Counties of Missouri—Their Ancestors and Descendants.* 2 vols. Eminence, MO: Self-published, 1977. With permission of the late Marjory Orchard and her heirs.

Reprinted a selection of the John J. Chilton memoirs, *True Tales of Bygone Days,* from the *Current Local,* Van Buren, MO.

1.51 Reprinted Williams, M. F. (great-grandson of Thomas Boggs Chilton). "Shadrach Fights a Bear." *The Shannon County Historical Review,* January 1965. Courtesy of James and Vada Chilton, publishers.

1.52 Reprinted the "Thomas Reed Letters" from originals verified by notary public, owned by Eleanor Jean Tobey, used with permission.

1.6 Shannon County Circuit Court Docket. State of Missouri vs. Andrew J. & Henry Chilton. Murder in the 1st Degree, May 20, 1879, Book "B",

p. 390. Indictment for murder, May 20, 1879, Book "C", p. 21. Nov 7, 1879, 6 for acquittal, 6 for guilty, Continuance. Book "C" p 35. May 6, 1880, Continuance. Book "C" p. 134, May 5th, 1881 to Page 140, May 8, 1881. Acquitted. See Index, Book "A", page 1.

1.7 Walsh, James M. *First Families—Shannon County Missouri.* Self-published on behalf of Friends of the Shannon County Library, Eminence, MO, 1992.

. . . .

2. DIGITAL MEDIA, by collection, date:

2.1 ABSTRACT OF DIVORCE RECORDS 1837–1899
Green County, Missouri, Circuit Court Divorces
Abstract Page 17, Chilton, Elizabeth/Chilton, Alexander, Interlocutory Decree, 17 May 1875, Book O, p. 137. Judgment dismissal 21 Nov 1876 Book P, p. 241. http://thelibrary.org/lochist/records/d1873.htm
2.2 ANCESTRY.COM—FOLD3.COM
Ancestry.com, http://www.ancestry.com/ Fold3.com, http://www.fold3.com Genealogy, Census, Marriage, Birth, Death, (many other collections), and Military Official Records linked to Fold3.com, http://www.fold3.com, membership required.
2.21 Sinclair, Louisa. Letters to Union Military Commanders, Fort Davidson, Pilot Knob, MO. Re: Plea for the release of Union prisoner, James M. L. Jamieson, Shannon County Subscription schoolteacher.
2.22 Chilton, Alexander and Elizabeth C. Nesbit. Lafayette County Missouri, Marriage Record and Certificate of Marriage. December 28, 1868.
2.23 Davis, Pvt. George. Seventeenth IL Company M, US CAV. Illinois Civil War Detail Report. Re: Killed April 3, 1865 by guerillas near Logan Creek, MO. Believed to be "the red-haired butcher who killed the Reeds." Discovered and copied from original by Jim Morris.
Note: Military service records/rosters were found for all main characters in this novel, with the exception of Capt. Shadrach Chilton and his

son, William Chilton. "Captain Chilton" was listed as enrolling officer on many soldiers' records. Confederate records are often incomplete.

2.24 Smith, David B., 1880 US census. Oregon, Marion, Mehama, 088, 1. Birth: Maine.

2.25 Smith, David B., Consolidated list of all persons, of Class II, subject to do military duty, 6 Sub District of 9 Ward, continued. Residence: Biddle St., bet. 17 & 18; Age 1st July 1863: 44; White; Profession: Engineer.

2.3 CORNELL UNIVERSITY LIBRARY, MAKING OF AMERICA DIGITAL COLLECTION

2.31 C., L. "Finding A Relic" by L.C., Serial: The Living Age Volume 0075 Issue 961 (November 1, 1862). Title: *The Living age... / Volume 75, Issue 961* [pp. 193-240, p. 194]. Collection: Journals: Living Age (1844—1900), Little, Son, & Co. Boston. Courtesy of Cornell University Library, Making of America Digital Collection.

http://ebooks.library.cornell.edu/l/livn/

2.32 Chilton, Robert. S. "The Crisis" by R. S. Chilton, Washington, 1862. N.Y. Evening Post. Chief Clerk United States House of Representatives. ------*The Living Age.*

2.33 THE WAR OF THE REBELLION: a compilation of the official records of the Union and Confederate Armies. Courtesy of Cornell University Library, Making of America Digital Collection.

http://ebooks.library.cornell.edu/m/moa/

2.34 Aug. 10, 1861. Series 1, Volume 3, p. 106. Battle of Wilson's Creek, MO. Brig. Gen. Ben McCulloch.

2.35 Aug. 10, 1861. Series 1, Volume 53, p. 434. Camp on Wilson's Creek, MO. Brig. Gen. J. H. McBride.

2.36 Sept. 2, 1861. Series 1, Volume 53, p. 435. Action at Dry Wood Creek, MO. Maj. Gen. Sterling Price.

2.37 Sept. 3, 1861. Series 1, Volume 3, p. 163. Action At Dry Wood Creek, MO., Brig. Gen. J. H. Lane.

2.38 Sept. 20, 1861. Series 1, Volume 53, p. 451. Siege of Lexington, MO. Brig. Gen. J.J. McBride.

2.39 Nov. 1, 1861. Series 1, Volume 3, p. 255. Expedition from Rolla MO, against Freeman's Forces, Col. G. M. Dodge

2.40 Nov. 30, 1861. Series 1, Volume 53, p. 395. Correspondence, etc. Acting Brig. Gen. J. B. Wyman. Re: Price into Kansas, John Ross, forced to remain neutral.

2.41 Dec. 5–9, 1861. Series 1, Volume 8. p. 36. Expedition through the Current Hills, MO, Maj. William D. Bowen.

2.42 Jan. 25–March 9, 1861. Series 1, Volume 8, p. 269. Pea Ridge Campaign. Maj. William D. Bowen. Re: Capture of Colonel Freeman and twenty-nine others on Feb 14. Report from Pea Ridge, AR, March 10, 1862.

2.43 Feb. 19, 1862. Series 1, Volume 8, p. 65. Skirmish at West Plains. Lt. Col. S. N. Wood.

2.44 March 4, 1862. Series 1, Volume 8, p. 67. Scout through Dent, Shannon, Howell, and Texas Counties. Maj. William C. Drake.

2.45 April 1, 1862. Series 1, Volume 8, pp. 195–204. Pea Ridge or Elkhorn Tavern, AR. Maj. Gen. Saml. L. Curtis. Re: rebels cut off from joining Price.

2.46 July 9, 1862. Series 1, Volume 13, p. 152. Skirmish at Inman Hollow. Maj. H.A. Gallup.

2.47 Aug. 24–28, 1862. Series 1, Volume 13, p. 260. Scout from Salem to Current River, MO, Lt. Herbert Reed. "Commanding Detachment. Re: Special Orders No. 11, Salem, MO, Aug 23, 1862" [see microfilm collection 6.1].

2.48 Aug. 29, 1862. Series 2, Volume 4, p. 465. Correspondence, etc —Union, Lt. Col. J. Weydemeyer. Re: Sen. Joshua Chilton, "King of Shannon County."

2.49 Aug. 30, 1862. Series 2, Volume 4, p. 471. Correspondence, etc.— Union, Lt. Col. J. Weydemeyer. Re: burial and justification, including murder of Worthington.

2.50 Aug. 30, 1862. Series 2, Volume 4, Page 472. Correspondence, etc.—Union, Capt. Geo. S. Avery, "Commanding Detachment. Re: Special Orders No. 103, Rolla, MO, Aug. 28, 1862.

2.51 Sept. 18, 1862. Series 2, Volume 4, p. 539. Correspondence, etc.— Union, Col J. M. Glover, Re: Lt Lacy, Col. Glover to investigate.

2.52 Jan. 20, 1863. Series 1, Volume 22, Part II, p. 64. Brig Gen Loan: J. Rainsford—Re: diabolical crimes.

2.53 Feb. 6, 1863. Series 1, Volume 22, Part II, p. 99. Brig. Gen. J. W. Davidson. Re: Leeper tried for abandoning Van Buren; Camp at West Plains, MO and Davidson move to Chiltonsville on Jacks Fork or Eminence on Current River, MO.

2.54 July 3, 1863. Series 1, Volume 22, Part II, p. 352. Col. W. F. Cloud, Springfield District, Re: Marshfield to West Plains scout, Coleman, Burbridge, and Freeman at Spring River Mills with force of 10,000.

2.55 July 3, 1863. Series 1, Volume 22, Part II, p. 383. Scout from Salem MO, and skirmish. Lt. William C. Bangs. Re: Colonel Freeman across Jacks Fork, high water.

2.56 Aug. 6–11, 1863. Series 1, Volume 22, Part II, p. 547. Capt. Richard Murphy. Re: scout from Houston to Spring River Mills, MO.

2.57 Sept. 13, 1863. Series 1, Volume 22, Part I, p. 618. Attack and skirmish near Salem, MO, Capt. Levi E. Whybark. Re: Colonel Freeman, William Orchard, Duckworth.

2.58 Sept. 28, 1863. Series 1, Volume 22, Part I, p. 681. Col. Clinton B. Fisk. Re: scout from Pilot Knob to Arkansas State Line via Centreville, Eminence, and Van Buren.

2.59 Sept. 29, 1863. Series 1, Volume 22, Part II, p. 580. Brig. Gen. Clinton B. Fisk. Re: Hundreds of deserters from Price's army back into this region; Bushwhacking extermination in Oregon, Ripley, Wayne, and Butler Counties for twenty days.

2.60 Oct. 28, 1863. Series 1, Volume 22, Part I, p. 682. Maj. James Wilson. Re: Expedition from Pilot Knob to Oregon County via Centerville, Eminence, Henpeck Creek, Current River, Eleven Point River, Alton routing guerillas including Duckworth.

2.61 Nov. 3, 1863. Series 1, Volume 22, Part I, p. 747. Special Orders, No. 43, Thos. B. Wright, Adjutant. Re: Scout from Houston to Jacks Fork, MO, via Lt. John W. Boyd., "clean 'em out."

2.62 Nov. 4–9, 1863. Series 1, Volume 22, Part I, pp. 746–749. Lt. John W. Boyd. Re: Scout from Houston to Jacks Fork, MO.

2.63 Nov. 18, 1863. Series 1, Volume 22, Part I, p. 747. By order of Major-General Schofield: J. J. Campbell, Asst Adj.-Gen. Re: Scout from Houston to Jacks Fork, MO.

2.64 Nov. 20, 1863. Series 1, Volume 22, Part I, p. 747. Special Orders, No. 186, by order of Brig, Gen Thomas A. Davies; Capt. and Asst. Adj.-Gen. J. Lovell. Re: Scout from Houston to Jacks Fork, MO, via Lt. John W. Boyd.

2.65 Nov. 23, 1863. Series 1, Volume 22, Part I, p. 748. Lt. John W. Boyd. Re: Scout from Houston to Jacks Fork, MO.

2.66 Nov. 25, 1863. Series 1, Volume 22, Part I, p. 748. Capt. & Asst. Adj.-Gen. J. Lovell. Re: Scout from Houston to Jacks Fork, MO.

2.67 Nov. 26, 1863. Series 1, Volume 22, Part I, p. 748. Brig. Gen. Thos. A. Davies. Re: Scout from Houston to Jacks Fork, MO.

2.68 Feb. 12, 1864. Series 1, Volume 34, Part II, p. 310. Col. R. R. Livingston. Re: Col. T. R. Freeman request for prisoner exchange, Monks treatment of prisoners, and glorious music of war.

2.69 –Aug.–Dec. 1864. Series 1 Volume 41, Part I, pp. 303–728. Maj. Gen. Sterling Price. Re: Price Expedition Summary. Page 640.

2.70 Sept. 12–Dec. 864. Series 1, Volume 41, Part I, pp. 652–662. Brig Gen. Jo. O. Shelby. Re: Price Expedition.

2.71 Sept. 20, 1864. Series 2, Volume 1, p. 454. Maj. James Wilson. Re: Price's Expedition, Re: Skirmish at Ponder's Mill.

2.72 Oct. 2, 1864. Series 1, Volume 41, Part III, p. 977. Brig. Gen. Jo. O. Shelby. Re: Price Expedition, Iron Mountain Railroad and Bridges, Pilot Knob, MO.

2.73 Jan. 2, 1865. Series 1, Volume 48, Part I, p. 17. Capt. Levi E. Whybark. Re: Scout in Shannon County, MO.

2.74 Jan. 16, 1865. Series 1, Volume 48, Part I, p. 30. E. B. Brown Re: Monks' men and fatal hits.

2.75 Feb. 23–March 2, 1865. Series 1, Volume 48, Part I, p. 547. Scouts from Salem and Licking, MO to Spring River Mills, AR, with skirmishes. Reports 1. Brig. Gen. Egbert B. Brown, 2. Col. Edwin C. Catherwood, 3. Capt. William Monks.

2.76 March 7–25, 1865. Series 1, Volume 48, Part I, p. 135. Capt. William Monks. Re: Operations about Licking, MO.

2.77 April 10, 1865. Series 1, Volume 48, Part I, p. 65. By order of Major General Dodge: J. W. Barnes, Asst. Adj. Gen. to Hon. Thomas C. Fletcher, Gov. of MO: Re: 200 gun salute to surrender.
2.78 April 10, 1865. Series 1, Volume 48, Part I, p. 65. Gov. Thomas C. Fletcher. Re: no guns "to sound forth the joyful news."
2.79 April 19, 1865. Series 1, Volume 48, Part II, p. 67. Brig. Gen, Clinton B. Fisk, Re: martial law and lawlessness in the border counties.
2.80 April 29–June 11, 1865. Series 1, Volume 48, Part I, pp. 227-238. Expedition from Saint Louis, MO, to receive the surrender of Brig. Gen. M. Jeff. Thompson, CS Army. Correspondence between the persons and armies of Maj. Gen. Grenville M. Dodge, US Army and Brig. Gen. M. Jeff. Thompson, CS Army.

3. MISSOURI DIGITAL HERITAGE—Secretary of State
3.1 The Chilton Murder Trial, *Phelps County New Era*, November 22, 1879. Volume 15, No. 33. Archived in Secretary of State, *Missouri Digital Heritage*, Hosted Collections. [Note: Index error for Collections/ Search: The Clinton Murder Trial.] Original source, *Eminence Argus*.   http://cdm.sos.mo.gov/cdm4/document.php?CISOROOT=/ phelpnewera&CISOPTR=11698&REC=9
3.2 Explore History of the Civil War http://www.sos.mo.gov/mdh/ CivilWar/
3.21 Soldiers' Records: War of 1812–World War I http://www.sos. mo.gov/archives/soldiers/
3.22 Missouri Provost Marshal Papers. http://www.sos.mo.gov/archives/ provost/
3.23 Leavitt, Nancy C., Statement in Court-Martial of Thomas J. Thorpe, Pilot Knob, April 14, 1864, Case NN 1815, Record Group 153, National Archives. http://www.sos.mo.gov/archives/provost/
3.24 Sitton, John J. Memoir—n.d. Hosted Collections. http://cdm.sos.mo.gov/cdm4/document.php?CISOROOT=/ mack&CISOPTR=4364&REC=9

BLUE & GRAY CROSS CURRENT

3.25 Union, Illuminated Rosters. Illuminated roster of Missouri troops (Union), 3rd (Glover's) Cavalry. 1862. Re: 1862 Raid on Joshua T., Shadrach, and Andrew J. Chilton farms, etal.
http://collections.mohistory.org/archive/ARC:A0286_4623
3.26 ------ Illuminated roster of Missouri troops (Union), 3rd Cavalry, State Militia. Re: 1864 Skirmishes at Ponder's Mill, Patterson, etal.
http://collections.mohistory.org/archive/ARC:A0286_4579

4. THE INTERNET ARCHIVE, DIGITAL LIBRARY
4.1 Wood, George B. (George Bacon), 1797–1879. Volume name: A Treatise On Therapeutics and Pharmacology or Materia Medica. J.B. Lippincott & Co. Digitizing sponsor: MSN. Book contributor: University of California Libraries. Collection: cdl; americana http://www.archive.org/stream/trea-tiseontherap01woodiala/treatiseontherap01woodiala_djvu.txt

5. NATIONAL PARK SERVICE
5.1 Stevens, Jr., Donald L. "A Homeland and A Hinterland: The Current and Jacks Fork Riverways." National Park Service, 1991. http://www.cr.nps.gov/history/online_books/ozar/index.htm
5.2 ------Map 3. Central Shannon County Settlement Pattern 1840 http://www.cr.nps.gov/history/online_books/ozar/images/map3.jpg
5.3 ------Map 4. Base Map 2 The Homeland: Early Settlement 1812-1860. http://www.cr.nps.gov/history/online_books/ozar/images/map4.jpg
5.4 The Civil War, http://www.nps.gov/civilwar/index.htm

. . . .

6. MICROFILM ARCHIVES: Military Official Records Collections

6.1 August 23, 1862. Special Order No. 11, US Military Post, Salem, Missouri, August 23, 1862. Record *Third Cavalry Company E, Orders* 177 J 37 F3, Missouri State Archives, PO Box 1747, Jefferson City, MO 65102. Discovered and copied from original by Jim and Barb Morris, 2010.

6.2 August 21, 1863. RG393 Pt. 4 Pilot Knob, MO Volume. 420 D MO [Old Books 1056A (Lexington, MO), 1057 (Pilot Knob), and 1058 (Pilot Knob)]. Union Correspondence. R. R. Livingston and Captain Finley, Centerville. Re: Theft. Arrest and question: Wilson. National Archives, Washington, DC Record of US Army of Continental Commands. Courtesy of John F. Bradbury, Jr., The State Historical Society of Missouri.

6.3 August 23, 1863. RG393 Pt. 4 Pilot Knob, MO Volume. 420 D MO. Old Book 1057 Letters sent Pilot Knob Entry 1004 R. R. Livingston to Captain Finley. Re: Theft by Alex Shelton, Jo Butler, John Story living near Jacks Fork. National Archives, Washington, DC. Record of US Army of Continental Commands. Courtesy of John F. Bradbury, Jr., The State Historical Society of Missouri.

6.4 Sitton, John J., Memoirs. R 1286 John James Sitton Collection, State Historical Society of Missouri. The State Historical Society of Missouri retains all copyright to the microfilm publication. There are no restrictions. Courtesy of John F. Bradbury, Jr., The State Historical Society of Missouri.

. . . .

7. SONG LYRICS: Original Recordings and Traditional Folk Arts.
7.1 Anonymous, traditional lyrics. "Johnny Has Gone For A Soldier."
7.2 Haverstick, Darren. "Pearl's Song". Words and music by Darren Haverstick, 5/5/2000. Registered with BMI, 6/9/2004. Recorded by The Bressler Brothers on their album *Taste of Life*. Shan-Co-Mo Records 7001, 2004.
7.3 Magliari, Michael; Goodall, Jim; Fleet, Tony. "Love Came Around" from their album *Love in Time~Life in Motion*. Words and music by Magliari-Goodall. M. Magliari / Published by MAGMUSIC, 1999. Courtesy of Michael Magliari.
7.4 ------ "Tale of Wind River," Words and music by Magliari-Goodall. M. Magliari / MAGMUSIC, 1999. Courtesy of Michael Magliari.

. . . .

8. AFTERWARD – Ongoing Collections at <u>www.blueandgraycrosscurrent.</u>
<u>com</u>.8.1 Biography and Photo of Characters and Descendants.
8.2 Chilton Family Tree – Expanded.
8.3 Chilton Homes and Properties.
8.4 Military Documents.

ACKNOWLEDGEMENTS

F ive cousins shared extensive Civil War research and collections of family letters, photographs, and stories: Eleanor Jean Tobey, descendant of Sen. Joshua and Betsy Chilton and Col. Thomas Roe Freeman; Jim and Barbara Morris, descendant of Col. Lucian Nester Farris; Olivia Dalessandro, descendant of Dr. Thomas and Polly Chilton Reed; David and Alice Lawrence, and Sue Lawrence, descendants of Shadrach and Patsy Chilton.

Also contributing were our local Civil War Roundtable led by Lou Wehmer; the works of Charles L. and Marjory Orchard, Genevieve Kile, and John Bradbury, Jr.; Ozark Scenic River Writers Guild led by Brigitte Harris; Steve and Brinda Orchard, Leroy and Susan Orchard, Allen and Nancy Brewer, and Alan Banks who shared their stories and sense of place at the rivers, family farms and graveyards.

We are grateful for the family storytelling by our own Aunt Betsy and Uncle Perry: Harriett Elizabeth Gates Rayfield and the late Perry Gordon Chilton.

Thank you to Sharon Kizziah-Holmes for critique; Hilary Clements and Jennifer Simler for the book cover, illustrations, and media; Col. Michael Roderman, Missouri 2nd Artillery CS and reenactors in the cover photo; Frozen In Time and Craig Shumate for photography; Mary McWay Seaman and Connie Crow for suggestions; Michelle Osborne Shedd, Sheri Horton, and Sarah Denton for proof reading; and the CreateSpace Project Team.

We appreciate the late John J. Chilton and his memoirs for enriched knowledge of our past. Major events and characters in this novel are real. Transitional events and characterizations are fiction, guided by historical documents and oral history.

We cherish our beloved Jacks Fork and Current River where millions enjoy renewal and seek solace.

Made in the USA
San Bernardino, CA
16 April 2014